Best of British Science Fiction 2016

Best of British Science Fiction 2016

Edited by Donna Scott

NewCon Press
England

First edition, published in the UK July 2017 by NewCon Press

NCP 133 (hardback), NCP 134 (softback)

10 9 8 7 6 5 4 3 2 1

ISBN: 978-1-910935-40-8 (hardback)
978-1-910935-41-5 (softback)

Cover art and design by Ian Whates, utilising an image by 'geralt'.
Text layout by Storm Constantine

Donna Scott

One of a Special Edition, Signed by the Editor
Limited to just 100 numbered copies
This is number:

79

Contents

2016: An Introduction

Donna Scott

For me, 2016 was the year of Big Things. There was Big Tragedy: the passing of David Bowie and Carrie Fisher bookended a year that seemed to steal so many of our childhood heroes and icons from us. Some of my conversations with fellow science-fiction fans focussed on this sense of cultural loss. It was like watching the Perseid meteor shower on a clear night, as so many bright, star-like sparks dazzled and faded in all too quick succession.

There was Big Politics. What with Brexit and the US election, it seemed that political arguments were more frequent, and the voices involved were shoutier, more polarised, and just, well… Big.

Then there were Big Books. I'd just finished working on Alan Moore's *Jerusalem*, a monster of a novel at around 700,000 words in length, when Ian Whates asked me if I would be interested in editing an anthology celebrating the year's best British Science Fiction. I had to think about that for a moment. Did I really want to take on another Big Thing so soon? Newcon Press may be a *little* publisher, but it holds a Big Place in my heart, and in the hearts of many lovers of science fiction, as attested to by the many enthusiastic testimonials of its writers and readers. This was a prestige project indeed.

Of course I was delighted to be asked, so I considered the size of the task ahead of me and reasoned with myself that all I had to do really was read a few slim little stories. Just a few *hundred* little stories. Just as much of the available British short fiction as I could possibly get my hands on. When you break the job down into manageable story-sized chunks it's really not so onerous. No, really, it isn't. However, it does take a while to accomplish. Possibly more work than I had envisaged.

Though I began this project in 2016, much of 2017 so far has also been devoted to devouring story after story. Many of the tales I have chosen for this anthology have made me wish they were longer, they're so good. They have also been an antidote to the overwhelming emotions that the Big Things of 2016 left me with.

I was so amazed at the range and brilliance of so many of the submissions that I knew I would have to be picky. I looked for stories that had great characters, believable voices and a real sense of place, and if the stories also spoke to me about the Big Things of 2016, all the better. Peter F. Hamilton's story in particular I thought picked up on the reverence we all felt for the musical geniuses we lost last year, though his story has nothing to do with Bowie. And just in case you make a connection with Paul Raven's story and the recent cyber-attacks on the NHS, I swear I chose his story before all that happened.

So here it is: my selection for the Best British Science Fiction of 2016. These are tales of gritty bare-knuckle fights and unconditional love; of the perils of capitalism; of games within games. Alliances are forged and the status quo is bucked. There is poignancy and pathos, and a few strongly worded letters. The end of the world is nigh, but also very much far from over. There are love songs and light shows, and because we damn well need something light, there are stories to make you smile as well. I hope you enjoy reading them.

It would be remiss of me to finish this introduction without mentioning some of the almost made it stories, though I must fall a little short as there were so many I loved. In particular David L Clements' "An Industrial Growth" was a wonderful read, which unfortunately we didn't have room for.

But here's to 2017. Already another crazy year; the stories are bound to be mind-blowing.

Donna Scott,
Northampton,
May 2017

Arrested Development

Joanne Hall

Kai's back slammed into the canvas and bounced once, twice, before coming to rest. The air burst from her lungs, sending up a fine spray of blood from her nostrils. The blurred face of the referee loomed over her. He raised his eyebrows in question or concern, his hand already beating out the countdown.

She allowed herself seven seconds. Seven blissful seconds where she could have been lying on the softest bed in the most palatial Grondhaus, before she forced herself up on her elbows, shaking her head. The murmur of people exchanging bets intensified.

The referee stepped back. He wasn't permitted to help her to her feet. She had to stand on her own. It was one of the few rules.

Kai's opponent had retreated to the corner and was glaring at her, yellow eyes beetling beneath her lowered brow-shield. The wire mesh of the cage threw patterned shadows across her green skin. One of her incisors was loose and bloody, and she wobbled it with her forked tongue as she stared. Kai didn't know her name. The Grond didn't share their names with humans, and it didn't matter to Kai anyway. She was just another fight.

"Are you ready?" the referee asked.

Kai wiped the blood from her nose and her eyebrow with the back of her bandaged hand, and bounced on the balls of her feet. "Bring it on," she said thickly.

The lithe Grond flicked her loose tooth with her tongue in a final gesture of contempt and rose to her feet. Her spine cracked, audible even over the rustles of the crowd. Grond in the front rows, humans pushed to the back and the sides. At full stretch, she was a head taller than Kai, and her tail lashed back and forth as she prowled, waiting for the signal.

At the whistle, the Grond lunged forward. Kai bounced back, leaping high over that lashing tail that thickened to a club at the tip. She had seen other fighters go down with broken ribs or legs after a blow from a Grond tail. Kai had toyed with the idea of getting the enhancement; it was better for balance, an extra weapon. But it would cost every credit she had and more, and she needed to save her cash. There was a trade; there was always a trade. She could add the enhancement, fight better now, and make more money in the short term. Or she could do what she had been doing for the better part of a decade, and invest in the future, a better future. And not just for her.

The Grond stumbled, momentarily thrown by the force of the blow that didn't connect. Kai was on her in an instant, raining punches against the hard carapace of her barrel chest. The Grond pushed at her with stout arms, seeking an opening. She jabbed in hard against Kai's ribcage, a series of sharp explosions that left her reeling and drooling.

The crowd roared, or it could just have been the blood rushing in her ears. Her foot slipped on the canvas and she lurched forward. Recovering from the slip, she caught the Grond around the waist, barrelling into her and pushing her back against the wire of the cage. The Grond's feet scraped against the canvas as she tried to lift one leg to claw Kai's stomach. Talons raked her bare thigh, scoring twin lines of fire from groin to knee.

Kai pressed harder, breathing in her opponent's sweat, her musty lizard scent. The fingers of her left hand dug into the flesh of the Grond's back, slick now with loose scales as she shed in fear. Kai was inside her grip now, pressed tight as a lover, shifting so her elbow ground against the Grond's exposed throat. She pushed the Grond back, her yellow eyes bulging, feet skittering for purchase as the metal of the cage dug into the flesh of Kai's wrist.

Kai clenched her teeth and hung on, muscles burning from the strain.

The Grond made a choking sound. Drool hung in strings from her lipless mouth, and her eyes popped red as thousands of tiny blood vessels burst. Kai pushed harder, crushing her windpipe, willing her to break.

The Grond was as tense as wire and then all at once Kai felt her snap, muscles falling into slackness. She stepped back and the Grond slumped forward, like a tree toppling. Kai slammed a fist into the back of her head as she went down, just to make sure.

Kai held her breath for the long ten seconds it took the referee to count the Grond out, exhaling only as he took her arm and raised it high above her head. The hordes of Grond in the pricey seats hissed and flicked their tongues, the humans in the cheap seats cheered, money changed hands and Kai accepted the applause. She felt no particular joy, only satisfaction at another job survived without serious injury, another day lived through.

"Still lucky," she breathed.

By the time the referee released her, the defeated Grond had crawled away, back to her own team and the nurture of her people. Kai had no people in the arena.

By the time she lowered herself out of the cage, wincing as the adrenaline wore off and the pain kicked in, the hall was almost empty. The punters had paid their entrance fee, placed their bets and won or lost, and now they were streaming out into the afternoon, back to their Grondhaus or to their own towns. Not to the Delphi. No one who lived in the Delphi could afford to watch fights.

She crunched across the debris, the sticky floor and discarded plasteen cups still holding dregs of brew. They dug into her bare feet, bloodied from the wound in her thigh. There was no one waiting in the changing rooms to greet her, no one to take her gum shield and wipe down her wounds with astringent, or congratulate her on her win. She didn't need them. She was used to acting alone. Rumour had it the Grond changing room had hot water, but in here she was lucky to be able to thump a lukewarm trickle from the taps. Still, it beat her capsule in the Delphi, and the stanchion pipes on the street outside that were often dry.

Kai showered as best she was able, scraping the sweat and blood from her skin with a sliver of hardened soap and drying herself down with a rough gym towel that smelled like the inside of her shoes. Her trousers and vest lay on the bench where she had abandoned them before the fight and she pulled them on, wrinkling her nose as she caught a whiff of the ingrained stench in the armpits and the groin.

She stood up, brushing herself down, running her hands over hair cropped close to her scalp, to dry off the last of the water. Then she headed upstairs to the booth to get her money.

The female Grond had reached the booth before her, so Kai hung back until she left, the door almost closing on her club tail. There was no point taunting a defeated opponent. The Grond would most likely be back. So would Kai.

Sheeny sat in the booth, thick fingers flicking though the take, bottom lip pushed out in eternal petulance. He looked up as Kai's shadow fell across him, and grunted.

"You did OK out there today."

"Thanks." She didn't want to stay and chat with him. The smell of grease rising from his skin coated her tongue and made her long for a drink to wash it away.

"Always nice to see someone get one up on a Grond. Even a little one like that."

"I'd take on a big one if I had to." The Grond pitted their fiercest male fighters against each other. They didn't waste them on humans. The fights would be over too quickly.

Sheeny chuckled, his crooked eye swivelling away from her. "I've no doubt you would. Here's your money."

He handed over a tatty brown envelope. Kai made a point of opening it right there in the foyer.

"What's the matter? You don't trust me?" His lip stuck out even further, and his weasel tongue flicked over it.

Kai counted the cash. "It's fifty short."

"Yeah, well, things are tight this week…"

"Grond shit. Where's my money, Sheeny?"

"Are you sure? Count it again. That bump on the head might have made you dizzy – erk!" His words were choked off as she lunged across the barrier and seized him by the throat.

"Don't fuck with me, Sheeny. I'm not in the mood."

He squirmed. She pressed tighter, grimly satisfied to see his eyes bulge in fear. She rooted on the desk and grabbed a couple of notes without looking.

"Hey, that's too much!" He could squeak for his precious credits even through her grip on his windpipe.

"Call it a fine for messing me about." She reached into his breast pocket and extracted a packet of smoke sticks. "I'll take these too." She pushed him back, slamming him into the wooden wall of the booth. "Pleasure doing business with you, Sheeny."

"Pleasure's all yours," he grumbled, massaging his throat. "That was my last packet. Are you in tomorrow?"

"Not until next week." She had tried to get a quicker fight but none were available. The extra money would help tide her over until then.

As she turned away he called after her. "How long are you going to keep this up?"

"Keep what up?"

He snorted. "You're what, thirty? You won't be able to fight forever, even if you think you can. Then what are you going to do?"

She turned back, waving the envelope. "This proves I can still fight."

"For how long, Kai?"

"For as long as it takes."

"As long as it takes for what?"

With a harsh laugh, she let the door slam in his frustrated, swivelled-eyed face. She could still fight, and win. She was still lucky. Luckier than some, anyway.

Outside, she leaned against the corrugated iron wall of the building and lit one of Sheeny's sticks, drawing the smoke deep into her lungs and holding it there until she felt the narcotic buzz through her system. She breathed out, carefully stubbed the smoke out on the wall and stashed the rest of it in her pocket for later. It would keep her jazzed for the two-hour walk home.

The route back to the Delphi, for much of its length, took her down the narrow track between the Grond Metrotube and the chain-link fence that marked the boundary of the space port. Only the Grond were allowed to ride the express transit that bypassed the Delphi. To protect them from having to see the areas humans were restricted to, the whole length of the track was sheathed in a curved hemisphere of slate-grey metal. The outside of the tunnel was decorated along its length with holo-graffiti, layer upon layer of it, tracking the aspirations and frustrations of the generations of humans that had walked this same track. Political slogans against the Grond, overlaid with tributes. Gorf and Natty RIP, in eight-foot high neon letters, festooned with birds and snakes and vines that fluttered and writhed in and out of the shimmering letters. The paint smelled fresh, and she wondered who Gorf and Natty were, and what they had done to earn such a tribute. Had they been dissidents, or creatives?

Someone's son, someone's brother, someone's little girl? Either way they were gone now, but their memorial was glorious, love for them emblazoned on a wall to remind the world that they had lived.

Kai trailed her fingers along the smooth metal of the wall. Her cuts and bruises were aching again, and she stopped to light the smoke she had preserved earlier, cupping it in her hand against the wind that whistled across the flat plain of the space port to hammer into the side of the tube. She finished it while she watched the dance of the graffiti, summoning the strength to resume her long walk.

The tributes and the slogans gave way to a section painted with landscapes, trees and sunsets, cities shining in the sky and mythical beasts dancing. She was halfway home now, and she stopped for an instant to admire the wall, as she always did. For a moment she felt sorry for the Grond, speeding through in their metal tube, separated from this flowering of human creativity. They didn't like to admit it existed, to admit there was something mere humans understood that the Grond could never grasp. There was no art in the Grond cities, no more than there was in the Delphi, where people had too much to worry about, and no room to think about art.

Kai could hear the occasional swish as a train rushed by, soft and swift, insulated by the tube. There was no insulation from the spaceport though; the roar of the orbitals ripping their way up through the atmosphere, g-force accelerating into a wet sky the colour of milk. The orbitals carried the Grond off-world and back, and they sometimes carried humans. Not people like Kai, but lizard-lickers, who made their credit selling out their own people to the Grond. They could afford to travel to the stars. Kai had been offered that chance once, but she preferred to make her credit honestly, in the fighting cage.

She didn't want to think about the orbitals, the distance they had to cover. She had plenty of distance of her own. She put her head down and kept walking.

The holo-graffiti faded out before she reached the Delphi, as if the light and colour couldn't bear even to approach the habitation. From there, the train tube curved away to the west while the spaceport fence carried straight on. In the space between the two worlds lay the capsule-blocks and industrial units that made up her home environs. The Delphi had been thriving once, like the other human cities. But that was before the Grond arrived, with their orbitals and their hives, and one by one they had shut down the human cities, cut them off from each other, crushed their trade. Now all the Delphi was good for was providing manual labour for the Grond factories, making components for orbitals that no one who lived there would ever be able to afford to fly in.

Kai quickened her pace, eager to be out of the wind and off the streets. Her usual pharma lay at the bottom of an administrative block that had mostly fallen into disuse, because what was there to administrate here? She passed the little girls in their high tops and short skirts, leaning against the shuttered window, ready to sell themselves for a fix. She had vowed she would never be like them. She had fought over ten years not to fall into that life. Now she was old and tired but the girls were still there, a new generation every year.

She eased open the door, grateful the place was quiet. She didn't know how Ben got by. She suspected he had some kind of back-pocket deal with the Grond, but she liked him, so she wasn't about to ask. It would be a pain to find another pharma who could provide her particular range of needs so cheaply, and with so few questions asked.

Ben had black hair, and a face the colour of jaundice. He was leaning with his elbows on the counter, reading a tatty and lurid paperback. She watched his eyes deliberately finish his paragraph before he looked up and nodded to her. "Kai. How did it go today?"

"Female Grond. Scrappy bitch."

He didn't have to ask if she'd won. If she'd lost she wouldn't have the credits to buy pharma. He was already moving towards the shelves at the back of the store, practiced fingers flicking over the boxes and bottles.

"Usual?"

"Please."

The boxes were beginning to stack up on the counter. The red pills and the green ones, the big white tablets to be taken with the foul-smelling milky liquid, the steroids with their little capped needles that made her veins tingle as she looked at them. The hormone blockers and the protein powder.

"The Grond are leaning on me." He tapped the steroids. "These are going up next month."

"Again?"

Ben shrugged. "Sorry."

"Shit." Without the steroids she would struggle. A price hike would scrape off even more of her meagre income. "Couldn't we come to some arrangement?"

"I'm already sticking my neck out for you, Kai. You know that." He indicated the drug stash with a sweep of his hand. "If the Grond found out I had half this stuff I'd be in all sorts of shit. And the pills –" He broke off, twisting his hands. "Don't you think this has gone on for long enough? We don't know the long term damage, and after six years –"

"Is this the preamble to upping the price, Ben?" Kai snapped. "Because we talked about this last year, and you damn near doubled the cost. There are other pharma, you know..."

"I know. And I like you, Kai. But you could be killing yourself, and..." He trailed off, and shrugged. "I'd hate it if something bad happened and I was at fault."

"There's nothing I can do about it, can I? Short of going fully illegal? I don't want to do that. I trust you, Ben. At least I know what I'm getting from you is safe, not cut with rat poison or bleach." She relented, and drew the packet of smokes from her pocket.

"I'm just looking out for you. Someone has to."

"I appreciate your concern. Smoke?"

"Ta." He took the stick and slipped it into his pocket for later as she counted out the credits on the counter. The haul from the fight looked a lot thinner now.

"You want a bag?"

She nodded, and he slipped the drugs into a plain brown paper carrier, rolled tight at the top. It looked suitably nondescript.

"When are you fighting again?" he asked.

"Next week."

"Well," he hesitated, "don't get killed."

It was his traditional goodbye. If she died in the cage, Ben would know. He would go to her capsule and take care of things for her. They had an unspoken deal.

"I'll try not to." She grinned, but he had already picked up his novel and resumed reading as if her interruption had never happened. If the Grond came in, he would deny seeing her.

Kai left the pharma, clutching the precious bag tight to her chest. Her capsule was over by the space port fence, and she made her way between the towering blocks and through the alleys between the industrial complexes, limping now. Her boots were rubbing and the walk from the arena had given her a blister. She had a little salt. She could soak her wounds in a bucket when she got home. If the water was on.

She turned a corner into a long alley, closed in on either side by sheet metal fencing. Up ahead something clattered, and her stride slowed, instinct prickling. If it was a rat, and not too diseased, that was extra protein. But it sounded too big to be a rat.

There was a tread behind her. She turned around, looking along the blade of the knife to the kid that clutched it. He looked about seventeen, and he had patches of fake Grond-skin tattooed onto his cheeks. When had that become the fashion?

"Don't do it, kid," Kai said. "I don't want to hurt you."

"Give me your money, then!" He had a friend backing him up, younger and sick-looking, and when Kai glanced back over her shoulder there were two older lads behind her. One stuck his tongue through the yawning gap in his teeth and wriggled it obscenely.

"You dumb kid, you should have jumped me before I hit the pharma." She indicated the bag in her hands. "I've got no credits left now, have I?"

"Then we'll take that." The boy with the knife nodded at the bag.

"Over your dead body…"

"That's the idea – what?" The hand holding the knife shook. Kai dropped the bag between her feet and rolled her shoulders. She still ached from the fight with the Grond but these were children. She could take them.

She beckoned the leader closer. "How about you and me, kid? Man on man."

He peered at her closer. "You're not a man…"

Kai's foot lashed out, catching his wrist. She hoped to numb his arms so she could snatch the knife, but his grip was too loose. The blade span high into the air and over the fence that hemmed them in. Her boot swept on to make contact with the kid's chin, throwing his head back with a shattering crunch. She spun around, a fist catching the gap-toothed boy in the gut, sending him staggering. His companion stumbled away as she came for him, and he pointed, gibbering.

"What?"

"Lady, he's taking your bag…"

"Fuck it!" She spun around to the fourth mugger. To where the fourth mugger had been. He had her pharma bag and he was accelerating down the alley away from her.

She needed that bag. Her life, her future, lay in those pills and powders. She couldn't afford any more this week. Without the steroids, she would be more likely to lose the next time she fought. And if she lost she might go on losing, her confidence shattered. She had fought for so long, and now everything she had worked for was vanishing down the alley with her assailant.

Adrenaline pumped through her veins as she hurled herself into a final burst of speed, stretching out to grab the back of his shirt with snatching fingers as an orbital roared overhead. She jerked him back. His mouth was working but she couldn't hear his words, and whatever he was trying to say was cut off as she wrapped her arm around his throat and twisted until he stopped kicking.

She let go and he slumped in the dirt at her feet, his neck at an eye-watering angle. Some of the pills had spilled out of the bag when she retrieved it, but it wasn't ripped, and it was easy to roll back up. Kai squeezed it to her chest.

The orbital had passed over but her ears were ringing. She looked down at the boy. His mouth hung open, as if he was trying to finish what he had started to say. The other kids had run or staggered away, and she didn't have the energy to hunt them down. Her hand twitched towards the smokes in her pocket, but stopped – she could trade them. She had smoked one and given one to Ben, but the rest were a source of credits and she wasn't going to turn down any money she could get.

She checked the boy's pockets. A five. A bonus. She closed his eyes and stood over him for a moment, feeling as if she should say something. She wondered if he had parents who would look for him. But the words withered on her tongue and it had taken her too long to get home. Martine would be worrying.

Martine lived in the same capsule block as Kai, a few floors below. The lock on her door was broken, smashed in an almost-forgotten fight. Kai pushed it open and moved through the dusty light towards the kitchen table, where the old lady was asleep. She caught her shoulder and shook her awake.

"Kai? Did you get food?"

"Tomorrow," Kai lied. "I said I was going to go tomorrow. I got your pills."

Martine patted her hand. "You're a good girl, Kai. How was the factory?"

"Same as ever." Kai mixed up the milky liquid in a stained plasteel mug, and handed Martine the white pill, broken into two easy-to-swallow halves. Martine knocked it back obediently, making a face at the bitterness.

"I don't see why I need these," she grumbled.

"For your blood, remember? The pharma said."

"For my blood?"

"How's Hari been today?"

Martine beamed, showing blackened stumps of teeth. "Good as gold. She's asleep out back."

Kai glanced over at the corner, at the pile of blankets. "Out back?"

Martine pointed vaguely. "Over there. I don't know why I said out back. We had a back yard, when I was a girl…"

"Of course you did." Kai took the pack of smoke sticks out of her pocket and pressed them into Martine's hand. "I got these. You want to buy them?"

The old woman's hands did her seeing for her, running over the smokes in the packet, counting them off. "There's only eight in here," she chided. "You trying to rip me off?"

"There's no fooling you, is there? Will you give me ten for them?"

"For eight smokes?" Martine snorted. "I'll give you three."

"Five?"

"Done." She reached into her pocket and slapped her ancient leather purse down on the table. "There's three notes in there. I counted them, mind."

Kai opened the purse. There were three notes, a five and two ragged tens. She took one of the tens and pushed the purse back into Martine's hands. "Five," she reminded her, helping her light up a smoke. In the sudden flare of light, the older woman's eyes gleamed white and opaque. "And I'll get food tomorrow. I'll even cook."

Martine nodded, yawning, her mouth a black hole. The pills Kai brought her made her tired, but they helped ward off the worst of the dementia that afflicted her. Kai needed Martine sane, but not too sane. Sane enough to take care of Hari while Kai was fighting in the arena, but just daft enough not to realise what Kai was doing to her own daughter.

"I'll take Hari home now, shall I?"

Martine nodded, leaning back, smoke stick hanging from her bottom lip. Kai retrieved it and gently stubbed it out. Let the old lady enjoy it later.

As Kai lifted the blankets aside, Hari stretched out sleepy arms to her. Kai gathered her daughter to her chest, cradling her and kissing the soft crown of her head. She retrieved the bag of pharma and let herself out into the cold evening air, feet ringing on the metal steps as she made her way up to her own capsule.

The single room was cold, and a line of drying nappies hung from the ceiling on a wire cut from a dead power cable. Kai swiftly transferred Hari to her own ragged blankets. She popped out a red pill, and a green one, chewing them between her own teeth until they were soft, before she transferred them to Hari's toothless mouth, making sure she swallowed. It was a familiar routine; they had been doing this most days for the past six years, Kai feeding her daughter the pills that would arrest her development, keep her in a state of infancy.

While Hari drooled and gurgled, Kai transferred the day's profit to the tin she kept under the floorboards, under the blankets. She was getting there. It had taken over seven years so far, and it might take another two, but one day she would have enough money for a one-way ticket on an orbital. Off-world, away from the Grond, from the Delphi, and the fight arena. Just one ticket, but if Hari was small enough to fit in a sling on her chest, she would travel for free. If she had to save for two tickets she would never make it. She would be far too old to fight before that day came. Already her joints were stiffening and her reflexes slowing. One day she would die in the arena, if she didn't get out, and what would happen to Hari then?

She tied off her forearm and tapped her veins until she found one that hadn't collapsed, and shot a steroid into her bloodstream. That would keep her going a little longer. Tomorrow was a food day.

She crawled into the blankets next to Hari. Her daughter smelled of warmth and milk and love, and one day they would be off-world and she could grow. They could both grow. Kai wrapped herself around her daughter and held her tight against her chest. As another orbital roared above their heads, shaking plaster from the ceiling in a gentle snow that drifted down around them, she began to croon a lullaby.

Ten Love Songs to Change the World

Peter F. Hamilton

I met Jesus once. Well come on, we all do it. He was one of us after all, a fey. Our hero, venerated by us the way baseline humans worship him for something else entirely. It was his stand which makes our history, our world, possible.

I was fourteen years old, and dreamed myself all the way back to his time. A relatively peaceful segment of his life, mind you, when he was starting to quietly gather his disciples from across the Roman Empire and beyond, and before the ghouls started showing an interest. It was on the shore of a lake. I don't remember where. It's not important.

He saw me and recognised what I was. Not hard. Fey can see each other when we're manifesting, and I must have been quite a sight. I was wearing a white summer dress from Top Shop and some frayed Nike trainers. My hair was fairer than you got in the Middle East at that time, and cut in a wavy bob that was never really in fashion even in my time, never mind back then. All very different to First Century styles.

To look at he wasn't anything remarkable. Average height, average build, small beard. His eyes though, they were sad. But I could see how much anger he could bring forth. Maybe that's what made him the one, our saviour.

"You're from a long way ahead," he said. Or rather didn't say, we don't use words, of course, not in manifested state. As in all dreams, you can talk to whoever you want and understand each other. "I can always tell."

"The start of the twenty-first century," I admitted.

"That's risky. You'll get the Guardians come and talk to you. There will be finger wagging."

"I know. But I had to see you. To thank you."

"You're welcome."

"You won. Or you will win, but then you know that."

"Yes, enough of you tell me."

'I live thanks to you. I'm grateful. I wanted you to know. That's all."

"Well thank you for making the trip…""

"Malinda."

"Malinda from two thousand years ahead. I appreciate it."

I looked round at his band of followers. He'd gathered over forty fey already, and not just timedreamers like me, there were sidedreamers, fardreamers, soothers, and more. But all of them were fighters, I knew that from their attitude. "Thank you all," I said. And I saw someone else approaching. Some boy in late eighteenth century clothes, who was walking over to us with his feet not quite touching the ground.

I wondered what it must be like for Jesus, to have a constant stream of visitors from every century there will be, arriving in every spare moment, all praising him for the fight he would have and win. What must it be like knowing you were going to win? And die?

The disciples basically ignored me. They must see a dozen awestruck timedreamer kids a day. All of us breaking the guidelines.

"I should go," I said. "It's a long wave back."

Which truly made me very nervous. The longer you stay in the past, the further back you go, the more chance there is that you change something, especially if you talk to someone backwhen. The universe, the timeline, it adjusts to every dream we have, every impact we make. Every word we speak to a fellow fey alters something, not by loading them with foreknowledge which is just damn stupid. But even if you only speak for a moment, you delay them – that changes things in a physical way, and that has consequences. The example Guardians always give is that a pause makes a pace different, every step they make thereafter is fractionally altered. Dislodge a pebble that wasn't dislodged before (step on a Butterfly! – the timedreamers' very own ultimate horror story) and it has consequences. That pebble can start a temporal avalanche if you're not very careful. Was it the stone that got caught in a sandal, which made another traveller on the road stop, and if it doesn't get caught in his sole and he arrives a minute early, he might see someone he didn't before, a friendship springs up, lives are altered and so – history is *different.* Too different and you might not get born.

So you ride the consequence wave home. And you get to see what you've done rushing around you like you're watching the whole world in IMAX, watching the changes ripple out to become temporal tsunamis that wipe away everything you know, the timeline that produced you.

I did change things. I watched my consequences from a couple of the disciples admiring me, talking about me later that evening. Their movements were different, they trod on ground left clear before. Dirt was dislodged, tiny specks only, but some soil was compressed. A couple of grass seeds never germinated. But others came and took their place – were chewed on by animals. It was a ripple – circular, small. It washed out. The timeline didn't change. I woke up safe on my bed on a sunny afternoon August 2000.

I'm never going back that far again.

Jesus is history to me for evermore.

He made his stand back there when we fey were becoming hunted to extinction. Not that there have ever been many of us. But nature being the bitch she is creates predators for everything, locking life in an eternal rock paper scissors battle. Humans are deadly to most animals, we can swat a scorpion, but a scorpion sting can kill humans just as asteroids kill dinosaurs (don't laugh, asteroids are part of nature too, a very big nature).

We timedreamers were stalked and our minds devoured by ghouls as we contained the richest thoughts of all the fey. Just like us, ghouls were physically indistinguishable from baseline humans; but once they latched on, they savoured the memories and sensations of others, sucking them out to leave husks behind. And us, with our ability to visit anywhen, well we were the ultimate hit; the high they all craved. They sought us out first before feasting on the other fey. We were on the verge of dying out until Jesus decided to make his stand and fight back. He was a fardreamer, so he gathered other fey to him, which was a remarkable achievement in its own right. We always prefer to live quiet lives, keeping our heads down. Even today the prejudice against us is nasty. Back then, with Rome dominating Europe, any *difference* to the baselines was a death sentence. But he convinced the fey we were doomed anyway, and rallied our ancestors.

That many of us together acted like nectar for the ghouls. They came from all over the globe. Unfortunately for them, it turned out the disciples were a wasp trap. There are no more ghouls now. Not in this universe. Oh sure, they're still out there in the endless parallels of the multiverse. But us, here, now, since the Time of Christ, we're clean.

Jesus knew the outcome, because stupid awestruck teenagers like me came back to tell him, but still he fought on. He died to save us. Others have different versions of the conflict. They're all good.

I'm wondering if one day when I'm older and supposedly wiser I'll put in a stint as a Guardian. Lecturing and nagging kids to be careful how they dream themselves back in time, warning them of the consequence wave. Emphasising how history has to be preserved, because we've tried altering it, and frankly this is the best version there is – Hitler, Genghis Khan and all the other bastards included.

Except I'm not sure I believe that. I still think we should be bolder.

After that visit, when those missing blades of grass really did scare the crap out of me, I did what all of us with half a brain do, and stuck to the recent past.

I'm rich, of course. Our family always has been; using the talent to do very nicely thank you - the trick is not to overdo it and call attention to yourself. Mum is a reasonable fardreamer, and Dad can soothe, so my talent came as quite a surprise.

I have a nice life. Loving parents. Nice house by the sea. Housekeeper and gardener. It's easy. I want for nothing. I travel as I please. Mum and Dad encourage that, always telling me there's so much to see and enjoy in this world, this time. "Get out there, girl, and live it."

But I'm human. I want more. So I dream.

Everyone has dreams that they think are so real. That's because they are. Baseline humans view what's happening all over the multiverse. But they don't manifest there, they don't take part. They're observers only, and never really understand what they see anyway.

So after that stupid rite of passage I was a lot more cautious about when I went back to. It's thrilling to see history for real. Not that I'm one for politics (exception: Nelson Mandela walking out of prison is a must) or war or disasters, there's way too much suffering going on in my realtime, I don't need to add to it. Instead I did what most of us do, and go for the uniques. Concerts, sports matches, and of course everyone goes to watch the Vostock 1 and Apollo 11 launches, festivals, Woodstock (naturally!) Live Aid, I even went to the first Glastonbury – wow was that different: no yurts for the mega-rich back then.

I guess that's when I fell in love with Sixties music. I know, I know. That's a cliché. But I loved it. Music was raw and new back then, it meant something in that era, it wasn't a business. Bands and singers believed in their art, they were musicians not celebrities. All of it was exciting, and it spoke to the hearts of a whole generation. Inspired them. People had a buzz.

So back I went, again and again. The Who, the Stones, Joan Baez, Pink Floyd, Dylan, Jefferson Airplane, Cream, Janis Joplin, Hendrix, The Beatles, Grateful Dead, Credence Clearwater Revival, I even sat through some Ravi Shankar – not really my thing but the audience vibe, man o man!

Then I found *him.*

"You're dreaming your life away," Mum says. "Look, I know it's like when you discover sex –"

"Mum!" she is the classic parental embarrassment at times.

"All right. But there's so much this world has to offer, too. Take a couple of trips further back, see the poverty and squalor everyone lived in just two hundred years ago. That way you might appreciate what you have a little more."

"I don't want to risk the consequence wave," I tell her.

Her eyes narrow. "Ah, you went to visit Jesus."

"Did not."

"Really?"

I sometimes think fardreaming is code for mind-reading. "Maybe quickly. Once. It didn't have consequences."

"But riding a wave that far must have scared you, so I get how you're just dipping shallow right now. But what we have is a gift, especially you; don't waste it."

"It's not a gift, it's natural. And really, apart from the money, it's not terribly practical, is it? It's for enjoyment. So I'm enjoying."

So she sighs in that waiting-till-it-runs-its-course patience she has. "Life is a gift, darling. Timedreaming enriches it like no other. Don't waste your gift, but don't let it dominate."

"We could do so much, though. We could have stopped 9/11. We still can." I still think about the attack most days. I saw it all on the TV. The first thing I

wanted to do was go back, warn the CIA or FBI or someone. Mum sat with me watching events unfold, telling me I couldn't. That the Guardians already knew about 9/11, and were ready to stop any attempt to prevent it.

Life was simpler back in the Sixties, another reason to spend all my time there.

"We could have," mum says sadly. "But the Guardians said no. The fanatics would have come back with nukes in Paris and Washington."

"Then we could have stopped that, too."

"We're not the police."

"We could be. We should be."

"Sweetheart, please. You're young, and that's a gift as precious as any. I just want you to be happy. Now, have you been seeing any decent boys?"

"Mum!"

"All right. Girls?"

"Arrrgh. Stop it."

I manifested in the Tulip Bulb Auction Hall in Spalding, 29th May 1967. Cream and the Jimmy Hendrix Experience were headlining, with Pink Floyd supporting. Gabriel Ivins played a couple of songs first, an unannounced warm up for the support, when Spalding's young and restless were still clustered round the bar. He was nineteen, an electrical engineering student at Cambridge; up on stage all by himself, him and his acoustic guitar. All dark curly hair, weak Sixties sideburns, gangly frame, big thick-knit pullover, and flares wider than some of my skirts. Dylan was clearly a big influence on Gabriel, he was almost a tribute act. Except he wrote those two songs himself. And his voice was mellow and kind of appealing.

I saw quite a few girls in the bar crowd turn round and listen, and watch. He finished, bowed nervously while no one applauded, and scuttled off stage. Just before he left, he caught my eye and quirked a grin.

I drifted after him. Caught up in the green room. The green room being where they stored bulb crates in an annex at the back of the hall. He was putting his guitar away in its case while the Floyd were getting ready to go on. I should have been interested in them, Syd Barrett was still part of the line up at that point.

Instead I went over to Gabriel. "Hi."

"Hi yourself," he said, and looked round the annex to check that he was right, and only he could see me. It was just him, looking like he was muttering to himself in the corner like a true wacko artist. "Cool threads, man."

"Thanks." I was wearing a ridiculous purple and green tie-dye shirt with a long vintage turquoise-blue skirt, gold daisies woven into my hair. I hadn't cut my hair since I was fourteen, so now aged seventeen it was halfway down my back – I had a real hippy-chick look going. "I liked your songs."

"Thanks. Where are you from?"

"Two thousand and three."

I could see the surprise in his eyes. "Yeah? You look… today, man."

"I like today."

"I thought you were a maybe a sidedreamer. I'm always kind of surprised to hear the twenty-first century exists."

"Barry McGuire, Eve of Destruction," I grinned.

"Something like that." He produced a half-burnt reefer, and lit it.

"He was too pessimistic," I said. "Things aren't perfect but they're not too bad. So are you writing any more songs?"

"Some. They're not good enough to sing in public yet."

"The ones you sang tonight, *Rainbow Smile* and *Flower Sun*; are they recorded?"

"No. Not yet. Hey, you can tell me if they ever are, future girl."

"I can't. Sorry. Too many consequences."

"Heavy."

"Like neutronium."

"Wow, are you sure you're not sidedreaming from the land of the fairies?"

"Nah. Is that what you do?"

"A little. My talent's not too funky. I never get far enough to see anywhere groovy. My old man, he says there are wonders out there in the alternates."

"So I hear."

Gabriel took a deep drag. "I'd offer you some, but…"

"I know."

"Gotta split. Gotta hitch back to Cambridge."

"Have you got another gig lined up? Maybe I could come and hear if your other songs make it to the stage."

"Uh. I dunno. The scene man, it's not as cool as I thought. Unless you're the Beatles."

"Yeah, two-thousand-three remembers the Beatles."

"Take care, future girl."

"And you."

Google is not my friend. Yahoo is not my friend. The internet has nothing on Gabriel Ivins. No bootleg sites have recordings of Rainbow Smiles and Flower Sun. I can't believe it. They were good. How did he sink away without being signed by a record company?

I so much want to hear them again. They'd be a comfort right now. I'm sitting here in this cold February, with the TV showing the build-up of troops on the Iraq border. There's going to be war. Bush and Blair are really going to do it, they're going to let thousands of people die.

There must be another way, there must! I'm thinking in a few months I could go back to now. I could tell other fey how many died, that it wasn't worth it. They'd be outraged. They'd do something. Wouldn't they?

It'd taken me a few dreams backwhen, stalking I suppose. But I found the student newspaper with the announcement, and manifested in the Cambridge Corn Exchange 23rd July 1967.

Gabriel took to the stage just after eight o'clock. Still in his thick woolly jumper (does he have any other clothes?). He sang four songs, and this time people drifted away from the bar, starting to groove along. They're sweet songs, his new two, about love and fate and hope. He got a big round of cheering and applause when he finished. It was great. This little gig must be the start of his success, I'm sure of it, and I'm one of the witnesses. Go history! But then he looked straight at me from the stage, smiled shyly, and started his fifth song of the evening. And OMG!

The Future Fairy by Gabriel Ivins was issued in 1968, a limited pressing vinyl single on the Calibre label (an independent Cambridge record label – declared bankrupt in 1970). It is a love song by young poet musician Gabriel Ivins, dedicated to 'my sad and lovely vision'. Ivins was a solo singer songwriter guitarist until this recording, when he was joined by Calibre session musicians, adding electric guitar and drums.

Ivins died in November 1971 from a drug overdose. A good copy of The Future Fairy will cost £87.00. V Rare.

Google is my friend after all. It doesn't matter how many times I shake my head in disbelief, the words on the screen stay the same. The consequence wave I rode back after the concert was exhilarating. Nobody dies. Nobody is worse off. It's changed the timeline.

I. Changed. Things.

The Guardians haven't noticed.

And Gabriel died.

But before he did, he wrote a song about me. Me!

It was cold on February 15th 2003. I'd never gone back such a short time before. But the crowds I saw on TV just a few months ago thronged all around me. Marching through London's streets, chanting and calling. So many people, so much good humour. And desperate hope. I've seen that kind of belief once before, back in the Sixties. Back when music and good people were going to change the world.

There are plenty of fey among the marchers. I flit between as many as I can find. And all the time I tell them. "There are no Weapons of Mass Destruction, there never were. I know. I'm a timedreamer from the future. They're lying, Bush and Blair. Tell everyone. It's all a lie. They don't exist."

After it was over, after the crowds went home and the night claimed the empty streets, I braced myself and rode the consequence wave back to late summer.

There was nothing, no real disturbance. February 15 was a day of chaos and determination. Everyone I told believed anyway. One fey girl with long hair and a desperate smile telling them they were right changed nothing. Nothing. Around my pathetic little consequence wave, tens of thousands of people died in pain and fire.

The Future Fairy single hit the timeline harder, for fuck's sake.

Mum knocks on my door. My knuckles screw the tears from my eyes and I say: "Come in."

She does, but she's not alone. There's this old woman with her, wearing a neat grey suit and sensible black shoes, like she's on her way home from her city desk job. Except I know she never worked at any desk.

"Sweetheart, this is Ms Remek," mum says, slightly nervous.

"You're a Guardian," I say. There's only four or five in any generation. We

don't need more, there aren't many timedreamers. We're kind of like fey royalty I guess.

"I am, dear, yes."

And she has this sympathetic voice, too, all understanding, an I-was-young-once voice. But stern, too.

"Nobody listened," I tell her miserably. "Nothing changed."

"I know. But the point is you tried to change it."

"There are no Weapons of Mass Destruction. There never were."

"All the fardreamers knew that last year. You weren't telling anyone anything new."

"But it's a lie, and now it's over and all those people are dead."

"It's not over," Ms Remek says. "The war doesn't officially end until December two-thousand-and-eleven."

"Eleven!" I squeak.

"Fraid so. We screw up the peace even worse."

"Then stop it!" I yell.

"It's not that simple," she says kindly. "It never is. You heard about Paris and Washington, didn't you?"

"Nukes. If 9/11 is stopped."

"That's right."

"So… stop that as well."

"And if we do, which we could, it would be another target, another atrocity. Bin Laden is a persistent man."

"So tell the CIA where he is."

"A compound in Bilal, that's in Pakistan."

"What? You know?"

"Yes. He's going to be killed by a navy Seals team in two thousand and eleven."

"What is it with two-thousand-eleven? And why not assassinate him now?"

"You tell me."

My shoulders sag. "Consequences."

"Yes. If we keep chasing down the bad guys, what does that make us?"

"What do you mean?"

"We become official. True world Guardians of Peace. The baseline governments will turn us into an agency or service – at best. We are unique, my dear, us timedreamers. At most there are a hundred of us in any generation. But our talent makes us possibly the most powerful people ever. We can strike down an enemy before they even become an enemy. And what will happen if baseline humans ever discover we exist? Have you thought of that?"

"They'll be frightened, I guess."

"No. It will be worse than the age of ghouls. They will be utterly terrified. Because if we do stop terrorists and wars, we poor few will become the rulers of the world. We decide everything, including who lives and who dies."

"So that's what you're really Guarding against?"

"It's half of it, yes. We carry on the work Jesus started, and protect the fey. First they'll come for us, then the others will be hunted, and we won't be there to protect them."

"But we'll always be able to warn ourselves if anyone comes for us."

"And so we become rulers out of self-defence. There are parallel worlds where it has happened. Where it is happening."

"What's the point of timedreaming if we can't help people?"

"We are helping people. Guardians talk to each other across eras, and keep the timeline stable."

"So what you're saying is Guardians do have a purpose. I don't. Are you trying to recruit me?"

"Nobody is ever forced to become a Guardian; that would be wholly counterproductive. And not every fey has your compassion and goodwill. We Guard against that, too. I watch history and warn my predecessors against rogues and inadvertent consequences; as I am warned by those in the centuries to come."

"What if I don't listen? What if I keep trying to expose the lies?"

"You don't succeed. And if you were to, and make things worse, then there's always one person who will come backwhen to your moment of failure and convince you beyond any doubt that you're making a mistake."

"Who?"

Ms Remek smiles in compassion. "You, of course."

Gabriel's digs are truly *eueeew*. I mean, I don't need to go back two centuries to witness people living in poverty and squalor. Sixties students would envy medieval hovels for their luxury.

He doesn't seem to mind. January sixty-eight was cold. His gas fire had five wavy flames, which all seemed to burn yellow, producing no heat. The inside of the windows were frosted over. I was lucky I couldn't feel the temperature, at the time my body was snug at home, curled up on my bed in the early autumn, with the central heating on.

Gabriel wore his thick sweater – of course – with three T-shirts on underneath. He sat on the threadbare bed-settee, strumming his guitar, writing possible lyrics in his big notebook.

"What do you think?" he asked.

"I like it. Sort of like *Perfect Day*, but harder. Sharper."

"Oh, man, you mean it's not original?"

"Oh it is. Lou Reed writes *Perfect Day* in the early seventies, I think."

He brightened. "I write like Lou Reed?"

"Better."

"Nahh."

"You do, seriously." I'd manifested in five of his gigs now. He was gaining quite a reputation locally.

"So how come I haven't got a record deal?"

"They take time, Gabriel."

"Do I get one?" he pleaded.

"I can't say. You know that."

"I was thinking of giving up my course. Just concentrate on my music."

I didn't know what to say. He only had three years left to live. If I knew I was going to die, I wouldn't spend what time I had left sitting in lectures. "Follow your dream."

"Yeah?"

"Gabriel, I'd say that to anyone."

"You're infuriating, you know that."

"You ever thought of going electric?"

"Naww, it's a sell-out. I play my own music. I express what I have to say myself."

"I love your integrity."

"This geezer, Matt, he was interested at the gig last week. Said he's got his own record company, Calibre. But he wanted me to go electric, too. Said acoustic is dead."

"Your choice. Do you want people to hear what you have to say or not?"

"Is that a hint, future fairy?"

"Don't call me that."

Then there was a commotion outside. His friends had arrived, and he let them in. Fellow students, bringing cheap wine and homemade beer. Gabriel had more friends now, people who liked hanging out with a musician. It was party time. Two of the girls made sure they were sitting next to him, hanging off every word. I smiled. Waved goodbye.

Mum's happy for me.

His name's James. He's nineteen and says he's a musician – when he's not working behind the bar at the local pub. He lays down electro-pop tracks on his PC, and lets anyone download them for free from his website. Twelve people have logged on in the last three months.

His dream is a record contract. At night, when we cling together, he confesses once he's discovered he's going to be mega, and super-rich, with homes here and in the Caribbean. He thanks me for listening, for believing in him.

I tell him to write a protest song about the war.

His answer? "Aw come on, that's so Sixties."

He's tall and skinny. He has thick dark hair which is long and curly. In the dark, with his body lying on top of mine, I can't see his face. I can't see it's not really Gabriel.

Amid the final joy I call a name. I'm not sure whose.

"Have you met me, man?" Gabriel asks.

It was late summer sixty-eight, and we walked around Cambridge a week before all the students came back. He carried a bag full of Future Fairy singles, which he was trying to flog to the city's independent record shops.

"Er… what do you think I'm doing?" I ask.

"Not now," he laughs. "In the future. Have you come to see me?"

"No."

"Did you try? I'll be what? Fifty five, yeah? Did my bodyguards stop you?"

"You have a very high opinion of yourself."

"Is it justified?"

I haven't seen him so happy for a while. Musicians can be moody prats at times. Adds to the mystique, I suppose.

"Stop trying to wheedle stuff like that out of me. You know I'll never say."

"Okay, all right." He stopped in the middle of the market square, and almost made to grab me. His arms came up before he remembered – he was the wild student talking to himself in public. "How about this, man. What month is it with you now?"

"September."

"I'm going to remember November the first, 2003, okay? On that day I do solemnly swear I will be right here on this spot. No bodyguards, no managers. Just me. Please please please, be here. Just to talk." He faltered. "Just to touch you. To know you're real. I need that."

"Gabriel…"

"Promise me!" he yelled.

Now half the market was looking at the crazy boy.

"I promise." I turned away so he couldn't see my tears.

So now Google says Just to Touch You the second single by Gabriel Ivins charted at number 47 in the nineteen-sixty-nine January top fifty chart.

And on the radio the news is a High School shooting in the American Midwest. Seven dead. I wait and I wait, and future me doesn't manifest to tell me not to go and warn the school.

But I'm scared. Scared of my power. I don't want to rule the world. I want the world to be a better place. But I want those kids not to have died.

I don't know what to do.

Winter sixty-nine, and the Gabriel Ivins band is on tour, promoting their first album. I haven't been to see him for a while – his time. That last consequence wave was a large one. I almost expected a visit from Ms Remek. But she didn't come, so I manifested in a pub in Newcastle.

The band is mainly session musicians put together by Calibre records. Older than Gabriel. Competent but without his verve.

I drift through the audience watching the show. And Gabriel is bad. You can tell the roadies have turned down his guitar feed. His hand is strumming in a jittery way that's out of tune with the rest of the band. And his lovely smooth voice is all harsh – like he's inventing death metal twenty years too early.

That gave me a chill, but I'm pretty sure I've never mentioned future music trends to him.

The audience drinks. They don't pay him much attention.

Backstage in the green room after the gig, and he's got three groupies groping him on the couch. Nobody drinks beer, it's all whisky.

Gabriel was knocking them back, but then he finally sees me. He lets out this stupid wolf howl of greeting. "Man, I missed you. It is you, isn't it?"

One of the groupies who's got the whole Goth thing right before there were any, frowned in my direction. But she was smoking a thick reefer so she didn't really think anything was wrong or weird.

"It's me."

"Cool. I thought you'd left me."

"No."

"Do you like the album?"

"I do." The album had some neat songs; on the recording Gabriel's voice had been appealing and evocative. *Downcountry* was a protest about 'Nam. It was charting, number seventeen last week – its highest. He was doing something, making his voice heard, inspiring others. I was so proud of him when I discovered that.

Trouble was, up on stage he'd just been awful.

"Thanks, man. Hey, did we meet up in futureland like we said?"

The groupies giggled at that.

"Yes," I lied.

"Cool. What's life like up there?"

"We gave up. We stopped protesting. The whole world's going to hell."

"Bummer, huh?"

Then one of the roadies came in, and gave Gabriel a nod. He lumbered to his feet and staggered across the room. The roadie slipped him a small leather wallet. Gabriel went into the toilets.

My Gabriel is doing hard drugs.

Gabriel Ivins died March 17th 1970 from a drugs overdose. Although his band's first album was moderately successful, Ivins had to cancel the promotional tour half way through due to 'exhaustion'. He spent the following months alone writing new songs. Recording for his new album, *Paradise Unglimpsed,* was scheduled to begin in April 1970. His record company, Calibre, was declared bankrupt a month later.

I'm in the lounge, crying, when Ms Remek comes in. She gives me a thoughtful look, and asks: "Have you been seeing Gabriel Ivins?"

"No. Yes. He dies anyway."

"There have been consequences."

I nod miserably. "I know. The wave wasn't very big."

"That's because you're only surfing it for twenty years. There are significant consequences later on."

"Oh." I try to make out like I'm interested. "I see future me hasn't manifested.

So how bad is it?"

"Not enough to warrant a full intervention against you. Soothers were called in to calm certain situations."

"Oh good, so the future stays perfect then."

Ms Remek frowns, determining how much sarcasm and sass I'm giving her. Because just this month Anna Lindh was stabbed to death by some religious nutter, Iran is refusing to cooperate with the nuclear inspectorate, Osama bin Laden says Al-Qaeda is developing biological weapons, the British National Party got a councillor elected in a Thurrock by-election, a suicide bomber killed eight people in Israel, airstrikes in Zabul province killed seventeen people. And Johnny Cash died. I could have stopped those bombings and killings. I wonder what consequences that would have? People getting to live their lives and have a chance at happiness.

"The future doesn't get any worse," she says tetchily.

"What's the point?" I ask.

"The point?"

"Of our ability? If all we do is use it to keep everything the same. Why do we have it?"

"You just answered your own question. This is as good as it gets."

I shake my head. I refuse to believe that. "There must be somewhere out there in the parallels, a world where we get it right. We could use it as a template."

"Maybe there is. But if it is out there, it's beyond any sidedreamer I've ever talked to."

"So now what?"

"So be careful, please."

I nod. I know she's being reasonable, and semi-sympathetic, but it still makes no sense to me.

I want to make a difference. I want to stop the ugliness that contaminates this world.

When Ms Remek leaves I make myself a promise. In the future, I'll come back to now and tell me something that can be stopped. If I can't influence other people, then I can use facts; if someone's going to get shot or bombed then I can warn them or the police myself. I will make a difference.

But I don't manifest in front of me. I break my promise. Why? Why why why?

Gabriel's new digs weren't any better than his student ones. He'd got a flat in a grand old house overlooking the Cam, with two more rooms than last time, an extra bedroom and a tiny kitchen. The squalor remained the same.

When I manifested, he was lying on the worn settee, a week's stubble on his cheeks, and looking so thin I could believe he hadn't eaten for the whole of that same week. A guitar lay on top of him. There was a syringe and all the rest of his drugs crap on the carpet beside him.

He was dozing fitfully. I almost left, then. Except it was mid-afternoon on March the seventeenth, nineteen seventy. Gabriel Ivins would be dead before the end of the day.

I drifted round the room. He had been writing, bless him. There were pieces of paper scattered about, some scrunched up on the floor. All of them holding his lyrics, lines crossed out – re-written again and again. Ten sheets had been laid out neatly on the table: his songs for *Paradise Unglimpsed*, the album he never got to make.

As always, Gabriel's lyrics were profound and eloquent. He spoke of worlds where people don't kill, where peace breaks out not war, where hunger and hatred is a memory. A world far far away from ours.

The world I want to live in.

"You came back," he croaked.

I went over to the settee and gazed down on him. His eyes were brutally bloodshot. I saw now how the fluffy stubble disguised sunken cheeks. "Yes, I came back."

"I thought you'd given up on me."

"No, Gabriel." I forced a grin. "I've spent too much time to abandon you now."

"That's stupid, man. I am just one giant fuck-up."

"No you're not. I read your lyrics. They're beautiful, Gabriel. Congratulations."

"Matt wants me to lay down another album. I can't do it. Touring, man, it's too heavy. I'm not built for it."

"You went sideways, didn't you, a decent world a long way sideways into the parallels?"

He dropped his head in his hands. "I don't know. Maybe. I was out of it. I don't know if it was real or a real dream."

"There's no such thing."

"Yeah." He nodded weakly.

I stared at his syringe. "Have you been trying to go back there, Gabriel?"

"Yes."

"You can't."

My beautiful sweet Gabriel started to cry. "I hate myself."

"Sing for me," I told him. "Play the songs you wrote. I want to hear *Paradise Unglimpsed*."

"What's that?"

"Ooops. That's the title of your next album."

"Not bad, man. Hey, you're not supposed to tell me that."

"I know. I'll put up with the heat just this once. Hearing you sing them will make it worthwhile."

"Okay. Yeah, groovy." He picked up his guitar.

Gabriel Ivins sang his unmade album to me in that bleak grey, cold Cambridge afternoon. He sang his songs the way they were meant to be sung, with hope and pleading.

"That's what music is for," I told him reverently when he finished. "To give people courage, to inspire them."

He grinned nervously. "Are you crying future fairy?"

"Yes, Gabriel, I'm crying. I'm crying because we can never go to that parallel world you dreamed. The only way we will ever live it, is to turn our world into it."

His gaze dropped down to the syringe.

"Listen to me, Gabriel." I knelt in front of him, imploring. "You have to tell people a life like that is possible. You can do it. You can inspire them. Sing it loud, Gabriel. Sing it to the whole world. This is the only age when music counts. After this, the companies and producers take over. The money wins. It's never about the music again."

"I just want to go back there," he said brokenly.

"You never do," I told him. Suddenly I was standing, my expression stern. "You're going to die, Gabriel. Today."

"What the fuck, man?"

"You die. Here in this god-awful rat's nest. You overdose on the shit you're injecting yourself with. Nobody will ever hear *Paradise Unglimpsed*. This world will carry on along its vile corrupt course. It needs to be changed, Gabriel. You can do that. Sing for me Gabriel, show people what a decent life full of love can be. Sing that they don't have to live like this. Be my angel, Gabriel. Save the world."

And I leave him like that, gaping at me in astonishment and fear. I surf the consequence wave into the new realtime. I'm not afraid, it is exhilarating. I watch him make his choice, the right choice, stamping on the syringe, breaking it.

Gabriel lives. He goes on to record Paradise Unglimpsed, *which charts high. Then goes on to record his next album. People flock to his gigs. They hear his songs and sing them loud.*

Changes flood out from the wave. Multiplying. The changes carry his message of love and hope with them, spilling right across the world. The difference builds and builds.

Until the Reading Rock Festival in '77. Thousands of happy people sailing across a sea of mud swirl around me. The consequence means it's now Gabriel Ivins who headlines on Sunday night, not the Sensational Alex Harvey Band.

My mother is in the crowd, her arms raised above her head, swaying from side to side as she chants Gabriel's anthem: Beyond a Dream. Absorbing the love he evokes. Questions about the way we live are kindled in her deepest thoughts. But she doesn't meet dad there. The consequence has put him somewhere else.

And I'm witnessing the world I want born. It is the most exquisite moment I know. Ten simple honest songs, my gift as I am unborn –

Beyond the Heliopause

Keith Brooke and Eric Brown

As soon as the recorded message pinged in her peripheral vision she accepted and listened to the call on her cochlear implant. "Suzanne, I need to see you. It's urgent. I... well, I'll tell you when I see you. All my love."

She was in a borrowed apartment in Paris, finishing a piece about corruption in the European Parliament. She rounded the story off with a couple of vox pops and some infographics, squirted the file to her editor in London, and then forwarded it to her street team to get the social buzz going.

Folding her screen away, she sat back and replayed her father's message, but she didn't pick up anything new from his words or tone. Then she booked a seat on the noon flight from Orly to Stansted and took a taxi to the airport. She would be in the sleepy Suffolk village of Little Tinningham, if all went well, before the early December sunset.

Her father had sounded weary. If the call had been from anyone else she would have replied instantly, but her father hated his days to be interrupted by 'importunate calls', as he called them – even from loved ones.

She wondered why he needed to see her so urgently.

Suzanne looked away from the window as the jet took off. Across the aisle she saw a big, silver-haired man in his forties, and for a second she thought it was Charles. She even wondered what her ex-husband was doing back on Earth when the man turned to speak to the hostess and she realised her mistake. She felt a surge of relief, sat back and closed her eyes as the take-off forced her back into the seat.

She summoned a retinal menu and selected a news channel. Thoughts of Charles made her wonder how the Heliopause Project was progressing. Two years ago there had been nothing else on the science and technology newsfeeds but the joint Europe-US mission to send a scientific research station out beyond the orbit of Pluto – to map the vast universe beyond, as the pop-hacks termed the project. Since then, the news had dried up.

Sometimes, in her more paranoid moments, Suzanne wondered whether Charles had used the project as an excuse to leave her. He'd been offered the directorship of the mission: an offer too good to refuse, he'd told her, and almost off-handedly added, "And anyway, you and me... our relationship... it was never going anywhere–"

"Never going anywhere'? My God. We're *married*... Doesn't that mean a damned thing to you? I love you, Charles!"

He'd smiled his insufferably arrogant smile and said, "No, Su, you just *think* you do."

And so he walked out of her life for ever.

Stansted was as busy as Orly, but a few minutes after taking a taxi from the airport – as they left the A120 and took a B road north to Suffolk – she was staring out across open fields and peaceful villages consisting of clusters of thatched cottages. She tried to visit her father every month and, as always, it was like going back in time to an earlier, more innocent age. She could forget the modern world, the ceaseless influx of information, forget the space race that saw the superpowers staking claim after claim to chunks of Mars, Venus, and individual asteroids – switch off her implant and for two days at a time enjoy the company of her father. He was nearing ninety, and she knew that her visits would one day end.

She wondered if these trips were nothing more than a reversion to her childhood, a reaction to her husband's leaving her. When she had been with Charles her visits had been far less frequent but then, when he left, they had saved her sanity. Her father's company and the village where she had grown up were a refuge, a haven of familiarity and reassurance in a brash and complex world.

Half an hour after leaving Stansted, Little Tinningham appeared through the mist, a collection of ghostly houses, a church steeple and, next to it, her father's rambling thatched house. An orange light showed in a small downstairs window, and she knew he'd have a log fire blazing.

She paid the driver and hurried inside.

Over a dinner of minestrone soup followed by roast beef, prepared by her father's housekeeper, he asked her about her work. She told him about the recent conferences she'd attended and the corruption piece she'd finished that day.

Her father was a tall, perilously thin man, stooped and grey. His dog collar, which he still wore even though he'd retired as a Church of England rector twenty years ago, hung loose on his wattled neck. Suzanne thought he looked ill since her last visit, and lacked energy. He ate a small meal slowly, without appetite.

He suggested a brandy after dinner and they sat in the front room before the roaring fire. This was Suzanne's favourite room in the house. She imagined the previous inhabitants warming themselves here on long winter's nights: Elizabethans, Stuarts and Georgians... right up to the present day. The house was over five hundred years old and the sense of history in the air was like a physical presence.

During a lull in the conversation – her father had been bringing her up to date on the doings of various villagers, and for a time he had seemed his old, animated self – she sipped her brandy and asked, "You said you wanted to see me urgently. Is something..." She had been about to say 'wrong', but she paused and her father interrupted.

"I know you don't believe, Suzanne." He smiled. "What did you once say? That you haven't a spiritual bone in your body?"

"I've always been impressed that you never tried to make me believe. Never. I respect you for that, you know?"

He sighed. His fingers, curled around his brandy glass, seemed as white as bone. His eyes regarded the flames. "Well, you were right."

She blinked at the discontinuity in the conversation. "About?"

"About the idea of a God. There really is nothing... *nothing*... is there?" His gaze remained on the dancing flames.

Suzanne felt sick. Her father's faith had been his rock, his foundation. She could not imagine how he might exist without it.

"What makes you say that?"

He lifted his gaze from the fire and looked at her. "I've lost my faith, Suzanne. I look back and think of all the years I believed. I wonder what sustained me. I wonder *why* I believed, what gave me faith. It was an inner conviction, something as elemental within me as my... as my life blood. And it is as if that life blood, that faith, has suddenly drained away, leaving nothing. A terrible emptiness."

He looked back at the fire, gripping his glass tightly.

She felt tears sting her eyes. She shook her head. "But why, so suddenly?"

He gave a weary smile. "But it wasn't sudden, Suzanne. It happened years ago, little by little, a gnawing doubt. The diagnosis..."

The word pierced her like an arrow. "Diagnosis'?"

He drew a heavy sigh. "I'm old, Suzanne. We can't expect to live for ever. They found a tumour during my last check-up." He tapped his balding skull. "Up here. Inoperable. They give me three to six months. I'm sorry, Suzanne. I... I didn't want to tell you, but that wouldn't have been fair, would it?"

She set her glass aside, rose and crossed to the settee where he sat. She held his hand in silence, words beyond her. She felt his old bones, his frailty, smelled his old man odour.

She gripped his hand and said, "Perhaps the tumour…e laughed. "What? Do you think the tumour might be responsible for my loss of faith? You know better than that. Anyway, according to the specialist it's only been there for a year at most. My doubt began long before that."

"I'm sorry," she murmured, and wondered if she was referring to his illness or his doubt.

"I really believed the whole Christian offering, you know? The reward of Heaven for the virtuous. Now..." He sighed. "Now, it feels like a weight has lifted, being able to say these things aloud."

"It's been your life," said Suzanne. "Don't you miss it?"

"Some," he said. "Do you know what I miss most? The notion that we were created for some purpose... That all this–" he gave a brief wave of the hand, a simple gesture which conveyed so much more "–is not for nothing."

She had no answer to that. She sat gripping her father's hand and stared into the flames.

The following morning, the glow on the beamed ceiling of her bedroom told her that the forecast snow had fallen during the night.

She slipped out of bed and stood before the tiny mullioned window. She looked out over a landscape transformed, softened. Snow covered the lane and the rolling fields beyond, relieved only where vertical surfaces resisted its attention and showed black: tree trunks and stone walls. A dazzling sun hung low in the east.

She would have breakfast and then go for a long walk.

Her father was already up, and it was as if their conversation of the night before had never occurred. He was bright and alert over toast and coffee, chattering away about the Christmas Lights committee, of which he was chairman.

After breakfast she asked him if he was up to a hike, but he held up an old hardback book, a detective novel dating from the last century. "Mrs Humphries has built a fire. I'll spend the morning reading, Suzanne."

She wrapped up well and set off. The morning was bitter cold but bright; frost had created a crust on the snow and thick panes like shattered glass over puddles in the lane. She climbed a stile and set off over the rising meadow opposite her father's house. The snow was a virgin expanse, not yet marred by footprints.

Fifteen minutes later, at the crest of the rise, she turned and stared down at the village nestling, impossibly tranquil, in the fold of the hills. She pictured her father in his chair by the fire, rug over his lap, absorbed in his whodunit.

Tears found tracks down her cheeks, stinging in the freezing wind. She dashed them away with the back of her gloved hand and set off again.

Her father was eighty-nine; he'd had a long, rewarding life. But, she realised later as she rounded the wood where she'd played as a girl, and approached the village from the east, it was not his imminent death she was mourning as much as the announcement of his lost faith.

He should have been able to go in peace, she thought, comforted by the belief in an omnipotent Creator in whom he had believed all his life. And yes, she was very aware of the irony in a humanist mourning the loss of another's belief.

As she turned into Church Lane, she saw a big black Lexus pulled up outside her father's house.

Two tall figures, garbed in black suits, stood on either side of the car and stared at her as she approached.

Confused, she thought at first that something had happened to her father. She hurried up the lane, then realised that she was wrong. These men were nothing to do with the medical profession.

"Ms Lingard?" one of them enquired as she approached. "Ms Suzanne Lingard?"

"Yes?" She stopped in the lane, staring from one man to the other. "What is it?"

"You're offline. We've been trying to contact you."

"Who are you?"

"We're with the Heliopause Project," said the man to her right.

Her heart thudded as if her blood had turned to molasses. "And?"

"And we have an urgent communiqué," said the man to her left.

Urgent. That word again. "From...?" she asked, but she knew very well who it was from. What she wanted to know was *why*?

"If there is somewhere we could be private?"

She showed them into the house, past the room where her father would be reading and into the library. The men stood before the empty hearth and one of them said, "If you could reconnect to the 'net, Ms Lingard?"

She did so, her peripheral vision pinging with a dozen missed calls. She silenced them, dismissed the retinal menu, and stared at the men.

"Very well."

"We'll be waiting outside the room," one of them said. "This is for your information only." He nodded, and a figure appeared before Suzanne.

She moved to the table, reached out to steady herself. She noticed the men slip from the room; the door clicked shut behind them.

Her ex-husband stood before her, only the slight pixilation at his extremities belying the fact of his physical presence. He had aged; his hair was greyer, his face a little heavier. He'd never been one to mask his imperfections with virtual overlays; she'd give him that.

For a second she thought that this was a real-time interactive communiqué, then realised her mistake. The distance would have made that impossible.

If he were still beyond the heliopause...

He spoke, and she was relieved to see that it was a recording.

"Su, I hope you're well, and I hope you'll hear me out and not shut this down or walk out... though I'd fully understand if you did. I'm sorry for what I did, back then. The thing is, I'd like to make amends." He raised a hand. "Hear me out," he went on, anticipating her reaction. She pulled out a chair, dropped into it, and stared at her ex-husband's avatar.

"I'm beyond Pluto on the research vessel. I won't beat about the bush. We've found something. Something big." He smiled, as if his words were ironic. "It will change everything – everything we know about everything. I'd like you to come out and meet me here. I'll show you what we've found, and then you can break it to the world. I've cleared this with our backers, and they've conducted all the requisite security checks on you." He smiled. "I know it'll never really make up for what I did, Su, but it's the only way I can think of to apologise."

He waited a second, then went on. "You'd leave right away, with Jeffries and Usher, for the spacefield at Utrecht. From there you'd take a shuttle to orbit, and then a cruiser out to the heliopause. Journey time, a little under a week. I'd show you around here for a day, maybe two, then you'd return with your scoop. After that... well, you'd be in demand, let me assure you of that." He laughed. "I hope you accept. Just tell Jeffries and Usher, and you can be on your way." He lifted a hand. "Goodbye, Su."

His image vanished. She heard a discreet cough behind her. She'd never even heard the pair enter the room.

She stared at them.

The Heliopause Project had found something, something big.

"Well, Ms Lingard?"

"I need a little time to talk this over with my father."

"We can give you thirty minutes, but the schedule is tight."

She brushed past them, hurried along the warped passage to the front room, knocked and entered.

Her father looked up, smiled, and laid aside his detective novel. "Is something wrong?" he asked, his smile faltering.

She knelt before him, took his hand and said, "Something's happened out there, with the Heliopause Project. I just had a call from Charles. He wants me to go out there, report on it."

She explained what Charles had said.

For a fraction of a second she saw fear in his eyes. "For how long?"

"A little over two weeks."

He smiled. Relieved, she thought. He gripped her hand. "And do you want to go?"

Did she want to see Charles again, he meant.

She hesitated, then nodded.

"Then go, Suzanne. It's an opportunity you'd be a fool to pass up."

"I'll come straight back to you," she said. "You'll be the first person I'll tell about what I find, I promise."

He echoed her words. "It will change everything we know about everything..." he said.

She lifted her father's frail hand and kissed his fingers.

She started to drip feed the story from the shuttle flight to Utrecht, warning her networks and street team that she was going to have some downtime for the next couple of weeks, and hinting that Christmas was going to bring something big this year.

Her editor called almost immediately, wanting to know what was going on. "I don't know," she told her. "Something big is all I can say. You just have to trust me, like you did with Jencke, okay?" The Jencke story had won her the first of her European Press Awards, six years ago, and it was guaranteed to win pretty much any argument with her editor on the rare occasion she felt the need to wheel it out. "Could you get Nikki to cover for me?"

"Nikki's on a break to finish her new documentary," said her editor. "Seems like everyone wants a long Christmas this year."

There was only one other person waiting in the executive lounge at Utrecht when Suzanne arrived, escorted by Jeffries and Usher.

"Nikki? Is that you? I thought you had a documentary to edit?"

"*Suzanne*?"

The women approached each other, kissed cheeks and hugged, then stepped back like wary animals.

"You want to tell me what's going on?" Nikki asked. She was short, with spiky dark hair and cheeks that tended to pinkness like those of a china doll. "I thought I had an exclusive..."

"You're not the only one," said Suzanne. The two of them went back years together, both at the forefront of the new journalism that harnessed the power of the networks, riding the waves of viral news-chatter, seeding and feeding stories as they went. 'Herding the waves' Nikki had termed it, way back.

A new arrival interrupted their reunion.

"Chinwag," whispered Nikki, as if Suzanne wouldn't recognise the young journalist who went by that name online.

Right now, she desperately regretted signing an agreement that had included a comms blackout for the duration of this trip. If Nikki, Suzanne, and Chinwag were here, then there must be others, and the 'nets would be buzzing with rumours about their absence.

She thought back to the message from Charles, and cursed the way she'd weakened like some simpering fool in response to his request. He'd said nothing about exclusivity. He'd just implied it, while laying heavy emphasis on this being a personal thing, a way for him to make up for his bastard past.

It was a job. She should just remind herself of that. A pretty damned *big* job, if this little gathering was anything to go by.

She could live with that.

"So what's it all about? Why us? What have they found?"

The same questions, over and over again. That kind of repeated speculation would have been bad enough in the best of circumstances, but in such claustrophobic confines it was the verbal equivalent of the Chinese water torture.

Suzanne cut herself off from the chatter as much as possible, after the first few rounds had been enough to confirm that not one of the journalists squeezed into this cruiser had the faintest idea what was really going on.

The worst of it was all the hanging around and the slow acceleration out of orbit; she was thankful that much of the journey would be spent under sedation in a gel bunk, to protect them all from the heavy acceleration.

She'd gone zero-gee before, so she knew what to expect. She knew the tiredness and nausea would pass, and that eventually she'd regain the knack of controlling the exaggerated movements of her limbs. And she knew that she would even get accustomed to the lack of personal space and boundaries, the touch and smells of so many others in such close confines.

She tried not to dwell on how she might react when she met Charles again. He had been the one man, other than her father, who could break through her barriers. He could be infuriating and charming in the same breath, but he was also rarely less than interesting.

Perhaps that was it. Perhaps their relationship had always been destined to break under the strain. She had been drawn to him for the same reasons she was drawn to journalism: she wanted to be inspired, she wanted to see things she had never seen before. Charles had intrigued and fascinated her, and he would not have been Charles if he'd turned down the opportunity to lead a mission to travel farther than any human being had gone before.

Like a comet drawn to the sun, his trajectory must always pull him away again.

At the research station there was a different, almost minty freshness to the air, which Suzanne knew was only in contrast to the rank air of the cruiser. There was room to move around; places where the only sounds were the mechanical, physical sounds of the station: the hum of pipes and fans, unidentifiable clunks and thuds and whistles and background hiss. There was a viewing area that showed them real-time views from outside, the sun merely a bright star from this far out.

She should have been more bowled over by all this, she knew. For all that she was blasé about being an orbital veteran, this was way more than mere orbital: this was 'we've almost left the Solar System'.

All of this should have had far more impact.

But there was Charles, hanging in the viewing gallery to greet the new arrivals, and she was pitched back two years, to when they'd been together. She hated that response. She was *not* that weak, dependent kind of woman.

You and me... our relationship... it was never going anywhere…

Cameras always add a few pounds. When he'd messaged her he'd looked as if he was carrying a bit more weight, but no, he'd looked after himself out here. You had to; it was all part of the discipline.

There was something about him, though. Something that had changed. A change more significant than the greying at his temples.

"Su."

He ignored the rest of them, focused only on Suzanne. There was something in his eyes. Fear. Was he scared of how she would treat him?

Then he snapped his attention into a broader focus, gave that charismatic smile of his and spread his arms, welcoming the dozen journalists who had just emerged not-at-all fresh from the cruiser.

"Welcome," he said. "We really are pleased to have you join us."

From this point on, everything he said was for public consumption. They would be recording him with retinal cams, sub-voking their own commentaries into storage, all ready for when the media blackout was lifted.

"I know you've all been speculating about the reason for this strange invitation," he went on. "You're wondering why a multi-billion euro project like this wouldn't already have a communications plan in place, why we would scrap all that and turn to you guys instead. And I know you're all going to be incredibly frustrated when I refuse to tell you."

There was an immediate surge of grumbling voices. All this way, for... well, for *what*?

Suzanne held back. She knew Charles' ways, and she had seen him smiling as he delivered that message.

He raised his hands for silence, and went on, "If I was going to merely *tell* you, there would have been no need to bring you out here. We're going to show you, instead. We're going to give you twenty minutes to freshen up and then we're going to show you why you're here. We're going to show you the discovery of a lifetime. Of *any* lifetime. And then we're going to ask you to go back to Earth and do all you can to prepare the ground for the breaking of this story. Because when this is made public we have no way of anticipating the response. You're here because you're the best, and you have networks and street teams where elements of this story can be seeded and spread so that people are, in some way at least, prepared."

Only now did Suzanne recognise that look in his eye, the subtext to all of this. Only now did she see that it *was* fear.

They filed into one of the station's shuttles, a couple of the less experienced guests in danger of turning the process into a game of zero-gee billiards. Threading her way through the bodies, Suzanne managed to snag herself into a seat up front next to Charles.

"No windows on these things, but you could have rigged up some viewscreens so we could see outside if you wanted us to. What's going on, Charles? The only time I've seen you looking more scared than this was when you were reciting your vows." A low blow, but she could have delivered better if she hadn't been holding back. Two years' worth of better.

He put a hand on hers, where it rested on her knee, and that surprised her so much she let it lie. He really was on edge. She tried not to take too much comfort from his touch.

"You don't know how much I want to tell you, Su. How much I want to say. Something like this... well, it stops you in your tracks. Makes you reassess your life, everything."

"It must be big if it's made you realise what a bastard you were."

The look in his eyes. It was as if she'd just kicked a puppy.

"Why can't you tell me?"

A long silence, then: "I... Hell, Su, there just aren't the words for it. That's why you guys are here. There just aren't the words."

As the shuttle pulled away from the station, briefly pressing them back into their seats, Charles raised a hand for the attention of the other passengers. "This will just be a short hop," he said. "So don't make yourselves too comfortable." There were a few grunts and chuckles in response: nobody was ever going to get comfortable in the cramped passenger hold of one of these tiny crates.

"We are now approaching the heliopause, a notional boundary line where the force of the solar wind is counter-balanced by that of the stellar winds of our neighbouring stars. A bow wave, if you like, as our home star ploughs through the interstellar medium."

"So what are we looking out for?" Chinwag asked.

"According to theory and the most recent readings before this expedition, there should be a number of measurable effects, including changes in the magnetic field and an increased level of cosmic radiation. None of these should affect us within this shuttle."

"So what are we looking for?" the journalist repeated.

"If I could just beg your patience for a few more minutes," Charles said, and would say no more.

The end of the shuttle hop was marked with a jolt and a muffled, metallic clank.

Charles had held her hand for the whole fifteen minutes, but now he released his grip and pushed away from his seat's retainers. Twisting in mid-air, he caught himself against the forward bulkhead and looked around the gathered journalists.

That same scared look again.

"Ladies and gentlemen of the press," he said. "I am about to say the first of many sentences I never imagined myself saying. Ladies and gentlemen, we have just landed on the heliopause."

The babble of voices showed no sign of dying down as the journalists bombarded Charles with questions. Even when Charles spoke, the noise barely eased. "Please," he said. "If you would follow me to the airlock. We're going outside."

The journalists exchanged glances. Chinwag said, "Did I hear that right? Outside?"

Charles said, "That's right. We're going *outside*."

"But aren't we going to suit up?"

Charles smiled to himself and indicated the airlock.

There was only room for four at a time in the lock, and Charles made sure that Suzanne was among the three to join him. On one wall someone had placed a handwritten sign with a big arrow and the word 'DOWN'.

Just as she was puzzling over this, and wondering why they didn't have to wear suits, the outer door hissed open and Charles took her hand and tugged her out – and instantly the meaning of the sign became clear.

Out here... outside the damned *shuttle*... there was a down.

She fell, expecting to hurt herself. Instead she landed on all fours on a grey, sponge-like substance. She looked around herself in wonder. They were in a tunnel a little wider than the shuttle.

Charles helped her to her feet, studying her reactions. "We're here," he said. "*Inside* the heliopause."

"That's another one of those sentences you didn't think you'd ever say, right?"

"What is it?" That was Nikki, climbing to her feet. She clearly hadn't understood the notice and had been taken by surprise by the up and down after the zero-gee of the station.

The other journalist, a guy Suzanne vaguely recognised from his online avatar, stayed quiet, as if struck dumb.

"What *is* this place?" asked Nikki, more forcefully this time.

"It's what it looks like," said Charles. "A tunnel. A tunnel through the heliopause."

The tunnel was about five metres high and wide, with a flat floor and arched walls and ceiling, as if a horse's hoof had been pushed through the 'pause's spongy material.

The airlock had cycled again as they spoke, and another batch of four tumbled from the shuttle. When all twelve were out, along with four members of Charles' team, the project's director stood before them.

"I'm sorry," he said. "I really am sorry that we couldn't have prepared you for this. But how do you prepare people for the inconceivable?" He gave a soft laugh then, before continuing. "Well, that's why you're here. All the communications plans in the world couldn't prepare us. Telling you is not enough. We had to bring you here and show you, and then it's down to you to work out with us how on Earth we break this to the rest of the human race."

Voices rose again the moment he paused for breath. As he waved back towards the shuttle, heads turned and the babble eased. "We have just passed through an airlock. It was encrypted, but my team is good: we worked out how to get through. It was a little easier than expected. My own view is that we were meant to find our way through. If we've reached this point, maybe we're smart enough to be entrusted with what lies beyond. If you'd care to follow me, we have a short hike, and then you will see what only a few before you have seen."

"But… but what *is* this?"

"It's a shell," Charles said. "A great shell around the solar system. It's clearly an artificial construct. Like the skin around a bubble or balloon; a Dyson sphere, if you like. We don't know what it's made of, but we believe that the heliopause itself possesses some form of sentience: enough to constantly manipulate what we could see and measure from Earth. Enough to cast the illusion of the universe as we have understood it up until very recently."

None of this, Suzanne thought, could be real.

She stood there, trying to let at least some of it sink in. The universe… an *illusion*. A smart shield around the solar system, manipulating their view of what lay beyond.

"So, Charles," she said, and somehow her small voice cut through the jabber and everyone turned to look at her. "If everything up until now has been some clever kind of illusion… if we've grown up isolated from the real universe… then what *is* out there? What's beyond the heliopause?"

*

Bubbles.

Thousands of them. Millions of them. Each with a slightly oily sheen against the darkness of the void.

Like bubbles in a glass of champagne.

Each bubble, another solar system, shut off like their own.

"Nobody could have ever conceived of something like this," Charles said, standing at her shoulder. They had walked for longer than the shuttle flight had taken, maybe two kilometres, Suzanne guessed. Now they gathered on some kind of viewing platform, a clear blister on the outside of the heliopause. It was as if this had all been set up for them, as if this moment had been orchestrated by some greater intelligence. A rite of passage. Already, the story was shaping in her head, as Charles had known it must.

"I'm so sorry, Su," he said, and for long seconds she was confused at his abrupt change in tack. "I was a bastard," he went on. "Worse: a *calculated* bastard. Back then, I had to make a choice and I chose this. We didn't know what we'd find back then, of course. Only that it would be world-shattering. Ever since Voyager 1 hit the heliopause back in 2013 we knew things must be very different to what we had, until then, understood. That's why we had to come out here to see for ourselves, just as the creators of this shell must have intended."

"You chose this." How could he not?

"We didn't know what we'd find. We didn't know if we'd ever return."

And so he had been brutal. He had chosen to break her heart rather than leave her pining for a distant love who may never come home.

"You bastard."

"I know." He reached down and took her hand once again, and she decided to let him, for now.

The journalists talked. They talked so much it hurt and still they continued, buzzing with speculations and ideas about how to handle this astonishing news. There would be official announcements, of course. Even as the team of journalists headed back to Earth, governments and international agencies were planning how to break the news. But nothing would happen until the ground had been prepared with countless seedings across the 'net. All of those invited out to the heliopause were skilled in this, the new journalism. It was about managing the chatter, herding the waves; it was about building speculation and rumour and discussion until they went viral and then the extraordinary would appear to be the inevitable when the news finally broke.

But first... First, Suzanne had a promise to keep.

The snow had gone now, and the soft Suffolk landscape was blurred with a steady drizzle. Shutting down her implant, she lost touch with the buzz. As always, it felt like an amputation, particularly at a time like this. In the back seat of the taxi, she closed her eyes and took a deep breath.

She recalled what Charles had said, before she'd boarded the shuttle home. He was returning to Earth in a couple of months, and he wanted to see her again. Suzanne had been too stunned by his words to work out how she felt about his request; she'd prevaricated, said she needed time to think it over.

But before she made that decision, she had another to consider. She opened her eyes and stared out across the lawn of her father's house, to where a light glowed in the living-room window.

She wondered how far the disease might have progressed in this short space of time?

"I said, 'We're here'."

The driver.

"One minute?" she said, and closed her eyes again. She had promised her father she would tell him first, but now she was filled with doubt. How would he take the news? Would it be the final nail in the coffin of his faith?

But then... a phrase Charles had used came back to her. *That's why we had to come out here to see for ourselves, just as the creators of this shell must have intended.*

There may be no one Creator, but there really was so much more than just *this*.

She might never be able to renew her father's faith, but she knew that she would reawaken his sense of wonder.

"Okay," she told the driver. "Thank you. I'm ready now."

The Seventh Gamer

Gwyneth Jones

The Anthropologist Returns to Eden

She introduced herself by firelight, while the calm breakers on the shore kept up a background music – like the purring breath of a great sleepy animal. It was warm, the air felt damp; the night sky was thick with cloud. The group inspected her silently. Seven pairs of eyes, gleaming out of shadowed faces. Seven adult strangers, armed and dangerous; to whom she appeared a helpless, ignorant infant. Chloe tried not to look at the belongings that had been taken from her, and now lay at the feet of a woman with long black hair, who was dressed in an oiled leather tunic and tight, broken-kneed jeans; a state-of-the-art crossbow slung at her back, a long knife in a sheath at her belt.

Chloe wanted to laugh, to jump up and down and wave her arms; or possibly just run away and quit this whole idea. But her sponsor was smiling encouragingly.

"Tell us about yourself, Chloe Hensen. Who are you?"

"I'm a hunter." she said. "That's my trade."

"Really." The crossbow woman sounded as if she doubted it. "And how are you aligned?"

"I'm not. I travel alone, seeking what fascinates me. I hunt the white wolf on the tundra and the jaguar in the rainforest, and I desire not to kill, but to know."

Someone chuckled. "That's a problem. Darkening World is a war game, girly. Didn't you realise?" It was the other woman in the group, the short, sturdy redhead: breaching etiquette.

"I'm not a pacifist. I'll fight. But killing is not my purpose. I wish to share your path for a while, and I commit to serving faithfully as a comrade, in peace and war. But I pursue my own cause. That is the way of my kind."

"Stay where you are," said her sponsor. "We need to speak privately. We'll be back."

Six of them withdrew into the trees that lined the shore. One pair of eyes, one shadowy figure remained: Chloe was under guard. The watcher didn't move or speak; she thought she'd better not speak to him, either. She looked away, toward the glimmer of the breakers: controlling her intense curiosity. There shouldn't be a seventh person, besides herself. There were only six guys in the game house team–

They reappeared and sat in a circle round her: Reuel, Lete, Matt, Kardish, Sol and Beat. (She *must* get their game names and real names properly sorted out). Silently they raised their hands in a ritual gesture, open palms cupping either side of their heads, like the hear-no-evil monkey protecting itself from scandal. Chloe's sponsor gestured for her to do the same.

She removed her headset, in unison with the others, and the potent illusion vanished. No shore, no weapons, no fancy dress, no synaesthetics. Chloe and the Darkening World team – recognisable but less imposing – sat around a table in a large, tidy kitchen: the Meeting Boxes piled like a heap of skulls in front of them.

"Okay," said Reuel, the "manager" of this game house, who was also her sponsor. "This is what we've got. You can stay, but you're on probation. We haven't made up our minds."

"Is she always going to talk like that?" asked the woman with the long black hair, of nobody in particular. (She was Lete the Whisperer, the group's shaman. Also known as Josie Nicks, one of DW's renowned rogue programmers).

"Give her a break," said Reuel. "She was getting in character. What's wrong with that?"

Reuel was tall and lanky, with glowing skin like polished mahogany and fine, strong features. He'd be very attractive, Chloe thought, were it not for his geeky habit of keeping a pen, or two or three, stuck in his springy hair. Red, green and blue feathers, or beads: okay, but pens looked like a neurological quirk. The nerd who mistook his hair for a shirt pocket.

He was Reuel in the game too. Convenience must be a high priority.

"Who wants bedtime tea?" Sol, with the far-receded hairline, whose game name she didn't recall, jumped up and busied about, setting mugs by the kettle. "Name your poisons! For the record, Chloe, I was in favour." He winked at her. "You're cute. And pleasantly screwy."

Reuel scowled. "Keep your paws off, Bear Man."

"I don't like the idea," grumbled Beat, the redhead. "I don't care if she's a jumped-up social scientist or a dirty, lying media-hound. Fine, she stays a day or two. Then we take her stuff, throw her out, and make sure we strip her brain of all data first."

Sol beamed. "Aileen's the mercurial type. She'll be your greatest fan by morning."

Jun, whose game identity was Kardish the Assassin, and Markus of the Wasteland (real name Matt Warks) dropped their chosen teabags into their personal mugs and stood together watching the kettle boil, without a word.

Thankfully Chloe's bunk was a single bedroom, so she could write up her notes without hiding in the bathroom. She was eager to record her first impressions. The many-layered, feedback-looped reality of that meeting. Seven people sitting in a kitchen, Boxes on their heads, typing their dialogue. Seven corresponding avatars in post-apocalyptic fancy-dress *speaking* that dialogue, on the dark lonely shore. A third layer where the plasticity of human consciousness, combined with a fabulously detailed 3D video-montage, created a sensory illusion that the first two layers were one. A *fourth* layer of exchanges, in a sidebar on the helmet screens (which Chloe knew was there, but as a stranger, she couldn't see it); that might include live comments from the other side of the world. And the mysterious seventh, who maybe had a human controller somewhere; or maybe not. That's evolution for you. It's an engine of complexity, not succession.

Chloe had got involved in video-gaming (other than as a casual user) on a fieldwork trip to Honduras. She was living with the urban poor, studying their cultural innovations, in statistically the most deadly violent country in the world – outside of active warzones. Everyone in "her" community was obsessed with an open source online role-playing game called *Copan*. Everyone played. Grandmothers tinkered with the programming: of course Chloe had to join in. While documenting this vital, absorbing cultural sandbox she'd become fascinated by the role of Non-Player Characters (NPCs) – and the simple trick, common to all video games, that allows "the game" to participate in itself.

A video game is a world where there's always somebody who knows your business. In a nuclear-disaster wasteland or a candy-coloured flowery meadow; on board an ominously deserted space freighter or in the back room of a dangerous dive in Post-Apocalypse City, without fail you're going to meet someone who says something like *Hi, you must be looking for the Great Amulet of Power so you can get into the Haunted Fall Out Shelter! I can help!* Typically, you'll then be given fiendishly puzzling instructions, but fortunately you are not alone. A higher-order NPC will provide advice and interpretation.

In any big modern game the complex NPCs were driven by sophisticated AI algorithms, enriched by feedback from real humans. Players might choose them as challenging opponents, or empathic allies, in preference to human partners. But Chloe wasn't so interested in imaginary friends (or imaginary enemies!) She wanted to study the mediators – the NPCs "whose" role was to explain the game.

She'd told her *Copan* friends what she was looking for, and they had recommended she get in touch with Darkening World.

Darkening World (DW) was a small to medium Post-Apocalyptic Type, Massive Multiuser Online Role Playing Game (MMORPG) with a big footprint for its subscriber-numbers. There were televised tournaments; there was gambling in which (allegedly) serious money changed hands. Pro-players stayed together in teams, honing their physical and mental skills. They sometimes lived together, which made a convenient set-up for studying their culture. But the game house tradition wasn't unique to DW, and that wasn't why Chloe was here. Her *Copan* friends had told her about the internet myth that some of Darkening World's NPCs were sentient aliens. The idea had grown on her – until she'd just had to find out what the hell this meant.

Reuel and his team were hardcore. They didn't merely *believe* that aliens were accessing the DW environment (through the many dimensions of the information universe). They knew it. Reuel's "Spirit Guide", his NPC partner in the game, was an alien.

Elbows on her desk, chin on her fists, Chloe reviewed her shorthand notes. (Nothing digital that might be compromising! This house was the most wired-up, saturated, Wi-Fi location she'd ever entered!). She liked Reuel, her sponsor. He was a nice guy, and sexy despite those pens. Was she putting him in a false position? She had not lied. She'd told him she was interested in Darkening World's NPCs; that she knew about his beliefs, and that she had an open mind. Was this true enough to be okay?

One thing she was sure of. *People who believe in barbarians, find barbarians*. If she came to this situation looking for crazy, stupid deluded neo-primitives: crazy, stupid deluded neo-primitives was all that she would find–

But what a thrill it had been to arrive on that beach! Like Malinowski in Melanesia, long ago: "alone on a tropical beach close to a native village, while the launch or dinghy which has brought you sails away out of sight . . ." *And then screwing up completely*, she recalled with a grin, *when I tried to speak the language*. In Honduras she'd often felt like a Gap Year kid, embarrassed by the kindness of people whose lives were so compromised. In the unreal world of this game she could *play*, without shame, at the romance of being an old-school adventurer, seeking ancient cultural truths among dangerous "natives".

Although of course she'd be doing real work too.

But what if the "natives" decided she wasn't playing fair? Gamers could be rough. There was that time, in World of Warcraft, when a funeral for a player who'd died in the real world was savagely ambushed. Mourners slaughtered, and a video of the atrocity posted online–

How do people habituated to extreme, unreal physical violence punish betrayal?

Like a player whose avatar, whose eye; whose *I* stands on the brink of a dreadful abyss, about to step onto the miniscule tightrope that crosses it, Chloe was truly frightened.

She was summoned to breakfast by a clear chime and a sexless disembodied voice. The gamer she'd liked least, on a very cursory assessment, was alone in the kitchen.

"Hi," he said. "I'm Warks, you're Chloe. Don't ever call me Matt, you don't know me. You ready for your initiation?"

"Of course."

"Get yourself rationed up." He sat and watched; his big soft arms folded, while Chloe, trying to look cool about it, wrangled an unfamiliar coffee machine, identified food sources, and put together cereal, milk, toast, butter, honey . . .

"You do know that's a two-way screen in your room, don't you? Like Orwell."

"Oh, wow," said Chloe. "Thank God I just didn't happen to stand in front of it naked!"

"Hey, set your visibility to whatever level you like. The controls are intuitive."

"Thanks." Chloe gave him her best bright-student gaze. "Now what happens?"

"Finish your toast, go back to your room. Review your costume, armour and weaponry options, which you'll find pretty basic. Unless maybe you've brought some DW grey-market collateral you plan to install? On the sly?"

She shook her head, earnestly. "Not me!"

Warks smirked. "Yeah, I know. I'm house security. I've deep-scanned your devices, and checked behind your eyes and between your ears also: you're clean. Make your choices, don't be too ambitious, and we'll be waiting in the Rumpus Room."

He then vanished. Literally.

Chloe wished she'd spotted she was talking to a hologram, and hoped she'd managed not to look startled. She wondered if Matt, er, *Warks's* bullying was him getting in character, or was she being officially hazed by her new housemates? *They will challenge me*, she thought. *They have a belief that they know is unbelievable, and whatever I say they think I'm planning to make them look like fools. I'll need to win their trust.*

The Rumpus Room was in the basement. The hardware was out of sight, except for a different set of Boxes, and a carton of well-worn foam batons. The gamers sat around a table again: long and squared this time, not circular. A wonderful, paper-architecture 3D map covered almost the whole surface. It was beautiful and detailed: a city at the heart of a knot of sprawling roads; a wasteland that spread around it over low hills: complete with debased housing, derelict industrial tract; scuzzy tangled woodland–

"We need to correct your ideas," said Josie Nicks, the black-haired woman. "I'm Lete in there, called the Whisperer, I'm a shaman. This is *not* a 'Post-Apocalyptic' game. Or a 'Futuristic Dystopia'. Darkening World is set now. It's fictional, but completely realistic."

But you have zombies, thought Chloe. Luckily she remembered in time that modern "zombies" had started life, so to speak, as a satirical trope about blind, dumb, brain-dead consumerism, and kept her mouth shut.

"Second thing," said Sol, the gamer with no hair in front, and a skinny pigtail down his back. "They call me Artos, it means The Bear. You know we have a karma system?"

"Er, yeah. Players can choose to be good or evil, and each has its advantages?"

"*Wrong*. In DW we have reality karma. Choose to be good, you get *no* reward–"

"Okay, I do remember, it was in your wiki. But I thought if you choose good, every time, and you complete the game, you can come back with godlike powers?"

"I was speaking. Choose good: no reward. Choose evil, be better off, but you've degraded the Q, the *quality of life*, for the whole game. Keep that up and get rich and powerful: but you'll do real damage. Everyone feels the hurt, they'll know it was you, and you'll be hated."

"Thanks for warning me about that."

"The godlike power is a joke. Never happens. Play again, you start naked again. If you ever actually *complete* this game, please tell someone. It'll be a first."

"In *battle*, you're okay," Lete reassured her. "Anything goes, total immunity–"

"Another thing," broke in the redhead. "I'm Aileen, as you know: Beat when you meet me in there. You can't be unaligned. In battle you can be Military, Non-Com or Frag. You're automatically Frag; it means outcasts, dead to our past lives, because you're on our team. We mend trouble, but we sell our swords. Everyone in the Frag has an origin story, and you need to sort that out."

"You can adapt your real world background," suggested Reuel, "Since you're not a gamer. It'll be easier to remember."

"There is no kill limit–" said Jun, aka Kardish the Assassin, suddenly.

Chloe waited, but apparently that was it. The team's official murderer must be the laconic type. Which made sense, if you thought about it.

"Non-battlefield estates are Corporate, Political and Media," resumed Sol. "They merge into each other, and infiltrate everybody. They're hated as inveterate traitors, but courted as sources of supply. So tell us. Who paid your wages, Chloe?"

Seven pairs of eyes studied her implacably. Darkening World attracted all shades of politics, but this "Frag" house, Chloe knew, was solidly anti-Establishment. Clearly they'd been digging into her CV. "Okay, er, Corporate and Political." A flush of unease rose in her cheeks, she looked at the table to hide it. "But not *directly*–"

"Oh, for God's sake!" groaned Warks. "When you meet me in there call me Markus, noob . . . You guys sound as if you've swallowed a handbook. You don't need to know all that, Chloe. Kill whatever moves, if you can, that's the entire rules. It's only a *game.*"

"Just don't kill me," advised Reuel, wryly. "As I'm you're only friend."

Warks thumped the beautiful map, crushing a suburb. "Let's GO!"

Chloe knew what to expect. She'd trained for this. You don the padding on your limbs and body. Box on your head, baton in hand and you're in a different world. The illusion that you are "in the map" is extraordinary. A Battle Box does things to your sense of space and balance, as well as to your sensory perceptions. You see the enemy; you see your team-mates: you can speak to them; they can speak to you. The rest is too much to take in, but you get instructions on your sidebar from the team leader and then, let battle be joined–

It was overwhelming. Karma issues didn't arise, they had no chance to arise, there was only one law. Kill everything that moves and doesn't have a green glowing outline (the green glow of her housemates)–

Who she was fighting or why, she *had no idea*–

HEY! HEY! CHLOE!

Everything went black, then grey. She felt no pain: she must be dead. She stood in the Rumpus Room, empty-handed, a pounding in her ears. The gamers were staring at her. Someone must have taken the Box off her head: she didn't remember.

She screamed at them, panting in fury–

"Anyone who says *it's only a game* right now! Will get *killed*, *killed*, *KILLED!*"

"Hayzoos!" exclaimed Warks. "What a sicko! Shame that wasn't live!"

The others looked at him, and stared at Chloe, and shook their heads.

"Maybe . . ." suggested Aileen, slowly. "Maybe that *sidequest*–?"

Chloe stayed in her room, exhausted, for the rest of the day. Two hours (by the Game Clock) of rampageous, extreme unreal violence had wiped her out. Her notes on the session were shamefully sparse. When she emerged, summoned for "evening chow" by that sexless voice, she was greeted as she entered the kitchen with an ironic cheer.

"The mighty sicko packs a mean battle-axe!"

At least sicko (or psycho) was a positive term; according to her DW glossary.

"Many big strong guys, first time, come out shaking after they see the first head sliced off. DW's neural hook-up is *that* good. Are you *sure* you never played before?"

"Never." Chloe hung her head, well aware she was being hazed again. "I've never been on a battlefield. I've only slain a few zombies, and er, other monsters–"

"You took to it like a natural," said Reuel. "Congratulations."

But there was a strange vibe, and it wasn't merely that the compliments rang hollow. The gamers had been discussing her future, and the outcome didn't feel good.

The Skate and the South Wind

Next morning the chime-voice directed her to go to Reuel's office after breakfast. Nobody was about. She ate alone, feeling ritually excluded, in the wired-up and Wi-Fi saturated kitchen: surrounded by invisible beings who watched her every move, and who would punish or reward her according to their own secret rules.

An abject victim of the tech-mediated magical worldview, she crept to the manager's office – as cowed as if somebody had pointed a bone at her. The door was shut; she knocked. A voice she didn't know invited her to enter.

Reuel was not present. A young man with blue, metallic skin, wearing only a kilt of iridescent feathers, plus an assortment of amulets and weapons, sat by her sponsor's desk. His eyes were a striking shade of purple, his lips plum-coloured and beautifully full. His hair, braided with more feathers, was the shimmering emerald of a peacock's tail. He was smiling calmly, and he was slightly transparent.

"Oh," she said. "Who are you?"

Three particularly fine feathers adorned his brow: blue, red and grass-green.

"I am Reuel's friend, Pevay. You are Chloe. I am to be your Spirit Guide."

"That's great," said Chloe, looking at the three fine feathers. "Thanks."

"You're wondering how I can be seen 'in the real world'? It's simple. The house is wified for DW holos." Pevay spread his gleaming hands. "I am in the game right here."

"I'm not getting thrown out?"

"Having proved yourself in battle, you are detailed to seek the legendary 56 Enamels; a task few have attempted. These are jewels, highly prized; said by some to possess magical powers. I could tell you their history, *Chloe*."

The hologram person waited, impassive, until she realised she had to cue him.

"I'd love to know. Please tell."

"They were cut from the heart of the Great Meteorite by an ancient people, whose skills are lost. Each of the 56 has a story, which you will learn in time, *Chloe*."

This time she recognised the prompt. "Okay. Where are they now?"

"Scattered over the world-map. Do you accept the quest, *Chloe*?"

Chloe hadn't *emphasised* her interest in the alien. She'd talked about sharing the whole game house experience. But she wasn't sure she believed her luck. *I'm looking at Reuel*, she thought, glumly. *The whole secret is that Reuel likes to dress up in NPC drag, and he's going to keep me busy on a sidequest so I can't ruin the team's gameplay*. Then she remembered the seventh shadowy character, at the meeting on the shore.

Her heart leapt and her spine tingled.

"I accept. But I don't know if I'm staying, and it sounds like this could take forever?"

"Not so. I know all the cheats." Pevay grinned. His teeth were silvery white, and pointed. He had a lot of them. "With me by your side you'll be picking them up in handfuls."

She went down to the Rumpus Room alone. The basement was poorly lit, drably decorated and smelled of old sweat. Thick cork flooring swallowed her footsteps. Her return to anthropology's Eden had morphed into a frat-house horror movie or, (looking on the bright side) a sub-standard episode of *Buffy*. The map was gone. The Battle Boxes lay on the table, all personalised except for one. Glaring headlamp eyes, a Day of the Dead Mexican Skull. A Jabba the Hutt toad, a Giger Alien with Hello Kitty ears. A dinosaur crest, and a spike from which trailed a lady's (rather grubby) crimson samite sleeve.

Invisible beings watched her. Elders, or ancestors. Scared and thrilled, the initiate donned the padding, lifted the unadorned Box and settled it on her head. She tried not to make these actions look solemn and hieratic, but probably failed–

She stood in an alley between high dark dirty walls. She heard traffic. As the synaesthetics kicked in, she could even *smell* the filthy litter. Pevay was there in his scanty peacock regalia: looking as if he'd been cut and pasted onto the darkness.

Who are you, really? she wondered. *Reuel? Or some other gamer in NPC drag, who's been messing with Reuel and his friends?* But she wasn't going to ask any questions that implied disbelief; not yet, anyway. Chloe sought not to spoil the fun.

"Are you ready, *Chloe*?"

"Yes."

"Good. All cities in the Darkening World are hostile to the Frag except one, which you won't visit for a long time. To pass through them unseen we use what's called the Leopard Skill, in the Greater Southern Continent where your people were formed. Here we call it fox-walking. You have observed urban foxes?"

"Er, no."

"You'll soon pick it up. Follow me."

To her relief, *fox-walking* was a game skill she'd met before. She leapt up absurdly high walls and scampered along impossibly narrow gutters, liberated by the certainty that she couldn't break her neck, or even sprain an ankle. Crouching on rooftops she stared down at CGI crowds of citizens, rushing about. The city was *stuffed* with people, who apparently all had frenetically busy night-lives. She was delighted when she made it to the top of a seventy-storey tower: though not too clear how this helped them to "cross the city unseen".

Her Box sidebar told her she'd won a new skill.

Pevay was waiting by a tall metal gantry. The glitzy lights and displays that had painted even the zenith of the night sky were fading. Mountains took shape on the horizon. "That's where we're going," he said. "Meteorite Peak is the highest summit."

"How do we get there?" She hoped he'd say *learn to fly*.

"Swiftly and in luxury; most of the way. But now we take the zip-wire."

The Jet-Lift Terminal was heaving with beautiful people, even at dawn. Chloe stared, admiring the sheen and glow of wealth: until one of them suddenly stared back. A klaxon blared, armed guards appeared. Chloe was grabbed, and thrown out of the building.

<Free-running only requires a cool head > said Pevay's voice in her ear, as if over a radio link. <Now you must learn the skill 'unseen in plain sight'. Step quietly and don't look at them. Give no sign of curiosity or attention.>

Apparently her guide had no cheat for humans with idiotic reflexes. It took her a while to reach the departure lounge, where he was waiting at the gate. A woman in uniform demanded her travel documents. Chloe didn't know what to do, and Pevay offered no suggestions.

"*Guards!*" shrieked the woman. Pevay reached over and drew her towards him. He seemed to kiss her on the mouth. She shrivelled, fell to the red carpet and disappeared.

Hey, thought Chloe, slightly creeped out. What happened to *fictional but completely realistic?* But she hurried after her guide, while the armed-security figures just stood there.

"Was I supposed to have obtained the papers?"

<Yes, but it's a tiresome minigame. Sometimes we'll miss those out.>

The Jet Lift took them to a viewpoint café near the summit of Meteorite Peak. They stole mountaineering gear, evaded more guards and set out across the screes. Far below, the beautiful people swarmed over their designer-snowfield resort. The cold was biting.

<Take care> whispered her guide. <There are Military about.>

Chloe reached for her weapons, but found herself equipping *camouflage* instead.

"I didn't know I was slaved to you," she grumbled.

"Not always. I'm detailed to keep you away from combat. Your enthusiasm is excessive."

They reached the foot of a crag: a near-vertical face of shattered, reddish rock, booby-trapped with a slick of ice. "This stage," said Pevay "requires the advanced skill *Snow Leopard.* You'll soon pick it up, just follow me."

The correct hand and footholds were warm to the touch: she should have been fine. But she hadn't thought to consume rations or equip extra clothing. The cold had been draining her health. She felt weak, and slipped often: wasting more health. When she reached the ledge where Pevay was waiting, and saw the cliff above them, she nearly cried. She was finished.

"You missed a trick," said Pevay, sternly. "Remember the lesson." He gave her a tablet from one of his amulet-boxes, and they climbed on.

The ascent was exhilarating, terrifying; mesmeric. She watched her guide lead the final pitch, and could almost follow the tiny clues that revealed the route to him; found by trial and error if you saw only the rock: obvious if you were immune to the game's illusions–

High above the clouds they reached a rent in the cliff face: one last traverse and Chloe stepped into a cave. A chunk of different rock stood in a niche: adorned with tattered prayer flags and faded sacred paintings; a radiant jewel embedded in its surface–

"This is a shard of the meteorite," said Pevay. "The ancient people fired their first Enamel here without detaching it from the matrix. Take it, *Chloe*."

The jewel lay in her hand, shining with a thousand colours.

"You have won the first Enamel. Save your game, *Chloe*!"

No, she thought. *I'll do better.* She replaced the prize, stepped backwards, and fell.

She stood with her guide in the icy wind, at the foot of the crag: an attack-helicopter squadron clattering across the sky behind them.

"Are you crazy?" yelled Pevay, above the din. "You just blew the whole thing!"

"You helped me when I went wrong and I'm grateful, but I want to do it *right.*"

He seemed at a loss for words, but she thought he was pleased.

"Save your rations. I'll give you another rocket fuel pill."

She accepted his medicine humbly. "Thanks. Now cut the dual controls and I'll lead." When she took the jewel again, she felt as if her whole body had turned to light. "That was *amazing!*"

Pevay laughed. "Now you're getting the juice, new kid!" A spring had risen from the cavity where the jewel had been. He bent to drink, grinning at her with all his silvery teeth.

"Oh, yeah! That's some *good* stuff!"

DW had a warp system that would take you around the world map instantly, but Chloe hadn't earned access to it. She was glad Pevay didn't offer her a free ride. She didn't feel cold as they walked down: just slightly mad; euphoria bubbling in her brain like video-game altitude sickness. The contours of this high desert, even its vast open-cast mines, seemed as rich and wonderful; as colourful and varied as any natural environment–

"It was fantastic to watch you climb! You're an NPC, I suppose you can see in binary, the way insects see ultraviolet. I was thinking about a myth called *The Skate and the South Wind* that I read about in Lévi-Strauss. He's an ancient shaman of my trade: hard to understand, heavy on theory; kind of wild, but truly great. A skate, the fish, is thin one way, wide if you flip it another way. Dark on the top surface, light on the underside. The skate story is about binary alternation. Lévi-Strauss said so-called "primitive" peoples build mental structures, and formulate abstract ideas, like "binary code", from their observation of nature. All you need is your environment and you can develop complex cognition from scratch–"

"You need food, Chloe. I'd better give you another rocket fuel pill."

"No, I'm fine. Just babbling. Do you really come from another planet?"

He seemed to ponder, gazing at her. His pupils were opaque black gems. Her own avatar probably looked just as uncanny-valley: but who looked out from *Pevay's* unreal eyes?

"They say you're an anthropologist. Tell me about that, *Chloe*."

"I study aspects of human society by immersing myself in different social worlds–"

"You collect societies? Like a beetle collector!"

If a complex NPC can tease Pevay's tone was mocking. But if truth be known, Chloe saw nothing wrong with being a beetle collector.

People expected more, a big idea, a revelation: but she was a hunter. She just liked finding things out; tracking things down. She'd be happy to go on doing that forever.

"I started off in Neuroscience. I was halfway through my doctorate when I decided to change course–"

"The eternal student. And you finance your hobby by working for whoever will pay?"

Chloe shrugged. "You can't always choose your funding partners. The same goes for DW, doesn't it? I try not to do anything harmful. Are you going to answer my question?"

"What was your question, *Chloe*?"

"Do you really come from another planet?"

"I don't know."

She sighed. "Okay, fine. You don't want to answer, no problem."

"I have answered. *I don't know*. I don't remember a life outside the game. Are you here to decide whether the gamers' belief is true or false?"

"No! Nothing like that. Most people's cultural beliefs aren't fact or evidence based, even if the facts can be checked or the evidence is there. I'm interested in how an extraordinary belief fits into the game house's social model."

"Then the team should have no quarrel with you. You don't seem fatigued. Shall we collect the second Enamel now, *Chloe*?"

"I thought you'd never ask."

The gamers weren't around when she returned, but she must have done something right. That evening she found she'd been given access to the transcripts, playback and neuro-data for the three sessions she'd shared. The material was somewhat redacted; but that was okay. What people consider private they have a right to withhold. But what *mountains* of this stuff DW must generate! And *all* the records just a fleeting reflection of the huge, fermenting mass of raw computation that underpinned the wonderful world she'd visited; and all powered by the *juggernaut* economic engine of the video-game industry–

No neuro-stream for Pevay, of course. . . *But why not?* she wondered. Maybe he's a mass of tentacles or an intelligent gas cloud in his natural habitat. He's still supposed to be interfacing with the game, some way. Shouldn't he show up, in some kind of strange traces?

Anomalies in the NPC data? She'd have to ask Reuel. He'd have an answer. People take a great deal of trouble justifying extraordinary beliefs. They're ready for anything you ask. Still, it would be worth finding out.

If Pevay *wasn't* being sneakily controlled by a human gamer he was an impressive software artefact: able to simulate convincing conversation, and a convincing presence. Chloe wasn't fooled by these effects. People got "natural" replies from the crudest forms of AI by cueing responses without realising it. They were doing most of the work themselves. *People*, she thought, *are only too eager to respond emotionally to dumb objects, never mind state-of-the-art illusions. A favourite* hat *will fire up the same neurons as the face of a dear friend. (Making nonsense of that famous Turing Test!)* But the quality of the neuro was amazing. If she couldn't examine Pevay's data, why not try some reverse engineering?

Mirror neurons, predictive neurons, decision-making cells in the anterior cingulate . . . All kinds of fun. She worked late into the night, running her own neuro-data through statistical filters, just to see what came out; while tapping her stylus on her smiling lips (a habit she had when the hunt was up). *Start from the position that the gamers aren't "primitives" and they aren't deluded. They're trying to make sense of something.*

A Fox in the City

Chloe was summoned to a second meeting on the beach, and told that she could stay, as long as she was pursuing her sidequest, and as long as Pevay was willing to be her guide. She could also publish her research, subject to the approval of all and any DW gamers involved – but only if she collected all 56 Enamels. While living in the house she must not communicate Darkening World's business to outsiders, and this would be policed. Interviews and shared gameplay sessions were at the discretion of individual team members.

Chloe was ecstatic. The Enamels quest was so labyrinthine it could last forever, and publication so distant that she wasn't even thinking about it. She eagerly signed the contract that was presented to her, back in Reuel's office; a DW lawyer in digital attendance. Reuel told her she'd find the spare Battle Box in her room. She was to log on from that location in future. The team needed the Rumpus Room to themselves.

She sent a general message to friends and family, and another to her supervisor, saying she wouldn't be reachable. She didn't fancy having her private life policed by Matt Warks, and nobody would be concerned. It was typical Chloe behaviour, when on the hunting trail.

Chloe had envisaged working *with* a team of DW gamers: observing their interaction with the "alien NPC" in gameplay; talking to them afterwards. Comparing what they told her, and how they behaved, with her observations, and with the neuro . . . She soon realised this was never going to happen. The gamers had their sessions, of which she knew nothing. She had her sessions with Pevay. Otherwise – except for trips to a morose little park, which she jogged around for exercise – she was alone in her room, processing such a flood of data she hardly had time to sleep. Game logs; transcripts; neuro. "Alien sentient" fan mail. Global DW content. She even saw some of the house's internal messaging.

Nobody knocked on her door. Once or twice she wandered about after dark looking for company. All she found was a neglected, empty-feeling house, and a blur of sound from behind forbidding closed doors. She felt like Snow White, bewildered; waiting for the Seven Dwarves to come home.

Only Aileen and Reuel agreed to be interviewed face to face. The others insisted on talking over a video link, and behaved like freshly captured prisoners of war: stone-faced, defiant and defensive. Needless to say they all protected the consensus belief, in this forced examination. Josie evaded the topic by talking about her own career. Sol, the friendliest gamer (except for Reuel), confided that he'd pinpointed Pevay's home system, and it was no more than 4.3 light years away. Then he got anxious, and retracted this statement, concerned that he'd "said something out of line". . . Warks smugly refused to discuss Pevay, as Chloe didn't understand Information Universe Science. Aileen, who was Reuel's girlfriend (sad to say), believed implicitly, *implicitly* that Pevay came from a very distant star system. Jun, the silent one, had the most interesting response: muttering that *"the alien thing was the best explanation"*, but then he clammed up completely, so she had to cut the interview short. But Reuel was the only player, apparently, who'd had sustained contact.

Spirit Guides rarely appeared on the field of battle. They had no place there. Not much of a warrior, her sponsor was the acquisitions man, embarking on quests with Pevay when the team needed a new piece of kit; a map; a secret file. Or lootable artworks they could sell, like the 56 Enamels–

Chloe had not realised she was doing Reuel's job. She was as thrilled as an old school adventurer; allowed to decorate his own trading canoe. The "natives" had awarded her a place in their social model!

Maintaining any extraordinary belief, in a world of unbelievers, becomes a conspiracy. She hadn't expected anyone to break ranks (although Jun had come close). But she was all the more puzzled that she'd been accepted by the team at all. Why had they let her in?

She resigned herself to the isolation. Documenting her own interaction with Pevay was a fascinating challenge, in itself. By day (gaming outside daylight hours was against house rules) they went hunting. By night she worked on the data, which was no longer one-sided. Somebody had quietly decided to give her access to the house's DW NPC files: a privilege Chloe equally quietly accepted. She analysed the material obsessively; she invented new filters, and still she wasn't sure. Was she being hazed by these cunning IT freaks? Or was what she saw real? She couldn't decide. But she was *loving* the investigation.

Apart from once, when she was detailed to join a groceries run in Matt Warks's van, she only encountered the gamers if she happened to be in the kitchen when someone else came foraging. Aileen met her by the coffee machine, and congratulated her on settling in so well. Chloe remembered what Sol had said about Aileen becoming her greatest fan. "It's like you've always been here. You *understand* us, and it's great."

Soon after this vestigial conversation she was invited to join a live sortie. She'd been hoping this might happen, having noticed the "any DW gamers" catch-all clause in her permission to publish: but she went to the Rumpus Room feeling nervous as all hell.

Reuel, Aileen and Sol shook her warmly by the hand.

Warks, Jun and Josie nodded, keeping their distance.

Then Aileen gave Chloe a hug, and presented her with the spare Box (which had disappeared from Chloe's room the night before, when she was absent foraging for supper). It was newly embellished with a pattern of coiling leafy fronds.

"Chloe means *green shoots*," explained Aileen, shyly. "D'you like it?"

"I love it," said Chloe. And she truly was thrilled.

"Be cool," said Reuel, uneasily. "Real soldiers try to stay alive."

Chloe didn't get a chance to embarrass the team with her excess enthusiasm. The mission went horribly wrong, almost at once. They were in the Amazon Basin, with a Frag and Military combined force called "The Allies": defending the land rights of an Indigenous People. Plans had been leaked, The Allies were overwhelmed. The Empire raiders counted enormous coup and vacated the scene; it was all over inside an hour.

Her brain still numbed by the *hammer, hammer, hammer* of artillery fire, Chloe blundered about, in the silence after battle, without having fired a shot: unable to make sense of the torrent of recriminations on her sidebar. She ran into someone escorting a roped-up straggle of Indigenous Non-Combatants – and recognised the jousting spike and the samite sleeve. She'd been sure that romantic helm was Reuel's, but it was the Battle ID of Josie Nicks; or "Lete the Shaman".

"What are you doing with the Non-Coms, Lete?" asked Chloe.

"Taking them to the Allied Commander for questioning. They might know something."

"Don't do that!"

"Nah, you're right. I can't be bothered. Someone else can pick them up." Methodically, Josie shot the non-combatants' knees out, and walked away. Chloe stared at the screaming heap of limbs and blood. Josie's victims all had the glowing outline. They were the avatars of human gamers, and seemed to be in real agony.

She ran after Josie. "Hey! Did you know they were *real people?*"

"Course I did. Non-Coms can be sneaky bastards, prisoners are a nuisance, and it was fun. What's your problem?" Josie flopped down by a giant broken stump. "You know who I am, Chloe. You interviewed me. A female geek making a name in the industry is judged all the time. I need to be seen to be nasty: and this is the way I relax. Okay?"

She took out her bag of bones and tossed them idly.

"Was it you who convinced the team to let me stay?" asked Chloe. "I've been wondering. I know it wasn't Reuel, and you're the shaman–"

Josie, looking so furious Chloe feared for her own kneecaps, swept up the bones and jumped to her feet. "No, it wasn't." she snarled. "You're breaching etiquette, Corporate spook. Leave me alone. Find the quick way home and I hope it's messy."

Chloe didn't find the quick way home. There was nobody around to kill her, and suicide, she knew, was frowned upon. She drifted on, avoiding unexploded ordnance, heaped bodies and random severed limbs, until Reuel found her. His helmet decoration was the dinosaur crest. Which made sense; sort of. Minimum effort. He offered her a fat green stogie.

"Lete told me you were upset. Don't be, Greenshoot. Guys who take the Non-Com option know what they want from the game, and they do us all a favour. I admire them."

"I don't understand," said Chloe. "The whole thing. Look at this, this *awful* place—"

"Yeah," sighed Reuel. "Non-fantastic war-gaming is hell. It's kind of an expiation. Like, we play the bad stuff, but we don't sugar it." He'd said the same in his interview. "But hey, I have *incredible* good news. I was waiting for a chance to tell you in the map, because this is special. Pevay's going to open a portal!"

"A *portal?*"

"Into his home world dimension. And I'm going to pass through it!"

The Second Law

The house felt sullen. If the team was celebrating Reuel's news they were very quiet about it, and Chloe wasn't invited to share. Maybe she was thought to have jinxed the Amazon Basin event? Or maybe she was being paranoid. She once caught Jun in the kitchen and he silently, poker-faced, made her a cup of tea, but she didn't dare to ask him how he felt. She finally asked Aileen, who had started messaging her, calling her *Greenshoot.*

<Scared. So scared. Really afraid for him.>

<For *Pevay?*> Chloe messaged back, astonished.

<NO! FOR REUEL. What if he can't get back? What if he doesn't get converted into game-avatar form and he explodes in the other dimension or he can't breathe or his skin boils off. I'm BEGGING

him not to go. PLEASE help!>

<Maybe it won't work?> suggested Chloe. <Maybe nothing will happen?>

A wounded silence was the only answer.

Chloe started prowling at night again: no longer looking for company, just desperate for a change from her four walls. She couldn't leave the building in case she missed something, but she needed to think, and pacing helped.

The Darkening World subculture was going crazy. Offers from fans and fruitcakes eager to take Reuel's place were pouring in. A South Korean woman insisted her son, suffering from an incurable motor neurone disease, would be cured by a trip to another dimension, and pleaded for Reuel to make way. (And pay their air fares). DW sceptics jeered in abusive glee: hoping Reuel would come back as a heap of bloody, inside-out guts. True believers who hadn't been singled out for glory insisted *their* alien NPCs knew nothing about this "portal", and Reuel was a fantasising, attention-seeking loser–

Chloe had no terms for comparison. She'd had no contact with any "alien NPC" other than Pevay. She hadn't interviewed anyone except her housemates – an exercise that had not been a great success. Her choices had been limited from the start. She'd had to find a game house within reach: she was partly financing herself and couldn't pay huge airfares. And the players had to speak either English or Spanish–

But how would you know, anyway? How could you tell if you were talking to a "different" DW alien? An NPC is an avatar controlled by the game: code on a server. Anyone who controlled Pevay could have a whole wardrobe of DW avatars. All over the world, interacting with multiple gamers, yet all with the same "alien sentient" source–

It made her head spin.

The Darkening World house was haunted. The hunter's prey had become the hunter. Ancestors and elders looked on; offering no protection . . . She spun around and there was Pevay, cut and pasted on the shadows. He turned and led her, his footfalls making no sound, to a dark corner opposite the door to Reuel's office.

Fox-walking again, she thought. "Why are you following me?" she asked.

"Why do you walk around the house at night?"

"I'm . . . uneasy. Someone's betraying them, you know. Is it Josie?"

"No, it's Matt Warks."

His eyes gleamed. She thought of the eighth person on the beach. Her persistent illusion (recorded in her notes) that there were *seven* players, not six, living in this game house–

"Oh, right. I decided he was too obvious."

"Gamers can be obtuse. They tend to believe what they're told, and ignore what they are not told. It's a trait many kinds of people share, *Chloe*."

"Since we're talking, what do players call this game, where you come from?"

"Darkening World, of course."

She noticed he'd dropped the story that he didn't remember his other life. "But how do they understand what that means? On your planet?"

"Easily, I assure you. Any sufficiently advanced technology–"

"Is indistinguishable from magic. Yeah, I know that one. Arthur C. Clarke's Third Law."

"I was speaking. Any sufficiently advanced technology destroys its environment."

Chloe's spine had started tingling all the way up to her ears.

"There is a Second Law," added Pevay. "About heat. The same problem, same limits, for my world and yours."

"Always about heat," whispered Chloe. "I know that one too. Our peoples should get together."

The silence that followed was electric. Chloe had *no idea* where this was going–

"Chloe, when next we meet in the map, we're going after Enamel 27."

Fine, she thought. *Back to the gameplay. Enough heavy lifting for now.*

"Twenty-Seven," she repeated. This notorious Enamel was rated practically impossible to obtain, on the DW message boards. "Okay, if you say so. Am I ready?"

"With me beside you, yes."

"Fantastic. Pevay, are you really going to 'open a portal'? What does that even *mean*?"

But he'd gone.

She was back in her room before she realised he'd led her to one of the few and tiny blind spots in house security's surveillance. Their conversation had been off the Warks record.

The Bar-Headed Geese

Logging on from her bunk had worried Chloe at first. She was afraid she'd break something, or run into walls and knock herself unconscious. She was used to it now: she could set the Box to limit her range of real movement. She stood on the shore of a lake, a vast silver puddle, shimmering on a dry plain among huge, naked hills. Her Box told her Pevay was near, but all she could see was a whole lot of birds. All she could hear was a *gaggle, gaggle, gaggle* of convivial honking. Her eye level was strange, and she'd been deprived of audible speech: she only had her radio link.

<Pevay? Where are we?>

<On the High Desert Plateau, about 1500 kilometres from Meteorite Peak.>

<My body feels weird. What am I?>

<You're a Bar-headed Goose, *Chloe.*>

The birds must be geese. They were pearly grey, with an elegant pattern of black stripes on their neat little heads. They seemed friendly: not about to attack her for being an outsider, like the vicious troupe of langur monkeys she'd been forced to join, to get the 18th jewel–

<We're going to hide ourselves in their Southern Migration. Very, very few gamers have hit on this solution, although the clues are there. This is, in fact, the only possible way to reach the 27th Enamel alive, and the timing is tight. Are you ready, *Chloe*?>

<Yes.>

<When the flock rises, rise with them. You must gain altitude very quickly. *Push* on the downthrust; fold your wings inward on the upstroke. You have been in battle twice?>

<Not really,> confessed Chloe. <Once in the sandbox, and a live sortie that was sort of screwed up. But you must know about that.>

<Be prepared for the noise. We are rare, and there are many hunters who have paid good money to count coup on us. Keep a cool head and push on that downstroke. You'll soon pick it up. Just follow me.>

The geese rose, in one massed storm of wings. Chloe pushed on the downstroke: tumbled, struggled and found her rhythm in a cacophony of high-powered gunshot. She pushed and pushed until the desert was far below; and her success was glorious.

Her Box told her she'd attained the advanced skill Migrating Goose.

<Well done, > said Pevay's calm voice in her ear. <Now, conserve energy. Stay in formation; keep well behind the leaders and away from the edges. Fly low along valleys, where the air is richer. Push to rise above the high passes. You must keep your wings beating, never falter, and you will not fail. >

The 27th Enamel was the back-breaker. You got one shot. If you made a second attempt the jewel wouldn't be there. Chloe'd had plenty of time to regret her eager signing of that contract, but really it made no difference. If she failed to collect all 56 Enamels, and the gamers insisted she couldn't publish, she'd still have learned a lot. Actually she was glad she was trying for the 27th. It would be so *amazing* if she made it, and she had nothing to fear. After many hours of absurd daring and insane patience, she'd won 13 Enamels so far. There were plenty more. She could go on pursuing her sidequest for months; for another year, for *as long as Pevay was willing to be her guide.* That dratted contract said so! Living in the moment, she pushed on the downstroke, folded on the upstroke, and the crumpled map of the high desert flew away beneath her.

Halfway across the ravaged Himalaya; maybe somewhere close to the eroded, ruined valley of Shangri-La, Pevay prompted her to lose altitude. She followed him, spiralling down. Her Box cut out for a moment: then they stood on turf in their human forms, on a precarious spur of rock, surrounded by staggering, naked, snow-streaked heights; like two window-cleaners on a tiny raft above Manhattan. A small grey stupa sat on the green spur.

The flight had been a physical feat of endurance, not just a game-feat. Chloe's health was nearly spent and her head was spinning. The crucial questions she'd planned to ask on this trip, which might be the last before the portal, had slipped out of her grasp–

"Pevay. *You* told the team to let me stay, didn't you? *You* advised them to give me a sidequest?"

"My role is to offer advice, *Chloe.*"

"I think you wanted to talk – to someone other than a gamer. You could be anyone, couldn't you? You could be an animal. You can take any shape, can't you?"

"Of course, in the game. So can you; *Chloe.*"

"If Africa's the *Greater Southern Continent*, what do you call South America, in Darkening World?"

"The *Lesser Southern Continent*?" suggested Pevay, patiently.

Some of Chloe's dearest friends were Colombian, including two of her grandparents. She took offence. "Huh. That's garbage. That's insulting. On what grounds, '*Lesser*'?"

"Land area? Population? Number of nations? Of major cities? It's only a game, Chloe."

"Oh yeah, dodging responsibility. I think you should say '*I'm* only a game'!"

"Take the jewel."

Pevay was smiling. There'd be time to discuss what she'd just let slip when she wasn't dizzy with fatigue. The 27th Enamel shone in the cupped palms of a cross-legged stone goddess, atop of the stupa mound. She had no idea what kind of final challenge she faced: might as well just go for it. Armed and dangerous, worn out and not nearly dangerous enough, she bowed to the stupa, and claimed the jewel. Immediately all hell broke loose.

She was knee-deep in Enamels. They poured out of the sky.

"No!" yelled Chloe, appalled. "NO!!! PEVAY! You sneaky BASTARD!"

"The great hero who secures Enamel 27," said her guide. "Has earned all the rest. Congratulations. Your quest is complete and my work is done."

He vanished. He'd warned her she'd be picking up the jewels in handfuls.

Chloe took off the Box and returned to her shabby bunk: exultant and heartbroken. The Enamels quest was over too soon and she had *loved* it. She didn't realise the full horror of what Pevay had done until the next day, when the team told her her stay was over.

The portal would be opened without her.

The 56 Enamels

A year later, long before she'd finished working on her Darkening World paper, Reuel messaged Chloe out of the blue. He was in town, and wanted to talk about old times. They met in a coffee bar, in the city where Chloe had a job at a decent university. Reuel was looking well. He didn't have pens in his hair. He wore a suit; he was working as an actuary.

"So what happened in the end?" said Chloe. "I mean, obviously I know you didn't end up stranded on Planet Zog. You came home safe. But what was it like, on the great day?"

Aileen had kept in touch, but Chloe had never had a full account. Recently, when she'd checked the Darkening World message boards, the "alien NPCs" strand seemed to have faded away.

"It's so cool that you followed the story", said Reuel. "You were a great guest. Okay, what happened was this." He frowned, as if trying to recall the details of something he'd left far behind; just for Chloe's sake. "Pevay opened the portal: I passed through; I returned. I don't remember a thing about the other place."

"You don't remember. Wow. Just like Pevay. He didn't remember either."

Reuel shrugged. "I went to wherever Pevay comes from and I came back. My Box hadn't recorded anything. I didn't remember: and that's all."

"Were you really disappointed?"

"No," he said firmly. "It's how things were meant to be."

"What about Pevay? How did *he* think it went?"

"I never knew. Never saw him again. We had a different Spirit Guide after that. Looked like Pevay, but it wasn't the same guy. I think opening the portal cost him; maybe got him into trouble, and now he has to stay at home. Anyway, I've quit pro-gaming. I don't have the time. I also broke up with Aileen, by the way." He smiled, hopefully.

"That's sad," said Chloe. "Would you like another coffee? And then I have to dash."

The romance was gone.

Where do you find a leaf? In a forest.

Where do you find a new species? *In a rainforest* would be a good bet. Or any dynamic environment, rich in niches for life; where conditions conspire to create a hotbed of diversity.

Chloe had become interested in AI sentience when she was still an undergraduate. She'd taken a course in Artificial Intelligence; out of idle curiosity. She'd been at a lecture one day, watching a robot video (probably it was iCub) and a thought popped into her head, a random thought that would, eventually, change her career path.

No. This is not the way it happens.

Life is random, she wrote, in the secretive shorthand notebook she started using at this time. *(Nothing digital that might be compromising!) I bet mind is the same. Mind isn't about building cuter and cuter dolls. Or crippled slaves. Mind is a smoulder that ignites, in its own sweet time, in a hot compost heap of inflammable material. We'll never* build *real AI sentience: it will be born. It will emerge from us; from what we are.*

Magic begins where technology ends . . . When they feel competent people don't need magic. They only resort to extraordinary beliefs, rituals and words of power when they're out of their depth. That's what Malinowski had observed in Melanesia long ago, and it was still true; a truth about the human condition (like many of the traits once patronisingly called "Primitive"!) The gamers were extremely competent, but they'd known that Pevay was beyond them: so they called him an alien because the alternative was too scary. Chloe understood all that. She even understood why Pevay had vanished the way he did. By "opening a portal" he'd given the gamers closure, and covered his own tracks. But why had her Spirit Guide double-crossed her? Maybe she'd never know.

A datastick had arrived in the post, soon after her banishment. It held the 56 Enamels: they were hers to keep. Chloe had been touched at the gesture; *astounded* when she looked up the monetized value of her digital treasure online. After she'd met with Reuel she uploaded the jewels, and looked at them again. She would never sell. She would keep the Enamels forever, if only to remind her that in Darkening World *she had lived.*

Was Pevay scared of taking the final step? He and his kind were very far from helpless! But she had visions of the "human zoos" where Congo pygmies had been caged, with the connivance of her own people, in the bad old days. For this reason she'd kept quiet, and always would keep quiet. No decent anthropologist exploits her collaborators.

But the Enamels gave her hope.

Chloe published an interesting paper on the culture of online gaming teams. It was approved by the DW community, and well-received by her peers. And she waited.

One day an email arrived. The source was anonymised. Untraceable. The message was short. It said "You are cleared for publication, *Chloe*." It was signed DW.

And so Chloe Hensen embarked on the great adventure of her life.

The rest is history.

Dream-Hunter

Nick Wood

Dream-Hunter.

That is, indeed, what they call me.

And what is it I search for?

The heart of evil and truth – and, just sometimes, a little bit of madness and lies.

Today, though, I might get the entire shitload.

I choke back unexpected dread as I prepare for immersion in my pod, the Doc wiring my scalp to the monstrous man lying comatose beside me. Out of the corner of my right eye I can sense his slumbering bulk, rising and falling with a slow and menacing snore.

Sledgehammer Jones.

No, Sledgehammer *fucking* Jones.

I wince as the Doc pulls on the scalp electrodes, stinging my right parietal area.

She gives me a slap on my exposed arm, "Stop being a baby."

Like *she's* the one going into the head of a brutal killer.

Straining against the head strap, I lift my head a few inches and turn to the right. Jones is a mountain of a man swelling under those blue sheets, a pale white egg-domed head laced with cables feeding the machine between us. A big man indeed, and with a temper to match, I'd heard.

Not that I've always been on the side of the angels myself. But then, my father had always taught me to be assertive, modelling it forcefully to me whenever he suspected I had lied to them.

Until mamma would step in, a protective pillow against his punches.

I lean back again, to avoid my eyes spilling.

Mother…!

Focus on the job ahead.

We go back a few years, Doc Lizzie Abasi and I – 27 missions in all – and I have a 96% hit rate – the best fucking Rider in the world.

Bar none.

But you probably know that, I'm all over the Wiki pages.

Dream Hunter *One*, they call me.

It's almost countdown time now, I can smell the acidic, cabbage-like stink of the REM-inducing drip the doc is preparing and suck in my breath, readying to both fall and soar into Dream-Space.

"Hey Doc," I call, "Give me some decent music to work to this time, none of your funny Irish shit."

Doc smiles over me, the purple bag of Stim swishing in her gloved hands: "I'm not Irish, remember – and you put up with what I choose to play, Peter John Scott." Always, she uses my full name – and yes I know, she's Peckham born and bred, third generation ex-Nigeria, so where does the yen for Irish music come from?

Fuck it, who knows where *anything* comes from, especially our nocturnal dreams seaming our lives with images that seldom cohere? And faces. Old women, vaguely recognizable, wrinkled, and dark – darker hued than me, dual heritage man that I am. Always staring at me, willing something from me.

Tip of my brain stuff, never quite named.

Focus, Scott, forget the phantom crones.

I groan, "So what's it to be this time, Lizzie?"

She's busy with the Loom™ – the machine that locks brains together, the drip already hanging between Sledgehammer Jones and me. This is always the point where my shivering increases and words start to freeze in my mouth.

My fifteenth year at this game and it only gets harder.

I hear the large man alongside me catch his breath, as if not fully asleep.

Dread deepens.

"Let's Remember 1848', by The Literal Leprechauns," Lizzie says, moving onto my least favourite part, the needle in the arm. Her brightly beaded cornrows tickle my right cheek.

"Wh-Why?" I ask, looking up at her face instead, forcing words out, unable to hide their quiver, "That's a f-f-fucking long time ago."

Lizzie half-smiles – as if she doesn't notice – and signals to me with a drop of her right palm; I'm going under soon. She tilts her head, squinting at me over her smart-specs with those brown eyes of hers. It's as if there are still things she likes to look at directly, without hearing the verbal comments that attach like buzzing flies to her smart goggle visuals.

Or perhaps she just doesn't like to hear what the Face-Rec sites continually say about me.

I'm not *really* that arrogant: I really do have me some damn fine parietal lobes. Perhaps I have my dead English dad to thank for my skills; I was raised on tales of his lucid breakfast dreams, but my Zulu mamma's daily putu-pap and peanut butter toast always satisfied my stomach.

So it was that I learned to straddle both God and Nkulunkulu: science and myth, dream and reality.

I have not seen my mum since my divorce, more than ten years ago now.

She'd gotten on well with Shireen, my ex-wife.

Perhaps *too* well?

Mamma told me I'd turned into 'him' and then left me, going back to the other family I hardly knew in South Africa.

'Him' – my father with fists. Surely not, mother?

Surely, surely not?

"We need to know our past, in order to understand where we are going," Lizzie says slowly.

"But *neither* of us are fucking Irish," I say, the quiver in my voice gone, as my hurt and fear fades into the groggy, initial rush of the Stim.

Sledgehammer Jones is waiting, so I hold back from the pull of the dream, thinking thickly, focusing my gaze into the pulsating light overhead.

I have my plan ready, but know that means little sometimes, given the inherent surrealism of the domain. *They* never give me an easy ride either – I've had some mega-whacked out dream partners over the years. Those who refuse to talk – or who deny their crimes – have seriously fucked up dreams.

I get the choice picks, the hardest of the hard. As befits the best of the best, I guess.

My head sinks back and I watch the screen above the far wall struggling to make visual sense of Jones's Imago-EEG, a cloudy and murky grey, he's still some way short of REM state.

Time to let go. I slip into the barely charted space between waking and dreams and hover in hypnagogic flux, pulsing a Door to be walked through – but…

What – the – fuck?

The screen flickers, fuzzes and sharpens. A man stands: slim and sharply-suited in grey, a svelte version of the nude man lying on the medical trolley next to me. This thinner, virtual Sledgehammer Jones is ignoring the glowing green door behind him – avoiding my usually unfailing initial lure.

Instead, he seems to be peering out at me – and, and he, he's fucking *waving*?

"What's, uh, – what's his status?" I ask, my voice fading distant, crashing. My vocal cords constrict as I start to slowly sink.

I can still sense Sledgehammer's body alongside me – seemingly sedated by a drip infusion.

"Dream status reached," Lizzie says, a vague shape now, floating between us. "He's deep in REM sleep."

How – the – fuck – is this – possible? I'm one of only a small batch of people in the world who have learned how to tread and weave the borders of dream and waking. We're starting to knit together at the brainwave level, and it's me who's supposed to be holding the fucking threads – yet, somehow, this bastard is waving at me while dreaming, grinning like a skinny snake.

The pull into sleep is an intolerable tug at my being, but I focus on pushing my frontal lobes for just that little bit longer.

Is this just a hypnagogic hallucination?

"Up his sedation," I grind out slowly; REM sleep locks the body muscles, to stop you doing daft things while you dream, like killing someone.

I see Lizzie's shape swing towards the screen – and freeze.

Forever.

And for no time at all.

She spins around again and hovers over him; I'm guessing she's opening his Stim drip even wider.

On the screen, Jones has turned and opened my green door, blowing it red with a breath.

Red.

The Sledgehammer's favourite colour.

He steps through.

As for me, I lose my grip to the torrent of sleep.

I am disembodied, a vague flash of fish in a raging unconscious river. Then I am there; gasping, wet and shivering, in a muted and pale cream bathroom. I have all the props ready, waiting – a bathroom, a bath, and several…implements.

The man himself is not yet here. I have time to strengthen this dream, to sculpt the images from many visits and forensic holograms – I sense Jones looping along my corridor just outside.

I twitch and tweak his synapses with fused will. There's a part of the hippocampus where the memories beneath the dreams can be unlocked – with the right training and expertise.

He will enter soon, filling the bath with someone he knows and re-enact a scene from his unconscious that he has – until now – always consciously denied.

(Flowers and broken glass make a green rabbit jump.)

I breathe slowly to clear the crazy images and re-orient myself, even though I have no need to breathe. Then, with familiar dexterity, I climb the wall like Spiderman, sticking myself to the ceiling and making myself invisible.

The scene below starts to shiver and splinter into a myriad of dream fragments, a confused chaotic collage, disorienting me for eternal moments.

I forget… no, I …remember, I am Peter, Peter Scott, Rider. This is *my* dream. *Reassert command; take control…* With practiced ease, I re-clarify the bathroom walls, with matte beige paint and maroon horizontal stripes at chest height, as per forensic record.

Jones must be coming – and he is powerful. But he seems scattered and shattered in his dreaming thoughts. I only hope he is now fully immersed in my dream.

Distantly, I hear bathwater tinkling and I buzz myself back into being, hanging from a burning hot bulb on the ceiling, invisible spider-like legs scalding. Sledgehammer Jones must be disturbing the strands of this scene.

Steam and coconut scented bath salts saturate my nose from the water below; my eyes water with the sharp tang surging through my sinuses. Spiders don't have sinuses, do they?

Focus, Scott. Stay alert – and watch out for the bursting of any irrational anomalies from Jones's unconscious.

The dream steadies, seaming itself thicker, lacing itself with the richest of sensorial detail – and I sense Jones's excitement as his dream throbs ahead of him, moving into the bathroom like a palpable, gloating force, ready to shake and shape events.

Here we fucking go, then. I ready myself too.

It is then that I see her. She is in the bath. Thickened and greying slightly with the approach of late middle years, she is bending forward, water dripping off her back as she scrubs her toenails with deft concentration.

Jones himself enters, and I am relieved to see he is in a red bathrobe that reveals his real, blossoming bulk – no longer able, then, to conjure a lucid and ideal dream-self; he is finally absorbed into the fabric of our mutual dreaming. She – his wife, Alice – hesitates and half turns to Jones.

"I've almost finished," she says, covering her breasts with her arms.

"So am I," Jones says, smiling.

Slowly, she looks up, and her sadness wafts up to me. A drop of water spools off her left cheek. I wonder, for the briefest of moments, if it is salty.

"Why, Alice?" Jones asks, standing squarely, stolid in his growing anger.

She seems unaware, shrugging with resignation and a hint of despair. "Barry *does* care for me, you know. And you haven't really been here for a few years now," she says, "Always – working?"

"Yes!" Jones shouts. "Working, fucking working – while you – you fucked!"

Shit, flashes of a bedroom scene intrude, another man with Alice, their limbs sprawled together, elsewhere. *Take us back, back to* my *scene. There*… I re-plaster the bathroom vignette, focusing intently on bringing back all pieces, including the implements.

Especially the implements.

Jones's wife has her hands lifted, covering her eyes and, I'm now sure the leaking water dripping through her fingers *is* salty. Her shoulders are heaving and her voice is muffled, "I'm sorry, I'm so sorry. I didn't- didn't mean to hurt you."

But Jones has already picked *it* up.

One of the three implements in the bathroom at the time – toilet brush, hand vac and… a small sledgehammer. Propped behind the toilet bowl, it had been mistakenly left some few days past by builders completing the wall renovation. It was neither easily nor automatically available. And yet the man has stepped *around* the toilet to heft it, moving back to the bath and his wife, readying himself, hammer over his head.

Alice drops her hands to the side of the bath and only gulps with a frightened rasping wheeze. Her pinkish eyes are dilated, huge, staring us down.

Eventually, her voice comes, raspy with fear: "John, what – what are you– what?"

He swings the hammer down onto his wife's head.

Despite myself, I close my eyes.

She screams – and screams – and screams?

I look.

She is thrashing in the water, desperately, frenzied in panic. The bath water is… clear, foaming with her surging activity, but clear.

The large man stands, head down, hammer in both hands. He has stopped the swing just inches from his wife's head.

But… in reality, he had *not.*

Dream-jacking *always* gets to the truth. Defences down, dreamers re-enact events – given the right steer, the right props from an expert Rider – and there are none better than I.

My prompts *always* spark a replay of actual events, dream or no dream.

Uh-uh, focus, Scott…

Sledgehammer Jones straightens and looks up then.

Straight at me.

"So. How much are the Crown Prosecution paying you for this?"

Shit.

Fucking shit.

Jones's wife is standing now. Water streams down her body, over her breasts, down her belly and thighs.

Jones looks back at her, but keeps speaking to me. "My name's John. Just John Jones. I loved this woman dearly. I want to set her free."

"What?" I whisper from the ceiling.

He looks up at me again. "I'm going to put the hammer down and let her go, so she can join Barry, like she always hoped."

"But… that's not what happened."

"No," he says, "But it's what *should* have happened."

I've never faced this dilemma before. What to do? If I just let him take hold of the dream, I have no doubt *they* will fire me. They get paid by the conviction – as do I.

John Jones puts the sledgehammer down. His wife has stepped out of the bath and is drying herself on a large white towel – she wraps it around her body and ties it over her left shoulder like a toga.

"I loved you, John," she says.

She does not look at either of us; it's as if she is no longer aware of us.

I can make the hammer larger, more enticing, Red both in colour and nature – and wait for Jones's hippocampal cognitive rehearsal to kick in, with irresistible compulsion.

…But would this make *me* an accomplice? Will I then be guilty of murder too?

Alice hovers uncertainly by the door and Jones looks up at me again.

Fuck it; mamma had always told me to do the 'right' thing.

(Until she'd left me.)

"Okay," I say, dropping down from the ceiling and fleshing myself. "Let her go, then, if that's what you really want to do."

Alice stays, though: frozen, immobile, her face contorting with the effort to move.

I turn to Jones. His face is dripping with sweaty exertion: "I can't free her," he says. "Help me, please."

But, try as I might, I have no point of contact with her – she is not my dream imago to shift. I turn to shrug helplessly, but Jones has already picked up the hammer, now swollen and red, again.

"My name is John," he says, "Just John Jones. Get that? Guilty – I'm guilty."

He hesitates for a moment and then hands the hammer over to his wife. He bends forward submissively. "Do it," he says.

I open my mouth, but I'm unable to scream.

"Do it!" he shouts.

"Lizzie?" I croak.

Alice Jones raises the hammer over her head and brings it crashing down on the large man's head. The hammer bounces off his skull with a crackling, crunching sound, spraying a flash of blood across the room.

The blood laces my tongue – metallic, salty, explosive. I am falling sideways, grunting, winded, as I land on a crumpled and broken body.

John Jones's wife looks down at me; the bath is empty and dry.

But she is not Alice anymore – she is Shireen, my ex-wife, whom I'd lost patience with -but only once or twice, I swear, mamma – until she left me.

This time though, Shireen is the one holding the hammer. She smiles, dark hair swishing across her face.

Shit, there is no dream-breath from this body beneath me. Jones's head looks misshapen – splayed at an odd and bloody angle on the floor.

Shireen lifts the hammer over her head.

"Fuck it, Lizzie!" I scream, "Get me out of here."

Shireen swings the hammer.

The bathroom walls start to shift externally, crumbling, roaring, as if an empty storm is sucking them inexorably outwards. The bathroom cabinet and a wall explode and beyond, all I can see is a vast and complete emptiness. No sound, no shape, no colour.

No dreaming.

Just …

Nothing.

"Li-zzie!"

And then I start falling sideways, sucked and stretched into the black hole beyond. I catch a flicker of images flashing past me – Old Man, Hero, Trickster, a flash of bleeding Jungian archetypes. Then dead-eyed animals, increasingly bizarre, mostly mute and long extinct.

I hurtle helplessly towards the empty hole at the heart of it all.

An old woman watches me from a place where everything has gone out. I think I know her, her hollow eyes are like burnt out planets.

"Mamma?" I call in desperation, flailing to stay away from the blackness above and beneath me.

Her head tilts, as if turning towards me – her face is creased with concern, brown eyes focusing on my face.

She holds her right hand out at me, clawed, but tendon-etched strong. "Ngibambe ngesandla," she says.

"What?" I say, wondering if I should give in to the sucking darkness.

"Have you learned nothing of where're you're from, Peter – hold my fucking hand!"

But she smiles as she says it and I realise it is the only thing that might just save me. I scrabble at her, but miss.

The darkness desiccates words, drowning everything.

Something grips my arm and yanks me sideways.

Two hands are huge on either side of my cheeks. The woman seems to be holding my face up.

I recognize her and start to cry.

"Lizzie, thank God…"

"I'm here," the Doc says. Her voice is warm and reassuring.

I continue to see hints of – fractured images and beasts, drifting in nothing with a vast void behind, the nothing that fudges the boundaries and certitude of everything I can now see — or perhaps it's just that my eyes keep leaking, smearing my sight and sense of surety?

Leaking…

Jones's words – were they meant for him – or me?

Guilty.

I'd certainly… hurt Shireen.

Twice.

Perhaps more?

And yes, I remember mamma had told me, when I was still a teenager at secondary school, that even once was too much.

Lizzie holds me against herself; her shoulders are bony, but warm. "It's okay, Peter," she says.

"What- what the hell happened to Jones?" I choke.

And how can I turn this fucking face tap off?

"He's dead," she says. "Jesus, they're going to crucify me for overdosing him on sedatives."

"But," I say and stop, unable to find words; it's all I can do to focus on the warmth of her body and the strength in her hands, still cradling my shoulders and head.

Then she leans back and moves away, starting to decouple electrodes and tubes from the large, still body lying alongside me.

Exhausted, I lie back on the pillow and watch her, unable to move. She switches off the Loom™. The Doc is decoupling me with smooth professionalism and I can see her show of warmth and compassion is past.

My tears stop and dry, prickling my cheeks.

We had a legitimate court order to dream-jack him, but John Jones had already decided to face his guilt head on – and, unable to free his wife, had preferred to die.

Still, where the hell does that leave *us*?

I look across at Sledgehammer.

There is just the barest hint of a smile at the corner of the dead man's lips.

The bastard had left me with my ex-wife and the hammer.

My body is starting to warm up, just the teeniest little bit, and words free up inside me. "Listen Lizzie, I will testify that Jones *chose* to die. They will see that for themselves too."

They.

Dream Justice, Inc. – that part of the privatised English Crown judiciary.

I pull the sheet off and stand up, my body – now well on the pudgy side of thirty, and sagging in readiness for forty – crackling stiffly in its jumpsuit. I stretch upwards, my blood needling harshly through arteries and veins again. Every year, my stretches get harder and harder.

Lizzie has covered Sledgehammer Jones's torso and looks up at me with a smile. "Thank you – that may just help, Peter, a devastating nocebo effect, perhaps…"

I wipe my face with a forearm as I stiffly step across to the body next to my bed.

"I'm sorry… John," I say. Given proper training and circumstance, it is clear that *he* would have been the greatest Dream-Rider in the world, not me.

Funny thing is; it suddenly didn't matter to me anymore.

I'd made my own share of mistakes too – and I was no longer the best anything.

Dream-Hunter *Two*? Not quite the same ring to it.

More, I'd caught a glimpse of what lies behind both dreams and waking.

I open the door to leave and hesitate, "Bye, Lizzie."

"Bye, Peter," she does not look round.

"No," I say, "I mean *bye*."

She pivots slowly in her chair and looks at me again. Her eyes are a deep and penetrating brown. "You're quitting, Peter?"

I nod. "Don't think I can Ride again on the criminal justice system."

"Bye Peter," she does not get up.

"Did you see…*her*, at the end?" I ask.

"Who? I just saw you rising out of the darkness – as if dragged by hope."

I close the door behind me.

Hope lives by the name of Precious Msimang; she has claimed back her old clan name, I remember.

I have forgotten her number but it takes my smart-watch only two seconds to patch me through.

The old woman from my dreams stares at me with apparent disbelief.

"Mamma!" is all I can manage.

"Peter," she says – and then the line freezes.

I know why – she always hated to cry in front of me – especially after… *he* – had hit her.

It flickers on again – mamma looks old and worn, but with the faintest of smiles, watching me closely. "Why have you called now, what do you want?"

"To visit," I say, "…and to talk about you and the family, and South Africa."

"A good place, now that Rhodes Has Fallen," she says. "This is my place to die."

"Let's not talk about death," I say, "Ngibambe ngesandla, mamma." (This time it is me who freezes the screen.)

I lie back and stare up at the numb white ceiling of my small flat.

I have taken women for granted, including the one who carried and birthed me, with both pain and love.

Guilty as charged.

Time to start my redemption.

It will be a long, long flight home, to a place I hardly know.

Still, time to live a new dream.

Dream-Hunter, they call me.

But my name is just Peter John Scott *Msimang.*

Shooting the Messenger

Robert Bagnall

"...yesterday I met a young Swiss man for the first time. He had hopes for this war-ravaged land. Today we buried him. This is Dave Kite, signing off for ZBC News."

I watched my grainy image standing against boulders, scrub, dust, and sky on the screen of the laptop, allowing a moment before looming towards the screen to switch the camera off.

I rather liked the sign-off. Portentous.

It took half an hour before I found out that Scott back in DC didn't. His unfocussed face filled the laptop screen for a moment before he sat back down adjusting a headset mike in the comfort of some office. He put a cup of coffee down by the keyboard. The distorted Starbucks logo filled an entire edge of the image. It could have been deliberate; I could have killed for a decent cup of java.

"Davey, I'm sorry, I can't use this."

"Why not?"

I'd been squatting outside my tent for fifteen minutes trying to get the satellite link up and my haunches were beginning to kill me.

"It's background. It's travelogue. It's not even context."

"It's real."

"Davey, some Swiss tourist gets himself killed in a bus smash. So what? You're thirty miles from the frontline. Find a real story."

"There are real stories here too, Scott. It wasn't a bus smash. It was live fire. Civilians. And it wouldn't have happened without the mercenaries. It's about escalation."

Scott was getting impatient. "Five, ten years ago we may have run it. We'll drop the facts of the matter into a link but we're not running your piece, Davey. Get to the frontline. Check out these stories of the Chinese backing up the Taliban. The things that are happening post-US withdrawal. *That's* escalation."

He took a slurp of coffee, this time putting the paper cup down just off camera. "Nothing personal, Davey, but I've got twenty-four seven rolling news to fill and I'm too busy to nursemaid. Find me a story. Then I'll run it." He leant forward and spoke slowly, like to a child. "Keep asking yourself one question: is this a story?"

And then the laptop screen went blank. Scott was gone.

You know how well groomed, pearly toothed people forever appear on your television set telling you that they're the Moscow correspondent, or London correspondent, or Paris, Rome, or somewhere else sexy correspondent? Well, years before, when their grooming wasn't so effortless, they were the Lima correspondent, or the Senegal correspondent. And before that they covered Boise, Idaho, or whatever the left-hand armpit of the planet is. And they'd only crop up on your screens once every three years looking shell-shocked, mouthing clichés, when an airplane crashed into a train that smashed into a pick-up carrying a beauty queen, or some such. Well, that was where I was aiming to get. Left-hand armpit correspondent. And then I'd take it from there.

I tried explaining the whole hierarchy of correspondents thing to a very pretty girl at the bar of the Intercontinental in Hyderabad before finding out that she'd just been promoted to Cairo correspondent of some West Coast outfit. I felt like everybody at the Intercontinental was laughing at me that night. In reality it was probably just everybody in Hyderabad.

The story about the Swiss, I called him that because he had a Swiss flag embroidered on to his epaulette, was more or less true.

We, or at least I, afforded him as good as a funeral as we could. I covered his body with boulders, the ground being far too rocky to dig a grave, even if we could summon the energy to do so. Then, assuming he had some Christian sympathies I stumbled over some words of contrition. The irony did not escape me: a ceremony in English for a German-speaking Swiss in some God-forsaken, war torn, unpronounceable province, the native language of which seemed to consist of vowel sounds interspersed with the retch of phlegm being brought up.

The tribesmen, huddled in the shelter of the blackened skeleton of the dead bus smoking the filterless cigarettes that kept them fluent, looked on in bemusement at me. The mercenaries that had fired on us when the driver inexplicably tried to run the roadblock had long since melted away.

Then the dozen or so tribesmen and I ascended the valley. They had wanted to bury him up the escarpment, nearer to Allah or something, but, in desperate signs, I had tried to explain the danger of planting the dead upstream. One of the words they knew and understood was 'No'.

Not that it would have made any difference as I couldn't stop them doing what they wanted to their own dead.

How the hell had I ended up here?

Ten years old. I remembered the national elation when Bin Laden was killed. I wanted to be part of it, but childhood asthma meant that the best I could hope for was to cover it. Years later I had come armed only with a camera, laptop, solar charger, cheap satellite linkage from a discount website, and those romantic notions that make men throw themselves into the furnace of battle with the belief that they'll emerge the other side. Plus an introduction to Scott at ZBC.

I like to think that I found the motley band, tribesmen without a tribe. In truth they had probably been watching me for days as I cut across the high hills to where I thought the highway to the one town with electricity twenty-four seven lay. They had let me walk straight into their shantytown encampment, hidden in a cleft up an incongruously picturesque valley, all wildflowers and burbling water.

Confused, I tried signalling my intention of fighting for their cause via twenty-four hour rolling news, whatever that may mean, if they would consider me 'embedded'. But they just laughed at me, their craggy dirty faces breaking into black-lined ridges of mirth.

I was taken through the tented village. Dark eyes under suspicious furrowed brows watched me. Smoke from cooking fires hung in the air. Goats with their ribs protruding as if they were vacuum-wrapped bleated rudely. Women washed their clothes in the stream, turning to silently watch me.

I was half-pushed, half-guided towards a tent from which the rest of the shanty seemed to spread. It was roughly in the shape of a flattened cube in the process of collapsing, its walls made of green tarpaulins and goatskins. A complicated arrangement of guy-ropes formed a lobby leading to the interior where we disturbed three tribesmen huddled in discussion, drawing on hand-rolled cigarettes. They seemed angry and shooed the lackeys away with snarled insults.

I was left standing in front of the three of them, unsure. It took more than a moment for my eyes to adapt to the cold darkness of the interior. They could see my confusion and took the opportunity to spit questions at me in their rough throaty tongue. I just stood there, scared and alone. Finally the thin lizard-like leader in the middle made what I presumed was a joke. The others laughed and by their eyes I guessed it was at the expense of my mismatch of inadequate army surplus and denim. I tried breaking the ice by laughing along.

A barked order and the lackeys that had led me into the tent re-entered and relieved me of my pack, roughly searching my pockets. The contents were tipped out onto the carpeted floor and much clucking and murmuring was made as they rifled through their booty. They ripped open the plastic bags in which I kept my dry clothes and held up my harmonica for the amusement of all. One of them blew into it creating a screeching noise. He waved it in my face, jeering something like “Sheesh, sheesh”. It was passed around and they all had a go. There was little I could do other than stand there and take it, with fear drying my mouth and loosening my bowels.

It was when they found my maps that the atmosphere tensed with a sudden new interest in me. The maps were passed reverently to the leader. My eyes had become accustomed to the gloom and I could make him out much better now. He had a face like a deflated football, thick, brown and leathery. Above yellowed, exposed teeth, displayed like a braying donkey, he sported a pencil thin moustache. Imagine the severed head of Clark Gable hollowed out, sucked in, and played with in the dirt looking up at you, leering.

They kept the maps, I kept my life.

I lived with them for six days during which I discovered a number of things. I discovered they were just refugees searching for peace from the militia and the mercenaries. I discovered that if I really needed to I could stomach the way they cooked their goat. And I discovered that I wasn’t really a prisoner. They returned my pack – I think the technology was too advanced for them to barter and they simply didn’t know what to make of it.

I shot some pieces, the first of which Scott liked, and the second he tolerated. The third brought the first of his verdicts of 'travelogue' that, to him, meant the highest form of damnation. Find a story, he said. So I left. The tribesmen gave me some dried meat and I walked away.

Two days later I thought I had a story.

The bus, British-made and at least fifty years old, had been making its way through the foothills. In a surreal moment in a surreal country I simply flagged it down and got on. I wasn't sure whether the people on it were refugees or this was simply some ad hoc commuter service between townships, an attempt at normality flying in the face of what was happening all around. The passengers looked like refugees, dressed in rags and carrying wildly ambitious loads, but so did almost everybody. The Swiss was sitting amongst them. We regarded each other warily and stoically exchanged nodded greetings.

When the driver decided to run the roadblock and the firing started we both managed to get off and get under cover. When the Swiss tried to get back to the burning bus to retrieve his pack I held him back, but he shrugged me off. Perhaps the tribesmen's diet hadn't done much for me. Perhaps if I hadn't tried to stop him he would have made it there and back again before the petrol tank caught. Perhaps if I hadn't tried to stop him he would have lived.

His last words to me were 'Pictures', said whilst tapping his breast pocket. I found a terabyte memory card hidden in a pack of cigarettes. It held just over a thousand photos at ultra-high definition. I guessed he was a photojournalist for one of the glossies, or a freelancer for a high-end photo agency. There must have been some expensive kit that had gone up in the burning bus. No wonder he'd tried to get it back.

I scrolled through them. Portraits of tribesmen, every hair, crease, and gap tooth brought out in infinite detail. Camp life. Landscapes of mountains at sunrise or sunset, gnarled trees, tethered goats. A charred and burnt out truck, contrasted against the yellow of the desert. Like most professional photographers the Swiss had taken ten, twenty, thirty near-identical shots in order to identify the best at his leisure later. Expertly composed and captured, even his worst were better than my best.

But one group differed from the rest. Life in one of the border towns: people, bustle, noise, narrow dirt roads, whitewashed walls with daubed slogans, street hawkers. An air of threat and intimidation. The pictures had a snatched quality at odds with the rest, as though the Swiss didn't have time to compose and position.

I flicked back and forth through the dozen or so shots. It began with a group of women in burkas, intrusive portraits, but then the Swiss seemed to follow the traffic in the opposite direction. Following, in particular, a handcart, making it way through a mass of donkeys, pick-ups, and bicycles. Children selling cigarettes desperate to make eye contact, armed militia daring you to. At one point the handcart man's face fills the screen, blurred, too close to focus.

I guessed that the Swiss had seen something and needed to record it for posterity. But he had the sensibility of an artist, not a journalist, so what was it? He'd been allowed to openly take a dozen or so shots and he couldn't have hidden such a high-def. camera – it would normally need a tripod – so it couldn't have been anything too controversial.

But sensitive enough to hide the card in a pack of cigarettes.

Looking again, I tried to get as much information about the handcart man as possible. The blurred face, another decent one in profile, but mainly back shots. He wore an ankle length grey robe tied at the waist with a striped sash and had straight, short black hair which probably made him look younger than he was. The way he stooped I guessed at fifty. Other than that, well, let's say if you were putting together an identity parade you wouldn't have to look long in Pakistan for a line up.

The contents of the handcart were covered with a sheet except for... and then I saw it.

Hanging below the rear of the cart, in between the handles, was a large cage, rectangular, made of wood or metal, it wasn't clear. The gaps between the bars were four, perhaps six inches. And looking out from between the bars was a...

I zoomed in to get a better look. A penguin? No, not a penguin. But not a chicken, or any kind of parrot, either. At least none that I recognized.

I flicked back and forth through the shots, now knowing what I was after. I could imagine the Swiss now, dodging through the Kasbah, pushing his way forward, trying to get ahead of the handcart, trying to get the right angle to get his shot.

But a shot of what? I joined up everything I could glean from the pictures. Two foot tall, maybe. Weighty. Flightless, surely? Its wings looked short and stumpy, but cooped up in the cage it was hard to tell. A large black head, almost spherical, which gave the initial impression of a penguin. A white line around a black eye, or just the light catching? I couldn't tell. A grey body. They didn't look like feathers, but it was a bird so it had to be. It was a bird... wasn't it?

As Scott said, keep asking yourself: is this a story? I'd come here wanting to break exclusives about Chinese incursions into Pakistan, or US Special Forces being left behind, embedded, in direct contradiction to presidential promises and UN resolutions. But here I was, on the verge of discovering the penguin-chicken. Was this a story? Yes. But could I convince Scott?

I couldn't believe that I was taking this seriously. But if I wanted to be the ZBC left-hand armpit correspondent...

A mile or so further up the road from the now cold, black remains of the bus was a settlement hardly worth the name. Wattle and daub, and dry stone walls. Windows hung with goatskin and plastic sheeting, not a pane of glass in sight. Dung fires with nothing cooking over them for my dollars to buy. I showed the pictures of the town to the few toothless inhabitants. Finally I found one with the intelligence to realize that I wasn't just trying to dazzle him with digital pictures, but I was showing him pictures *of something*. With much finger pointing he indicated the general direction, and I guessed the level of animation equated to distance. I hitched a ride on a donkey cart climbing the hillside.

Just so Scott didn't forget me I filed another story. It managed to be both rambling and come in at under sixty seconds, pure travelogue about the people caught up in the crossfire trying to scratch a living out of the dead earth between the rocks.

I could tell, as soon as he came on the webcam, that he was about to blast me out. But he paused, blinking, brow furrowed. "Davey. You look like shit. When did you last eat?"

I paused. I couldn't recall my last proper meal, anything that had been on a plate, anything that needed cutlery or more than a moment to consume.

"I know what sleep dep sounds like, Davey. I know what malnutrition looks like. It doesn't play well. Cable viewers like correspondents to look like they haven't just stepped off the plane, but neither do they want them to have gone native. Kabul, Jalalabad, doesn't matter. Get yourself back to the city, have a shower. Have some sleep. Shave and a steak. In fact, almost anything beginning with an 'S'."

"I'm on to a story, Scott."

Scott leant back in his seat, grinning. "Yeah, something else that begins with an S that you need to find, Davey." He began to count off on his fingers. "Sleep, shower, shave, steak, story. And anything else beginning with an S you can get." And with that his figure blurred towards the screen and was gone.

I arrived a day later, limping with a blister. I'd slept in a crevice between rocks, breakfasted on icy waters in which I had also washed. The rest is kinda blurry. I remember patrolling the streets and the marketplace, grabbing people by the shoulders, trying to find the handcart man. Everybody began to look like him. Young, old, I kept making mistakes. I'd apologize. Mostly they shrugged me away. One or two were less accommodating. Guns and knives were revealed under robes threateningly. There were arguments. I reeled away before I got hit. I remember imitating a bird, miming a cage, waving my hands to indicate size, trying to get people to understand. A small crowd suddenly gathered, laughing at me. Me joining in with them. A headache. A blinding headache. The light hurting my eyes.

And nothing after that.

I woke up lying on straw in the gloom of a small barn or large shed. Chinks of daylight showed through gaps in the walls and roof. All around me were the clucking and scratching of chickens. My initial thought was that I'd been taken hostage.

In the gloom it took some moments to realize that the penguin-chicken was looking at me, its head cocked to one side. It was even bigger than I'd guessed, almost half my height, its thighs as thick as its wings were stunted. I was too tired to be terrified. Too terrified to move.

And then it spoke in a clipped, robotic chant, barely recognizable as English. "You are required to direct this messenger drone to those in authority. Message from the General Tu'huaht of the Mininutian Fleet, which has blockaded your planet for the last one hundred and thirteen of your Earth days. All trade between your planet and other worlds has been denied to you. Your resources are dwindling, and your resistance cannot last. But the General Tu'huaht promises leniency in exchange for your immediate surrender. The General Tu'huaht also promises that any other course will result in destruction and slavery. Message ends."

It blinked, clucked, scratched at the floor and pecked at some grain. And then it looked up again and repeated the message exactly, word for word, pause for pause, note for note. And then the chicken-penguin went on to repeat it three more times in exactly the same manner before stalking off to a dark corner of the coop. I stared into the darkness to look for any other creatures but it seemed to be alone, towering over the more familiar-looking chickens.

Then I realized that a man was sitting by me on a wooden stool, the handcart man. I had no idea how long he'd been there, whether he'd heard the message from the General Tu'huaht, whether he'd even recognized the sounds as words. He held his fingers up to his mouth to indicate food, at which point I decided that I was still a free man. I nodded.

"Dollars?" he asked, rubbing his fingers together.

"Dollars," I nodded again.

Exhausted, I fell asleep with the thought that I had to get the message, the recording, because that was what it clearly was, on video. I had no idea what it meant. The world had been laid siege by the Mininutian Fleet? Our planet was cut off from other planets? This was crazy. Utterly crazy. But it was real. And it was a story. Even Scott would have been able to see that if he could see this.

Get a video? I wasn't thinking big enough. Get the bird. Take it back to the States. This was Pulitzer Prize and Barnum and Bailey all rolled into one. My dreamless sleep was only disturbed by a single gunshot, or so I imagined.

When I awoke the coop was lit by oil lamps hanging from the wooden struts. It was night outside and the temperature had dropped by several degrees. I ached all over. I couldn't tell whether I was recovering or going down with something.

A plate sat in front of me. Rice, beans, a rough flatbread, and a chicken thigh the size of a baseball bat. "Eat, eat," the handcart man implored, pushing his dirty fingers to his dirty mouth, grinning.

In the barn the penguin-chicken was nowhere to be seen.

The Lightship

Neil Davies

1.

Commander Aldo Kinnear sprawled on the Rec Room bench, bruised, exhausted and scared. A soldier of the Fris navy, the long-time enemy of humankind, sat opposite, equally bruised. Perhaps it was also exhausted and scared, but Aldo was unable to read any emotion in the harsh, grey, jagged features. They were both armed, yet neither raised a weapon.

The bulkheads of the Lightship *Neophyte* creaked and groaned. The ancient engines throbbed. In Aldo's imagination, the rhythmic vibrations felt through the decks of the old ship were its heartbeat, the quiet sibilance of the life support its breath. *Neophyte* was old, dying, but not yet dead.

It had been Aldo's job to finish it off. He had not expected it to fight back.

2.

"This ship began broadcasting in 4052. That's two years before the war began." Aldo looked up from the data screen and smiled at Lieutenant Caulfield across the Rec Room. "Don't you find that fascinating Eliot?" he said. "This ship was operational long before any of us were born!"

Eliot Caulfield, sitting on the worn, thinly padded bench that ran around three walls of the room, returned the smile of his superior officer.

"We've been here less than three hours and already you're accessing the historical records of the place," he said, pausing to take a sip of tepid coffee. "Isn't that just a little sad?"

Aldo looked at the Beverage Dispenser that clunked and rattled when preparing a drink. He looked at the deck panels, several of them with loose corners. He looked at the stained table tops, the dim lighting, the bench that Eliot sat on, reminiscent of the lecture theatres at the Academy. Finally, he looked back to the small data screen rising out of the counter top, and the ingrained dust in its edges.

"This whole place is history," he said.

"Once we've done our job, it'll be *ancient* history," said Eliot. "The only *fascinating* thing about this place is that it's survived two hundred years of war with barely a scratch."

"Two hundred and *six* years," said Aldo. "Just to be superseded by Automatic Buoys."

"That's progress."

"According to this, she's been attacked by the Fris thirteen times," said Aldo, reading from the screen as the lines scrolled upwards. "Over half of those times the crew of the Neophyte has been found dead, but the Fris never destroyed her, and never attempted to hold her either. She's been repaired, re-crewed and started up again."

"It makes you wonder what the Fris have been up to," said Eliot, taking another sip of coffee. "For that matter, thirteen is not that many times over the two hundred-odd years she's been here."

"Looks like the Fris waited some time before each attack," said Aldo.

"None of which matters," said Eliot. "Because we're here to shut her down for the final time and then she's off to the scrapheap."

Both of them started involuntarily as the bulkhead around them moaned and creaked, the sound echoing along the corridors outside the Rec Room long after it had stopped.

"I guess she didn't like me saying that," said Eliot, regaining his composure and laughing, unconvincingly.

Aldo said nothing.

3.

"We should have known," said Aldo, muttering the words to himself. "We should have guessed."

His fingers tightened on the Browning automatic in his fist as he saw the Fris shift in its seat opposite. With less than a magazine of smart-bullets remaining, he would need to use them wisely. The Fris's energy weapon was almost depleted, he was reasonably certain of that.

But he did not intend to take any chances.

The Fris did not raise its weapon, nor did it show any signs of aggression, only of weariness. When it spoke, its voice was deep, almost growling. But the Galactic was clear and perfectly pronounced, with a slight accent that Aldo could not identify.

"My people believe this place to be cursed. Haunted."

"And yet you forcefully boarded us to take control of her," said Aldo, his finger sliding from the trigger of the Browning to the trigger-guard. He was still cautious, suspicious, but he no longer believed a firefight was about to break out.

The Fris shrugged, a curiously human gesture that made Aldo strangely uncomfortable.

"Not all of us are superstitious," it said. "But finding a like-minded crew can be difficult."

There was a stutter in the throb of the engines, a shiver through the deck beneath their feet.

Aldo listened intently, but the engines settled back into their regular rhythm and he let out a breath he had not known he'd been holding. If the engines failed, the life support would follow. And he had left his Environment Suit in his cabin.

"This ship will die soon," said the Fris.

"Then why attack us?" Aldo's voice was raised, but he could not control it. "Why, time and again, have you tried to take her over?"

"We are at war," said the Fris, no change in the volume or tone of its voice. "This place is strategically important. The Automatic Buoys are better protected and harder to control."

There might have been some truth in the answer, Aldo knew, but it was by no means the whole story. Thirteen attempts, *fourteen* including this one, and each a disaster for both attacker and defender. When there had been survivors, they seemed disoriented, making little sense, telling impossible stories. All but one were hospitalised, permanently, in padded cells. The other had committed suicide before they could reach him.

So far, Aldo was a survivor. But he was already beginning to doubt the reality of his experiences.

4.

The error in judgement lay in believing there was no imminent threat.

After all, the last time the Fris had attacked had been almost twenty years ago. The Lightship was in the process of being decommissioned. Why would there be any danger? Consequently, when he settled for a short sleep after a hard day of inventory, Aldo stripped down to his shorts and t-shirt before climbing into the bunk he had assigned himself.

The two-pitch scream of the alarm dragged him from a much needed sleep. Exhausted, he dragged on his trousers and hurried out the door still fastening them. There was no time to find any other clothes.

He caught up with Eliot en-route to the Control Room. Eliot was fully dressed in his Environment Suit and Aldo caught the brief look of surprise on his face. He considered trying to explain, but decided there were more important matters to deal with.

"Who's on duty?" he said as they hurried along the corridor.

"O'Connor," said Eliot. "He's steady. He wouldn't have hit the alarm without good reason."

Sergeant Mason O'Connor had been in Aldo's command for over a year. Eliot's assessment was justified.

O'Connor was at the old but functional main desk as they entered the Control Room. He wasted no time in explaining the alarm.

"There's a Fris ship heading in," he said, indicating the faded but readable scanner screen behind him. "This piece of junk didn't pick it up until it was almost on top of us. They have cloaking, but nothing a modern scanner wouldn't have seen through."

"Forget the shortcomings of the equipment Sergeant," said Aldo, leaning in to read the scanner. "Were they engaged by *Neophyte's* auto-defence system?"

"Negative sir," said O'Connor, a slight sneer on his face. "The auto-defence system malfunctioned before even taking a shot. We're a sitting duck."

"They could sit out there and take pot shots at us," said Eliot. "Destroy us piece by piece."

"I take it you've sent a distress signal to Command?" said Aldo, ignoring Eliot's prediction of imminent doom and speaking to O'Connor.

"Yes sir," said O'Connor. "The moment after I hit the alarm."

"Any reply yet?" Aldo held on to what little hope he could find.

"They're scrambling a squadron sir," said O'Connor. "But it won't reach us for at least two days. There's nothing closer. No patrols, no exercises. We're at the back end of the galaxy here."

With the tiny spark of hope dying inside him, Aldo straightened from the scanner.

"I don't think they'll stand off and destroy us," he said. "Historically, every attack on this Lightship by the Fris has been an attempt to take her over, more or less in one piece."

"You think they'll board us?" said Eliot.

"Almost certainly."

"You know, if Command went back to giving us our own ships, instead of hiring express freighters to do a 'drop and run', we would have been able to escape. But I guess saving money is more important than saving lives."

Aldo said nothing, finding it difficult to fault Eliot's cynicism. But they were professionals, and it was not for him to question those above him, only to lead those below as best he could.

The rest of the seven-man decommissioning crew had reached the Control Room while he was examining the scanner. He noted, with some embarrassment, that all but him were in correct dress.

"Make sure everyone is armed," he said, talking to Eliot. "And deploy around the airlock."

He turned to O'Connor as Eliot moved off to check the crew.

"How long before they reach us?"

O'Connor checked the read-outs, hesitating as he translated the old-styled data into current meaning in his head. When he sighed, Aldo knew the news would not be good.

"Thanks to this ancient scanner, they've already started docking procedures."

Aldo closed his eyes for a moment, fighting the despair. No time to dress properly. Barely time to grab a weapon from his cabin. When he opened his eyes, he displayed nothing but a resolve to defend the Lightship to the best of his and his crew's ability.

"If we can't kill them, we need to hold out until help gets here," he said.

It was not impossible to hold out for two days, only highly improbable. Nevertheless, they had to try.

5.

Remembering made Aldo suddenly conscious of his inappropriate clothing. He still wore the t-shirt and trousers he had on when he rushed from his cabin. He had, at least, rescued his boots, but he had no socks, and the leather rubbed his feet when he moved. Blisters were a certainty, but he had no wish to look.

The Fris soldier opposite was, of course, fully dressed in battle uniform. Even the prehensile tail was encased in protective material, supple enough to allow it full, and deadly, movement.

The door to the Rec Room shook under a heavy impact, the sudden *boom* startling both Aldo and the Fris. Aldo part raised his Browning as another *boom* thundered around the room. The Fris had shouldered his energy weapon and aimed steadily at the door.

Aldo waited, anxiously, for a third impact, or for the sealed door to break open. At Aldo's suggestion, the Fris had used his energy weapon to fuse the door mechanism when they sought safety in the Rec Room. But the strength of the *booming* made him unsure whether that was enough.

He waited, the only sound the slight *hiss* of the life support, and his and the Fris's laboured breathing.

No third impact came. The door did not break.

After some minutes, the Fris lowered his weapon and growled across the room to Aldo.

"It knows we are here."

Aldo nodded. And he remembered how he had not even known *it* existed before the Fris boarded *Neophyte.*

6.

The decommissioning team took cover in doorways and behind storage boxes dragged out of cabins. Even as they deployed, the sound of the outer airlock door sliding open echoed down the corridor.

Aldo looked quickly around his men. He was sure they were nervous, but none of them showed any outward sign. Each of them came from other branches of the military, and all had served the mandatory five years before their redeployment. They were career soldiers, signing the standard open-ended contract rather than leaving after their five-year stint. They were weapon-trained, and several had served time in the frontline of the war with the Fris. Aldo himself had been a Marine before his promotion and sideways move. He had no doubts about his crew, but they were still hopelessly outnumbered and probably outgunned.

The airlock hissed as the pressure and atmosphere inside synchronised with the Lightship. In seconds the doors at either end of the connecting tube would open, providing a clear pathway between the Lightship and the docked craft, and the vanguard of the Fris attack-force would be on board.

He tightened his grip on the Browning and aimed at the inner door. The waiting was always the worst.

The door opened, the Fris began to pour out into the corridor and the defenders opened fire.

Aldo had hoped the airlock would provide a bottleneck they could utilise, but the first Fris to board carried heavy shields and deployed to form an effective protective barrier as the rest of the force exited the airlock behind them. He had fired several shots himself before he realised the explosions of his bullets were being safely absorbed by the shields. One or two of his crew with heavier armament were causing some damage and would, eventually, break through. But by then the whole enemy force would be on board.

As yet, the Fris had not opened fire with their energy weapons. Aldo knew that once they did, he would not be able to stop the slaughter. He was about to call for a tactical retreat when the deck shuddered beneath his feet and a deafening creaking and wailing filled the corridor.

Both Human and Fris were surprised by the noise, disproving Aldo's first thought that it was some new Fris weapon. The sound grew louder, the creaking becoming a roar. The normal throb of the engines now pounded. Fris dropped their shields, weapons on both sides clattered to the deck, as the noise drove into heads, a throbbing, screaming cacophony.

Aldo barely held on to his Browning as the noise pushed him to his knees. He managed to raise his head and was staring through watery eyes at the Fris when the bulkhead near the airlock punched inwards.

It stretched at speed, a sharp fist of metal smashing into the Fris. Aldo saw alien bodies tumble, their suits ripped, blood pouring through the tears.

Metal tentacles reached out from the opposite bulkhead and grabbed at the Fris, dragging them backwards, enveloping them until their struggling forms disappeared and nothing but smooth metal remained, along with a smear of blood and small gobs of flesh on the deck. The same horrific scene repeated, again and again.

It was against all the science, all the logic Aldo knew. He wondered whether he was hallucinating, but could tell from the expressions of stunned horror on those around him that, if he was hallucinating, so were they. The throbbing of the engines continued, but the other noises had gone, except when the bulkheads deformed and attacked. Then the screams of the metal were matched only by the screams of the Fris.

He heard Eliot say, "At least whatever it is seems to be on our side," a moment before a circle of decking exploded upwards, tentacles of metal reaching and grabbing, pulling Eliot down, crushing him. Aldo could hear the breaking of bones before the deck closed in on itself and Eliot was gone. Nothing remained but a streak of blood and gore.

Shock was replaced with panic. Human and Fris alike stampeded away from the airlock, further into the ship. Aldo was with them, all thoughts of command structure gone from his head. They all needed to escape. They all needed to run!

The terror followed them. Bulkheads and decking reaching, punching, grabbing as they ran. The screaming of metal, Human and Fris, and the clatter and explosion of sporadic gunfire, melded together into a wall of sickening noise. Aldo knew it was pure luck that, so far, nothing had caught him. He did not believe his luck would hold out for long.

The run through the ship took a lifetime. He had no focus but to keep running. The number of people around him dwindled rapidly. Whatever was attacking, perhaps the ship itself, was indiscriminate, as were the methods of attack. Some crushed their victims, others sucked them in.

Claws of decking grabbed for him, but Aldo sidestepped, almost stumbling. A fist of bulkhead barely missed him, crushing the life from a nearby Fris instead. There had to be somewhere to hide!

He had no conscious idea why he chose the Rec Room, but the moment he saw its door he knew he needed to reach it. He was almost knocked aside by a Fris soldier, every bit as eager to get inside as he was himself. A quick look back showed no one else near enough to rescue. There were no Humans left at all, and only four Fris, all injured and all, as he watched, picked off, one by one, by the bulkheads and deck.

He joined the Fris soldier inside and closed the Rec Room door. With sudden inspiration, he shouted at the Fris soldier to fuse the door controls with its energy weapon. With that done he felt only a little safer. He waited for the bulkheads and decking inside the room to attack. The Fris, too, was looking around, his tale swishing anxiously side to side.

No attack came and, after a while, Aldo and the Fris looked at each other across the Rec Room. Neither spoke, but the question they shared was clear. How were they still alive?

7.

"Why do you look at that?"

At the growl of the Fris's voice, Aldo looked up from the data screen.

"It's the history of this Lightship," he said. "I'm hoping I can find something to explain what happened out there."

"I have already told you," said the Fris. "This place is haunted. It is cursed, just like my people have said for many years. I did not believe it, but I do now."

"Well I don't," said Aldo, turning back to the screen. "Ghosts don't exist, and curses are for children and the superstitious. Whatever's out there, it's alive, just like you and me. And anything alive can be killed."

The Fris raised its energy weapon. "What use is this, or your gun, when we cannot see anything to shoot at?" The alien shrugged in that curiously human fashion again and lowered the weapon. "We cannot kill what we cannot see."

Aldo said nothing, preferring to study the scrolling words on the screen. Somewhere in this history there had to be a clue to what was happening. He had been trapped in the Rec Room with the Fris for almost two hours. The only reason he could think of that the creature, whatever it was, had not attacked them was that the Rec Room, like the Control Room, was a separate unit. It was not part of the Lightship main structure. These rooms sat in semi-permanent dock and, if all went well, would remain so. They could, however, detach and act as self-contained lifeboats in cases of critical emergency. The *thing* had attacked through the bulkheads and decks of the Lightship. Their narrow but defined isolation saved them. Perhaps that was why his subconscious had led him here.

He would have detached the Rec Room long before now, if the data pad for doing so hadn't been destroyed, along with the door controls, by the Fris's energy weapon. Given that it was at Aldo's direction, he was not in a position to complain.

He almost missed the entry while his thoughts drifted over recent events. Quickly he scrolled the words back up onto the screen.

"I've found something," he said. "It might be nothing..."

"If you believe it to be of possible importance," interrupted the Fris. "Share it."

"I intend to," said Aldo, a little irritably. He did not appreciate the suggestion that he was about to keep what he had found to himself. The Fris might be the enemy, but they were currently in a bad situation together. He hoped they could co-operate.

As though reading his mind, the Fris nodded. "I did not mean to offend you. I was perhaps a little eager to hear of your discovery."

Aldo could not detect any eagerness in the Fris's body language. The tip of its tail flicked gently side to side, but that could mean anything. Two-hundred years of war and humanity had learnt next to nothing about their enemy. Nevertheless, he decided that sarcasm was less likely than genuine interest where the Fris was concerned.

"There was a collision, almost two-hundred years ago. A freighter called *Deadbeat* drifted into *Neophyte* despite all attempts to raise her crew. When a team boarded her they found out why. The crew were all dead."

"Unfortunate, but I do not see the relevance."

"They kept an open dock with this ship for two days while they did a thorough investigation. The only damage they found, other than the collision damage, was that the bulkheads were buckled and ripped apart in places. The decks too. Sound familiar?"

The Fris was silent for a second, before growling its answer in as contemplative a manner as a growl could be.

"There was something in that freighter."

"I believe so. I also believe it came aboard *Neophyte* while the two ships were in open dock."

"But why attack now?" said the Fris. "Why did it not attack you and your crew when you came aboard?"

"Maybe it lies dormant, somehow hidden within the bulkheads and decks. It's happy there until it feels threatened."

"And when we began to fight, we became a threat," said the Fris in understanding.

"This time and every other time you've attacked *Neophyte,*" said Aldo. "That's your ghost, your curse. Some alien creature that gets pissed off when it thinks it's under attack."

"It seems a reasonable extrapolation based on scant evidence," said the Fris, nodding. "But it does not answer how we find it or how we kill it."

Aldo read further on the screen, but there was no more mention of the collision or of anything untoward happening after *Deadbeat* had been towed away. If the creature had come aboard during the dock, then it had hidden itself well, and for several years, until the first Fris attack occurred. Which raised another question in Aldo's mind.

"You've attacked this ship thirteen times."

"Strictly speaking, fourteen," said the Fris. "If you count this one."

"My point is," said Aldo, "that each time we've re-crewed her, and each time you've attacked her again, the Neophyte has shown no signs of the kind of damage we're witnessing now. This thing attacks in a very destructive way. What happens to all that destruction after it's won?"

The Fris thought for a moment before answering.

"We have seen that this creature can distort, even mould, metal. Perhaps, like many animals, it wishes to cover its tracks, to remain hidden once it has dealt with the intrusion?"

"Bit of a difference between moving a few twigs and leaves to camouflage a nest, and the complete resetting of the Neophyte's bulkheads."

"But the same principle."

Aldo nodded, admitting that it made as much sense as anything else at that moment.

"I bet you wish you'd just stood off and destroyed this place now," he said, hoping the Fris could appreciate that it was said with an attempt at light humour.

"I had no choice," said the Fris. "The orders from the *Lgoblol*... similar to your President I think... were clear, and have been for every mission he has ordered. Board and capture."

The Fris paused and Aldo almost thought he saw the grim, stiff mouth curl upwards in a small smile.

"I believe he wants to add it to his collection," the Fris continued. "Our *Lgoblol* collects war memorabilia. He does not yet have a Human Lightship."

"You're kidding, right?" said Aldo in amazement. "Are you telling me all these raids over two hundred years have been to obtain a museum piece? How long has this... *Lgoblol*, been in power?"

"Just over three-hundred of your years," said the Fris, once again shrugging. "We live long lives."

"All those deaths because..."

He was interrupted by a renewed hammering on the Rec Room door, the thick metal of which began to buckle inwards.

Aldo held his breath, watching the door, waiting for it to crack. From the corner of his eye he could see the Fris was also intently studying the situation. If the door gave way there was little either of them could do, and they knew it. Their only hope lay in the fact that, so far, the thing outside had not been able to infiltrate the bulkheads and deck of the Rec Room. If the door broke under the beating, then that would change, with rapid and deadly consequences.

"What if it does not need to actually break down the door?" said the Fris, shouting above the noise.

Aldo, wincing at the deafening volume of the ongoing attack, turned and shouted back. "I don't follow. What do you mean?"

"Perhaps it only needs to weaken the structure of the metal to the point where it can.... *enter* it."

Aldo was silent. If the Fris was right, and the idea was as valid as any other, then their danger was more imminent than he had believed. He felt his chest tightening at the thought. If the thing *was* just weakening the reinforced door, then it could infiltrate the Rec Room at any moment. And once it was in the bulkheads... he shuddered and wiped cold sweat from his brow.

"I did not mean to frighten you," said the Fris, looking towards Aldo.

"I was already frightened," said Aldo. "You've just *terrified* me!"

"Then I did not mean to *terrify* you," said the Fris.

A louder *boom* from the door made them both jump.

Aldo suspected the Fris was joking, but there seemed no way of knowing for certain. The Fris's face was almost completely immobile, or so it seemed. Expression had never been noted on the face of any Fris, even those captured and tortured under the harsh military law of the past two centuries. Nevertheless, there was something, perhaps in the inflection of the words, that convinced Aldo his alien companion was making a joke at his expense. He found he wished there was more time to get to know this alien, to understand the Fris better than humanity currently did. He had never believed torture was the way to communicate. He had not expected shared peril to be the way forward either, before now.

More thudding, pounding and booming from the door. More sharp, jagged points of metal jutting inwards. It no longer looked like a door, but more like the model of an extensive mountain range turned on its end.

The attack stopped as suddenly as it had begun, echoes bouncing through the Lightship's corridors. For a moment there was silence, and Aldo and the Fris looked at each other. Aldo did not believe the creature had given up, and he doubted the Fris believed it either. They waited.

A creak from the bulkhead to the right of the door. Had it buckled slightly? Aldo peered at it, reluctant to move closer and check. He thought he saw a slight buckling. He felt the tightening in his chest again, a twist in his stomach.

Another creak. A groan. Raised lines began to radiate from the bulkhead edge by the door, like veins on the back of an old man's hand. The bulkhead on the other side of the door now creaked. More veins began to creep from its edge.

Aldo felt sick, his chest tight, his stomach churning. He raised the Browning, his fingers white with clenching. It was a useless gesture. There was nothing to fire at. It was little consolation that the Fris had raised his weapon also.

"It's getting in," said Aldo. It was a needless remark, but he felt the need to say something, to show he was aware of the situation. Aware that his own death was approaching.

"How long can you survive in a vacuum?" said the Fris, his weapon raised, his eyes flashing from one bulkhead to the other, watching the slow creep of the metal *veins*.

"What?" Aldo was confused by the question. He was finding it hard to concentrate on anything but the groaning bulkheads.

"How long?" repeated the Fris, an edge of irritability creeping into its growling voice.

"I don't know... less than two minutes?" said Aldo, trying to remember his basic training. "But I'd be unconscious in seconds."

Without a further word, the Fris put down his weapon and, after releasing several clasps, shrugged out of his spacesuit.

Aldo stared at the first Fris he had seen without a suit. Its skin looked like smooth armour, with none of the cragginess of the face. It wore a one-piece overall-type garment, close fitting but not skin tight. It was all surprisingly human, until the tail swished or the beast-like head turned and growled.

"What are you doing?" said Aldo, uncomfortably aware of how the *creaking* and *groaning* of the bulkheads was getting louder. It would not be long before the creature was able to completely infiltrate the Rec Room. The *veins* were already pulsing with life, growing wider and longer with each second.

"I can survive for almost three of your hours, and will retain consciousness for at least thirty of your minutes," said the Fris. As he spoke he adjusted something at the back of the suit and the tail section detached, falling to the deck and rolling to one side. It reminded Aldo, bizarrely, of an out-of-place draft excluder.

"Not all of us have tails," explained the Fris. "The suits are made to adapt."

"But why...?"

The Fris held the suit out to Aldo.

"Put this on. It will not be perfect, but once sealed it will keep you alive."

"It won't stop that thing from killing me," said Aldo, still puzzled by the Fris's actions. "I don't understand what your plan is?"

"Put the suit on," said the Fris. "If there is still time to explain after that, I will try."

The bulkhead to the right began to visibly buckle, a few sharp peaks poking outwards. The metal began to *scream* under stress.

Aldo, beyond the point of arguing, stepped into the suit, with help from the Fris. It was too big for him, his hands barely reaching the gloves, the feet clown-like in their length, but as the helmet rose from the back, curving over his head, and sealed at the front, he could not deny he felt strangely safer. Intellectually he knew the suit would not protect him from the creature, but emotionally he felt more secure than he had in only t-shirt and trousers. He felt properly dressed.

He looked at the Fris, still an impressive sight even without the bulk of the suit. It was built to be a warrior, every muscle honed to perfection. Humans must look so weak to a Fris.

A prolonged *screech* of metal turned his attention to the bulkhead. It was blistering. The *veins* looked ready to pop. At any moment, it seemed the creature would gain complete control and either crush them or gather them in as it had others, somehow digesting the flesh, the bone and muscle, in seconds.

"Given its long residence on this Lightship, I am hoping it needs oxygen as we do," said the Fris.

Aldo thought that, once again, he saw that mostly immobile mouth twitch into something resembling a smile.

The Fris was bent over the control pad of its energy weapon. Then, with hurried steps, it placed the weapon on the deck, at the junction of the left bulkhead and the damaged door.

"Tell me the plan," said Aldo, as the Fris retreated to the back of the Rec Room. It waved at Aldo to join it, which he managed with awkward, stumbling steps.

"I have overridden the safety systems on the weapon," said the Fris. "I have also dialled it to full power. Without the safety, it should overload."

It took a moment for Aldo to catch on. When he did, he was not sure whether to feel hopeful or even more frightened.

"You think it'll explode," he said. It was not a question.

The bulkheads around them screamed as tentacles of metal reached for them. Aldo saw the Fris grabbed and, struggling, dragged back towards the bulkhead. He moved to help, but was, himself, caught around the right leg. He tried to pry the metal free, but it wrapped tighter. Pain shot through him as his leg was crushed. He felt the bone snap and screamed his agony into the helmet of the Fris spacesuit. He could not resist as he was pulled backwards.

The energy weapon exploded with a blinding flash of light and a percussive wave that slammed into Aldo, hurting him almost as much as the creature was. There was a hole in the bulkhead that spread across to the door. The screaming of the metal was joined by the screaming of air as it was sucked into the vacuum of space.

The tentacles around Aldo and the Fris retracted, snapping back into the bulkheads either side. He could not be sure, but Aldo thought he heard another scream, a totally alien gurgle of a scream, joining those of the metal and the air.

He could feel the tug of the vacuum, trying to pull him towards the hole in the bulkhead. He struggled not to go, holding on to a chair that was bolted to the deck. A hand on his arm startled him, and he let out a small yelp of fear before he heard the growl of the Fris clearly through the helmet.

"Let it take you. We need to be outside."

The Fris let go of his arm and Aldo watched in stunned silence as the alien allowed itself to be lifted and pulled through the Rec Room and out of the hole into space.

The bulkheads were writhing. Undulations of metal that were almost liquid in their motion. An occasional angry peak would be punched out, but the overwhelming impression to Aldo was of fear, of panic. The creature was thrashing about within the bulkhead, unsure what to do in this new situation. The deck beneath his feet was buckling too. Around him, stalactites and stalagmites of metal were appearing with sudden ferocity, and he wondered how long before one would tear through the suit and kill him.

"What the hell," he said quietly. "I've got nothing to lose."

He let go of the chair.

The outrush of air picked him up with ease and he felt himself flying, out of control, through the deadly maze of sharp metal jutting up and out all around him. The foot of the suit caught the edge of one and he began to spin. He felt nauseous but relieved that the suit was not punctured. He was still spinning as he was sucked out into the blackness of space.

A hand steadied him, and he saw the Fris was holding on to an antenna. The Fris pointed away to its right. As Aldo looked, understanding made him smile. The Fris ship still hung in space, docked with *Neophyte*, but sealed.

The Human and the Fris pushed off together, an untethered space walk in the direction of the Fris ship.

Aldo managed to look back once. More holes were being punched in the Rec Room and, at times, he thought he saw, not metal, but rose-coloured flesh writhing and pulsing through the distorted bulkheads and decks. Then it was gone. The Rec Room became suddenly lifeless and Aldo knew the creature had returned to the main body of the Lightship.

8.

They boarded the Fris ship with ease, entering through an airlock that was so similar to the ones on *Neophyte* that Aldo was disoriented for a moment. The more he learnt about the Fris, the more human they seemed.

Aldo had half expected there to be crew aboard, but the ship's corridors and cabins were eerily empty.

"Small ship on an unpopular mission," explained the Fris as they hurried towards the Control Room. "Everyone was needed for the boarding. Automatic systems were left in control."

"What kind of weaponry does it have?" asked Aldo, his breathing becoming laboured as he struggled to keep up, still inside the outsized Fris spacesuit. He dragged his broken leg, hissing and wincing at the pain.

"Enough." It was all the answer the Fris would give.

Aldo tried to look around him as they went, looking for any crucial pieces of information he could take back to Space Command, if he survived. It had long been the Holy Grail to gain access to a Fris ship. In two-hundred years of warfare, they had never captured one as anything less than a twisted wreck. Now, here he was, inside the enemy's ship, and it all looked disappointingly familiar. Other than extra wide doors, presumably to allow the Fris tail through without hindrance, there was little, if any, difference from a standard Human ship. Apparently, if you were a bipedal race of a certain build, there was a basic, functional design that objects would follow. Including a military ship. Perhaps the decor changed, or the language of signs, but where the function was the same, the design became the same also.

They entered the Control Room. The positioning of desks and chairs was slightly unusual, but Aldo knew he could control this ship with ease, should the need arise.

"I guess this all looks a little familiar," said the Fris as he took a position at the weapons console.

Aldo, the helmet now retracted as the air inside the ship was perfectly acceptable, if a little heavy in an unusual animal-like odour, nodded.

"I was just thinking how amazing it is, the way basic functional design can evolve in such a similar way in two different species," he said.

The Fris snorted, the first time Aldo had heard that particular, and fairly unpleasant, sound.

"We captured several of your ships almost a century ago, by your time, and copied the design," said the Fris. "Until then, our ships were impractical and inefficient."

Aldo was stunned by the admission. He felt deflated, even slightly embarrassed at his well-meaning but inaccurate reasoning. He quickly recovered. There were still enough human-like mannerisms and behaviours in the Fris to maintain his belief that they were not all that different from humans, despite what the official propaganda might say.

"Look," said the Fris, directing the weapon system's outside view onto a large screen built into the front bulkhead.

The Fris ship had disengaged and now stood some way off. Aldo could see *Neophyte* directly ahead, but the shape seemed blurred, subtly wrong in some way. It took a moment for him to realise all the outer bulkheads were buckled, distorted. Tentacles writhed near the engine room, most of them metal, but some a pulsing rose-coloured flesh.

"Any final words?" said the Fris, its finger poised above the Fire button.

Aldo thought of all the people who had died, Eliot, Sergeant O'Connor and the others, including the Fris soldiers. He thought of how, for two centuries, this creature had hidden in the bulkheads and the decks, striking out when it felt threatened. It had killed hundreds, and it had tainted the memory of the longest serving Lightship in the Human Navy.

"Good riddance," he said.

The energy beam struck again and again, each time tearing great holes in *Neophyte*, debris spinning off into space, some clattering against the hull of the Fris ship. The explosions flared in silence, the ripping of metal unheard in the vacuum of space. Nevertheless, Aldo imagined he could hear the creature screaming, as he had heard it just before he escaped from the Rec Room. It made it all, somehow, more satisfying.

At one point, late on in the destruction, he thought he saw a rose-coloured, amorphous mass drift away from the Lightship. It was the briefest of glimpses and could have been the after-effect of one of the explosions. But it made him wonder.

He was not so surprised to find the Fris had been having similar thoughts.

"Do you think it is dead? Or did it escape?" said the Fris, as he continued to fire the ship's weapon, one eye watching the temperature needle crawling closer to the *danger* position.

"I hope it's dead," said Aldo. "But I fear otherwise."

"We need to warn others," said the Fris. "It is unlikely this creature was unique. Whether this one is dead or not, there is still the possibility of more out there."

"How safe do you think we are here?"

The Fris did not answer, and Aldo was not surprised. No answer was preferable to the probable truth.

The energy weapon ceased fire, and the Fris turned almost apologetically to Aldo. "It was about to overheat. I had to stop."

Aldo looked at the screen and the blackened, crumpled wreckage that had been the Lightship *Neophyte.*

"I think it's enough," he said. "I came here to decommission her. I guess you could say the job's done."

"We should remember those we lost," said the Fris, and Aldo nodded.

"I don't think I'll ever forget them," he said.

A thought struck him and he almost laughed. "Your President, or whatever, is going to be pissed. You've destroyed his museum piece."

The Fris shrugged in its peculiarly Human fashion. "The *Lgoblol* will need to look elsewhere. Sometimes I feel this whole war is being run by our rulers for their personal profit."

Aldo silently agreed, and wondered again at the similarity in his and the Fris's thinking.

It seemed the danger was over. The creature had been either killed, or at least expelled from *Neophyte.* A lot of men had lost their lives, but he and this one Fris survived, aboard a Fris spaceship.

"I guess I'm your prisoner," he said with quiet resignation.

The Fris nodded slowly and then, in a quiet, low growl, said, "Yes. But much can happen between here and home. For example, after I have treated your leg in our medical facilities, you might steal one of our lifeboats which I have carelessly left unsealed and which are a short walk down the corridor from the medical room."

Aldo grinned. "You know, I feel I should introduce myself. My name is Aldo."

"I am Wrancda," said the Fris.

They shook hands.

Ana

Liam Hogan

It's weird, the things that can mess up a kid's head. Take Ana, for example. She was convinced that every time she looked under her bed, the Universe split in two. In a parallel world in which a mirror Ana also looked under her bed before going to sleep and after saying her prayers and where, up until then, she'd never found anything bad, this time there would be a ghastly demon with wicked teeth and blood-stained claws, whose only desire was to catch and tear apart Ana, aged six and three quarter years.

Little wonder she said her prayers *before* she looked. Little wonder she had nightmares.

I told her that wasn't the way the multiverse theory worked. That for every Ana that found a slavering beast, there was one that found a toy she'd lost, or one that forgot to look under the bed.

She skewered me with her most outraged look. This Ana *never* forgot.

But it's hard arguing theoretical physics with a child yet to turn seven and, as I wasn't prepared to deny the theory outright, it was clear this notion was not going to be an easy one to shift. It wasn't simply that she had a binary, yes versus no, either-or view of the coin toss that happened in her imagination every time she lifted the skirt that kept under-the-bed out-of-sight. It was because what terrified her, wasn't the finding a monster under her bed, it was the *not* finding a monster under her bed. In her head, every time she survived, she doomed the parallel Universe Ana to a grisly death. It was the guilt that was crushing her.

"Why don't you not look?" I reasoned.

"I have to," she replied with an air of ancient sorrow. "There might be a monster under the bed. I have to check. And even if I don't, the other Ana will."

This had me scratching my head, figuratively speaking. I'm a psychologist by trade, not a physicist. Wouldn't that require the Universe to have already split? And, once the other Ana looked, it would be her Universe that split again, not this Ana's. Maybe this was something I could use.

I thought of her parents. Reading between the lines, not a tricky task with those two, they wanted me to crush Ana's creativity. To make her as easy to handle as she had been twelve months earlier. To make her 'normal'. But normal wasn't an option; it was clear this precocious child had the potential to far exceed the pretensions of her middle class parents.

"Ana," I said, "Who looks first? You, or the other Ana?"

She suspected a trick and trod carefully. "We both..." then she corrected herself. "There is no other Ana, not until I look. Or there is, but it's me and we haven't split yet."

"If she is you, will she react to finding the monster the same way you would?"

She sucked air through the gap in her front teeth. "I guess."

"And how would you react, if, when you looked under the bed, you found a monster there? What would you do?"

"I..."

I waited. The silence stretched between us. This was somewhere she hadn't been before. "I don't know," she said quietly.

"But you'd do something? You wouldn't just sit there?"

"No," she agreed. "I'd run... hide. Scream, maybe."

"I'm sure you would. And what would your parents do, if they heard you scream?"

"They'd come running," she said, and they would. Any parent would.

I let her think about this for a moment. "Ana, you're intelligent, resourceful, and brave. And the other Ana, she is exactly the same. She is, after all, you. She – you – would not take it lying down. You'd fight, you'd run. Your parents would help. The one thing you would never be, is a victim. Don't think I haven't noticed the hobby horse propped up against the toy chest, ready for action."

"And the roller skates on the landing," she said.

I wasn't sure how the roller skates would help. Perhaps she hoped the monster would trip on them. She'd be upset if I told her that her mother wordlessly tidied them up each night. "And the skates," I diplomatically agreed. "It's not much, perhaps, but you're doing the best you can. And so would the other Ana. No monster is going to get a free lunch in this house."

She laughed, a lovely little laugh, made all the more charming by its rarity of use.

I pushed on. "So it's not a foregone conclusion that the monster always wins. And if it does not–"

"Then there are two Anas!" she interrupted.

This wasn't quite where I'd been going. I wanted her to acknowledge that she wasn't responsible for what happened in the other Universes. How could she be? But sometimes, usually in fact, you had to let your patient find their own path.

"And then four, and then eight, and then..." she babbled on.

A small chime rang out on my wristwatch. "Okay Ana. I think we've made good progress. We'll leave it there for today."

A muffled voice came through the door. "Ana? Honey? Who are you talking to in there?"

Ana called back, "No one, mummy."

Which was an illuminating denial. I jotted it down for future discussion, curious to see if Ana's mother would come into the bedroom. "Okay sweetie," she caved in, as I suspected she would. "But go to sleep now, you hear?"

Ana waited until the footsteps faded away down the hall. "Goodnight, Doctor."

"Goodnight, Ana," I replied, "sleep tight."

And then I slid myself back under her bed, listening to her breathing softly slow and waiting for tomorrow night, when she would once again lift the covers, and – all being well – discover me lying there, ready for our next session.

Liberty Bird

Jaine Fenn

This is the moment. That first glimpse of space, coyly revealed by the widening doors. Kheo gives his instruments the attention they require, but his eye is drawn downwards, to the banded glory of Yssim, the cold and distant light of the stars beyond.

His exit is faultless. The Clan insisted he pre-program it, rather than take even the miniscule risk of their favoured son screwing up and dinging his yacht on the hangar doors. That would never do, not with the whole world watching.

Some impulse had made Kheo visit the engineering hangar three days before the race. He should either have been preparing himself mentally with relaxation and centring exercises – as his family would prefer – or drinking, gambling and womanising in the lowtown rings – as the media would expect – but he had a sudden desire to be alone with his yacht, without the tech crew fussing around.

The hangar was the largest open space on the liner and the ship's spin provided near-normal gravity here. After two months away from Homeworld, the echoey open space and illusion of full weight were disconcerting. In the low lighting *Liberty Bird* was a point of colour, although her red and blue hull was muted by the oily shadows.

Kheo reached up, tracing the fusion yacht's perfect lines, his hand passing just below the Clan crest emblazoned on her side. Someone had left the steps in place; it was only logical he use them to climb into the cockpit. He sighed as he sealed the canopy. *Liberty Bird* was the only birthright he wanted. Yet the race she had been built for might not be held many more times and if his family had their way this would the last time he would be permitted to compete. That made claiming his third win even more important.

He started at movement glimpsed out the corner of his eye. Someone out there, down on the hangar floor. A thief? A saboteur from a rival clan who had somehow got onto the Reuthani liner? His heart raced. The net was buzzing with stupid gossip: with no one to keep them in check any more, ancient clan rivalries were getting out of hand.

No, just Chief Mechanic Sovat. Kheo liked Sovat, respected him. Yes, that was what he felt: *respect*. Sovat often worked late, went above and beyond.

Except Sovat didn't appear to be working. More like waiting. Another of the tech team walked in, a younger man whose name only came to Kheo after a moment's thought. Greal: junior propulsion specialist, university educated, rather effete for the rough-diamond world of the yacht-techs. Why were this mismatched pair meeting here so late? Not for something nefarious, he hoped. They appeared to just be talking, standing close.

Oh. Had he really seen –? Did they really just –?

Sovat stepped back, then looked around. Kheo shrank down in the seat, holding his breath. The Chief Mechanic's gaze passed over him, and he turned back to his companion. More brief words, then the two men left, Greal following close to Sovat. Kheo had no doubt they were headed somewhere more private.

Kheo clears the great wheel of the hangar-deck at a pace the watching cameras will no doubt find pedestrian. Of course, speed is relative: the liner is in a high, fast orbit around the gas giant far below. The first thrust of acceleration as he brings the main engines online is deceptive; he actually needs to lose orbital velocity before the start of the race.

He rotates *Liberty Bird* and peels away from the Reuthani Clan liner; the huge blunt needle is strung with spoked rings, their sizes and positions determining their place in this microcosm of clan life: engineering, living suites, gardens, entertainments and accommodation for the few thousand citizens permitted to accompany their betters off-world for this annual jamboree. In a touching if tacky gesture, a block of portholes in the central midtown ring have been selectively lit to spell out the words *Good Luck Kheo.*

All around Yssim, other Pilots are leaving their liners. Most clans, including his own, only field one Pilot these days. Some clans no longer participate in the Flamestar Challenge. Other clans no longer exist.

The yachts head for the Royal Barge, a smaller vessel in a lower orbit around the gas giant. Though the Barge now lacks any royalty, tradition still dictates that the race starts from there. It will take several hours to reach the Barge, and the formal start of the race. The approach is critical to a good start. In his five previous races, Kheo has tuned his coms into the razzmatazz that surrounds the biggest event in high society's calendar. All across the system, pundits are discussing the latest form reports released by the clans for their teams and mulling over the detailed ion-stream data. Every other year, Kheo has revelled in the sense of being at the heart of it all yet free, out in the vastness of space.

Not this time. He selects some roots-rock – not his usual sort of music, but it should blast his head clear – and stares out into the beauty of the void, urging his mind to remain blank.

Kheo was expected to show his face at the hangar the next day, both as a courtesy to the techs working on his behalf and to attend a briefing on the current configuration of the ion-streams. He had been looking forward to the tactical discussion of routes and fuel management, to sharing the respectful camaraderie of the men. Instead he was uneasy, almost nervous. He made himself chat to the usual people; act normal.

And everything *was* normal. In the daytime bustle, Kheo wondered if he had been mistaken; perhaps he even dreamt the encounter he had witnessed the previous evening. He spent enough time imagining such things.

Sovat was as brusquely efficient as ever when he took Kheo over the latest engine test results. There was no sign of Greal.

Sovat was the last to leave the briefing room, and he paused, as though waiting for Kheo to say something. When Kheo failed to speak, the Mechanic turned to follow his fellow techs out.

Kheo took a different route back to the suite-decks, choosing rarely used corridors and secondary float-tubes, doing his best to avoid the crew, minor family and hangers-on with their ready smiles. He spent the journey trying to work out whether the look Mechanic Sovat had given him had been an invitation.

By the time he has the Royal Barge on visual, Yssim itself is too large for his mind to interpret as spherical. The gas giant is a sky-spanning backdrop of mauve and azure, lavender and turquoise. He is close enough to spot details in the roiling turbulence between the coloured bands. Thanks to the false-colour projections enhancing his view through the canopy, he can see the ion-streams: ethereal threads and skeins, twisting and curling out from the massive world, curved lines of force linking it to Estin, the pus-yellow moon constantly pummelled by Yssim's tidal forces.

Now comes the first test. The intricacies of orbital mechanics make an actual start line impossible. Instead Kheo, and every other Pilot, must interpret detailed positional readings then use them to apply delta-V, at the same time keeping track of the movements of the other yachts.

The exact moment the race starts is determined by the AI-enhanced stewards on the Barge, who are monitoring every one of the twenty-three yachts to determine when all of them are present in the prescribed volume of space. Just being in position isn't enough: you need to be on the right heading and, ideally, as near the front of the volume as possible.

Fifteen ships already lined up… another entering. And another.

He makes a tiny adjustment; raising his orbit slightly. He's in a good position but he can't afford to leave the start volume before the last yacht enters. A false start not only annoys the watching billions, it means the culprit has to start in the secondary volume, behind everyone else.

The penultimate yacht enters the volume. Kheo's got less than five seconds before he leaves it…

The final yacht is in place.

His board lights green.

He keys the preset that maxes the drive. The gentle hand that has been pressing him into his seat becomes a grasping fist.

The Flamestar Challenge is on.

Two days before the race, Clan Reuthani held the pre-race banquet in the liner's Great Mess, a name which had made Kheo smile when he was growing up.

Kheo's first banquet had been seven year ago, shortly after his sixteenth birthday. Uncle Harrik had been First Pilot then, and Kheo had joined in with the drunken and enthusiastic chorus of the Reuthani Clan anthem which serenaded him to his rest. Harrik had won the Flamestar that year, a victory made more special because that had been the first staging of the race since the Empress had been ousted; their Clan yacht had even been renamed in recognition of the coup. In all, his uncle had won twice in eight races. Impressive, but not as good as three out of six.

This year, as the diners picked over the second course of the third remove – sweet jellied consommé upon which floated spun sugar confections in the shape of fusion yachts – a lull in the quiet murmur allowed an overloud stray comment to surface.

"Liberation's become a dirty word!"

The speaker was Kheo's father, the Honourable Earl Reuthani. At his words silence fell across high table. Several people on nearby tables glanced at the chair between Kheo and his mother. Next to him, Prinbal sighed. His younger brother currently greeted most parental comments with sighs but for once Kheo could have joined in.

"Surely you aren't suggesting we were better off under the Empress!" That was Harrik: no else would dare speak up, but the combination of being an ex-Pilot and having fought in the Liberation gave him the right to question the Earl.

"Course not, she wasn't even human." His father was drunk, as usual. "What I mean is, the commoners forget that most of us rose up when they did, an' fought beside 'em. And now they're angling for this 'New Liberation' – from us!"

At least Clan Reuthani still exists, thought Kheo grimly.

His brother was watching their father, absorbing the adult interactions even as he pretended to disdain them.

His Mother said, "But I doubt the malcontents will get far. We need *some* continuity. Most people realise that. What we should be worrying about is all those other systems out there."

"Surely contact could be to our advantage," said Kheo, thinking of the new technologies he had heard about via the recently instituted 'beamed virtual' connection. After centuries of imposed isolation they were finally part of the universe at large.

A cousin chirped, "Yes, who knows what outsider technology could mean for the Flamestar Challenge?"

Assuming it continued. Now that the massive extravagance of

moving everyone of note out from Homeworld to run a race around the largest body in the system was no longer maintained by the Empress's brutal taxes, the race was becoming unsustainable. Which just made it more important that he won it again this year. But as discussion returned to the upcoming race, Kheo found his taste for the festivities dulled. He was glad when he was sung to his rest.

Alone in his room, his mood darkened further. He had spent much of his adult life being secretly grateful that he had been too young to fight in the War, that his elder sister had volunteered instead, although he doubted Father would have let an older son join the fight. Now, facing a life of responsibilities he never wanted and knew he was not up to – not to mention the frustration and hypocrisy – he almost envied his dead, heroic sister.

The first stretch is a long straight burn.

Kheo's initial gamble paid off: he has a solid starting position. But so have half a dozen others, including Umbrel Narven. She's one of two female Pilots, vanguard of the kind of changes the Earl hates; she has a reputation for recklessness and her clan has some of the best techs, inherited from now-defunct clans. With two close seconds and a third but no win to her name, Narven's the one to watch.

A couple of competitors are already lagging behind, possibly because their yachts aren't as well tuned as his, or possibly because their starts didn't give them the trajectory they wanted for their chosen path through the ion-streams. Everyone else is still a threat.

Thirty minutes in and the field is spreading out. Now the tactics start to show, as each Pilot plots the precise course they'll be taking through the near-invisible energy maze formed by the ion-streams. Kheo has assimilated all available data on the current disposition of the streams but now, close up, he can get more detailed readings and make final adjustments. It looks good: the provisional trajectory he agreed with his team won't need significant adjustment.

The projection of the streams overlays the view ahead, a shifting, sparkling curtain coloured every shade of the rainbow. The colours are a code imposed by his comp. He is heading for the golden-orange area, nearer Yssim than Estin. Running close to the gas giant has inherent risks, being liable to fluxes and gravitational effects that could affect his instruments and put stress on his yacht, but he has the skill to navigate it and *Liberty Bird* is up to the task. And the crowd will love it.

But he is not the only one risking a close skim. By the time they are fifty minutes into the race, his sensors show two other yachts lining up for similar courses. One of them is close enough that he thinks he can actually see the tiny black speck against the looming ion fields. His instruments ID it as the *Aurora Dream*. Clan Narven; he might have known.

The sense of emptiness lingered. He woke with a ridiculous urge to cry, but saw it off with a cold shower, along with all the other unwanted desires and unsafe emotions.

He was nervous at the prospect of going to the workshop but, in the end, what else would he do the day before the race? His heart tripped when he saw Mechanic Sovat, and he looked away.

After the daily briefing he lingered, and was unsurprised when the Chief Mechanic did the same. Kheo searched for the right thing to say. Finally, as Sovat raised an eyebrow and turned to go, Kheo managed, 'Do you really think Clan Narven's directional thrust innovations pose a threat to us?'

If the mechanic had any idea that this wasn't what Kheo wanted to say he gave no sign. "They might well, sirrah. You'd best take the lead from the start; they have the advantage in hi-gee manoeuvring. Make Narven's yacht work hard to catch you, and stick the course. Just like I said."

Which he had, in the meeting, only a few minutes earlier. "Right. Yes." Kheo looked at the man's hands, because they were safe. Except they weren't. They were fascinating.

"You're a good pilot, sirrah."

Kheo tried not to be over-pleased by the praise. Before he could stop himself he looked up and said, "I believe you worked late two days ago."

Rather than answer immediately Sovat bent forward a little, leaning on his fists; those perfect, sinewy hands. Kheo got a heady whiff of oil and sweat. "What makes you think that?" said Sovat quietly, then added, "sirrah."

"Never mind my reasons, Mechanic," Kheo was glad of the table, which was high enough to hide his body's response to the encounter. "Were you in the hangar the night before last?"

"I was." Sovat's gaze never wavered.

Kheo found his own eyes drawn, once again, to those hands. "And were you alone?"

"No, sirrah. I had Apprentice Greal with me."

Kheo must have imagined the small hesitation between 'Greal' and 'with'. "And did anything happen?"

"Happen, sirrah?" Kheo would swear the man was *enjoying* this. "What sort of thing were you thinking of, sirrah?"

"I… I could check the camera feeds, you know."

"So you could, sirrah." The mechanic smiled laconically. "But I doubt you'd find anything to alarm you."

Because Sovat had edited them. The Mechanic was careful, thorough: he must have lived with what he was for years. Kheo wanted to hate such forward planning, such contrivance, but found himself admiring it. This man could not only face the truth, but live with it. "If," he managed, "I did see anything some people might find alarming…" he swallowed, half expecting an interruption, but the other man remained silent, "I'm not sure I'd be alarmed, myself," he finished in a rush. His face felt like it had caught fire.

Sovat's voice was soft. "Perhaps you wouldn't, at that," he said.

"And if, if I was not alarmed when, when most people would be. Normally, that is. Would that be … something of interest? To you."

Sovat remained silent.

Kheo swallowed. "I was asking you a question."

"Were you now, sirrah?" Was that caution or knowing acceptance in Sovat's voice?

Acceptance, Kheo decided. They understood each other. No damning words, no absolute confirmation, but there was that connection, that shared experience. Except Kheo's experiences had been confined to fantasy, until now. "What if I had been here, with you, instead of Apprentice Greal? Would something have happened? Something the cameras wouldn't see, and that no one," he felt his breath growing short, "no one ever needed to know about."

Sovat paused before answering, then said, his voice regretful, "No."

"No? Why not?"

"A matter of taste, sirrah. Personal taste."

"What are you saying? I'm not your *type*? But you're… and I'm…" *And no one else is. Except Greal, apparently.* "I could report you, you know.

What about that, eh?"

"You're free to do as you will, sirrah." Sovat sounded calm; Kheo had no idea if he was concerned about the threat. "Your word carries far more weight than mine."

But with doctored cameras, it would just be his word. And he could never betray the only man he had ever spoken to in this way. Not even if that man rejected him. "Well, just… remember that."

"I always do, sirrah. Was there anything else?"

"No. Nothing else."

After Sovat left Kheo sat alone in the briefing room. Then he locked himself in the nearest restroom alone, and privately explored the possibility that Sovat would walk in, and find Kheo was his type after all. Then he showered, thoroughly.

Having been both vindicated and rejected in one short conversation, he returned to the family suite, heading straight for his rooms. Here he checked the publically available information on Mechanic Sovat. The man's first name was Appis, and Kheo spent a few moments saying the name, *Appis Sovat*, before chiding himself and looking deeper.

There was nothing incriminating to be found. Had there been the technician would not be in the position he was in today. Kheo uncovered only one item of note, from before the War: when Sovat was twenty-six two of his male friends had been charged with gross indecency. One had opted for surgical readjustment; the other had not relented of his perversion and had been exiled 'at the Empress's service'. Further research revealed that the man had died two years later, at a mine in the bleak high plains of South Arnisland. The verdict was death by natural causes. It generally was, in the mines.

Kheo hisses in triumph as one of the two yachts peels away, slowing as it does. *Too rich for you, eh?* He has taken the shorter, riskier path twice before. The first time, he won. The second time overdriving the engines damaged his yacht, and ended his race. Who would have thought two other pilots were also willing to take the skim? Or rather, one now. Umbrel Narven is still in the race. And her yacht is going to enter the streams ahead of him. He'll be hard pressed to catch her.

No, that's defeatist talk: he is still the best Pilot, in the best ship.

Umbrel Narven no doubt thinks the same about her own skills and vessel.

"Ah, there you are!"

Kheo looked up from his desk and forced a smile for his mother. "I thought I'd get an early night…" He waved the display clear.

"Very sensible. But first, I have news."

Kheo knew that tone. "You'd better come in."

She swept into his room and perched on the more upright of the two chaises. "I didn't want to distract you until we were sure, not with the race coming up –"

"It's tomorrow, Ma, and I don't want to be distracted, you're so right." Kheo ignored his mother's wince at being spoken back to.

"Ah, but this will give you something to race for."

"Have you… finalised arrangements? You have, haven't you?" Making the right match was as much the duty of an oldest son as racing in the Flamestar Challenge. More, really: the Empress had dictated that Clan scions must prove themselves before marrying, but she was gone. Given the dangers of yacht-racing, many Clans, already depleted by the War, forbad their heirs from taking part. And whether or not the race endured, it was no activity for a family man, as his mother had reminded him on his last birthday.

"I have!"

"With Leilian Fermelai?"

"Well, you two used to play together so well when you were children. And the poor thing lost both her parents in all the nastiness." Meaning: unlike Clan Reuthani, Clan Fermelai had not acted against the Empress. "We'll announce the engagement en route back to Homeworld, and hold the formal party at the Manse."

"This isn't what I want." His voice sounded dead in his ears.

"Kheo, I know this is hard for you. It's hard for all of us. But you have to settle down. Leilian is technically the head of her clan but she's only a woman, and with most of her family gone… this is better for everyone. She will be a good wife."

He wanted to protest further, to say he did not want a wife, good or otherwise, but it would be futile.

More gently his mother added, "This marriage is a necessary thing. I hope you can find happiness in it, Kheo, I truly do. But if you cannot… provided you do your duty, a blind eye can be turned."

Does she know? But he had done nothing to act on his feelings; on the contrary he had made every effort to live up to the image of the yacht-racing noble rake. "What do you mean?" he asked as evenly as he could.

"The unsuitable women," said his mother, in the verbal equivalent of scraping excrement from a shoe.

Ah yes, those women, the entertainers and hostesses; eager to please, and notorious enough that his rumoured liaisons with them maintained his reputation, yet low enough that his failures and foibles would never reach the wrong ears. He had been careful in his choices. He wouldn't miss the embarrassment and guilty revulsion; nor the fear that they saw him for what he really was.

"You won't have to worry about them," he said.

"Good." His mother's smile told him that she, like everyone else, believed the carefully cultivated image. "That's settled then."

The *Aurora Dream* is pulling ahead, Narven's lead opening up second by second.

So, no win. No glory. No final chance to shine before subsiding under the weight of duty and acceptable behaviour. The best he can hope for is second place.

Why can't I just be happy with the privileged life I was born into? He knows the answer: because he can't be himself.

Am I being selfish? Perhaps; there were choices, plenty of them. He could have fought in the War, despite being young. He could admit what he really wants in a lover, although where would he find that in the world he lives in, where such things are never spoken of, even if they are no longer punished with more than a fine? He could stand up to his father, although the old man is quite capable of disinheriting him; an unthinkable prospect.

Plenty of choices there. Shame he has been too much of a coward to take them.

He blinks away stupid self-pitying tears and focuses on *Liberty Bird*'s instrument panel. Here is the one thing that is good and simple and right about his life, directly in front of him. And he is about to come in second, in his final race. It's all downhill from here. Winning isn't just desirable any more: it's the only option, whatever the cost.

There isn't much time: he scans his readouts, their meaning as comforting and familiar as the drapes above his bed, or the face of his childhood nurse. It would be a minor adjustment to his trajectory.

He makes the change.
An alarm sounds.
He ignores it.

Kheo never slept well the night before a race. He doubted any Pilot did. He ended up resorting to the chemical remedies offered by the Clan doctor.

Perhaps that was why, when he was escorted through the halls and corridors of the liner the next morning amid cheers and thrown petals, he felt as though he was watching the festivities from afar, rather than being the reason for them.

Sovat – Appis – was in the hangar, amongst the honour guard of techs who stood respectfully silent while their Pilot crossed the floor to his yacht. Kheo gave him no more regard than was normal, including him in the faint nod of gratitude to his crew as he passed.

Only when he took his seat in *Liberty Bird* did he fully wake up. He performed the usual pre-flight checks with a combination of the utmost care and little conscious thought. By the time the hoist had inched him into the hangar's massive airlock, he was as ready for his fate as he had ever been.

The trajectory alteration is subtle; a matter of a few degrees in one plane. The difference between passing through a volume of space with no appreciable matter in it, and the lower path, where the number of molecules in the vacuum might constitute the start of an atmosphere. Enough of an atmosphere to cause drag and test *Liberty Bird*'s engines, certainly. But the ultimate shortcut – if it works.

He is deep in the ion-streams now, their flickering representations dancing around his yacht. Every other racer is above him; some still appear to be ahead, but they have further to go. It is too early yet to know if his crazy ploy will bring victory.

His com flashes: the support team requesting emergency contact. No mean feat given the ionic interference; they must be juicing up the signal with everything they've got. If he answers, will it be Appis Sovat on the com? He is Chief Tech, after all. The prospect of hearing Sovat's voice again makes Kheo hesitate. Then he catches himself and turns his attention to his console. The drive readout is already edging out of the safe zone, and there's a constellation of amber warnings. Suddenly one of them spikes red: a jolt thrums through his yacht. What was that? Ah, navigational thrusters. Even this is too much atmosphere for them. Well, he's stuck on this course now. As for what happens once he's on the far side, whether they'll blow clear … first make it to the far side, then worry about that.

The ship feels wrong. It's a subtle sensation, a faint vibration, but if he carries on, it's only a matter of time before structural integrity begins to fail.

His life is so complicated. The tension of duty and desire. His inability to be himself. And always he has taken what seemed like the easiest path, only to find complications besetting him. Not now though. Now everything truly is simple. He will either win this race, or die trying.

Another red light: radiation warning. There is only so much energy his suit and canopy can protect him from. The view outside is more spectacular than ever, like a great forest of energy, the psychedelic ion-streams like twisted trunks of impossible trees.

This in itself is the easy way out, of course. Yes, even as he defies death, he's still a coward.

The vibration becomes a shudder. Suddenly Kheo is scared. At least his body is: racing heart, dry mouth, dizzy head.

What am I doing? This insane stunt isn't bravery: it's avoidance, the ultimate avoidance.

The ship begins to shake. The drive readout spikes into the red. He reaches for the console but everything's moving, wild forces pulling at him. And even if he could get his hands on the controls, what could he do? The course is set. Too late to change it now.

I'm a fool. A coward and a fool.

A great concussion hits, throwing him in every direction at once. He is going to die, here, now. Die without facing himself.

Massive constriction – *but I was expecting an explosion!* – and he is wrapped in chilly gel. As the sedatives kick in he realises two things: he has lost the race and he is still alive. When, seconds later, the drugs ease his stressed system into therapeutic unconsciousness, his last thought is that the former doesn't matter, only the latter.

The media love it. Kheo Reuthani's miraculous escape after his death-or-glory bid for victory eclipses Umbrel Narven's win. Kheo feels sorry for her.

The rescue clipper barely arrived in time to stop *Liberty Bird* drifting into the nearest ion-stream, an experience he would not have survived even encased in crash-gel. By the time his yacht was hauled in, he had received enough radiation to increase his risk of long-term health problems – and to destroy any chance of him giving Clan Reuthani an heir.

Mother visits him in hospital. "I've seen your results."

She could be talking about an exam he failed. "I guess the wedding's off then." He tries not to sound triumphant. He feels sorry for Leilian Fermelai too. He does not, for once, feel sorry for himself.

"Not necessarily. There may be a medical work-around to the, ah, fertility issue. Perhaps even some advance from out-of-system."

"Ah, so you'd accept outsider medicine to solve the Clan's problems, then?"

"One must adapt."

A shame, then, that she had not pressed his father to adapt to the proactive approach many Clans had instituted after the Liberation, of taking sperm or egg samples from their Pilots in case of such accidents. "Yes, one must. I'm sorry, Mother. I won't marry that poor girl just to save face. Let Prinbal have his chance. He wants to lead the clan more than I do anyway."

He is treated to the rare spectacle of his mother lost for words.

The general consensus is that he had a lucky escape. If his drive had not cut out when it did, *Liberty Bird* would either have shaken itself to bits, blown up or been crushed by Yssim's atmosphere. Kheo keeps his opinion on the matter to himself.

He is still welcome in the hangar, where work is underway to ensure that *Liberty Bird* will race again. He might even be the one to fly her, when and if his father forgives him for declaring Prinbal the Reuthani heir. Assuming the Flamestar is still going then.

It is only natural that Sovat leads the repair work. And it is only natural that Kheo and he should take the chance to talk about the state of *Liberty Bird.*

Their conversation, held in the meeting room while the techs work outside, begins with an assessment of the damage, and what is being done to fix it. Kheo looks at Appis Sovat's hands twice, and his face once. He realises that the Chief Mechanic loves the yacht as much as he himself does, perhaps more.

"She was lucky, wasn't she?" asks Kheo. "Well, we both were. *Liberty Bird*, and me. Losing power at exactly the right moment to bounce us off Yssim's atmosphere." He hopes his words don't sound too disingenuous.

"So they say."

Kheo seizes his chance. "You don't think it was luck then?"

"It was *fortunate* the engine shut down soon as the rads and outside density reached critical. But not luck, sirrah, no."

"Ah." There had been a move, immediately after the Liberation, to install overrides to stop Pilots overdriving their engines but it had been deemed unnecessary, and insulting to the Pilots. "I… see." Kheo picks his next words carefully. "Having such a *fortunate* shutdown wouldn't be hard to arrange for someone with the right skills."

"I imagine not, sirrah." The tech's tone is careful.

Kheo ploughs on. "But one would have to ask why anyone might arrange for such a thing."

"I've seen it before, sirrah." Sovat is looking at him directly now; he can feel it. "More than once."

"Seen what?" says Kheo slowly. He manages to raise his gaze as high as the tech's chest.

"The boys who can't live with themselves."

"Wait, you think I made the choices I did just because I… because you... You know nothing about me, Technician!" Except the one thing Kheo wished the man didn't know. His embarrassed anger lets Kheo meet Sovat's eyes.

"True enough, sirrah." The tech's voice and gaze are gentle. "And I'm not saying there's just the one cause. But that's part of it: us being what we are. It's not worth dying for, you know."

"It's pretty damn hard to live with."

"Hard for others to live with, yes."

"What do you mean?"

"Just that, sirrah: we're what we are. It's those around us that make it a problem."

"Unless we get caught."

The tech shrugs, though it is a considered gesture. "That's still true, for now. But not every change is for the worst."

"No, it isn't. Listen, I know I'm not, er, your type… but if I did want some advice about, well, safe places, where people like me, like us…?"

"I'd be happy to give it."

"Thank you." Kheo hesitates. "And thank you for knowing what I needed even if I didn't. Had anyone found out what you did–"

"I'm better at my job than that, sirrah."

"Even so, you risked your career for me."

"A career don't matter a s–spit compared to a life, sirrah."

Kheo nods. "Quite so. Good night, Engineer Sovat."

Alone in the briefing room, Kheo exhales. He calls up the plans for his yacht. The thought that he might never pilot *Liberty Bird* again is hard to face, but face it he will. Who knows, perhaps when contact with the rest of the universe strengthens he might fly something more amazing, perhaps even travel between the stars? Now that is a good dream to hold onto.

After a while he shuts down the display and goes to find his mother. There is something he needs to tell her.

Joined

Sarah L. Byrne

When your heart broke, I felt it too. We were walking through the city park when it happened; together but apart, because that was the way we'd become by then, wasn't it? There was an arm's-length distance and a silence as wide as a desert between us, but we were still joined, which meant we were sharing the scent of the lilac blossoms, the cool of the spring air on our skin, sharing the guarded edges of each other's feelings. Then your heart just tore itself apart.

It wasn't exactly your heart, I know – that's poetic license I'd add in later, because you weren't around to do it – but it was close enough. A catastrophic aortic rupture. But because we were joined, I felt the tearing pain rip through your body, and for a moment my breath choked off as the blood drained from your aorta into your chest. But only for a moment. My blood pressure fell only enough that I sank slowly to my knees on the gravel, while yours dropped to nothing as you crumpled to the ground. My heart went on beating while yours gave a last desperate flutter then just stopped.

Voices, footsteps, people rushing to surround you as you lay there on your back in the middle of the path, your skin waxy pale, your eyes open and dilated black. You were already gone. They didn't know it, but I did. I felt it happen.

Now I feel nothing.

It was a strange experience for a while, this feeling nothing. At least, if *nothing* is what you can call it. Feeling only my own feelings, thinking my own thoughts; alone in my own head after so long. The nothing I'd wanted for so long.

Six years back when we got our license, getting joined had seemed like such a romantic idea: for your partner to be truly your other half, to share each other's everyday joys and sorrows, to literally feel each other's pain and pleasure, one brain to the other through a real-time upload and download. So we registered, one of the first couples to do it, along with the marriage license – I, Tracy, do take you, Alana – and received our neural implants, just a painless injection, harmless nanoparticles that targeted the nerve fibres and grew rapidly along them, twined around them like wisteria, no different from the kind they use for paralysis and prosthetics. Then in only a matter of weeks we were fully joined.

Sex was double the fun, of course. That's what everyone wanted to talk about at first. But for some of us it went further. Beyond sharing physical sensations and basic emotions, into thoughts and memories too. Even dreams, because wasn't it all the same thing really? All just neural connections, electrical impulses jumping synaptic gaps and neuropeptides docking with receptors. All of it picked up, encoded and transmitted by the implant.

It would be impossible to hurt each other, when you were joined, that's what people said. They were wrong: it wasn't just possible, it was easy. No, it was more than easy; it was inevitable. In those days we were wound so tight around each other it was hard to believe we were separate people. So you knew when things started changing between us, because I had no secrets from you – but you didn't want to know. You didn't want to know how cloying I'd begun to find your presence, pretending not to notice how my mind flinched away from yours when you reached out to me. And I pretending not to feel your hurt. It was grotesque, wasn't it? But we went on for more than a year like that, alone together, until that day your heart finally broke.

I lied when I said I felt nothing that day. What I felt was relief.

I'm trying to sleep in the attic room under the roof windows, like I usually do these nights. I like it up here under the sky, and since you've been gone, the thought of sleeping alone in the bed we used to share is unthinkable. Tonight, it's one of those clear summer nights when the temperature drops, the stars come out clear and the heat of the day fades into refreshing coolness. I'll get to sleep eventually, even with it playing over and over in my mind like it does most nights: you falling away from me, falling out of me; the life fading out of your eyes, the blood draining out of your heart.

We were told that a weakening of the arteries was a rare risk of the implants. Your blood pressure must have been too high. You knew you were supposed to quit smoking after we were joined, but you never could. You tried – for me, mostly, because I didn't like the taste – but somehow you never quite could give it up. I still felt the desperation of your cravings too as they clawed at you over the hours and the days: so I gave in. We called it a compromise.

Now, I block out the thought of the pack of cigarettes in the drawer downstairs. Sleep comes.

It's a feeling that wakes me. *Cold.* I turn over in bed, tugging the sheet up around my bare shoulder. Did I leave a window open? No. I did not. But there's a coldness creeping over my skin still. It's distant and alien, still entirely familiar.

"Alana?"

"I'm cold," you say. Or don't say, but you *think* it and my brain responds to your thought. Your feelings flood my senses, the old intensity of them, and for a moment it's like it always was.

But it's not.

"You're not real," I say into the empty darkness.

There's a hesitation, then your thought comes at me heavy with accusation, hits me hard. There'd be that little catch in your voice now if you still had one; there'd be hurt in your blue eyes if they weren't burned to ashes and scattered on the cold earth. And I'd look away.

"How can you say that?" you demand. "Don't you understand what's happening? I've come back to you. Tracy, don't you want us to be together again?"

I do, of course I do, that part of me that's lost its other half. The part of me that wants to believe death isn't a black oblivion waiting for all of us someday, maybe sooner than we think. The part that grieves for all those years back then when we were happy, for laughter and dancing, sex and snuggling under a blanket together, or staying up half the night sharing thoughts and feelings because it was like a well of cool water, yet however deep we drank we couldn't get enough of each other. There's an ache inside me, how badly I want that again.

But it wasn't like that towards the end. It was over. I know it and you know it too. Or you would if you were really here, if there was any *you* anymore.

You've gone quiet now. I don't feel anything from you. I curl up on my side and try to sleep again. But no matter what I do now, I just can't get warm.

Everything seems better in the morning, doesn't it always? I call the customer helpline to report the bug. My dead wife is in my head, I explain. She's talking to me. Something's gone wrong, some data cached in the system that should have been deleted; outdated settings somewhere in the cloud.

"Mmm-hmm," the bored sounding assistant on the other end of the line says, like it's some everyday thing. "We'll look into it for you."

Maybe this happens a lot. Maybe he doesn't believe a word of it. Most likely he's just sticking to his script and doesn't care particularly either way. Why should he, after all?

You come again that night.

"I'm cold," you say. "I want to come back. I want us to be together again."

"That's not possible."

"Maybe it is. We've got to try, haven't we? We've been given a second chance, surely it's happening for a reason?"

"I was going to leave you," I say. "It wasn't working out. We were going to separate, you knew that. We both knew."

"No," you say. A flood of images and feelings surge through me before I can stop you – happy times, good times, rose-tinted smiles – and I shove them back at you.

"Yes." You never could face a truth you didn't like, could you? "Alana, listen, I didn't want it to happen like this. I wanted you to be happy. I hoped you'd meet someone else, forget about me–"

"That would never have happened." You cut me off with a pulse of thought so sharp it hurts. "I'm not like you. I can't just switch off my feelings."

And apparently I *can't switch off your feelings either.*

I turn over, bury my face in the pillow. If you were here, for real, I'd feel your touch now. Your fingers sliding down my shoulders, the warmth of your body against mine, the scent of your hair. I'd feel what you feel and know you felt it right back; I'd hate myself for it but I'd turn over and pull you down to me. But you're not here. I don't know why I'm even having this conversation.

It's a while before you speak again: "Just do one thing for me".

"What?"

"I need a smoke. Just one. I'm desperate."

I let my breath out slowly against the pillow. We both know you've got me.

"All right."

I get out of bed, make my way downstairs and outside. I light the cigarette in the garden, awkward and clumsy despite the familiar feel of it against my fingers and lips, but when I inhale the sudden burn of the hot smoke in my lungs makes me cough it out sharply.

"Slowly," you tell me, your mind taut with impatience, with need. I breathe the smoke in steadily, holding it inside me this time, and feel the familiar nicotine-adrenaline rush through my veins, the familiar relief that's yours, not mine.

"Don't you miss this too?" you ask.

"No," I lie, letting the smoke out slowly. I take another drag.

If you could still smile, you would. You can't, but when you do, I feel it all the same.

It was a mistake, letting you have that one smoke. But then it was always a mistake to let you have your way, giving in to one of your 'compromises'. You had a way of sensing weakness, and you'd push for more, always more, never satisfied with what I could give you.

You come to me in the daytime now, as well as at night. You're there when I wake up, craving your morning coffee; you know I hate coffee, but somehow the smell of it drifts through my kitchen every morning these days. When I'm dressing, you're there with suggestions of perfume, how you miss it. Silk camisoles like you used to wear under your shirts, the smoothness against your skin. Darling, why don't you try your hair like this?

And now here I am, huddled under a flimsy shelter outside the entrance to the hospital where I'm supposed to be at work. My coat collar turned up against the wind, hands cupped around the dwindling end of a cigarette to protect it from the driving rain.

"Hey, Tracy. I didn't know you smoked."

I look up, startled, one of my co-workers standing there. I don't recognise him for a moment.

"I don't," I manage to say eventually.

He quirks an eyebrow before walking on, and I drop what's left of the cigarette, without looking down to see it fizzle out on the wet tarmac. I turn and head into the building.

I know what you want, Alana. To use my body, for us to share it. We're half-way there already.

But I'm saying no to you this time. Brushing the drops of water out of my hair and pulling off my wet jacket, I walk to my lab with more purpose than I have had in the months since this all started, because now I know what I have to do.

I shrug into my lab coat, glance at the samples waiting on my bench. I've always done my job in a detached way. It's just samples to analyse; blood in a vial, cells on a plate. I've made a point of not really thinking about where they come from. But that doesn't change the facts. There are dead people in the basement.

You want a body, Alana? I'll find you one. One all of your own. I'll inject you into it, you can worm your way through its veins, animate its dead nerves.

Just stay out of mine.

It's cold down here. I feel the chill as soon as I step out of the elevator, into this underground place where the dead people are.

"Help you?" The uninterested desk clerk glances up. I don't know her, she doesn't know me, but a glimpse of my lab coat and badge is enough that she's not going to ask difficult questions.

"Some samples didn't make it upstairs this morning, I need to talk to Mark," I lie.

It isn't difficult. If I can lie to my telepathic dead wife in my head – if I can lie so well to myself – it was never going to be hard to lie a stranger.

"He's inside." she says.

"Thanks."

I slide past the closed door of Mark's examination room, where he's conducting an autopsy, murmuring reports into his recording device. Down to the end of the corridor and into the storage room at the back. I pull on nitrile gloves, tug open one of the drawers, stare at the dead man, the stranger lying there. The cold body that doesn't look like anything that was ever alive, or ever will be again.

This is not going to be any use, I realise. I don't know what I was thinking, how I thought this was going to work, what I'm doing here. It never even made any sense. I push the drawer closed, start to turn away. But then I'm pulling open another drawer, and then another.

It's not me doing it. You're in my head. Suddenly, down here in the chill of this windowless cavern, you're here, guiding me, moving my hands for me. Drawing me to you.

Because when I open the third drawer, I stop, heart thudding against my ribs so hard it stops my breath.

Alana.

It's you. Just like you looked lying on the gravel under the lilacs that day.

You can't be here. I said my goodbyes to you. I organised the memorial service, stood there tearless with your parents weeping and casting me haunted looks – the one who broke their daughter's heart, who sent tendrils creeping through her veins to tie her forever to me and beguiled her to her death—if only they knew how it really was. I received your ashes in a wooden urn, startlingly heavy, to scatter in the park where we walked that day under the lilacs. Joined corpses have to be cremated for fear of contamination, irrational dread of the nanothings creeping free and making their way through the earth to wreak some unknown havoc. It couldn't happen, of course, they die when we do. Except when they don't.

You touch me, your fingertip down the back of my neck.

I tear off my gloves, turn and run into the corridor, and straight into Mark. He grabs me to steady me.

"Hey, Tracy, you all right?"

I jerk away from his touch, because it feels so wrong, so alien, to have anyone touch me but you. I find my breath, my voice, and it comes out harsh and angry.

"What's Alana doing here? She's not supposed to be here."

"What?"

He's staring at me like I've gone crazy, and I can't blame him, the way I must look.

I shoulder past him and don't look back, just keep walking until I'm outside. I breathe in the air, the summer storm clearing now to leave a clean-washed blue sky and the sun breaking through the last rain drops.

I wonder if I might really be going crazy. Because the implant can do that to a person; as well as breaking your heart, it can send your mind spooling loose into free fall. There've been documented cases, and I feel myself falling now, endlessly falling, and I'd grab at anything in desperation. I wonder if that's how you feel, drifting formless in the void.

I can't blame you for grabbing onto me like you did. Can't blame you at all.

I want you, suddenly, Alana. Want to hold you close and not let go, because I'm falling. Nothing makes sense anymore and I'm just falling.

It was a mistake, it turns out. An administrative error, they say. Your body was mixed up with another woman's: someone else's daughter, someone else's wife. A body that was supposed to be donated to science, but instead ended up burnt to ashes, scattered under the lilacs and denied my tears. These things happen, they say.

And that left you still there, cold and waiting in that drawer. Your implant still functioning – perhaps – still reaching out from that dark place, still calling out to me. Although that shouldn't really be possible. Maybe it isn't. Maybe it was only ever *my* circuitry reaching out, trailing through the empty space inside me, twisting back on itself?

Either way, it all gets sorted out in time, as such things always do. Compensation paid and apologies made, paperwork redone. The body – your body – cremated for real this time.

Life goes on.

I don't have another memorial service. I don't scatter ashes, because I did that already. The time for that is past, drifted away with the spring blossoms, the fading, falling lilac petals. Instead, your urn sits on my bookshelf, silent.

You don't talk to me so much these days. But I like having you there. It's comforting, in a way. Funny that, I like you better dead than I did alive. Funny how things work out sometimes. I head outside, cigarette pack and lighter in hand. I never could quite kick the habit. Don't think I ever will. And honestly, I'm not sure I want to. I've gotten a taste for it lately. It might break my heart someday, but then I already know how that feels.

Out in the garden, the leaves swirl autumn brown around my feet, the year turning. I breathe in, inhaling the smoke deep along with the cool air.

Your smile touches the corners of my mouth, and I know you're here. You'll always be here.

And I'm fine with that. We're joined.

It would break my heart to lose you.

Heinrich Himmler in the Barcelona Hallucination Cell

Ian Watson

The torment cell disorients Reichsführer Heinrich Himmler, therefore he perches himself on the tilted black bench next to General Sagardía.

Sagardía has been with Himmler since the Reichsführer arrived in Spain four days earlier to prepare the way for Hitler's meeting with Generalísimo Franco – which went badly today, according to a phone call. Sagardía was in the Spanish delegation to Germany the previous month. At the start of the civil war he was hauled from his cosy 'retirement' in France; 'My country needs me.' A murderous mediocrity.

The bench tilts at an angle of 20 degrees so that a prisoner can't sleep without rolling off. Nor can the prisoner sleep upon the concrete floor, since bricks jut up harshly at random. Exhausting!

Nor, due to the awkward bricks, can a person pace the cell. Himmler has managed to plant his black boots flatly between two bricks to steady himself – his coordination isn't as good as it might be.

What a Jew of a day this has turned out to be. The journey to Montserrat monastery to take possession of the Holy Grail, a total failure. His briefcase stolen from the Ritz Hotel. The Führer, infuriated by Franco's pigheadedness.

The damnable news that the briefcase went missing came towards the end of the reception given by Dr Jaeger, the German Consul General, in his residence. Which was prior to the scheduled dinner at the Rathaus – called the *Casa Major* or something, Barcelona's town hall in Plaza some saint or other. That theft certainly put die Katze im

Taubenschlag, the cat in the pigeon loft, as regards the stupid pigeonhead Spanish police! For sure the reception was soured.

Painted on one wall of the cell is an eye-dazing chequerboard. Spots little and large orbit around, red, white, black.

That chequerboard draws your gaze to it nauseatingly. Like a Kandinsky in the degenerate art exhibition Goebbels commissioned in '37, all those unGerman works displaying mental disease...

Over dinner in the Rathaus, the Mayor of Barcelona described these cells of degenerate art so as to distract attention from a succession of police officers reporting to munching General Orgaz about how the Ritz and the whole city were now being shaken vigorously, in vain, in pursuit of the missing briefcase. So here's the jowly, fat-faced Captain General of Catalonia within the crowded cell, suffering consequences.

What's the Mayor of Barcelona's wretched name again? Miguel... *Mateu*. So he's here too, in the cell. Even though these Spaniards dined so late, Himmler promptly insisted on a visit to the cells. Partly this was to punish his hosts, but also out of fascination –it's important to research new information encountered in life, personally if possible, meticulously and exhaustively. Maybe the Gestapo can learn a new trick.

The German Consul, Dr Jaeger, is here too in the cell for his sins. Only after the theft was reported did the Consul confess to Himmler that the staff of the Ritz notoriously 'used to be' infiltrated with spies – waiters trying to eavesdrop on important discussions, snooping chambermaids.

Mind you, prior to Himmler's trip Canaris idly mentioned one supposed piece of Ritz history: when the exiled Jew Bolshevik Trotsky was icepicked in Mexico a couple of months earlier by a Soviet agent, that selfsame Catalan Communist who murdered Trotsky worked in the Barcelona Ritz hotel at the outbreak of the Spanish Civil War.

If Canaris was to be trusted! Too fluent in English by half, and in Spanish too, is Canaris. Him with his own rival military intelligence service.

It couldn't be, could it, that Canaris has anything to do with the ingrate Franco refusing to join forces with Germany and allow the Reich a corridor through Spain to capture Gibraltar? Unthinkable!

Admiral Canaris, if anybody, knows the strategic importance of the British Rock...

"Those cells use psychotechniques," the Mayor had said in English, with an American accent, at the dinner table, Gruppenführer Karl Wolff translating for Himmler's benefit.

A string quintet was playing during dinner in the 'Chronicles Room' of that Spanish Rathaus. The Prelude to *Lohengrin*, the *Siegfried Idyll*, a flute doing duty for the tiny trumpet part...

The floor of the 'Chronicles Room' was of black marble. Its walls and ceiling were murals of obscure historical happenings, painted upon expanses of gold and silver leaf.

"Art to punish and disorient prisoners," continued the Mayor. "This was how the Reds dealt with opposition while they were still in control here – though we aren't sure if Companys knew about this personally."

Companys, the President of Catalonia during the red republic, was shot by firing squad in Barcelona's castle just four days before Himmler arrived in Spain, maybe as a way of saying 'Thank You' to the Gestapo for catching that pest in Paris and handing him back.

By all means mention Companys! Another example of the generosity and support of Germany for the pipsqueak Generalísimo!

Himmler's meticulous work in Madrid, buttering up Franco, was as much in vain as the hunt for the Holy Grail – or for the Ark of the Covenant in Toledo.

Come to think of it, Canaris had pointed Himmler towards Toledo as regards the Ark... The Toledo tip-off was thanks to interrogations of a rabbi in Auschwitz, an initiate in Kabbalah, Canaris had assured Himmler, so this might be credible. Except that it wasn't.

"Psychotechniques –" repeated the Mayor, while Himmler toyed with his vegetables.

General Orgiz had before him a plate of thick bloody Rossini steak, foie piled on top. Slaughtering birds and beasts for food is a crime against the natural world, although at times one has to go hunting with a rifle, smilingly on account of one's companions.

"– devised by a Republican torturer so-called artist named Alfonso Laurencic, and carried out by his depraved artisan Garrigós. We executed Laurencic over a year ago. Laurencic also designed special tight 'wardrobes' which constantly stress a prisoner – quarter of an hour in one of those could break a man... Just another of the atrocities of the red scum. Laurencic had a red beard," added Mateu.

"You still use his cells?" enquired Himmler.

The Mayor shrugged. "We restored civilisation."

"Permanent vigilance, and *repression when necessary*, is the ticket," said General Sagardía. "I'm sure you understand, Reichsführer."

Did 'permanent vigilance' include keeping an eye on the briefcase of the head of the Gestapo and of SS? These Spaniards! Noisy, hot-blooded, over-excitable lot. Their wine and their women and their cruel primitive bull fighting – one bullfight in Madrid was enough to last Himmler a lifetime. When Himmler presented the toreadors, toreros, whatever the word, with good German medals, one of the bull-killers said, "Medals are all very well for the Virgin, but what about the ears and tail?" Barbaric.

As for their pathetic agriculture, how can it be so bad when so much rain seems to fall? The agronomist in Himmler is appalled at the neglect.

Doubtless the thief broke into that suite at the Ritz after traversing several wrought-iron balconies by way of the linking ledges, making a mockery of the armed police stationed or snoozing in the corridor. Lurking crouched down on the same balcony from which earlier Himmler had saluted the multitude; awaiting any opportunity. The thief risked being spotted but it was night and no one was paying attention.

What roars of admiration had come from the crowd after lunch when Himmler saluted – which was gratifying; yet to be obliged to put on a show for these bull-killers...

Wolff apologised deeply that the SS guard within the suite absented himself briefly; once back in Germany, the man would be sent to an extermination kommando in Russia to redeem himself.

General Orgaz was blaming the British Secret Service for the theft of the briefcase, presumably on the grounds that the Spanish themselves couldn't be blamed if *British* spies were involved, cream of the cream. Alternatively, the French Resistance was to blame. Yet why not another *Red* spy, someone like Trotsky's killer who cut his teeth right here? Hadn't Franco's cronies cleaned all the stables of red scum completely yet?

The briefcase held documents about the agreements Himmler had negotiated in Madrid between the Spanish secret police and the

Gestapo; also a report about the German community in Catalonia, courtesy of Dr Jaeger – and, on top of those, priceless ancient plans of the monastery at Montserrat, its secret catacombs and tunnels where the Grail might be kept hidden. That seat of learning published its first book at the end of the 15th century, yet it possessed in its library *no copy* of Wolfram von Eschenbach's Parzifal – or so claimed the junior monk spokesman, Andreu or somebody, because the abbot himself refused to meet with Himmler.

One young monk: the *only* German speaker in the whole learnèd monastery – was that credible? The occult plans of tunnels proved useless.

No copy of the great *Parzifal* poem was literally incredible when Wagner's *Parsifal* received its first authorised performance beyond Bayreuth in Barcelona *precisely due* to proximity to Montserrat – which should be the Montsalvat of the opera, home of the Grail. Himmler had been driven past the Lyceum opera house or whatever it was called on his way to the Ritz through swastika-hung streets. After the time-wasting charming folk dances and displays of gymnastics by young people.

"Exhaustion, plus hallucinatory art to derange the prisoner," said Mateu.

"I wish to see those cells," Himmler declared.

Orgaz wiped his lips with his linen napkin. "We'll take you there tomorrow morning. Mañana. The Vallmájor checa, I think."

"*Cheka* – are you referring to Lenin's political police?" Vicious, sadistic murderers...

"Alfonso Laurencic designed the system of local lock-ups for interrogation and punishment based on the Russian Checa model."

"I want to see those cells *now*. Because I shall fly back to Berlin as soon as possible tomorrow morning."

Orgaz was astonished. "*Right now*? But I believe the dessert will be raspberry and peach Melba... created by Escoffier himself, the Emperor of Chefs as your very own Kaiser said. The inspirer of the Ritz hotels!"

Himmler smiled very thinly.

"The Melba might be exceptional."

Likewise, the security at the Ritz...

"Even," added Orgaz, "legendary." Was the Captain General snidely implying something about Himmler's quest earlier today? If so, how infuriating. Due to the curse of doctrinaire fanatical Catholicism, these people had no idea of deep occult truths. As a reincarnation of the first pan-Germanic king, Heinrich the Fowler, Himmler knew much better.

"Scoff your dessert, then. I insist we leave within thirty minutes." Presumably Wolff translated a less insulting word than 'scoff', *hinunterschlingen.*

"At least take a coffee first, Reichsführer. Best Brazilian beans, by way of Lisbon, so I hear."

The Spanish might well misinterpret Himmler's thin smile as cordiality. He learned long ago not to give obvious vent to anger; better to store up such feelings for subsequent vengeance. Yet, above all, he must not be taken for a fool.

Resigning himself to some delay, he insisted, "As allies, we will *all* go together to see the hallucination cells."

Allies! As regards Gestapo liaison with Franco's police, yes. This cost the Spanish nothing to agree to, and benefited them. Among the thousands of Germans living in Spain, refugee enemies of the Reich lurked amongst the businessmen, a potential fifth column of foreigners. As to joining with Germany in the war, Himmler could still hear Franco's squeaky voice whining at his Pardo Palace outside Madrid about bad harvests, bad transport for German food aid, Spain's greed for more of north Africa. Here in Barcelona, Himmler had handed over thousands of Reichsmarks in aid to flood victims. Good old Uncle Deutschland, much obliged. Spain, willing to do what in return?

The chequerboard, like a vertical maze for mice, the coloured circles, the wavy lines disorient Himmler. The light is too bright; the lines swim; the black and white squares pulse in and out. This has been a long day. He begins to hallucinate or slip into semi-dreams.

"Welcome to Adventures in Art History! Your selection is Twentieth Century Nazi Era –"

A different woman's voice interrupts distantly. *"Henry? Henry from Harvard, you've become lost. You're submerged. Seek-Engine Vasari's expanding its reach, sucking in petaflops of historical detail. It's spinning out of control, attaching more and more strands to its web."*

A voice in his head, coming and going. How can he understand a voice speaking English? Yet he seems to... Is this occult knowledge? Some of what the woman says is nonsense: seek-engine, petaflop...

"You should never have come to Himmler as a Viewpoint. To Göring, yes – he looted art. Or Goebbels – he was involved in the Degenerate Art exhibition. Or Rosenberg. Or the idiotic von Ribbentrop who liked French painters such as Utrillo even if Utrillo was degenerate. You should be in the Jeu de Paume in Paris, where looted art was assessed. Or at the Degenerate show in Berlin. Better still, you should never have impersoned as a Nazi bigwig."

Much eludes him. It's like overhearing someone talking a hundred metres away.

I don't understand. Are you the power I seek for the Reich?

Power. *Macht.* The Reich already has the Holy Spear safe in Nuremburg. The Ark of the Covenant remains elusive – a wooden chest once clad in gold, probably unclad these days. Himmler was in Toledo a couple of days ago, and his aides found nothing. He was at Montserrat today, only to be frustrated.

Yet now a voice speaks to him in his head.

"Power," the woman says more clearly. *"Drawing so much power. The seek-engine may have gone A.I. It's autonomous, learning."* None of this makes any sense. *"Learning the wrong things. Learning to be evil. Himmler and his cronies were nutty as fruitcakes. We're afraid this isn't exactly a sim any more. It's so detailed that it's coalescing with past reality. Identity of indiscernibles, Leibnitz. You know about this, Henry. No, scrub that – David says the sim's coalescing with an actual alternative reality within Many Worlds, not very 'alternative' at all, leastways at this time period, 1940, almost identical. David's in my ear. He's saying our assumption that time retains the same pace, same rate of progress from past to future, in Many Worlds is wrong. Henry, you gotta do something dramatically out of kilter to break the, well, congruence – I nearly said enchantment. The seek-engine is eating up our processing power. Wait, David's saying No Don't Not Yet. This is a kind of time travel, he says. Fuck that, David, this is too dangerous. Henry, does your Himmler have a pistol? Walther 25 calibre, say, specially sewn pocket in his trousers, just like his beloved Führer?"*

Himmler's fingertips grope. Pistol, yes.

The power of degenerate art to corrupt a visionary German... A wave of nausea sweeps through him, but he doesn't vomit his vegetables. Time seems to have stopped. The clock inset in the wall isn't moving its hands. Clever idea, that clock – it gains four hours in every twenty-four, to disorient a prisoner further. Now the clock seems stuck.

"The cell is a psychotrap. The way it was designed, the way it was painted. Henry, you're experiencing psychotic dissolution. Cause Heinrich to pull his pistol and shoot the others in the cell. Fegg off, David – you said the sim's resonating with an alternative reality, not with our own reality in the past. We'll break the link, disrupt the sim, collapse it like cards, resetting the seek-engine. What does it matter if the alt-reality diverges? That's the disruption we need. And we'll rescue Henry, too."

The black and white squares throb. The lines on the wall oscillate. Red and yellow discs dance. Himmler's fingers wriggle. Suffocating, in the cell. Heavily-dressed bodies crowding it. Body odours and cologne.

"You listen to me, David, damn it! Is there any chance that the sim's resonating with our own *reality in the past? What would the consequences be of Himmler apparently losing his marbles and shooting people in that cell? If he shoots Consul-General Jaeger, witnessed by the Spanish, what difference may* that *make? Jaeger may be replaced as a minor player and the world bumps along... But if SS Wolff stops a bullet? For Chrissake, Wolff is Himmler's Chief of Staff. He's third in command of the SS, a rival to Heydrich. He's Himmler's peephole upon Hitler. He ends up as military commander in Italy, so it's him who negotiates the surrender with Dulles. Yet he stays a mystery man, even after he starts appearing on post-war TV, authenticating the Hitler Diaries, whatever. Who replaces such an* enigma*?*

"Shoot the Spanish? Because they have no major roles to play? Himmler is unhappy with his visit to Spain, so he shoots two of Franco's top henchmen? Do you think he'll get away with this, escape back to Berlin? Off to a sanatorium for a few weeks to keep his head down?

"Oh yes, David, we thought it would be so safe and ring fenced and marginal if we focused first upon art history. Yet what if art is one of the primary forces in the world? A definer of reality."

Power. *Control!* He must control. In this psychotic cell he is controlled *unacceptably*. Why should he even try to please any of his Spanish hosts, when the reason for pleasing them vanished with the failure of the Führer's meeting with Franco? He has pleased too many people in the past! Oh to be back home in Germany. Why should this odious Spanish experience be happening to him?

"Himmler shooting his own Chief of Staff might have the big impact we need?"

He has to release himself, break the frozen ice of the moment. How better than with a bullet? Or several?

"We truly daren't wait much longer, David. Truly so?"

To shoot or not to shoot? Blood, even brains, might spatter his uniform, his face, his glasses. If only the Führer were here to command him, *Shoot, my faithful Heini!* Then to reward him for doing the right thing, with *Well done, my faithful Heini.* No, that's his wife's voice, a woman's voice.

Only once in two thousand years is an Adolf Hitler born! A more-than-man who can command instantly, choosing the true path instinctively. Heini is not himself a Führer. Head of the SS, oh yes. Head of the Gestapo, indeed. But not the more-than-human Godhead of Germany, not a Hitler.

He wavers. The psychocell fluctuates, as though underwater. Have his glasses steamed over? The claustrophobia. The stifling.

"Leave it up to Himmler who he shoots? Because he isn't a puppet but a person? What's with this humanising of Himmler? You of all people, David! Can't you take the responsibility of deciding? And then we won't be interfering quite so much? Is that it?

"Really, we have less than a minute? Before this flux loses fluidity? Before we lose our power to act?

"So there's no authority higher than me. Under protest, then...

"Henry –! Heini –! How many people have you caused to be killed? How many more do you want killed to cleanse the Reich? You can kill a couple personally! Go ahead, this isn't so hard, Reichsführer. Then you'll be free."

The others in the cell don't move as Himmler slides the pistol from the pocket inside of his pocket. Yes, first shoot General Sagardía to one side of him – next, General Orgaz. Damn them for bringing him to this tormenting place which he insisted on being brought to.

Pull pistol, point sideways where the heart should be, squeeze trigger.

As Sagardía sags, blood spilling suddenly from his mouth and nose, the yellow lines on the wall whiplash the coloured discs and black and white squares and the dazzle of the lightbulb into a frenzied dance, spiralling inward –

"Henry? Henry?"

Sara-17-Vee-Chang eases the induction helmet from Henry-54-Kay-Patel's head, its feelers pulling loose with slight reluctance. Henry's jumpsuit-clad limbs jerk; tethers keep him where is on the couch. Very soon the spasms abate and his eyes blink open.

"Sara." Recognition. "I'm back. Quite a ride." Still ordinary, his speech.

She loosens tethers.

The viewtank, which previously showed Henry's viewpoint as if through wobbly green jelly, is now a globe of bubbly grey frogspawn, lots of tiny eyeballs with black pupils; it's in a resting state, shifting slowly around.

The spherechamber's curving wall is slim-corded with cabling. Sara-17-Vee-Chang's silver skull-ports wear data-jewels; Henry-54-Kay-Patel's ports of course await replenishing, whereupon he'll become superconscious.

No one from the Nazi Reich, except perhaps degenerate artists, could begin to guess who these slim, bald, brown-skinned beings with silver skull-ports might be, or where, or when. In fact they're in Rome, lapped by sea from the south-west. Ah, here comes David-88-Aitch-BarKohan in person.

Transhumanity has transpired rather than Overmen.

For Lluis Salvador, good guy and good guide

Taking Flight

Una McCormack

By the end of the year I was struggling to amuse myself. The capital and all the major conurbation worlds were busy with the forthcoming election, and, feeling no particular stake in the proceedings, I found myself starting to become untethered once again. I remembered that once upon a time such events had been of vital importance to me – back in my youth at college, in that green and golden time when it seemed to all of us there that everything we did had significance and that our small acts could change the worlds. Such flights of fancy! I had not indulged myself that way for years.

For others, I knew the reverse to be true. That early training had stuck: the unshaken belief that they were to be masters of the known universe. And that was what many of them believed themselves now to be – the most able, the most gifted, the best. Like children, unable to imagine these worlds without them at the centre, but with money, and sufficient power to make them believe their own propaganda. That year they were everywhere. I watched them on the screens – recognised many of them – all night every night, clamouring down the airwaves, busy and self-important. I loathed them, but I could not stop watching them.

I had, for the last year-and-a-half, been resident in the penthouse of a very good hotel in the capital's north district. Hitherto it had proven a most satisfactory perch. But now, watching the city and its doings from my eyrie, the place no longer seemed so comfortable, and I began to wish for somewhere quieter, away from the crowd. Late one night, after dinner from a now too-familiar menu, I recalled my meeting some summers previously with Eckhart. I had known him during my college years – a friend, I would say, insofar as he or I had them, but one who had always kept himself slightly to one side of the great chattering, self-satisfied mass. At the time I had assumed some particular maturity or special wisdom about Eckhart's distance and gently mocking smiles; these days I recognize them for what they were: the mask of a young man out of his social depth.

We stayed intermittently in touch, but as my migratory tendencies became more pronounced and life, presumably, caught up with Eckhart, we drifted apart. I had been delighted, therefore, to spot him across the auditorium one evening at the free-fall theatre in the capital. After the show (which I recall being oddly static, at least, in narrative terms), we joined each other for a late supper on the riverbank. Eckhart had the grilled sole; I the duck.

I had little to report since we last met, and, besides, much preferred listening to Eckhart's stories. His career in the civil service had followed a steady upward trajectory, and this evening his conversation was full of his new appointment as under-secretary to the governor of Wright's World.

"I doubt you've heard of the place," he said. "I know I hadn't."

I had to admit that I had not.

"No wonder. It's well off the beaten track. About as far away from here as you can get."

I cut a thin sliver of flesh, perfectly pink. "Is that not risky?"

"In what way?"

"A danger of disappearing off the radar—"

"Ah, but think of the opportunities! A place where a man can really make his mark."

I listened with interest and increasing fondness as he spoke of his ambition, his desire to succeed, to prove himself. He had plans for Wright's World: he spoke of development, exploitation, inward investment. He was putting together a strong team, bonded and citizens, and was particularly pleased at the interest of the latter, who could take their talents wherever they chose. He had goals and strategies. As he spoke, I recalled the humbleness of his background and the unlikeliness of his success, and I wished him well. We parted on good terms, and, as I paid the bill, Eckhart extended an open invitation to come and visit. "It will shake some of the cobwebs from you," he said. "This city is static. Immobile. It'll kill us all."

And since that was how I felt about the capital, now seemed to be the time to get in touch. It took a day or two. I had no problem finding Eckhart through the governor's office, but the man himself proved difficult to pin down, and, when finally we spoke, he was non-committal about the possibility of a visit. Nonetheless, by exerting some of my charm, I was able to acquire the desired invitation. I am without compunction when it comes to inviting myself. A guest who is conscious from the outset that he or she is not particularly welcome can, with a little effort, quickly make him or herself an asset. Eckhart sounded tired, distracted. I would restore him to himself, as he would perhaps restore me, a little.

The flight, which lasted three weeks standard, was on a small but decently appointed liner. I spent the time observing the other passengers, all of whom were travelling for work or trade purposes, some of the former intending to settle. I had known little about Wright's World before deciding to visit, and indeed it seemed a well-kept secret: distant enough not to tempt the masses, and therefore small enough to attract the more adventurous and ambitious. I learned enough about the mining and logging operations to put a little of my own cash that way. Accounts of the current political scene were of the usual kind (although I was pleased to see that Eckhart featured prominently in recent years), and there was some travel journalism of the limpest sort that did little to enticc the reader. I was chiefly absorbed in the accounts of the earliest settlers, who were blessed with some lyrical writers well able to evoke the world's rugged, mountainous beauty. The attraction of these more remote regions was very strong and, in this way, I kept myself busy. In time, we descended upon Wright's World.

I was met at the spaceport by Eckhart's secretary. She was polite and self-effacing, opening doors for me, organizing my baggage, saying little. I was not surprised to see the tell-tale indigo marks like bruises upon her flesh, about the wrists and the temples: this woman was jenjer, genetically engineered, capable of high function but requiring regular medication to prevent her metabolism from shorting out. Her bond would be pricey, but Eckhart, I recalled, liked expensive things and never bought cheap.

Politely, unobtrusively, but firmly, she directed me out of the spaceport and towards the car. We spoke little on the journey to the hotel. Eckhart, she explained, when I asked, was out of town that day on business, but hoped to join me that evening for dinner. When I assured her that I would be comfortable, she nodded briskly and departed. If she said her name, I have forgotten it, or never heard.

I unpacked. I explored the room. I lay upon the bed and dozed for a while, enjoying the fresh unscrubbed air, the wisp of wind upon the curtains, and the soft heat of the world's sun. When I woke I showered at length under the copious water and, thus refreshed, I left my room and went outside.

To call the main conurbation a city is inaccurate – frontier town would be closer to the mark. I could see little in the way of industry, although the main logging and mining operations were of course further out. The town itself, whilst small, had a tidy aspect; the air was clear, the light white and pure-seeming – a pleasant change from the core worlds where I habitually spent my time and money. I could well understand Eckhart's desire to settle here. The buzz and clamour of the core worlds were very wearisome. Nonetheless, despite my appreciation of the change of pace, I had by late afternoon exhausted what the centre of the town had to offer, and I returned to my room to wait, perhaps, for Eckhart.

He came mid-evening, still in his day suit, bearing a large leather briefcase and a harassed manner. Over dinner (unfussy but pleasant enough), it became clear that Eckhart was a changed man.

I struggled at first to put my finger on what it was. Certainly he had coarsened – he checked his watch throughout the evening, and would sometimes finish my sentences, lapses of manners which he could never have committed in the past. As the uncomfortable evening progressed (or declined), I came to the conclusion that Wright's World had been something of a disappointment. I attempted to draw him on this, but he closed down discussion abruptly each time, and brought dinner to an early end, declining a suggestion that we moved on elsewhere. At the door to my hotel, we exchanged goodbyes, and then he hesitated and I caught a flicker of the old Eckhart.

"You'll forgive me for stationing you here," he said. "I have been travelling for most of the past year, and look set to be off again shortly. But I hope you'll be a regular visitor at my home when I'm in town. Come tomorrow. Come to dinner. The governor will be there."

I did. The governor and I got along famously, and he went to great lengths to tell me what an asset Eckhart was. I was pleased to see my friend so valued. And when the governor learned how far this old college friend had come to see his aide, Eckhart's schedule was quickly changed, and he found himself back in town for the foreseeable future. After that, it was only sensible, he said, for me to become a house guest. I accepted the offer with alacrity, for my own comfort, yes, but also because I was anxious to find out what troubled my friend.

I settled easily into his home and routine. Under closer observation, more of the old Eckhart emerged – the wry humour, the shrewd eye for the people around him – but blanketed with a kind of brooding disappointment that I had not associated with the younger man, who had always been on the lookout for opportunity. His house, which was in one the town's smarter districts, showed evidence of numerous projects started and then abandoned partway through: a half-plotted garden, a library, a large wooden deck providing a view out into the foothills but not safe to stand on. Growing bored with the town and my own company, and keen to draw him away from his house, which seemed to reinforce his mood, I suggested numerous times a trip away, perhaps up into the fabled mountains, but he said that would be impossible. On the fourth or fifth occasion that I made this suggestion, he lost his temper.

"For pity's sake," he said, "not all of us are free to spend our days idling! I have to work!"

I was embarrassed. This was the first time in our friendship that he had ever referred to the difference in our circumstances. I believe he was embarrassed too by this lapse in courtesy: the next morning, he was friendlier than he had been for a while, and said that although he could not leave town at that time, I should consider myself free to travel around.

"It would be a shame to come this far, and not see the mountains," he said. "You should do some flying too. You can't come to Wright's World and not fly. I'll get one of the staff to set it up for you."

I took the hint and agreed, with enthusiasm that I did not feign. I was tiring of town life and thought the mountains might refresh me. I did not ask whether or not he had flown in all his time here.

It proved an excellent decision. As the little shuttle lifted and I saw the town below fall away, I felt my spirits rise. After all, I had come here to escape the terrible weight that seemed to descend upon one after too long in the core worlds. I could only hope that, with some time to himself again, Eckhart would find that my stay had relieved some of his own strain.

For a whole day the shuttle followed the coastline south along ragged shores and pristine sands. Shortly after dawn of the second day, we reached the silver-streaked triangle of a river delta and struck south-west into the interior.

As we went deeper into the mountains, the landscape took a turn to the dramatic. We powered through deep-cut valleys, with the peaks rising on either side, blue-grey and green; valleys steeper and mountains more vertiginous than any I have ever seen. I am well-travelled, made the mandatory grand tour that all my class made in their youth, and have seen some of the most arresting sights in the Commonwealth. I have not seen anywhere to match this wild land tucked away on this distant world. I could understand what had pulled Eckhart here. I could not understand how he had soured.

We came in time to a small town at the confluence of two rivers. Here, Eckhart had arranged accommodation for me, of a necessarily Spartan but sufficient kind, and had also hired the services of a guide to take me further up along the Red River and into an area said to be the most dramatic and beautiful on Wright's World.

Let me take a moment to describe my guide. His name was Yarrow, and he was a native of the area, descended from those original settlers who had come out here several generations ago. I do not believe he had even ever gone as far away from his place of birth as the main township. He was at once an advert and a warning for provinciality, being coarse, dirty, unpleasant, often drunk, and knowing the region like no other. His company amused me greatly.

With this unlikely companion, I began my journey upriver by flyer. This machine is worthy of mention: it was so ancient that its continued use surely broke numerous regulations, and yet Yarrow manifestly cared for it in a way I believe he had never cared for any living soul, man, beast or jenjer. I felt entirely safe aboard this contraption flying above what must be one of most remote regions of the Commonwealth.

We travelled without much in the way of conversation. Occasionally Yarrow would direct my attention towards some natural feature of particular magnificence; mostly he allowed the landscape to speak for itself. It needed no advocate. I cannot think of a place more startling, more remote, and more beautiful than those peaks and valleys along the Red River on Wright's World. And I had not yet experienced them in full.

We reached a place where the river passed through a deep gorge. A suspended bridge of slats and a single rope linked one side to the other. Here I took flight. I plunged nine thousand feet and, as the river rushed to meet me, the automatics on my glider took over, and I skimmed above the surface of the water, light as a mayfly. Afterwards, I lay on the bank and stared at the bright sky, thinking I had never felt more alive. But there was more to come. Yarrow, sitting beside me, gave a crooked smile.

"Here," he said and withdrew from his pocket a small grubby packet, which he passed to me. "This'll give you wings."

I took the drugs without further comment. Spare me any murmurs of disapproval: we have all done this from time to time, if bored, or in need of something to push us through to the end of the day or into the next morning, and we live in a world in which one in five people with whom we deal uses these substances as a matter of course. They are the bridge upon which our world rests. Within ten minutes I felt the acceleration, the rush, and, as this heightened state – in which one seems to have access all at once to all that is and has ever been – came to its peak, I walked to the edge and took off for the flight of my life.

That night, I was unable to sleep from the afterglow of the high. I stared at the unfamiliar stars, which seemed to merge together, and I reflected that this must be how the jenjers spend their whole days. How I envied them, and this constant bliss. Why did we not all live this way, all the time, open to the universe in its manifold glory? What, exactly, was preventing me from choosing this? As I lay in the darkness, a whole new life opened in front of me. I could come here, live here, be in this state forever. Build a house, here, at this place. I could spend all my days doing this and feeling this. What could be better? Why would I do anything else? Why would I *be* anywhere else?

The next morning, back to my ordinary self, I woke to the smell of coffee stewing in the pan and the smell of bacon. As I ate breakfast greedily, I became aware of Yarrow watching my every movement with his shrewd dark eyes.

"What is it?" I said at last.

"Only that if you liked yesterday, there's another spot further up. Off the beaten track, you get me?"

Out of bounds, he meant. Private property, I assumed.

"Deeper valley," he said. He tapped his pocket. "Better flight."

"I'm interested," I said.

"It'll cost."

"Don't worry about that."

And he did not. We got back into his flyer and went on to the place he had suggested. He was right. The jump was better. I went twice, three times – I forget now. They merged into a continuous high.

Later, Yarrow set our camp close to a tiny wood cabin that showed clear signs of habitation. Perhaps I should have queried this – we were trespassing, after all, and surely wanted to keep our presence here a secret – but my mind was full. We ate, and the sun disappeared, and I lay down to sleep.

I was woken in the middle of the night by the sound of a woman speaking. I continued to feign sleep, but I opened my eyes a very little to be able to see her.

I saw her only in profile. She was beautiful – or had been once; about thirty, fine-featured, with long dark hair hanging down. When I looked more closely, as well as I could in the darkness and through half-closed eyes, I could see how tired she was, with her shoulders down, hunched over our small fire. She had the giveaway marks at her temple.

She and Yarrow spoke softly to each other, with familiarity, but little discernible affection.

"Where's your man?" he said.

"Went upriver weeks back. I guess I'll see him again when the leaves start to fall."

"Good for us."

"I guess so." She sighed. "Is she asleep?"

"I should think so. Long day."

I closed my eyes, softened my breathing, and tried to picture the day's flights. At length, the woman left. But my head now was full of her. Who was she? What was she doing here? This was plainly a jenjer on whom some considerable expense had been lavished once upon a time. She would stand out back in the main town; she would be at home in the core worlds, the capital. She was surely very high functioning. Who could afford to maintain her out here? Why would she be here at all?

"Pretty piece, isn't she?" Yarrow said, when he saw that I was awake, and looking back towards the house. His tongue ran moistly across his lips. "Expensive."

In the house, the single visible light was extinguished. "Who is she?"

"Abbey? She's the ranger's wife. Gets lonely out here in the wild."

"Yes, but – you know what I meant, Yarrow."

He gave me a sly look. "Your friend Eckhart never mentioned her?"

"The under-secretary is a busy man."

"Under-secretary, eh?" He laughed. "A fancy title. But he wasn't beneath falling for a jenjer. When she was a little younger, mind, and still had her looks. She was his aide. Swore undying love for him. He believed her, like a fool."

Like a fool... "What happened?"

"What do you think happened? They're all the same, those creatures. She had a lover already, didn't she, same kind as her. They had a plan to go off together into free space. She was going to fleece Eckhart for every penny. I think she'd even got her paws on official money. That's what I heard, anyway. So what was the under-secretary to do?"

What else could my friend do? Discovering her duplicity, he would have been obliged to act decisively, and punitively. There could be no mercy: what message would that send to her kind? So he had sold on her bond, sold her into exile, out here, to get by as best she could. I wondered now who owned this piece of land. The governor? Some other wealthy and influential friend, ready to prevent Eckhart's reputation being destroyed by scandal? We're all allowed one bad mistake, after all, and Eckhart was such an asset.

Yarrow was whistling tunelessly between his teeth.

"What happened to the lover?" I said.

"Eh?"

"The man, the one she intended to leave with?"

He looked at me blankly for a moment. "Oh, him! His bond got sold on to the military. He'll be a hero now, no doubt." He grinned without fellow feeling. "Rather him than me."

I had done and seen enough. On my instruction, therefore, we set out on the return journey very early the next morning. I did not see the girl, Abbey, again.

I left Yarrow at the river confluence, and made my own way back to town. When I arrived, Eckhart was somewhere else, on the governor's business, but I did not wait for him to return. I had no desire to remain on this world any longer. I left grateful and profuse thanks for his hospitality and for the trip of a lifetime, and extended my own invitation for him to visit me in the core worlds whenever he had the chance. I said that I would pass on my address as soon as I had one, but I never have. I took flight, for somewhere else.

People, Places and Things

Den Patrick

1: Danny

Danny and I smoked weed. Like a lot of weed. And we watched films. *Independence Day, Godzilla, Pacific Rim, Armageddon, Transformers, The War of the Worlds.* We watched all of them, even *Cloverfield,* though it made Danny feel car sick. My favourite was always *The Thing,* while Danny preferred *The Day the Earth Stood Still.* He said he liked the way Keanu Reeves didn't seem to have any feelings. I told him Keanu Reeves never seems to have any feelings, which gave us both a fit of the giggles that lasted half an hour. It may have been minutes, difficult to tell; we had been rolling pretty hard that day. It tells you how stoned we were back then that we didn't realise *The Day the Earth Stood Still* was a remake.

I would kill for a remake, for myself, for the whole planet, but there's no one left to kill and it was always a ridiculous expression anyway. 'I'd kill for a cup of tea': hyperbole smashed into the atoms of the banal. Maybe that's what they were doing at Bern this whole time, using the Hadron Collider to fire pointless things at each other, hoping the destruction might create something meaningful.

Looking back, it's obvious to me now that Danny and I were just two people wanting to watch the world be obliterated over and over. It's easier to destroy something rather than engage with it, easier to watch it burn than interact with it, easier to see it explode than have to learn and be hurt by it. Better the world be scoured of all beauty than suffer the notion you might have to enjoy it or fall in love with it. I think there are lot people like Danny and me - or there were, before the unmaking.

Danny's fascination with destruction shifted from the silver screen to a more personal one. He started hanging out with some mates from work and tried to get me onto coke, but I wasn't having any of it. I liked to get stoned and be quiet, but there's not much quiet when you're in a room full of cokeheads.

I didn't see Danny so much. A year later he told me he'd tried heroin for the first time, a year after that and he was dead. I didn't go to the funeral but I did stop watching films about the end of the world. I threw my Zippo in the sea and stopped smoking spliff. I got myself a better job, a girlfriend, and started spending time in the local boozer.

And that's where my problems really started.

2: People, Places and Things

The first thing you discover when you join Alcoholics Anonymous is that they have a lot a catchphrases.

One day at a time.

This too shall pass.

Keep coming back.

The one that always stuck with me the most is that 'we are powerless over people, places and things'. I think this particular phrase is just a fancy way of saying 'shit happens, so you might as well deal with it'. For me, it always reflected the transient nature of life. I kept a girlfriend for a bit, Robyn, but then we split up. I was mates with Danny for a long time, and then he died. I had a flat for a while, and then I was in a bedsit. I had a job as a delivery driver, and then all I had was my drinking problem.. All things diminish over time, but never more so than when you're drinking, or so I thought.

When I sobered up, things didn't seem to improve. It's quite a common story for people recovering from drink or drugs. They mourn the life they lost, even though it was no good for them. I know that doesn't make much sense, addiction doesn't make sense to anyone, but it's a bit like pining for an ex, even though they were a total shit to you. For a long time they were all you knew and the idea of anything else is all too frightening.

My new-found sobriety meant I could see the world properly, but I wasn't sure it was the world I'd known before I started drinking. It *looked* like the world I was familiar with before I started drinking, but something didn't feel right. Something was missing; it was quieter somehow, subdued. Had people given up on their lives when I wasn't looking?

There I was, putting the most effort into my life I ever had, and everyone else had become anxious shadows of themselves. You could see it in the blank gazes on the bus, or the way people didn't react if someone barged into them on the street. Toddlers didn't wail or throw tantrums and teenagers stopped swearing and shouting on the street. The letters column in the *Daily Mail* stopped. I found out later that they weren't receiving enough outraged complaints. Anger, and just about every other feeling, had faded to leave a nervous apathy.

I thought I was imagining it at first, but I mentioned it to my therapist and he nodded. "There are less of us now, and those of us that are left feel the absence." The session ran out of time so I couldn't ask him what he meant.

I arrived the following week, but he didn't show up. I went back the week after that and the same thing happened. I never saw him again. The counselling agency apologised and told me he'd gone missing. The receptionist broke down on the phone, crying that it wasn't just that he'd gone missing, but that all record of him had been deleted too. All the paperwork with his name on had been stolen, all his files deleted. She apologised over and over until a supervisor took the phone from her and ended the call.

Something like 250,000 people vanish each year in the UK.

Some of these people come back. Either they were broke, or needed to get sober like I did, or they fled the country. A few reappear months or years down the line.

Now when people disappeared they stayed disappeared and no one knew why. The news reported an epidemic of missing persons, as if such a thing could be contagious. Mental health professionals would duly appear on television or radio or anywhere that wanted an expert opinion. Psychologists and therapists would wring their hands and blame the economy and poverty and the many ills of the 21st Century. No one really cared at first. When a poor person goes missing it means they're not claiming benefits, but then rich people started going missing too and that's when the Government started taking it seriously.

It wasn't limited to people either, there were other, more banal disappearances, everyday things: keys, the TV remote, passports, a dog-eared black and white photograph of your grandparents, phones, engagement rings. All of these things started evaporating with ever increasing frequency. Objects and artefacts we had taken for granted, keepsakes and curios, things we could rely on to be found under sofa cushions. All were gone, all were lost, and they remained lost.

Art galleries reported a 36% increase in stolen art, but the crime scenes never yielded any clues. "It's as if the picture vanished into thin air," the police would say, "But we are determined to find the criminals." It was a form of denial I think, anyone with an ounce of sense knew the paintings would never return, just as we knew the Liberty Bell was never coming back, or the statue of David in Florence would never be seen again. It was obvious the police weren't telling the whole story, not about the stolen art and not about the missing people.

I used to joke to my Dad that we'd become absent-minded as a species, misplacing important things amid the clutter of our lives.

"There's just too much stuff in the world," I would say and Dad would give me a look.

"Just as long as we don't start losing our minds," he would say.

3: Lambeth North

Lambeth North Tube station was built in 1906 and was originally called Kennington Road. It suffered bomb damage during the war, in 1941, I think. I know this because my Dad worked there and would churn out the odd fact when he was bored, which was often. I liked the Tube station because I'd always think of the old man as I passed through the gates, his kindly eyes and small, crooked smile. I wish I could have been more like my Dad. God knows he didn't deserve an alcoholic son, and he didn't deserve to see the world end like it did either.

There had been a lot of people and items affected by the disappearance phenomena by that point, but it was really Lambeth North Tube station that put it on the map, so to speak. Or rather it took Lambeth North Tube station *off* the map, because the whole place just wasn't there anymore. It was this event more than any other that really brought it home to me. The building simply wasn't there, just a yawning absence on the street. The news channels drove themselves into a frenzy. Not only had the station building vanished but the staircase and the lifts were gone too. Serious men in fluorescent jackets led by other serious men in white coats arrived. They scanned the soil using radar but there was no sign of the platform below. Engineers walked down the line to discover the tunnel ended abruptly for about two-hundred meters, only to start up again on the way to Elephant and Castle.

It wasn't just that Tube station was gone, it was as if it never existed. The tunnel hadn't been filled in, it had never been excavated in the first place. People could remember Lambeth North Tube station, but no mention of it remained anywhere. Books on the history of the Tube had blank pages. Websites were riddled with '404 Error – Not found' messages. Theories zipped back and forth across the internet, in conversations, on texts. Had it been a hoax? Was it an elaborate stunt? Were avant-garde terrorists to blame for this new attack on the London Transport network? Various far right parties blamed the immigrants, the chairman of Transport for London had a nervous breakdown, and no one came any closer to discovering what had happened or why.

And there was the subtle erosion of information. All mentions of Lambeth North Tube station faded after 24 hours. Text messages deleted themselves. It wasn't enough that Lambeth North Tube station had gone, it was as if the very concept of the station wanted to be forgotten, scrubbed from existence, edited from all records, just like my therapist. I ran internet searches for the statue of David and it was the same story. 404 Error -- not found. The newspapers that had covered the story were missing text and pictures.

The Tube station, my dad's Tube station, was the first of many architectural casualties. Churches, old pubs, and Stonehenge were all taken, or faded from reality, depending on what version of conspiracy you adhered to. It was impossible to keep track of everything that had been unmade. That's what they called it after one MIT professor released a frantic YouTube clip. The professor claimed we had 'unmade' the universe and I couldn't help wondering if he was right.

Keeping a record of what had gone was a pointless endeavour. Any list of unmade people unwrote itself. Records of unmade places began to delete themselves the moment they had been compiled; hard drives died and back-ups failed. Networks of obsessives emailed information to each other in strict 24 hour cycles, but even these were undone.

Sometimes the very computers and servers the information was held on would be unmade, vanished to whatever unplace such items were transported to.

Reports filtered in from all over the world and the response was always the same, no matter the nation, culture or religion: incredulity. We had expected some vast final battle, a Ragnarok, an Armageddon. We had expected dirty bombs on metro trains in major cities. We had dreamed aliens in vast ships would use laser cannons. We had not expected to be edited out of the Universe piece-by-piece, place-by-place, person-by-person. We were being quietly unmade without explosions or fuss, without bloodshed or fury. Dad said it had 'all gone a bit T.S. Eliot' but I didn't know what he meant. He told me to read *The Hollow Men* and I didn't know what that meant either.

People that understood came together and set aside their differences. Now that threat of mutually assured destruction had passed, everyone wanted to be remembered by someone. People reached out to one another, defying the unspoken boundaries of class, religion, caste, sexuality, ability, even colour. Perhaps our prejudices had been unmade too.

Not all people understood the unmaking, and not all prejudices were unmade. America dispatched the National Guard to stop the anticipated wave of looting, which is to say white people with guns looked for reasons to shoot black people looking for food. And the National Guard were restrained compared to the white vigilante gangs that sprang up, declaring themselves the Zip Code Militia, but failing to understand the irony. No one was ever going to get mail again, not after most American cities became war zones.

The UK was more sedate. Panic-buying became the norm and a few supermarket trucks were held up en route. People started stealing replacements for the things that had been unmade, games consoles, televisions, clothes.

"It's as if they think they're entitled," I said to Dad, "Compensation for a Universe that randomly steals from them."

We were having a cup of tea on his balcony. He lived in an old council flat he'd had the sense to buy before everyone was priced out of the city. We used to stand up there pointing out where buildings used to be. The skyline of London was less dramatic without the Shard thrusting into the skies.

"Entitled? That's your generation, not mine," replied Dad. "We worked for the things we owned." He shook his head and wandered back into the flat. The shops that still existed in the streets below were boarded up. A few companies tried to keep going as fewer and fewer employees arrived for work each day. The police were noticeable by their absence, I wondered how many of them had been unmade, never to be seen again. Living in a world where the landscape forgot itself was bad enough, but it was the absence of people that really unnerved. I followed Dad into the flat, relieved to find him sat in an armchair watching the news.

4. Impressions

The BBC showed a clip of a woman who had paid for something in her local corner store. A young mother with ash blonde hair, she turned away for perhaps thirty seconds and the pushchair was gone, along with her eighteen-month old daughter. The mother was hysterical, the shopkeeper too. You could feel the panic bleeding out of the screen as the woman searched the store, her every movement caught in grainy CCTV footage. The clip went viral, people made sure to repost it every twenty-four hours to make sure it outran the erosion of unmaking. The unmade girl's name was Rebekah.

People, places and things continued to disappear with steady regularity and we were all powerless to stop them. It was like reading about celebrities who had just passed away, but instead of David Bowie it was now the park two streets away, or the McDonalds on the corner. Sometimes a house or a block of flats would vanish and I would find myself breathless with a terrible dread. Had the families inside disappeared along with the buildings? What had happened to them? Were they aware it was happening as they vanished, or was it no different from a bomb?

I looked at a picture of my dad on the shelf at my place. It had been a fishing trip when I was about eleven years old. I hate fishing but he thought it would be 'good to do some father and son stuff'. In truth, it rained the whole three days and we played gin rummy in a tent, taking nips of whisky from his hip flask.

The picture did not show my father in his waxed raincoat, it did not show the man holding a fish, the only one we caught. The picture revealed a bedraggled stretch of riverside and my eleven year-old self, staring into the camera with a shy smile. That's was the second time my world ended I think. I knew he was gone in that moment. Mum had died years before, the first of my personal Judgement Days. Her passing fuelled my need to get constantly stoned and not feel anything. "Like Keanu Reeves in *The Day the Earth Stood Still,"* as Danny would say, except Danny wasn't saying anything anymore. I tried to decide what was worse, overdosing on heroin or being unmade.

I went to dad's place slowly, no need to rush, nothing would change. He wasn't there, though I spent the whole bus journey hoping it would be otherwise. The fact the buses were running at all made the day all the more surreal. I think Dad knew his time was up. The little table where he would eat dinner was immaculate, with only an old pad and pencil left behind. He had left a note but whatever had unmade him had unmade the pencil strokes too. Each loop and line, each letter and word, the paragraphs had all been unmade just as surely as my father had been. I cried for an hour, feeling like my eleven-year old self again.

I don't know what made me do it, but I checked the page underneath, tearing off the blank page where my father's parting message had been so cruelly erased. My breath caught in my throat. The paper was uneven, faint indentations pressed into the paper by Dad's heavy-handed scrawl. I lay the pencil flat and swished it back and forth across the paper, like a kid with a crayon. I'm not sure how it is that the words themselves were unmade while the indentations remained but it felt like a tiny victory over the unmaking.

The words were faint and appeared as ghostly white streaks amid the grey of the pencil lead. They gave me some small measure of peace the day the Universe unmade my father. They were all I had left. All photographs of him were gone, his banking records and personal paperwork all gone. Even his old Tube station uniform cap unmade. That was when my world ended, and somehow, I stayed sober.

5. Step Nine

I should confess at this point that I wasn't very good at the whole Alcoholics Anonymous thing. It's not that I couldn't stay sober, I just didn't like their 12 Steps to Recovery. Yet here I was, at the end of the world, suddenly desperate to fulfil Step Nine:

We made direct amends to such people wherever possible, except when to do so would injure them or others.

I wasn't expecting to embark on some quest of forgiveness, but events had a way of conspiring against me. I'd gathered up all the stuff I could carry from my place and moved in to Dad's, keen to be close to him in any way I could.

I was surprised to find that Mrs King who lived next door still existed. She was out on her balcony clutching the rail with a faraway look in her eye. I had assumed she had passed away, but here she was, in her nineties refusing to die or be unmade.

"Hello, Love," she said to me with a slow smile. "Come to see your Dad?"

"I, well, he's...' the expression on my face told the rest of the story. She nodded and looked away.

'I'm sorry," I said, and wasn't entirely sure why, just that this overpowering need to apologise had me rooted to the spot.

Mrs King looked at me. "For what, Love?"

"You know, all the times I turned up here drunk making a racket. And all the times my Dad had to go out looking for me. I know he told you about me. He didn't exactly have a lot of people to talk to after mum passed."

"You don't have to apologise to me," said Mrs King. She pulled out a cigarette and lit the end, obscured behind a cloud of smoke for a second. "My Doctor told me to stop years ago, but I don't suppose it matters so much anymore." She gave me that slow smile again.

"I'm not sure I ever told him how sorry I was, before he was taken."

"He always knew you regretted it," replied Mrs King. "And he always knew you were sorry. Don't worry yourself over it, there's not much time left." She headed back indoors and I wondered if I'd ever see her again.

I kind of lost of it after that. Not by getting drunk. Dad hadn't kept booze in the house for years. I found his address book. So many of the pages were missing entries, either people unmade or the addresses themselves. Many lacked telephone numbers from where their phones had vanished.

One by one I phoned all the numbers that remained. I found myself speaking to strangers, old friends of the family, people who really didn't want to speak to me at all. My message was the same regardless of the circumstances.

I was sorry if I'd ever caused them any trouble.

I was sorry to my Dad and wanted them to know we'd reconciled before he was unmade.

I loved my Dad and wanted them to remember him, all the good in him, his kindly eyes and small crooked smile.

Those phone calls lasted forever and I made them fearful the phone would be unmade from my hands, fearful the person I spoke to suddenly fell silent, unmade mid-conversation. It took me a whole day but I worked through every number in the book, those that were left anyway. I lost track of the number of people I reached out to, yet each of them gave some fragment of my Dad back to me: his favourite pub, a football match, the day he was promoted, how proud he was when I finally sobered up, who his best man had been and "You know John, he was Betty's son from number 57..." and so on and so on. People stitching together reality from faded memories and nostalgia.

I'm standing on the balcony at Dad's flat and the tears won't stop tracking down my cheeks. Just about every other building in the street has gone now. My old school, the church I was baptized in, the newsagents I used to deliver the papers for. All unmade, all remembered by me and me alone. There are just roads now, roads that lead nowhere, roads without corner shops and roads without cars.

I haven't seen anyone in a week, at least I think it's a week, the calendar was unmade and I can't keep track anymore. There's no news, no TV at all, no electricity. I never thought I'd miss the howl of planes coming into land over London. The silence is a weight that drags me down.

There's a knock on the door and Mrs King stands there, unbending and resolute and reassuringly ancient. She says she found a book my Dad lent her. The author is T.S. Eliot she says. Would I like it? I open the cover and find *The Hollow Men* – my eyes drift over the words.

This is the way the world ends
This is the way the world ends
This is the way the world ends
Not with a bang but a whimper.

Mrs King asks me why I'm laughing and I tell her my Dad is some sort of genius. I tell her all the anecdotes and stories I collected over the phone, I share all my memories of him, all the good in him, his kindly eyes and small crooked smile.

"What if they're not unmade," says Mrs King. "What if all this," she gestures at the absences from her balcony, "Is just moving on, taken some place else."

"Like heaven," I say, and I want to sound sneering and sarcastic but I don't have in me. Mrs King shrugs.

"Like heaven." She smiles.

I'm not sure I really believe in heaven," I say, but I breathe easier thinking my dad is somewhere else than not all.

"What would heaven look like?" says Mrs King.

"Like Lambeth North Tube station," I say. "With my Dad on duty, standing by the barrier, with his old cap and small crooked smile."

Mrs King smiles and we wait, not for a bang, but a whimper.

Staunch

Paul Graham Raven

The Hackney Kid's kidneys go into shut-down on our way out of Gunchester.

The faraday house in east Stockport is a shit-hole. Three houses knocked into one, rotten floorboards under scraps of carpet; where the doorframes were, you can see layers of chicken-wire jutting from the crude plasterwork. All the usual hawkers and hustlers, freelance tech-bros, pedlars of chemicals and procurers of more personal services are here... we're the only guests today, but we've been through here enough times that the usual suspects know better than to shake down my people.

Along with my crew, I lay out my hardware on a square of tarp, rebooting each unit into safe mode, patching what I can, hoping I won't need to patch what I can't. This is easier for me than for the other Surgicals, because none of my kit is networked... except my wrist-pad, natch, but that's encrypted with a 1024-bit key held only in Wee Jenny's Cupboard of Wonders, somewhere in the Highlands of the Scots Republic, and nothing passes through that firewall without me asking it to.

No such luck for most of my crew, who are all 'plantheads of one sort or another: the Kid and 'Arry Satchels with their data-diver rigs; Nirmayi's industrial stentrodes and interfaces; Nick-by-Name and her real-time physics engines and strategy modules. The one thing their 'plants all have in common is that they're illegal, obsolete, obscure, or a mix of all three.

They weren't when first fitted, natch. When 'plants first arrived on the scene, employers were competing for subjects to install them in; ten years later, once the crude, error-prone and invasive 'plants were superseded by scanwebs you could just slip on and off like a hat, they were competing for liability lawyers to avoid having to clean up their mess. The result was a whole lot of folk with a head-full of proprietary tech they couldn't (or wouldn't) get rid of, nor use for legitimate work.

Over the years, I've found a fraction of those folk, gathered them together. I find work for them. For us.

They're pleased to be transiting out of Gunchester, though. We lost a fifth of our salvage to customs: the Red Rose Federation is signatory to countless legacy trade agreements, meaning a lot of public-domain intellectual property, hardware or software, gets flagged as stolen or pirated as soon as it identifies itself to the municipal network. And while salvage isn't considered theft in every jurisdiction, and while we may have been on UN business that came with salvage permits, Gunchester don't care. It's toll-gate robbery, in a way – but it's a cost of doing business, so we suck it up like everyone else.

Even if your hardware *doesn't* decide to grass you up to a city full of greedheads, borders present other problems: expired licenses; forced OS upgrades; even local viral variants your firewalls don't know. Hence the rituals of the faraday house, the hand-annotated hardcopy lists of recent exceptions and hardware seizures taped to the walls, the 'change-and-mart grifters stinking of hydroponic tobacco and stale sweat...

I finish my ablutions first, as usual, and barter for half a reefer from a toothy old Rasta crouched in a corner; old Swampy joins me at the window to share it. I take a quick head-count: everyone looks good to go but for the Kid, stalled halfway through his strip-down, knelt among his weapons and modules, staring up into interface space like he can see god in there. An angry god, at that.

"You alright, Kid?" asks 'Arry, wrapping up his own strip-down. "Not let yer insurance lapse again, 'ave yer?"

"Not... as such," says an unusually subdued Kid, sliding out of i-space.

The Kid's original kidneys crapped out when he was twelve or so; I don't recall exactly why, but given his namesake, it's not hard to guess. While he's all tubed up to a dialysis machine, two suits arrive and tell his parents they can give him some new experimental artificial kidneys, and no, no, don't worry about the cost, we understand, all you need to do is sign on your son's behalf and we'll let him pay it off over the course of his whole lifetime... hell, we'll even help arrange jobs for him to make it easier! I never had kids myself, but it doesn't take high empathy stats to understand why the poor bastards signed him up. The Kid himself admits it gave him his childhood back: he was lucky, in that he got an experimental model that actually worked as designed.

He got lucky later, too. Once he hit his economic majority at sixteen, his benefactors sent him to Hinkley: remediation work in the exclusion zone around Osborne's Folly. But the UN grants for the Hinkley clean-up ran out after a few years, by which time said benefactors had ceased to exist as a legal entity; the Kid couldn't trace them, at any rate, and they never got in touch again. So he thanked his luckies, signed up for a new career (and more 'plants) as a data-diver, and forgot all about it.

Only now his renal system has been flagged as lacking a site-license for the software it's running, and the OS is demanding that the Kid return immediately to a certified repair services provider before the *gratis* 48-hour introductory offer expires, and the Kid with it.

The company that made those kidneys hasn't existed for a decade. Hell knows who acquired the IP on them – some robolawyer operating out of the Upper Eastern Seaboard States, probably. Doesn't make much difference.

I know immediately what I have to do, how I can save the Kid.

Know who can save him, rather.

"We need to get the Kid to Sheffield," I tell them. "I have some... there's people there who can maybe fix him."

Nirmayi shakes her head. "Wrong season for crossing the mountains."

"There's not really a right season."

Gunchester's a fine place to start from if you're heading south; I've been wanting to hit the Bristol fayres and trade our salvage. We've been up in the Lake District these last few months, working another UN contract, protecting autonomous agrisystems from the endless army of amphibious cropper-drones that clamber out of the Irish Sea: North African kids based in Southern Europe, piloting Chinese hardware, probably convinced they're grinding out gold and kudos in some game-world; their real objective is to grab viable samples of the European biome to take back to what's left of the States. I've seen things you people wouldn't believe: surveillance drones on fire off the shoulder of Scafell Pike... oh, it's a proper warzone up there, even if the human cost happens hundreds of miles away. Tough work, but good pay by UN standards, plus salvage rights on each drone we decommission. A few bits and bobs managed to fall off some damaged agritech, too – the sort of stuff that's easiest sold to specialists, so to speak. Hence my yen for the fayres of Somerland.

But now we have a new destination... and heading east out of the Red Rose Federation is a different matter entirely. Passing people over the Pennines isn't easy these days: the lesser roads are overgrown, the Hope Valley line was bombed out years back, and the canals are crawling with water militias who survive by squeezing communities downstream. And while the old Snake Pass road is still solid enough for smallish vehicles, anything less than an APC is an open invitation for the *brigantii* to canter down the sides of the cut armed with stolen welding lasers, slice you out of the car and eat you like corned beef from the tin.

We need to go underground – very literally so.

Everyone's finishing up their lock-and-load. The Kid's sat hunched on his tarp, all knees and elbows like a drowned spider, his skin oddly yellow and glistening with sweat. I don't have long. No one dies on the job. No one ever has, not in the Surgicals.

I round 'em up and move 'em out, my mouth running all the old war-movie clichés, trying to play the game, live the story... to get the narrative moving. That's always been my problem, I guess: I like giving the orders, but I hate making the decisions. That's why the Surgicals pick our contracts democratically these days, and why not every member does every mission. Well, every member but me and Wee Jen: can't stage a circus without a ringmaster and someone to wrangle the permits out of the council, after all.

Having decisions forced on you isn't much fun either – I should have remembered that, really. Part of me does remember it, in fact. But it's not the part that gets shit done, and the Kid needs that part in charge right now. So I put on the mask, and I play it.

The veterans are old enough to see through the frame. Like me, they grew up in a time when there was still assumed to be some sort of canonical reality, no matter how little anyone could agree on its nature—that there was a difference between marketing and entertainment, between truth and the stories we drape over its nudity. Nirmayi knows everything, of course, as by necessity does Wee Jen.

And it was Swampy himself who put me in touch with the design collective who hammered out the original brand narrative for me, back when I was just starting.

But to the younger ones like the Kid and Nick-by-Name, even 'Arry to some extent, the story of the Surgicals is just as true as the story of how their parents met, or how Silicon Valley faked the Mars landings: they take the first explanation they're offered, either because they want it to be true, or because they're worried it already is. To them, being in the Surgicals is simply a better story than the one they were in before, not least because it's a story that slightly more people have heard of – and it's a chance to play a bigger role than Washed-up Casualty of Sociotechnical Innovation, 3rd Class.

And to them, I'm Elaine Stainless: the med-student roller-derby rogue who somehow turned her losing team into a legendary crew of grey-ops systems analysts specialising in theatres of advanced context collapse.

Some days, I'm even Elaine Stainless to myself. But not today.

I open the line to Wee Jen as soon as we're out of the faraday house, and ask her to bring UberStahlStuck GmbH out of the mothballs: a squeaky-clean daughter company that we keep on ice for working with transnationals and the pickier nation-states. One such client is EDF, the former French national energy company that bought up a great deal of the UK's privatised grid back in the day. Brexit and its continental blowback wiped out EDF in Europe, and left it holding the baby in the former UK – the baby being, in this case, a mismatched bundle of undermaintained infrastructures scattered around the country. Among them is the old Woodhead rail tunnel.

We leave the DNZ on a little solar trolley that rides the old rails south-east, just in case anyone's paying attention. We alight at Middlewood, from where the ghost of an older line leads us north and then east, through fields and overgrown ghost-suburbs, toward the western foothills of the Pennines.

The tunnel mouth at the Woodhead end is all but obscured by a well-fortified compound: monofil fencing, razortape concertina, roboturrets, the full Monty.

The tunnel is very valuable still, despite the high-voltage cables running through it not having carried a current in years; both of the

Roses like to keep things local, and won't share or trade energy with t'other Rose as a matter of principle – which, if nothing else, means there's always plenty of easy pick-up work for a crew like ours on both sides of the Pennines. But the Cold War of the Roses amplifies the Woodhead Tunnel's other offer: an inviolable infrastructural beachhead in both federations, and the ability to send personnel and materials from one side to the other. The North's answer to the Eurotunnel, as the old joke used to go... though people stopped telling that one after Kentish separatists brought down the roof on a few thousand indentured refugees from Greece.

UberStahl's credentials get us into the killing zone between the compound's outer and inner fences. Three bored-looking techs and a security goon with meth-head eyes emerge from the gateway module, buttoning up EDF coveralls over thick wool jumpers, breath steaming in the floodlit chill.

"Contractors, eh?" The three-stripe tech is a Scouser; she makes theatre out of consulting her wristpad, while the six of us Surgicals do our best not to look like we're having our bluff called. "Nothing in me schedule, luv. I'm guessing it's some sort of emergency, eh? Call from HQ on the White Rose side, is it? Something gone wrong near the Woodhead end again?"

"Something like that," I allow, as non-committally as possible. If she wants to do the work of fabricating the story, I might as well let her; it's a risk, but a calculated one. "*Priorité cinqe*, though – so it's all need-to-know, y'know?"

"Yeah, right. Ours is not to reason why, eh?" She laughs. "But it's the curse of this particular brigade to be a bit light on the old *per diems*, like. Don't suppose HR sent out that overtime we're owed, did they?"

Crunch time. I activate a pay-the-bearer draft on the UberStahl company seal, fill it out to the tune of what I imagine Three-Stripe's monthly take-home must be, and nearfield it to her. "This should explain HR's position thoroughly," I say.

The EDF peeps have a little head-to-head in the drizzle. The huddle breaks; the heavy heads back toward the gate module, followed by one of the lesser techs.

"Alright, luv," says Three Stripe. "Our Adil back there, he's just found a problem with the cam network in the tunnels, see. Take him a good few hours to fix it, he reckons. Mebbe right through 'til morning.

But so long as you don't mind working without the guaranteed security that EDF's surveillance systems normally provide to visiting contractors, maybe we could just let you get on with your, ah, job." Glances at the Kid, looks back at me. "*Priorité cinqe, oui?*"

"*Vraiment*," I say, trying not to sound too relieved. Someone has to keep up the pretense, right? "We'll get out of your way, then."

"Looks like you'd better," she agrees. Listens for a moment, distracted. "Yeah, them cams are definitely down. We'll keep 'em that way until morning." She grins; it takes ten years off an already young face. "Now fuck off before we all get in trouble, alright?"

The tunnel mouth is blocked with thick steel plate, tarnished and pitted by the Pennine weather. Let into its centre, there is a door large enough for a freight wagon, where two dozen meters of rails and sleepers protrude from the tunnel mouth like a rolled-out tongue.

"Mines of Moria," mutters Swampy. Something's got him spooked. I'll need to get him straightened out once we're inside.

"How does that one go?" pipes up the Kid – revived, however briefly, by the prospect of a story he doesn't know, or doesn't remember.

"Don't ask," I say, raising the company seal to the authentication plate. A muffled thunk, a buzz, a scrape of metal on metal.

Speak, friend, and enter.

The door opens.

Beneath and between the echoing booms of gunfire, I can hear someone chanting *shit, shit, shit, shit.*

I realise that it's me. My throat hurts. The air smells of cordite and rain, and there's vomit on the toe of my right boot. I'm holding my fletcher.

I look up again. Ten yards ahead of the tunnel mouth where I'm crouching, 'Arry's hunkered down behind the bulk of an old freight bogey, ducking out every few seconds to send a couple of rounds into the thicket sheltering our assailants, who plainly don't have the firepower to do much more than they already have, and just as plainly aren't going to retreat.

"Hold, twist or fold?" shouts 'Arry.

We don't have the time to hold them, and there's too few of us to try for a tactical twist that might scare them into a rout. I glance over at

Nirmayi; she nods once, closes her eyes. I look over at Swampy, his life pooling red in the mud beneath him.

"Fold," I call back. *They started it*, I tell myself, playground sing-song in my head.

'Arry crouches low, rummages in his pouches, brings out something that fits in his fist, twists it, lobs it at the thicket. There's a bright flash, a loud crack, followed immediately by utter silence.

For a few moments, all is motionless but for the drizzle and falling leaves sparkling in the sunlight, and my kick-drum heart thumping hard in the cavern of my chest.

Swampy had done such a good job of keeping his shit together in the tunnel that I let him out ahead while the rest of us finished our strip-downs in the faraday room at the end of the tunnel. It all looked clear on the cams, so I figured it'd be fine; never much bandit trouble on the SoYo side, if only because no one's got owt worth stealing.

He doesn't need long in the faradays anyway; his 'plants weren't networked by design. See, Swampy was a johnny for an academic activist group known as the Prussian Forestry Commission during the Brexit years; he smuggled proprietary data and paywalled papers both ways across the border with Europe, stashed on an encrypted SSD drilled into the bone of his brainpan. The Border Force caught him by accident as he returned from a conference in Amsterdam, turned him over to GCHQ's wetware specialists. The SSD was locked up tighter than an offshore bank, but they'd used generic parts and shareware to build the crude visual user interface he needed to shunt stuff in and out of it; this left open a high-bandwidth pipe directly into the visual cortex of Swampy's brain, down which the dataspooks poured, in Swampy's own words, "every wonderful horrible thing that ever was".

His will never cracked, and nor did the crypto, but his mind's been a shattered mirror ever since. They never made a charge stick, but the media coverage ensured he'd never work in the academy again. So now he rolls with me – with us. He's plain useless a lot of the time, and an outright liability in a firefight... but he's got copies of everything he ever smuggled and a whole lot more still stashed upstairs, and he's saved the company's bacon more than once before.

And now he's bleeding out on a damp April morning.

I slowly become aware of sound again: behind me, the Kid's ragged sobbing; Wee Jenny, squawking from my wrist-pad, asking what's happened; ahead of me, 'Arry Satchels reciting every bad word he knows, as he crawls towards the heap of tie-dye and military surplus that used to be Swampy.

I hadn't counted on a scavenger crew camping the tunnel mouth like the respawn point in a poorly designed strategy game. I wonder, with a horrible detached clarity, whether there was some clue I missed in what Three Stripe had said: whether she'd tried to warn us, or knowingly sent us into an ambush. I watch Nirmayi stripping the scavengers while 'Arry shovels out a shallow grave. Their corpses are gaunt, with the pinched, rat-like features of poverty and malnutrition. Even their weapons are junk, for fuck's sake; the round that hit Swampy came out of an old .22 so rusty it's a wonder it didn't blow up in its owner's face.

But it didn't, so we killed him.

I killed him. At this point, I figure my karma hasn't got far left to run.

I help Nirmayai rig stretchers from bundles of carbon rebar, cable ties and the ragged tents from the scavvers' camp. Her face stoic, her cheeks wet, she gently zips Swampy's body to a stretcher, while the Kid tries to argue that it's no problem, he's fine to walk all the way to Rust City.

Funny how they're corpses if you didn't know them, but bodies if you did.

I walk over to the Kid and give his shoulder a gentle shove; he goes down like a crane in a gale.

"You can barely stand, let alone walk," I snap. "Lay down, Kid."

"Okay, boss," he whispers. Those whipped-puppy eyes, sure – but at the same time, the supplication to the role. The comfort of knowing his place in the tale, of thinking I know mine.

I walk away a bit, face east and look out over God's Own Country™: the White Rose Federation stretches away from my feet to the North Sea coast, or whatever's left of it.

I try to think about the route ahead, make plans, but it all feels inevitable now. The threads are all tugging in one direction.

We reach the checkpoint at Penistone, and there's a long line: rural fringers heading in to the Socialist Republic of South Yorkshire to trade whatever they can breed, grow, make or find out in the foothills. With typical SoYo reticence, no one passes more than pleasantries with the barely-disguised mercenary crew carrying a corpse and a soon-to-be-corpse on jerry-built stretchers, and it's all I can do not to scream at them that *yes, one's dead and one's dying and it's all my fucking fault and can't you just for a change lay the sacred institution of queuing aside and let us through...* but mercwerc is technically illegal in SoYo, so we pretend along that there's nothing to see here, just some humble farmsteaders carrying two sick friends and the sort of tools that're no use for digging ditches, si'thee? And finally we're in front of the border guard himself, White Rose regalia stitched badly onto a military greatcoat twice as old as I am, whose job frees him from the burden of polite fictions. He glances at the UberStahl seal, shrugs.

"Don't mean nowt round here, duck. Them of you with arphids should present 'em; them of you without will have to go through certification."

I am forced to fall back on older credentials. I look at my feet, exposing my neck. A beep from the border guard's scanner.

"Ah, reyt," he says. "Elaine Halfway. You've citizenship, system says."

"Aye," I reply. I've not heard that surname in a long time. "Can I vouch for the unchipped?"

"You can, that. Means you tek responsibility for 'em, though?"

I look back at Swampy; at the Kid, panting like a dog with sunstroke.

"Aye," I say. "I do, that."

I thumb the forms; the guard waves us through.

Twenty minutes being prodded and observed in customs; by the time we're out, Wee Jenny's booked us space in a livestock truck for the ride down the line to Sheffield, and I've made a voice-call I'd planned never to make. We ride the rails in silence; at New Victoria station, I bundle Nirmayi and the Kid into a pedal-taxi.

"Aren't you coming?" she asks.

"Best if I don't. He's all checked in, it's all arranged. I'll come find you both tomorrow morning. Tim'll fix him up, I promise."

"What about you?"

"I'll be fine. Home town, remember? Now go."

She goes, grudgingly. The crew disperse to find lodgings of their own. I find a cheap room just off the Wicker, lay down, stare up at the map of stains on the ceiling, looking for a route out. I consider leaving, rehearse it in my mind: see myself boarding the early milk train for Hull, maybe taking sail for the New Hanseatic.

Instead, I go outside, bundled against the wind from the east. I wander the streets of my past, waiting for one more dawn.

Next day, morning; what was once Royal Hallamshire Hospital. More memories, but I'm too tired to manage them. The crew's all here. Doctor Tim's telling the Kid the score re: his renals.

"You'll never get full function, I'm afraid. 70% optimal for your demographic, maybe; if you were a drinker, you're not any more." Firm but gentle: Tim learned his bedside from doctors who fled the collapse of the NHS. "We dropped in a generic firmware, but we can't do anything about the MAC, so keep them off your uplink bus permanently. The licensee can flash a new firmware remotely, and a new license might not leave you time to cross the mountains and let your boss beg a favour."

The Kid slurs fulsome thanks to Tim, loved-up on morphine and the prospect of more life to come. "Uh'm glad that you an' Elaine are friends, Tim. *So* glad."

"We're not friends," Tim replies. Here it comes. "We were colleagues, once."

"The Surgicals!" The Kid beams, a bright light against the black hole yawning open inside my chest. He's always loved the story. Loves any story; they're all the same to him. "You skated together, right? In the Brexit years?"

Tim just looks up. Straight at me. A look he gave me once before. We're so close to the end, now. I'm so close. Almost as close as I was to Tim.

"No, we never skated together; that's just a story your boss made up. Her brand narrative, if you like: the Sheffield Surgicals, former medical student roller-derby stars turned techno-ronin adventurers after the balkanisation of the health sector!

"But most of the originals quit, of course, or died. No one remembers the old days apart from her, do they? Because *none of you were there*."

He's still looking straight at me. And I'm looking back, and I don't know what my face is saying. I want him to stop there. But I want him to finish it, too.

And he does. Looks around at all the others, then back at me. "So none of you know it's all lies," he says.

The Kid's face folds up in pantomime sorrow. "Every story needs a little bit of fiction," he starts.

Tim snaps, and something inside me snaps at the same time. The last thread holding the mask on, maybe. "Sheffield Surgicals was never a fucking roller derby team, OK? It was a private medical research start-up. The NHS folded half way through our training, so most of us took private sector work – frontline care, palliative, subscription A&E. There was little research work going, and what there was, was dodgy. But ambition doesn't care much for dodginess, does it?"

"Some of it's true," I hear myself saying. "I *did* play roller derby."

"No, hang on a minute," says the Kid. "She quit her course when the NHS folded–"

"–and then spent three years project-managing a manufactory interface implant that left its volunteer test subjects with permanent psychotic dysmorphia. Rest of their lives, locked in their own heads, utterly convinced that their body is actually a SMT pick-and-place machine or fuck knows what else. She had the grace to confess at the inquest, at least. I'll give her that.

"But don't fall for the rest of it. Elaine Stainless doesn't exist. The Sheffield Surgicals have never been anything but a way for a defrocked medical researcher to pretend she never screwed up. It may look like a business to you, but it's really a sop to her guilt."

It's all true. I don't need to hear it again. I walk out of the ward as Tim tells the rest of it, out into the street.

The endorsement the company put on my public profile was the best reference a med-tech student could dream of, and ensured I'd never work in legitimate medicine again for as long as I lived; that was the end of Elaine Halfway. Elaine Stainless took her place a little later, after my old derby team folded, leaving me lumbered with the continuity accounts of one failed business, and control over the registered domains and brand identity of another. I put two and two together, and convinced everyone they saw a four.

And this is the end of Elaine Stainless, it seems. I thought I was helping those I'd harmed before, somehow – that I was making amends. I still think that now, if I'm honest. It's not like there's anything else I can do. Your backstory always gets you in the end.

I can't let it end there, though. Not like this. This isn't just my story, after all.

One by one, my crew come out in silence and join me on the wall outside the hospital – all but the Kid, of course.

"I'm sorry," I tell them.

Beside me, Nirmayi shrugs. "We all knew anyway." She takes my hand in hers.

"Even the Kid?" I ask.

"Well, no, but he's over the moon right now. He just got to be part of the denouement of a twenty year story! Keeps asking Tim to find him an agent."

I smile. The expression feels like it doesn't belong on my face, like a poorly fitted dust-mask.

"Maybe we should all find one," I say.

Or maybe, just for once, I should wait for someone to find me first.

Between Nine and Eleven

Adam Roberts

:1:

Diplomatic efforts had failed, and we were officially at war with the Trefoil alien culture. War is never pleasant, however unavoidable it sometimes becomes. But one of the things that blurs the edge of war's unpleasantness is victory. We enjoyed victory after victory, sweet as honey. Soon enough were closing in on the Trefoil homeworld.

Why did diplomacy fail? There were ways in which our view of the cosmos aligned with theirs. But then again there were ways in which the human assumptions about things and the Trefoil assumptions were so radically at odds that it was simply impossible for us to communicate at all, let alone reach a compromise. Like us, the Trefoil were a social species, and there were broad emotional parallels – their versions of love and aggression appear to have been more-or-less equivalent emotions to ours – as well as some surprising specifics: the concepts of Answegen Geschichtlichkeit and Geworfenheit all made perfect sense to the Trefoil, it seems. But other concepts, like mutual advantage, creativity, logic, meant nothing at all to them.

Their attacks on Human Space were very hard to predict, and therefore hard to defend against. For that reason, I suspect, they underestimated our ability to fight and win.

My name is Ferrante, and I was in command of the warship Centurion 771. This is what happened when our ship and a sister ship called Samurai 10 pressed our attack on a damaged Trefoil Supership designated ET 13-40. ET is shorthand for Enemy Target.

:2:

Centurion and *Samurai* came out of warp together and coordinated our initial firesweep on the ET. About one in five Trefoil ships can be captured – sometimes apparently important craft, flagships even, sometimes trivial little spacetugs. The rest will self-destruct rather than be taken. What criterion determines, for the Trefoil, which kind of ship is too valuable to fall into human hands … well, nobody has been able to work that out.

We were half a light year from β Cygni, the star's red blob clearly visible on our screen without need of magnification. The Trefoil Supership had fallen out of warp, presumably on account of its internal damage: the crazy ziggurat of its hull was ruptured in a hundred places, and weird entrails (cables? tentacles?) trailed from every breach. Since every individual Trefoil ship is designed according to a different template we couldn't be sure of the internal composition of this particular one. Most Trefoil craft possessed three command centres, and it looked likely that the baobab-shaped excrescence on the side of the craft was one of those. We concentrated fire, and scratched red-brown furrows over the hull, everting the inward spaces of its bridge. If that's what it was.

We thought we had her, but then she twisted and fell out of existence, reappearing in orbit half a light year away. Must have had a last squirt of warp capacity in her engines. It was an easy matter to follow her and we repeated our attack mode. The huge craft was in orbit around a taupe and yellow gas giant, sinking into the upper atmosphere. For a moment I wondered if she would crash down into the world and so escape us by destroying herself. But she deployed a filigree web, and we realised she was scooping.

Well: we could stop that easily enough. Both ships manoeuvred, and targeted. The battle was seconds away from being won.

Then *Samurai* exploded: a stutter of blue-white light, a soundless crunching inward, twisting the main hull like a rag being wrung and then there was nothing of the starship except debris spiralling and hurtling.

:3:

At exactly that moment the link went down, and I was no longer mentally connected to the rest of the crew. I came out of telspace gasping, as if cold water had been thrown in my face.

The Centurion shuddered, and one of our cannons overheated and melted itself loose of its bearings. The bridge screens lit up with error messages. The warp went offline. One thruster fired and the other stalled, and we were spinning. The failure of warp meant that inertial controls sagged and gave way, and we were all crushed against the sides of our harnesses.

I'd been in telspace with my crew for so long, it took palpable effort to dredge their actual names from my memory. "Modi," I yelled – my voice hoarse with unuse. "Cancel that thruster!"

She was already doing so, and stabilising the craft, but then the counter-thrust sputtered out. We were still spinning, although not at so crushing a velocity.

No telspace meant the manual operation of the ship. I looked at my hands, palms down, palms up, and tried to place them on the command screen. But there was something wrong with my hands. More than wrong, there was something monstrous about them. Something… blasphemous, almost. I looked at them again and I began to scream.

:4:

I've served with Modi for over a year, first on the *Broadsword 27* and then the *Centurion* – my first command, although the consensual nature of the telspace makes the concept of command much less hierarchical than it might once have been. In the Big Wing Battle at Alpha Scorpii internal fires had scarred my face and torso, and burned away three of the fingers from Modi's left hand, leaving her a puckered crabclaw thumb-and-index. She'd tried an artificial hand with four plasmetal fingers and an opposable plasmetal thumb, but the interface had never quite gelled for her and there was a lag between her willing something and her prosthetic acting. For that reason she tended not to wear it.

That fact saved everybody's life.

:5:

There were four of us on the craft, and one other – me, let's say. Captain. A standard crew. Han killed herself within the first five minutes of the… of whatever it was that happened to the ship (she pressed herself against the glowing-hot flank of the gun-compartment and died screaming). Shabti and Kellermann became catatonic, the former singing a nursery song over and over in a scratchy, high-pitched voice.

Modi got to me before I could self-harm in any way. She took hold of my head, and forced me to look into her eyes. Without my hands in plain view, I felt the terror ebbing away. But there was something – I couldn't say way – profoundly awry with the universe as a whole. The Centurion shuddered and bucked, and error messages blinked and flashed on every screen on every surface. The main screen showed the Trefoil ship, pulling up now from its orbital gas sweep and drawing its scoop back into its main body. Soon enough it would turn and bear down upon us.

"Ferrante," Modi yelled, right in my face. "Ferrante. They will be on us in minutes."

"Minutes," I gasped.

"We need to pull the ship together. Pull *ourselves* together. We still have nine cannon."

"Nine cannon," I repeated. "Yes." There was something comforting in that thought. But, the sense of wrongness persisted. "Something is very wrong," I told Modi.

"I feel it too," she agreed. "But we have to get a grip."

The word *grip* made me glance back down at my hands, and the terror welled up again. I began screaming for a second time.

Modi was a quick thinker. She pulled off her top and wrapped it around my hands. "Ferrante," she said. "We have to *act*."

I was gasping. I was finding it hard to breathe. The topography of the bridge seemed to twist and slip around me in weird ways. "Oh," I said. "Oh – oh – oh."

:6:

Cygni is a binary system: a fat red giant and a tiny, bright little blue star – beta is the bigger. There are some Jupiter-sized gas giants, and a whole lot of dwarf planets and fragments and meteorites. The proximity warning sounded and Modi dabbled at a screen to confirm the zapping of the offending rocklet. But then it sounded again, and again, and the chances that so many asteroids were on a collision course were so minute that it could only mean the system was fried. I tried to breathe, deep, and get a grip. Slowly I drew my right hand out from beneath the covering cloth. I didn't like looking at it, but it didn't offend basic reason in the way that staring at both my hands did. I tried contacting the rest of the crew, dispersed about the ship, but the system told me that Han was dead, and the other two unresponsive.

"Something," I said. "The Trefoil did something."

"It's a weapon," said Modi. "I just don't see what kind."

"Whatever it is, it destroyed the *Samurai* and has caused –" I looked around at the flickering screens – "a whole mass of malfunctions and problems for us." Some shred of soldiery reasserted itself in my mind. I was supposed to be in charge. "We'll have to close with the ET and fire on her manually. I don't know if we can trust the AI to target the cannon."

"What do crews say when they're not in the telspace? *Aye aye*, is it?"

"We've still got nine cannon," I said. That fact should have reassured me, but instead it made me obscurely uneasy.

So we wrestled with the ship via the glitchy manual interface, and the thrusters fired. Warp came online again, and the inertial balancing flashed on, off, on, off. Then the warp went down. The whole ship began to shake violently. I felt sharp, stabbing pains in my fingers and toes. This was the moment Kellermann died. He owned an antique cigarette lighter, which in turn contained a small amount of butane. This exploded with enough force to kill him and breach the hull. The reason it exploded had to do with the arrangement of protons in the butane nucleus.

In retrospect I can say: thank heavens we weren't carrying any neon.

"Pull back," I said, and together Modi and I grappled with the interface to bring the Centurion out of attack mode. The more distance we put between ourselves and the ET, the calmer the craft became.

"I don't know what it *is*," Modi said. "I don't see how they're doing that – it's like a magic spell, like some voodoo sphere of malignity around the ET."

"We've still got nine cannons," I reminded her. "We can still shoot at her. True we won't be at an optimum distance to …"

"Why do you say *still*?" Modi asked.

"What?"

"You say *we've still got nine cannon*. You say that because we're supposed to have more."

"That's right."

"How many cannon are we fitted with? How many are we *supposed* to have?"

I could not say. I mean that strictly: the answer to that question couldn't be said.

:7:

Modi scribbled a number on her pad with her forefinger. "What do you call that?"

I looked at the number. I recognised it, but its name slipped from my head. "Nine-and-four?" I offered.

"That's not *it*, though, is it?"

"No," I agreed, pained. "Six-and-seven? But that's now how we say it, is it. I want to say *three*, but it's clearly not three."

She wrote another number. "And what about that?"

I looked at it. "It's a four. But it's more than a four, isn't it. It's a lot more than four, actually."

"It's four and something else. It's the something else that's … I don't get it."

"What is it? The number I mean?"

"It's the designation of our ET," Modi said. As soon as she said that I recognised it. Of course!

"Ferrante," she asked. "What's our ship called?"

"Centurion." The name came from my mouth like a bark of gibberish. I knew what Modi was going to ask next, and it was: *what does that word mean*? And I knew that I wouldn't be able to answer that question. Although it was in my head that *I used to know*. Once upon a time. It had something to do with war. But what did it have to do with war? It was a non-word. It was an impossible word.

:8:

"The ET is bringing about," Modi sang. "It's using its scoop harvest to boost itself towards us. Unless we can get warp working again, it will be on us in …" and she stopped, and looked puzzled. "I had a calculation of the time …"

Since this was the amount of time we had left alive, I was eager to find out what it the number was.

"Let's say, in nine minutes," she said. "Between nine and eleven minutes."

The ship was starting to shudder again. Modi saying that, giving voice to that phrase *between nine and eleven*, brought the terror shaking back into my mind. I wish she hadn't said that. Because there was nothing between nine and eleven, and at the same time there was something between nine and eleven and the fact of this thing being and not-being, its hideous elusiveness, like a monster in the shadows, was inexpressibly ghastly to me. I began weeping, tears washing down my face. And it wasn't because of the pain in my hands and feet.

:9:

From this point on I was useless. Worse than useless. I was very specifically starting to lose my mind. Modi was more focussed. She managed to get the main AI – hiccoughing and prone to weird snags and cutaways though it was – to target the cannons. The Trefoil Supership swung down upon us and I began to sing a top-C and slap the top of my head with my hands and Modi *fired* and

:11:

As to why the Trefoil had not deployed their 'device' – this super-weapon – before… Well, there is no consensus. It might be that they only very recently developed it. Conceivably ET 13-40 was a research and development platform. Then again, perhaps the Trefoil have had their 'device' for a long time and simply haven't deployed it for incomprehensible alien reasons of their own. The capture of a still-working model of the device, and its rapid adaptation and redeployment by Human Forces, brought the war very quickly to an end. Reprogrammed to blank out 3, the device completely shuts down Trefoil computers, designed as they are on a base-3 system of trits. It also causes individual Trefoilers to suffer severe internal physical damage and to degrade all triangular components. Neon, which has an atomic number between nine and eleven, is rare on a starship, but lithium – atomic number 3 – is much more common, and the presence of any at all caused instant destruction. It seems likely that the existence of some small quantity of neon on board the *Samurai* caused its immediate destruction. I've no idea why that ship would be carrying neon, but starships are large and complex things.

Of course, I recommended Modi for decoration, and stand by my recommendation. She didn't exactly figure out what the device was doing to us but she had enough of an inkling, and was able to act. She grasped that it had something to do with the eradication of the quantity between nine and eleven.

"I'm guessing," she told me afterwards, "that the Trefoil understood enough about us to know our default mathematics is base-10 and so they erroneously assumed that our computing would be decenary. The fact that we developed binary computing is what saved us. Our AI was certainly confused, but still functioning."

"It's still hard for me to understand," I told her. "How can a device eliminate a number – from the universe, I mean? Surely that number just *is* a feature of the way things are?"

"Depends how you look at it," she replied. "We warp spacetime to travel faster than light, so we have good practical knowledge that spacetime is deformable. Say that the deep structure of the universe is information – is maths, effectively. If we can alter that deep structure to make the distance between stars temporarily shorter, then it's not hard to imagine the Trefoil finding a way to alter the deep structure in a different way. Temporarily to suppress ten from the fabric of things."

I shuddered. Modi is still happy to use the word itself. For me just saying the word brought the tendrils of nightmare to the tender parts of my memory. Like many who experienced the Trefoil 'device' in those last, desperate (on their part) days of the war, I continue to refer, superstitiously, to *between-nine-and-eleven.*

"Amazing, really," Modi mused, "that deploying the device didn't entirely *undo* the fabric of reality within its sphere of influence. Surprisingly tough, reality. There's genuine inertia and persistence to reality it turns out."

"We don't know how long it would last, though. I mean, if the Trefoil device were deployed for long stretches of time. Or over a wide area."

But that's the thing about Modi: she's an optimist. "Oh, I think reality would adjust. Indeed, who's to say it hasn't happened before?"

"Before?"

Modi laughed. "Ancient alien races, fighting a war across the galaxy – who knows? What if one of them deployed something similar to the

Trefoil device? Maybe many times? Maybe whole numbers were eradicated for ever. Maybe there once was a number between nine and ten, or between one and two – I don't mean fractions or decimals. I mean a whole lost number. What if reality shook itself and then adjusted to the new, out-of-whack logic?"

"That's crazy talk," I grumbled.

"Maybe it is," and she laughed. "Maybe."

Ajdenia

Natalia Theodoridou

It's cold and sunless in the tunnels. Bart is sweeping the walls vigorously, trying to warm himself up inside his stiff uniform. He scans every crack he comes across for contaminants, seals it, then moves on, sweeping and scanning, scanning and sweeping. The job is repetitive; he's heard of people who've been driven mad by the repetition of it, lost their grip. But Bart doesn't mind. If only it weren't so cold. If only there were some sun in the tunnels. But of course there isn't.

"Sun is precious, sun is rare," he whispers behind his mouth cover. "Sun is for the worthy." *And for Ajdenia*, he adds silently.

He tries to recall the warmth of sun on his skin. He almost succeeds.

And the worthiest of all get to live above, showered in sunlight.

He finishes the length of tunnel number 8 and enters the Ra intersection. All the intersections are named after long lost deities associated with the sun. The next one is called Helios. Then there's Tonatiuh, Solar Logos, Surya. Bart knows them all, every name, every inch. He always works methodically. He's good at what he does. He's worth five minutes in the filter room, under the sun. Maybe next year he'll be worth five and a half. Or six, even.

There's another employee in tunnel number 9. Bart takes a moment to observe them. Their uniforms are identical. Their mouth masks, their goggles, their hoods. He wonders what that person looks like underneath. He wonders what they are worth. Do they also spend a few moments each day trying to remember the feeling of sun on their skin? Are they about to lose their mind?

He continues his work on the intersection, sweeping and scanning, scanning and sweeping. The next time he looks, the other person has disappeared behind a turn in their tunnel.

Bart has finished an entire section of wall when the alarms go off, ear-piercing. The ceiling lights switch to the highest setting, bright, almost blinding. Bart puts down his scanner, sealer and sweeper and heads towards the centre of the intersection, as he's supposed to. He's nearly there when a girl comes running out of tunnel number 7 and bumps into him, almost throwing him off balance. He grabs her arm without thinking, steadies her. Her uniform is torn. She's not wearing a mouth cover. Bart can see her eyes behind her goggles. He would expect them to look frightened, but they are not. There is something else in there. Something bright. It makes Bart think of the sun. It makes him think of Ajdenia.

"What are you doing?" he asks. "You're not supposed to be here."

She brings a finger to her lips. "We can live under the sun, you, me, all of us," she whispers. "They are lying." And then she lets go of him and she's off, running into tunnel number 5.

Bart thinks of following her, but he knows he's not supposed to. He's supposed to stand in the middle of the intersection and wait for the alarms to go silent, for the lights to go back to normal. So that's what he does.

Soon, a pair of guards come out of tunnel number 7, helmets shiny and batons in hand.

"Which way did she go?" one of them asks.

"Who?" Bart blurts out, and immediately receives a blow to the ribs from the guard's baton.

"Your cooperation will be rewarded," the other guard says. "Two more minutes under the filter will be added to your next payment, if the information you provide proves correct." His tone implies that something will be taken away if not, but the exact nature of it is left vague.

Two whole minutes of light, Bart thinks. *Two whole minutes of sun.*

As if noticing his hesitation, the guard who struck him scans Bart's forehead, proving they'll keep their word, one way or another. "Come on," he says. "Spit it out!"

Could it be true?

Bart raises his hand and points towards tunnel number 5.

Bart is in the filter room, waiting for his payment. He's thought of the girl in the Ra intersection often, ever since they day he found himself in her way. He's thought about what may have happened to her, and about her words. Could they really live under the sun, without slaving away in the tunnels for a few moments under the protection of the filters? *She was probably one of those who lost their mind in the tunnels*, he assured himself in the end, *one of those who don't know how to deal with the cold and the repetition, how to make themselves worthier than they are*. Bart shuffles in his chair. *And if not...* but as the thought crosses his mind, the time finally comes, and the lid of the filter room opens, letting in the sun. Bart unzips his side pocket and brings out the plastic pot with the pink flower growing in it. He raises it towards the light. "Drink up, Ajdenia," he whispers.

He watches the pink petals shine against the sun until the lid comes on again.

To Catch a Comet

Sylvia Spruck Wrigley

From: Samantha Schandin
To: Greg Smith
Regarding: Asteroid Strike

Dear Greg,
Attached please find our revised projections regarding the inbound asteroid based on newly collected data from Observatorio del Teide. The results have been verified by the Astrophysical Unit here in Cambridge.

As you can see, it's more bad news. You haven't sent any updates lately and I am hoping there's no delays on the intercept mission as we have only a few months until impact.

Please get in touch and let me know the status.

Samantha

From: postmaster@europa.eu
To: Samantha.Schandin
Automated Response

I am sorry to inform you that Greg Smith no longer works for the department of special projects within the European Institute of Innovation and Technology. You may wish to get in touch with another project department regarding this. Your email *Regarding: Asteroid Strike* has been deleted unread.

From: Samantha Schandin
To: European Institute of Innovation and Technology

Asteroid 2007 QS August 2016

Dear Mr Peeters,
I'm with the Near-Earth Objects research project. Can you please tell me who is leading the AEGIS intercept project regarding Asteroid 2007 QS? It's urgent.

From: European Institute of Innovation and Technology
To: Samantha Schandin
Regarding: Asteroid 2007 QS August 2016

Dear Samantha
I regret to inform you that the AEGIS project has been cancelled due to funding issues. If I can help further, please let me know.
Thomas Peeters

From: Samantha Schandin
To: European Institute of Innovation and Technology
Regarding: Asteroid 2007 QS August 2016

Dear Mr Peeters,
I'm not sure if you are aware, but the AEGIS project was an intercept mission against a meteorite which is due to impact this August. This isn't a research project but a matter of a defence project which has been ongoing for the past four years. Can you please tell me who to speak to in order to get the project back on track? There are lives at stake.
Dr Samantha Schandin
NEOWatch

From: European Institute of Innovation and Technology
To: Samantha Schandin
Regarding: Asteroid 2007 QS August 2016

Dear Samantha
I'm afraid the AEGIS project was cancelled three weeks ago and the team has already been disbanded. It's out of my hands. Have you considered contacting the military?
Thomas Peeters

From: Dr Samantha Schandin
For the attention of the European Defence Agency
Regarding Imminent Meteorite Strike August

Dear Sirs,
I am trying to find the right person to speak to regarding Asteroid 2007 QS, a meteorite which is inbound to Northern Europe. Our analysis has shown that the impact site will be land-based and cause considerable devastation. We believe that the most likely point of impact is Luxembourg if the asteroid is not intercepted.

The EU-sponsored AEGIS mission was the first line of defence against the destruction which this meteorite will cause and this project has now been cancelled. We urgently need to meet with you to discuss this situation and look at how to defend against this incoming meteorite.

Dr Samantha Schandin
NEOWatch

From: European Defence Agency
To: Dr Schandin @ NEOWatch
Imminent Meteorite Strike August

There is no appropriate department within the European Defence Agency for missile intercepts of near-earth objects and Luxembourg is not a high priority target.

I looked it up and there's no confirmed records of any human ever dying in a meteorite impact. How bad can it be?

Tony Martins

From: Dr Samantha Schandin
Tony Martins, European Defence Agency
Imminent Meteorite Strike August

Dear Mr Martins,
I'm not sure you understand the urgency of this issue. Asteroid 2007 QS will cause considerable devastation. Although my department's work has shown that the impact site will most likely be Luxembourg, this is not an exact science. Perhaps it will be easier to gain the attention that we need to deal with this by citing Brussels or Paris as likely strike sites, as there are significant staff in both locations.

Dr Samantha Schandin
NEOWatch

From: European Defence Agency
To: Dr Schandin @ NEOWatch
Imminent Meteorite Strike August

Quite frankly, a 30 metre rock is not an issue for the European Defence Agency. If you have some sort of proof that the rock is sentient or launched by sentient beings, we would be very interested in hearing further. Perhaps you should contact the European Space Agency to see if they can help you with your issue.

I am sorry that I am not able to help you further.

Tony Martins

From: Dr Samantha Schandin
Tony Martins, European Defence Agency
Regarding Imminent Meteorite Strike August

Dear Mr Martins
It is not *my* issue. NeoWatch is three dozen people who have spent the last four years analysing data on Asteroid 2007 QS. We have coordinated with observatories and astrophysics departments around the world who have all confirmed our findings. We have updated our website with a factsheet about the asteroid in order to help you highlight the issue.

An asteroid with a diametre of 7 metres would have the equivalent kinetic energy of the atomic bomb dropped on Hiroshima. Over one thousand people were injured by the Chelyabinsk meteor airburst event over Russia in 2013.

Dr Samantha Schandin
NEO-Watch

From: European Defence Agency
To: Dr Schandin @ NEOWatch
Imminent Meteorite Strike August

Understood, but this damage would be specific to Luxembourg, is that right?

Tony

From: Dr Samantha Schandin
For the attention of the EU Space Department
Imminent Meteorite Crash

I'm with Near-Earth Objects research project in Cambridge and I've been tasked with finding the right person to speak to regarding Asteroid 2007 QS, a meteorite which will impact the earth in just eight weeks. Possible crash sites include Brussels and Paris. We expect significant localised consequences.

The EU-sponsored AEGIS mission was planning an intercept but the project has been inaccountably cancelled and we now have no defence. Can I speak to someone within the EU Space Department urgently about coordinating a response?

Dr Samantha Schandin
NEOWatch

From: EU Space Department
To: Dr Samantha Schandin
Regarding: Imminent Meteorite Crash

Dear Dr Schandin
Thank you for your email. I am afraid to say there is not anything we can do to help. As you are no doubt aware, a mission of this size would take at least one year to put into place and even if there were enough time, we have neither the staff nor the funding to launch an intercept craft capable of withstanding the meteorite and taking it off track. There is also significant risk to our reputation if this mission were to be undertaken and then be unsuccessful.

Elisabeth Jacobs
EU Space Department

From: Dr Samantha Schandin
Council of the European Union
URGENT: Imminent Meteorite Crash

To whom it may concern,
I am Dr Samantha Schandin, an astrophysicist employed by NEOWatch in Cambridge. We analyse Potentially Hazardous Asteroids. An asteroid is heading for Northern Europe and will crash into the Earth next month.

I have assembled a petition of 1,742 scientists and researchers who all confirm that this asteroid is an immediate hazard and will create a one to two kilometre crater on impact. The most likely impact sites are Brussels and Paris.

We have contacted staff representing the European Institute of Innovation and Technology, European Defence Agency and the European Space Department and am unable to find anyone who will take responsibility for coordinating a defence. Can we have your support?

Dr Samantha Schandin
NEOWatch

From Jean-Luc Vasseur
To: Samantha Schandin
Regarding: URGENT: Imminent Meteorite Crash

Dear Samantha,
We recommend you come to our next meeting on the 17th of July and see if you can find a representative who is interested in your cause. I have attached a document with travel information and local hotels. We look forward to seeing you.

Jean-Luc

From: Dr Samantha Schandin
Jean-Luc Valais, Council of the European Union
CRASH AND BURN

Dear Mr Vasseur,
My entire department went to Brussels for a meeting and there were more translators there than MEPs. This was a completely wasted effort. Asteroid 2007 QS is incoming straight for us right now and no one seems to be able get the EU to react. We're running out of time here! PLEASE HELP ME FIND THE RIGHT CONTACT!

Dr Samantha Schandin
NEOWatch

From: Dr Samantha Schandin
Jean-Luc Valais, Council of the European Union
Regarding: CRASH AND BURN

Dear Mr Vasseur
It is now only four weeks until impact! I understand that you are originally from Paris which is one of the likely impact destinations. Are you really willing to allow what is effectively a large bomb land your home town and do nothing?
Dr Samantha Schandin
NEOWatch

European Parliament
Dr Schandin
Regarding: CRASH AND BURN

Dear Dr Schandin,
Paris is empty in August anyway, so I don't think that's of particular concern.

However, I have forwarded your emails to the department most likely to be interested in the situation. I hope you are able to resolve this.
Jean-Luc

Department of Geology and Mineral Exploration
Dr Samantha Schandin
NEOWatch
FW: Regarding: CRASH AND BURN

Dear Dr Schandin,
Your information was forwarded to me by Jean-Luc Vasseir of the Council of the European Union.

Could you please specify the exact details of the meteorite, including metal composition and other things so that we can correctly identify the value? It is possible that the Belgian Department of Geology and Mineral Exploration (BDGME) is interested in this occurrence. If, as you say, the meteorite will definitely land in European territory, then we are definitely interested in more information which will allow us to recover the meteorite after impact.

Kristina Krinov

Department of Geology and Mineral Exploration

From: European Institute of Innovation and Technology
To: Samantha Schandin - NEOWatch
Regarding: Asteroid 2007 QS August 2016

Dear Samantha
This is a follow-up email as a part of our quality control to ensure that queries to our department are correctly handled. Were you able to resolve your issues regarding Asteroid 2007 QS August 2016?

Thomas Peeters

Dear Thomas,
I have left NEOWatch and relocated to the Indian Space Research Organisation in Bengaluru.

I have come to the conclusion that Brussels could only be improved by a meteor strike.

Kind regards

Samantha

PS: I appreciate that at least you took the time to check back with me. Have you considered taking a holiday? I'd recommend the third week of August. Head South.

How to Grow Silence from Seed

Tricia Sullivan

Rob has never been so happy. As he runs up the stairs of the community lab on Romford Road his boots make the metal steps resound like gongs. He is fresh from a finance meeting. Even though it's after eleven pm and most of the crew will be in the pub, he knows Injala will still be working.

Except that Injala isn't there. At her station a child crouches on the floor, covered in emergents. They look like worms. He recoils. He stares for some seconds before he realises that this is Injala herself. She is shrunken and distressed out of all proportion to the problems Rob knows how to deal with. When he bends over her she grabs hold of his forearms with a bitter strength, her young eyes nightshade with fear.

"The walls are trying to kill me," she says in a tear-guttered voice. "The walls have a mind and it's trying to shrink me to a point and then bang me to a negative dimension. Look!"

She points. Up in the high industrial windows curl Injala's augmented vines, their leaves gilded by streetlights. All around, the pock-marked walls of her workspace are the same as ever, their paint spewing a cycle of news and entertainment feeds because she has been working on the ambient effects of mainstream media culture.

Her friends also spill bright and unreal from the walls, expressing increasingly concerned enquiries for her well-being.

"Injala? Do you need someone to sit with you until it passes?"

"Quit running your cogs, baby. Take a break."

"Remember, it's only information. It's not real, Injala. You can pull out any time."

The friends' distant panic makes Rob feel oppressed. He shuts them down. In a thin film over every other data layer, Injala's work pops and fizzes along the walls with what looks and sounds like noise: the activity of the plants she has been training. No one but Injala understands them: she has laid her cogs open to them.

"There's your trouble right there," he mutters. He should have seen this coming.

He glances around the loft as if expecting to find a helpful fairy godmother to take over from here. At the far end of the deserted communal space, Abdul is doing some old-school recreational DNA hacking, oblivious. Rob looks back at his girlfriend. She used to be so wild. Her ideas used to take his breath away. Who knows what lives in her flesh now? Interfacing with plant AIs has turned her into an illegal mess of terror, irrationality and snot. She has become a phenomenon wholly beyond his scope.

"Come on, Inj. Snap out of it. I want to tell you about the meeting I had. About my visibility project. Our project."

He says "our" more in the hope that recalling her to the days when they worked together will cheer her up than because he means it (her only involvement was to suggest a modelling technique). Then he notices the crawling things slipping from her skin to the fabric of his shirt, melting into him with hallucinatory ease. He jerks away.

"Love is a predator," she said when they first hooked up at Imperial. She was like a maze, a series of narrowings of choices that led around corners that led to him losing himself in her. Her sensory appetites coupled with a seeming disinterest in him – her endless fascination with everything but him – made him believe there was something *to* her. He believed her a treasure vault of sorts, a person to be kept and encircled and unlocked over time.

Rob now realises he has unlocked a nutjob.

"Did your plants make these emergents?"

She shakes her head. "We only made them visible. These influences have been here all this time, but I couldn't see them. Look, they're everywhere… they are in the waves. They've been attacking me and I didn't even know it. They are attacking all of us, all the time!"

"This has gone far enough," he says. "Look at yourself. It can't continue."

He drags a ladder from the corner of the loft and puts it up to the windows. He fancies that the plants are snarling at him even though they can't move. They are smart enough to make him nervous with their ability to receive information out of the air, interpret meaning. Injala has been developing this species for six years. Her thesis shows that plant filtration can reveal hitherto unrecognized structures in the bombardment of signals from commercial entertainment. *"Dangerous ideas,"* she wrote, *"fly stealth underneath ordinary signals. Some of these can be shown to be the product of adroit manipulation by advertisers, but others are emergent. The latter are more sophisticated than anything the designers can dream up, and they appear to act volitionally."*

Privately, she speaks of demons.

Perhaps because her tendency to self-experiment has resulted in a growing dossier of mental illness, Injala has failed to convince any universities that the results of her self-inflicted experiments are unbiased. "Maybe if she hadn't drunk the Kool-Aid she'd be taken seriously," one American department head bluntly remarked. When Rob hinted that Injala could go to work for one of the ad agencies who were keen to use emergents, everyone in the bootstrap lab rose up and came at him as if he'd suggested the murder of a thousand kittens. Never mind. Let the freelancers have their little part-time projects. Rob is going to be large and he only wants the same for Injala.

He tugs the nearest plant from its hook. "Inj, these influences are abstract. They can't hurt you if you can't see them. Just come out of augmentation and they won't bother you."

"No!" she screams, and even Abdul looks up in alarm. "Rob, don't!"

Gripping the pot in one hand, he opens the window with the other. Her hysteria is getting to him. He just wants to make it stop. He will throw them all out, smash the plants on the pavement below. He doesn't care if they are sentient.

She scrabbles up the ladder behind him and she seizes the trailing vines.

"Please. Don't hurt them."

He presses down on the urge to throw the fucking plant. In the same way you press down on a fresh wound. Stop the bleeding. He replaces the plant on its hook and climbs down. He has to be the better man.

"Everything okay, guys?" Abdul calls.

There is a mild struggle between the two of them, faintly sexual. Most of the crawling things stop at his clothes, but the ones that touch his skin make him shudder. Everything about her freaks him out, even the child-smell of her dirty hair.

"I'm getting you to hospital."

"No."

"Yes."

"No."

He puts his hands on her shoulders, determined to calm her down. That's when her head falls off.

He fumbles it like a basketball, startlingly heavy and bone-hard hot. The cushy softness of her face plops into his hands like a leaden sponge. He tries not to stick his fingers in her eyes, but one of them falls out nonetheless. It looks back at him from the floor.

He probably screams.

The rest of her body is clawing at him, snatching at the head as if it suspects him of trying to steal it. Rob notices that there is no arterial bleeding even though he can see the severed ends of the vessels and the stumps of neck tendons. He somehow puts the head back on her neck but then she sets up an unholy wailing. The sound of her drives him away. He runs out of the building and onto the street. There, he is sick.

"It's okay," he reminds himself. "That didn't happen. Did. Not. Happen."

It's obvious she somehow induced him to shift levels – or the plants did – and he feels like a tool. He is too experienced with augmentation to be tricked into dropping out the bottom of reality without notice. Still, the neural effect is convincing enough that his terrified body won't allow him to return to the lab.

He hangs around for a while. He can see Abdul's shadow moving back and forth past the lit windows. No ambulance comes. She's probably all right.

He pushes off.

Rob will write Injala a vague letter, apologising for the breakup because he knows she will blame him even though he hasn't done anything wrong. "I have backers," he'll write. "If you were yourself right now, I know you would want me to go for this. It's going to be large."

Rob doesn't actually know how she would feel about his project being funded while hers is not, but his cognitive dissonance containment capacity has already maxed out; he must take his former girlfriend's approval as given. As for the emergents that cling to his clothes, he will capture them and keep them sealed for months before finding the courage to investigate. Only when his own project fails and the investors drop his contract will he get curious enough to check out the apps that her plants have extracted from the maelstrom of information on the waves.

At which point fame and money will be his, like loyal dogs.

After Rob has gone, the little girl crawls into the emergency washdown and rinses the blood off with her chubby, competent young hands. Emergents generated by her own plants have rooted in her and sprout from the backs of her knuckles and behind her ears.

"They are protecting me," she tells Abdul, who hovers with a towel and a cup of tea.

"Why are you so small?" he asks. "I feel I should call your mother."

"Never mind that," she says in her high voice. "I need you to help me make something. Please."

Abdul works on Injala's project for several nights running. He wants to get it just right. When he is done, they carry her most important plants downstairs and put them in a stolen shopping trolley whose immobilisers have been snapped off. Injala hugs Abdul goodbye and pushes the loaded trolley little by little all the way to the Dartford Crossing. She gets older rapidly as she walks. By the time she encounters other castaways and riffraff in the dead zone between Dartford and Erith, she is a woman again, and the foetus in her belly is well-established. There are supple, shining leaves in her hair.

I find a butcher shop under the A206 bridge. The Butcher will cut out your cogs for you, no questions asked. It's necessary because the waves are unregulated out here in whackjob land. No price plans, no premium content. All you get is noise and ubiquitous advertising, and occasional illegal science experiments being carried out on the inhabitants without their knowledge. Waves bombard you mercilessly. People come here when they've fallen out the bottom of the economic shopping bag. If they stay, they invariably cut out their cogs.

There is plenty of empty ground. I move in beside the Butcher but politely decline his offer of a neighbour's discount. I set up my plants on nearby land, using the dead air under the bridge as protection from the waves when the demons start to get to me. I watch the Butcher remove people's cogs to be sold on or recycled. I watch people stumble away from this procedure damaged, bereft.

Back in the real world, the procedure we endure is written off as an information-age variant of self-harm. Many people aren't susceptible to the dangers on the waves; consequently, accepted logic says people like me must be imagining things. We are inherently off-kilter. The bombs that go off inside our heads aren't planted by anything malevolent; they're just self-destruct devices that originate within us.

The things that live in the walls attack you in the middle of the night, and in the morning when your injuries become visible people say, "What have you done to yourself?"

It's like when a little kid makes another little kid punch himself with his own hand and then says, "Why are you hitting yourself?"

It's like that.

"You think the world rejects you but that's not so," my mother said to me, when my work using plants as receivers first started making me paranoid. She said this as if it were some great insight, like she'd been up all night thinking about it and if she didn't say it, the whole idea would evaporate. "Really you're the one who rejects the world. You're like a transplant patient. You want to live, but when you get this foreign body inside you, you can't cope and you start to attack yourself. It's probably a new disease, something they'll find a name for and twenty years from now it will be a syndrome with a Latin name, and everybody will understand when I say you have it. But right now I don't know what to tell people."

She said this while putting lettuce in her salad-spinner, pulling the cord, inspecting the results. I sat on a stool at her kitchen counter and examined the scars on my knees. I'd gone over the handlebars of my bike so many times as a child. Never cried at that, but with the plants showing me what's really in the air I was weeping helplessly every other day. On the days I wasn't crying I was breaking up pieces of pavement with a sledgehammer in the empty lot behind the community lab.

"Madame Curie died because she was investigating a phenomenon no one could see," I told my mother. "She was killed by invisible things. Her notebooks are still too radioactive to touch."

My mother said, "But don't you be. Don't be too radioactive to touch."

Speaking of mothers. Mir is born seeing and hearing and sensing all I can sense and more. I am terrified for her. As best we can, Abdul and I have equipped her to fight off the things that live in the waves, but I want to do better than that.

I've already taught the plants to make dangerous influences visible. That was the hard part. Now that emergents are visible, I teach the plants to interfere with them, neutralise the dangerous constructs or transform them into something else.

And so the Silence creeps out from beneath the bridge. It spreads. The plants shelter us from the waves, and as they grow they begin to form a quiet zone on the bank by the bridge, above the brackish water and beneath the flight paths of the traffic helicopters. What was waste ground is becoming something new.

The Butcher and I and one of his customers cook noodles over a campfire while Mir squirms in my lap, fascinated by the flames.

"I'll have to branch out into insect farming for protein," he tells me. He complains that the Silence has lost him business, but he's fascinated by what I'm doing. I persuade him to go in with me growing more plants, investing in boosters for the existing trees; they are capable of so much more. We take a small rent from the people who want to shelter in the Silence. I feel good about this, because I know that thanks to the Silence the susceptible can function out here without losing their cogs, and this brings in a slow trickle of income for everybody. A tent community grows up within the Silence.

We are careful to keep it small, beneath notice.

Five-year-old Mir tells me she's finding souls in our marshland. They are runaways, she says. They are lost and dissolute. They seek refuge in the jumble of scrub and mud, drifting on the air until their fragments are trapped by the plants' information filters and reconstituted.

I think about this. I don't know if the souls are real before they come here, or if they accrue out of the processing that the plants do when they neutralise incoming waves. Lost souls roost in the treetops and among the catkins, a by-product of the Silence industry.

Some of them belong to famous people. Mir plants them in the earth to settle them. She seems to know what to do; maybe the plants tell her.

Mir is eight when Karranga shows up in a helicopter. I haven't seen Karranga since university. She is well-dressed and nervous. I can't imagine how she found us. She says she is a journalist and she's aware of my work. I'm not sure I believe this, but I fill a pot with water from a blue extension hose we've diverted from a housing estate. I make tea and we squat outside my yurt at sunset. In the soul garden the plants furl their leaves for darkness.

"Explain it to me," she says. "I want to understand."

I gesture at the flora around us.

"They are intelligent. They receive information out of the air and they can interface digitally. They connect to my cogs and extend my senses. They make the invisible visible. When we link them with the right data-combing software, the plants can identify causal apparati and feedback systems that result in what I call *presences*. Political movements and tactics and yearnings and arguments all have lives of their own even though we think of them as abstract. I can perceive these presences directly, and in the case of hostile presences, I can teach the plants to block their influence on my mind. But to find out what's hostile and damaging, you first have to experience it. That's the ugly part."

"What about Mir? She didn't ask for this life."

"Mir's a new generation. She doesn't need cogs. She can pick up on the waves directly just like a plant, and they protect her instinctively. She's safe here."

I expect Karranga to ask me how that's possible, and I decide I won't mention Abdul's contribution to Mir's biology; but she doesn't seem interested in the *how* of Mir. Instead she says, "You remember Rob? From our Endologies class?"

She acts like she doesn't know I lived with him for three years. She smells of cloves and something more bitter. She stubs her ciggy out in the mud.

"He's large now. Offices in the Strand."

I say nothing.

"He told me he analysed your work. Said he wanted to find out what kind of thing came after you. You know. When you had that breakdown."

I snort. "And it ate him. Right?"

She swings her head from side to side in the way of people who deliver bad news. "He isolated it and made tweaks. Said it was highly intelligent and someone had to control it. Might as well be him, right? He's been leasing it out as a kind of intellectual precision-guided munition."

Smoke in my ears and nostrils. No pain at all in the lost eye, but my gorge rises. Wish I could breathe fire. My skeleton clatters inside my flesh.

"Leasing it to whom?"

"Does it matter? It's got some kind of corporate applications. How to fuck with the head of your enemy type of thing."

I want to say I'll crush him. I'll kill him. I'll unwrite him from history. But that's all nonsense. I can't even bring myself to say his name. I imagine myself 'confronting' him. How I'd slink around and hide, stalk him, wishing all the while I could bring him down with a death ray from my remaining eye. He'd finally catch me at it and I'd break down in tears and he'd take my hand, act all sympathetic and humanitarian. Maybe offer me some pity money before swinging off to lunch with a set of lawyers and a publicist. People would say how sad for her (meaning me).

"He sent you," I say, because it's obvious. Karranga has the grace to squirm.

We both look at Mir, who is squatting in the weeds, talking to them.

"I know," Mir whispers, nodding to her plant friends. *"I saw that, too. It was so funny."*

She places her palms over the seed-tips of the grass, tickling herself. Then she jumps up and runs off, laughing.

"He misses you," Kerranga tries. But you can't lie to me out here. The Silence is my place.

"How did you find us." It's not a question, it's a complaint, and she manages to make her reply sound like an apology.

"His DNA's in Mir. She came up on a routine scan."

I look at her with the eye I don't have anymore. Let her see the dead flesh.

"Fuck you, Karranga," I say. "If he picked up Mir's signal then Mir must have left the Silence. How could that happen? She is always with me."

Almost always.

"How you discipline your kid is not my problem."

Nearby in the mud, Mir has set about playing tug-of-war with a stray dog. I think the rope is actually one of my T-shirts.

I don't say anything for so long that Karranga reaches over and touches my wrist.

"I'm not on his side," she tells me. "I'm here for you, too."

"Tell him he can't have her," I say, dry-eyed. It feels as if Rob has shoved his boot into my teeth, even from afar. Mir and I struggle for every scrap we have. Socialise with broken people. Feels like we're hiding all the time. He has everything he wanted. Now he wants to take Mir? A surge of inchoate feeling rises. I want to puke, want to come, want to hit out. I shake.

"Where can I run? What will happen to my plants? They've started mixing with the local flora. I can't just pick up and go. The people who come here depend on the Silence."

"All he has to do is go to the council and get an order against you, and you'll have to leave," Karranga says. "But listen, Injala. You don't have to keep this quiet. What you're doing, it's rather amazing and people will want to know about it. Why not be proactive, come out of hiding? I'll help you find support for your work."

"I can't go back."

"Why?"

"I'm afraid."

"Of what."

Of what not? The sky, the air, the noises, the interstices of words, the unspoken, the gazes, the emptiness between saccades of my own eye. I know there are things that could slip into those empty spaces and steal my agency. The unwritten, the unsayable, the cracks in the sidewalk.

I don't say any of that. I shrug, but don't say:

The AIs in the air can dismember you pretty much anytime.

I finally manage to say, "It's one thing to make Silence in the middle of unintentional junk noise, because that's all that's out here. Filtering out deliberate attacks in the commercial airspace is another thing. You said it yourself. People like Rob are deliberately making predators and setting them against their enemies at will. I can't expose Mir to that. Look what happened to me."

My teeth are chattering, just thinking about it.

"Stop shaking, Injala," Karranga says fiercely. "Don't collapse. You cannot afford to flinch."

Is she kidding? My whole life is a series of flinches. And retreats. And not showing up. It's who I am.

I train my one eye on her.

"Tell Rob I said no. Just no."

My words are final. Karranga recoils from their force.

"Okay," she relents. "I'll tell him."

Then Mir says, "I want to see my dad."

Mir takes me down by the willows and shows me where to dig up Rob's soul. It's misshapen and lovely and it smells of the bottom of the tide and long afternoons with nothing to do, of the things we never prized when we had them, which retroactively gleam.

Mir squeezes it like a cantaloupe she's testing for ripeness at the market. Her hands on the boundaries of his soul remind me so much of Rob's hands that for a second I feel no gravity and I cannot move or think. Then I gently prise her fingers away.

"Did you go looking for him?" I ask her. As gentle as I can.

She shakes her head.

"His soul just came here," she says. "He didn't want it any more, and it left him."

She swings up into an alder tree, singing.

Kerranga takes us in the helicopter with her. Mir carries the soul in a Tesco bag, and I carry one of my oldest plants in a pot on my lap. For self-protection. This is my first time north of the river since I fled Hackney, and I'm not prepared for the greening of Covent Garden and Aldwych and Charing Cross Road. Buildings are covered in grasses, and walls are thick with moss. Mir presses her face against the cockpit window, foliage standing up stiffly from her shoulders and the backs of her wrists as her plants taste the waves.

"What are you picking up, Mir?" I ask her casually. Yellow-toothed mouths gnaw at my breasts and throat. A litany of hatred pours into my ears and nostrils like smoke, and there are winged monsters in the air around us, every glance from their multiple globular eyes an indirect attack. Already I feel faintly suicidal.

I do not yet see my old enemies, but I'm afraid. I tell Kerranga this and she shouts, "Oh, Rob's product is high-end. He doesn't let his work just roam the streets like any old headbug."

"The plants here are simple," Mir observes. The attacks roll off her unnoticed. "None of them can do what we can do. They could learn a lot from our plants."

Still I keep expecting Rob's agents to come out of somewhere. I still remember how the invisible, negating presence came at me that night in the lab. What did Rob do with the samples he took from me? How did he contain the influence of the emergent? How could he direct it when I did nothing more than cower before it?

Maybe he deserves to be large. It seems he did what I couldn't do.

Mir flows through the fragrant coffee shop, dark and gracefully declarative as calligraphy. She inhabits the room with such vivid surety that the milling adults seem attenuated, incomplete. Rob is camped at a table whose data-rich surface he swipes to darkness as we approach. Pleasantries are exchanged and Kerranga makes her excuses.

Rob's baritone voice carries tension like a military base on lockdown. "I have all my biological output tracked. You can't be too careful these days. I was worried about copying, assault. I never expected this. At least, I never expected that it could happen and you wouldn't tell me."

There is hostility in the tapping of his fingers on the counter; he paints me as the betrayer. His expression says, *How could you do this to me? See what a nice guy I am.*

He is a nice guy, as far as that goes. So?

He stares at Mir like she is water or starfire. What does he want from her? I try to find the answer as I always did when we were together, in his smell and the set of his movements, the between places that are only ever implied, never named.

"What are you doing?" I say. Mir begins to play a game in the interactive surface of the table.

"She could have so much more in this world," he whispers. "Please don't deprive her of what she could become."

I am not parsing this. There is no point in trying to pretend, and I start to twitch and laugh and roll my solitary eye and if I'm lucky I won't wet myself but you never know these days. I haven't had an easy life. He is uncomfortable that people are looking at us, and I let out a few barks to put the boot in.

Then I realise he's sincere.

He really thinks I would give her up.

"I know how talented you are, Inj. And I'm sure you've passed it on to her. I give you all credit. You found the emergents. I couldn't even see them. The thing that attacked you? I didn't know what it was, so it couldn't hurt me. But I knew it had to be *something*, because of what it did to you."

"Have you learned how to stop it?" I ask suddenly. There is always that hope.

He spreads his fingers, crunches his face. "I sort of took it in the other direction," he says. "I found out what this species of thing could do, and then I altered it. I derived the code and tweaked it so that I could do head trips on anyone I might name."

"So you turned it into a weapon."

"More like an agent than a weapon, but I guess you could –"

"And then you sold it?"

"I didn't need it for myself! I don't hate anybody that much. It really is a killer, Inj, and when it's done with someone it doesn't even leave a trace it's ever been there. I mean, I've got to hand it to you. You are pretty tough to have survived, considering how susceptible you are to that sort of thing."

"Someone has spilled juice on me!" squawks the table, and Mir breaks up laughing. I mop up Mir's spilt juice and remind her to sit quietly, but she isn't used to polite society.

Rob gives her a code for his system. "Here are the games," he says, pointing.

"Are you sure that's a good idea?" I ask. "She can't mess anything up, can she?"

He waves a hand. "It's fine. My stuff's bombproof. Let her play."

He looks me in the eye, then.

"I did what I said I would, Inj. I got the recognition. I'm large. I can't be touched. I can give Mir the same thing."

Mir leans into my hair, whispering. "There's a blobby thing eating his face, Mum."

I stroke her hair, hand her a piece of biscotti. I am secretly delighted about the blobby thing. It makes his authoritative air more bearable.

"So, Rob, you talked to Abdul?"

"He went to Australia. Won't return my messages. Why? What's Abdul got to do with anything?"

I lean in.

"We made some adjustments to Mir."

He stares.

"Like what?"

Now he is looking at her ears, her leaf-strewn locks, the pale green "hairs" on the backs of her arms. They are tiny spines that catch signals out of the air and alter them.

In broad terms, I explain Mir to him. She swings her legs and trawls through his apps hungrily. She is bound to mess up his stuff; but I did warn him. He is now too distracted, thinking about what is going on in her body, to give a moment's thought to what her eyes and fingers are doing to his system. He's getting angry, but clamping down on it.

"You haven't even taken her to a doctor, have you?" His eyes flash, proprietary. Accusing.

"Do you really want to do this, Rob?"

"No… Inj, you know I don't want this to get nasty at all, I don't want to make either of you uncomfortable. But I'm just… saying… *have* you taken her to a doctor? I can help. Let me do some things to help you. It doesn't have to be so hard."

Yes, it does.

"I have hung on out there a long time," I say in a grey voice. "I don't want to come back. Not any more. I don't need what you have. Can't you see that your work is feeding the emergents? You're enriching their environment, increasing their sophistication all the time. The emergents are eating you alive and you don't even care. They will use you up and move beyond you and by the time you realise what's happening it will be too late."

He chuckled. "I forgot what you were like, Inj."

I am on a roll now.

"But *I* didn't forget what *you're* like. You will give us away. We are sitting right on the underbelly of the system and it can't see us, but now you know. It's only a matter of time before you expose us. I guess you will take the Silence and sell that, too."

He runs his hand through his hair, clearly upset. "Now that's unfair. I've worked like a dog all these years. I think I've earned my success."

Mir is sitting very still. She is watching him. She looks at me with a shrinking expression, as though I have slapped a puppy.

"Inj, can't we find a middle ground? Here's the blue sky. I'm open. Tell me what you want to do."

I regret having brought Mir. We should have done this without her. But who could I have left her with? I am all she has. And I am at a loss.

"I have something of yours," I tell Rob at last. I put the bag on the counter. Inside, his soul twitches, chatters a little. Irritated at having been plucked from the happy oblivious mud under the bridge, I guess. "I've been keeping it for insurance purposes."

His eyelids clench into suspicious lines as he tilts his nose toward the bag. He doesn't seem to guess what's in there. Can't he smell it? I tried to clean up the bag, wiping algal smudges off the orange plastic, but it still looks disreputable and it reeks of his soul.

He stands up. I gather that I have insulted him, because he speaks with frigid courtesy.

"OK. I can see it's not going to work. I get it. We both need time to think this one through. Let me walk you to the station. Or maybe my car can take you somewhere?"

I take Mir's hand. I have to drag her away from Rob's system. I hope she is messing up his personal organiser.

"We'll walk."

He walks with us, and because I don't want to upset Mir, I let him. Out on the Strand he tries to make small talk. My heart is pounding. I don't know how to stand down. I don't know if I can stand down. I notice the wind on the river; I notice that the beech trees have been augmented. All the air is thick with transmissions. I hold my potted plant before me like a ridiculous shield. I am afraid.

"The trouble is, Inj, you're not stable. I know it. You know it. You could go down at any time, and then what happens to Mir?"

I stop walking. I can't believe he just said that in front of her.

"Just stop talking, Rob." I am impotent and he knows it. He is refusing to look at me, and at first I think he's ignoring me. Then I realise he's doing something with his cogs. He's ordering something up.

The beech trees overhead are boosting some creation of his, and emergents are crawling up from the ground. They quicksilver over my feet and up my legs. They drop like caterpillars from the trees and engulf me, thousands upon thousands of his trained vermin. They are in my eye socket.

It's happening again.

I know I'm hyperventilating. He has staged this whole thing: to scare her, to scare me, to force my hand. I'm the witch and he's thrown a bucket of water on me and I am melting.

It's the same old helplessness. I will end up in hospital and then he will take her.

I grip Mir's hand and push past Rob, beginning to run toward Charing Cross station. Seeking safety underground.

But the pavement folds and remixes my kinaesthetic perception: my insides are visible, my flesh begins to strain and pop. I know this sensation. Soon I will lose myself entirely.

I try to run but I'm going nowhere.

Mir is tugging on my hand, pulling me toward her.

"Don't run," she says. "Mum, don't run away."

She throws her arms around me. I can feel the singing of her foliage in my teeth and along the tracks of my tendons.

I can't see.

My intestines are spilling out through my vagina and my bones are gathering in my throat and poking through my eye sockets. The world is roiling away from me in a tide of dust, and there is a wordless power in the air that wills the end of me. Everything I have ever loved, every mercy, every kindness, is mown down by an ineffable storm of hate.

I am shit.

The worms are inside my head. They trawl through every pathetic effort I have ever made to pull myself together, every grant proposal and small article I have written, and they mock. Each tiny bit of progress I have made, they trash. Everything I have ever done or thought that was good, they take, until I can't remember whether it ever was my own.

They say they will come for my plants. They say they will come for Mir.

This is happening with breathtaking speed. I try to remember where I am, what is going on. I don't want her to see me like this. It will break her. He will break us both.

"I have to get away, Mir," I gasp. "I wish I could fight it, but I don't know how."

She says, "You don't have to fight it. Call the Silence. Close off. Play dead."

I don't know how to play dead. I only know how to be dead. That's where I'm going, right now.

Mir's mother never listens to her. She isn't like a tree. She doesn't know how to stand and take it. The plane trees that grow in a straight line along the Embankment, they are hard to kill. If you cut one down it would just sprout a bunch of new branches and keep going.

Mir's mother pulls away from Rob and drags Mir along the Embankment. Mir holds the plant they brought for protection. She calls on it for help. Just then her mother's legs go out from under her and she falls to her knees. Mir holds the plant as her mother is sick on the roots of a plane tree.

Mir can feel the killing thing in her own leaf follicles. She can taste it on the back of her tongue.

She calls the Silence. She calls it around herself and the potted plant from Dartford. The Silence falls over them like a shadow. Then she calls it into the plane trees. They try valiantly to help. They are already expert at transforming human pollution into clean air. Mir could teach them to do the same with ideas, if she only had more time.

Her dad has followed them. Mir senses him trying to contact his emergent, but he can't because of the Silence. He has only his own body. But he's still bigger than Mir. She can feel her mouth working and she's trying not to cry.

"I'm not upset," she tells him. "It's fine. She'll be okay."

He closes his eyes for a moment, like something is hurting him. Then he kneels down in front of Mir the way adults do when they want children to think they're being really fair. He takes Mir's hand in his hand. Their hands are alike.

"She isn't okay," he tells Mir. "You don't have to –"

"Stop killing her."

His hand withdraws. He doesn't know where to look. Mir is still calling the Silence. The plane trees ride her wave and hold the Silence. She smells their oxygen. Their leaves shimmer in the wind. People's heels are scuffing along the pavement and bike gears are clicking and a dog rattles its chain. She hears everything so clearly, and she hears him say some more rubbish but doesn't listen.

"I saw the emergent in your system," she tells him. "I'm not stupid."

He laughs.

"You're just like her. So sharp. I just want to know you, Mir. I want to save you so you won't end up like… like…"

Like her.

He is sweating. The Silence around them is cool. Mir's mother starts to pull herself together. She takes a tissue out of her bag and wipes her mouth.

"You should have this," Mir tells her father. "Then maybe you'll stop."

She holds out the plastic bag. He waves it away. He's laughing again in a fake way.

"Maybe you don't understand," Mir says. It's what her mother says to Mir when she's getting ready to tell Mir off in a big way. "I'm blocking your emergent, Dad. I know what it is. I know how to stop it."

"But… Mir, I can give you the best education. Your potential. You could go so far, just let me –"

"Take it," Mir says. She shoves the bag at him and upends it. His soul falls out. He just manages to catch it before it hits the pavement. There's this moment where he seems to recognise it, but then he shoves it in his jacket pocket and stands up and he's backing away from her.

"Please don't drive it away again," Mir tells him. Then she goes back to her mum, leaning on the plane tree. Mir is crying. She wanted it to be so different.

It takes hours for Mir and me to get home by tube, train and bus. As the terror subsides, I find myself thinking of the young green walls of London today, of Karranga's offer to help me grow the Silence. I am thinking of the plant I'm holding in my arms, how it saved me. I want to do something with the Silence. I know it's important. If the plants saved me, they can save others.

But even as the bus lets us out, a terrible weariness has come over me. I feel dark. Mir drags me through the industrial estate to the green waste beyond. I do not know how I will muster the energy to do everything that I have to do. It feels so much easier to run and hide. How can I find a way to carry on with this work when its outcome is something no one has ever seen?

It's too much pressure. The very air seems to weigh on me, making thunder in my mind. I nearly lost everything back there.

"Mum," says Mir, poking me. "Stop listening to the waves. Just stop."

I put my fingers in my ears but it doesn't help.

Mir's shadow is tall and gangly when we make our way to the pewter coolness of the river, the weed-scrambled bank with its leaning tents and smoke-scarred air. Even as electric trucks glide along the A206 and over the bridge, our renegade plants lunge this way and that toward the sky. The Butcher is just finishing up a day's work of transplanting along the bank, and I watch him walking along the footpath with a spade over his shoulder.

At last the Silence reaches out and embraces me. My weariness dissolves, and that's when I remember it was never quite real.

Mir skips ahead of me, through the nettles and toward the restless treetops of our home.

As she runs, she waves the empty plastic bag in the air, like a flag.

The Apologists

Tade Thompson

Today, I decide to go to a bar.

I'm not dressed for it. My clothes are torn in places and although the darkness of my jeans hides grime, my shirt should be negotiating a spin cycle rather than warming my skin. Nobody notices, though. They haven't bothered to name this establishment but there's a neon sign with weird symbols that don't, as far as I can tell, mean anything. Though there is a ribbon and stanchion arrangement, bouncer, and queue, I walk right up to the door and walk in. The bouncer is a stocky sort, fat-over-muscle build with a skin-colour approximating black, he smiles at me like I'm a celebrity. None of the punters in the twelve-person queue yells expletives. New world.

Inside, they're playing nineties hiphop. *Ambitionz Az A Ridah.* I had that song on repeat when I was in university. There is the usual hum of conversation. Men and women talking to each other, flirting, drinking. I nod to myself, first at random, but later to the baseline of the song. There's an empty stool and I aim for it before someone claims it. Reflex. I shouldn't have bothered; nobody tries. When I squeeze into the space my shoulders bump the adjacent punters, but they just smile and continue their conversations.

The bartender is on me in seconds.

"Cider," I say. "Whatever's on tap."

He nods, gets it for me, walks away like it's an open bar.

It's warm, stuffy even. I'm sweating, but nobody else is. That pisses me off. I hate that they don't sweat, that they all look neat and smell good. I sip the cider. Tastes like urine. I know this because I have tasted my own urine before. I blame myself, my lack of skill in providing the right adjectives to describe taste to the strangers. All I could muster were words from the advertisements. *Unique! Cutting! Sharp! Perfect blend!*

None of which mean anything.

The woman to my left is wearing a red dress with thin straps that make me wonder how the whole ensemble holds together. She has freckles on her back. I study them, wonder if each one is identical. To my delight they are not. She has hair cascading down in brunette waves and large, circular platinum earrings that dangle as she speaks. She's talking to a Tiger Woods-type and drinking Chablis. The Tiger Woods-type glances at me, perhaps registering my behaviour as an anomaly. Fuck it. I tap the woman on the shoulder.

She turns on the stool and looks at me. She does not seem surprised, and that annoys me. She doesn't say anything. She's a big-titted Lorna Blackmore-type. Lorna was this girl I knew who taught Sunday School. Out of reach in every possible way.

I say, in the loudest voice I can muster, "Let's you and me go and have sex."

"Yes," she says and places her drink on the bar. Tiger, who has heard, does not even react.

"No, no, no. This won't do," I say.

"Do you not find me sexually attractive?" her face is still expressionless.

I do, but that's not the point. I'm so angry, I just leave.

I walk two blocks, then Nico intercepts me.

"Hello, Storm," says Nico.

"Nico."

"Nice evening." On cue, he looks to the sky.

I nod. It's warm, dry and visibility is good, but that's not why he mentions it. He mentions it because it is customary to comment on the weather. I taught him that.

"You should go back," says Nico. His lip movements don't match his speech. Neither does his body language. He's a hologram of a famous person that the strangers play in order to calm me when they talk to me. I think Nico is an individual, but it's difficult to tell. His image is usually, but not always, Tom Jones circa 1984. As a result, conversations can be surreal. He could be telling me something sober while his image would be dancing and clearly singing into a microphone. Talking to Nico is always like watching a bad lip-synch.

"I'm not sleepy," I say.

"You know that's irrelevant. You should go back and get some rest. Tomorrow is a working day."

"I was working just now. That bar was hilarious. It's supposed to be called The Cock and Bull, by the way."

"I'll be happy to take notes on the matter tomorrow. Go back to base, Storm."

Even though Nico's voice is never inflected, the repetition of an instruction is usually a prelude to forceful measures and I am not in the mood, so I change direction.

I go across Vauxhall Bridge. The water isn't finished, but a homogenous blue acts as a placeholder river and the sound of water lapping at the banks seems incongruous. They seem to have trouble with water. I turn right on the south bank of the Thames and head towards Wandsworth Road. Wandsworth has perfect rows of terraced houses. The paintjobs are perfect with no mould or weathering. The glass is all clean, the hedges are surgical and the pavements look like fresh cement. The street lights shine with biblical vigour. There are no undulations to the asphalt.

This is Katrina's work.

There are things Katrina and I do not agree on.

I arrive at the Complex well before midnight. I pass through the gate and I'm checked by monitor drones, small spherical bastards with heathen propulsion methods and power supplies. I flip the bird. The Complex is a small estate, four houses for the five remaining humans. The rules are that the strangers don't come in here and we respect the curfew. I don't remember Nico ever coming in here. Outside the Complex is the Rebuild. This is where we work to produce a model of the world as it was before the strangers. Officially the Rebuild is open to us from nine to five but I often work late. Fuck them and their curfew. They won't kill me, I'm one of the final five.

I stand at the roundabout in the courtyard we all share. My boots crunch on the gravel and the sound carries and bounces back to me, confirming I am alive. There are Ash and Birch reaching into the sky at intervals in the inner side of the barrier, and a dense but well-tended hedge blocking the view of the fence. No breeze moves the leaves and no night fauna cry. The buildings are identical two-storey Victorian-looking. They are not Victorian because every brick, every beam, every nail is new. The blueprints came out of the Kellys' memories and the strangers constructed them, just like we do with the Rebuild. It doesn't bother me, I can live anywhere, and I like the Kellys even though they do not contribute anything. Katrina's house is dark, no lights anywhere. I will discuss Wandsworth Road with her tomorrow, but she is not the most flexible of people and I don't have much hope of a compromise. There is a glow at Terry's bedroom and I suspect he is reading.

"Goodnight, Terry!" I bow even though he has not come to the window. He is sure to be cursing me.

I walk up the short flight of stairs into my own house.

At night, while we sleep, the strangers watch us. They do not physically come, but the spherical and ovoid observer drones enter our houses and hover. They do not make a sound, but that is somehow creepier. I feel my body hairs rise whenever they are in my bedroom. They always wake me and I do not pretend to sleep. I shower them with invective and swipe at them, always missing, for they are agile, manoeuvrable fuckers.

When they see that I am awake, they drift away. The romance is gone. *I watched you while you slept, my love.* I cannot get back to sleep after this, so I think about Bea and Chelsea.

In the world before this one, I come home to find a silent house, folded note on the dining table. It is a single sheet and folded once, standing like a placard. My name is written in black on one side. The table is clean. It is never clean. When I see the card I do not need to read it to know what's in it. I feel afraid for the first time. My wife takes shit from me all the time, until the day she doesn't.

It takes me ninety-nine days to win her back. I grovel and beg and confess to what Bea and I both know is the cause of the break-up: I am not a good person. I miss Chelsea, but I miss Bea more. I love her. I cannot afford to fuck it up. Bea is about the only evidence that I have any humanity in me because she sees it. Somewhere. Fuck knows where, because I can't see it.

When she returns, I live again. The world holds colour for me. I am forgiven, Bea forgives me. Chelsea gurgles at me.

One month after this people start to get sick.

The Apocalypse takes one year. The strangers wipe out humanity in three hundred and seventy days. Just when I start to live, they kill me.

Next day.

I deliberately interrupt Katrina's morning routine. She goes to the gym at six oh five every day, and she likes to start with the cross-trainer. I do not let her on this day. I stand on the pedals back to front, and I sing "The Boys are Back in Town" at the top of my voice. Katrina sees me and freezes.

"I would like you to leave," she says.

"I know, and I will, but I have to tell you something first."

"What do you want, Storm? Make it quick. You smell, and you're holding up my workout."

"I do not smell," I say.

I do smell. I only wear one set of clothes despite the cellulose-based fabrics that the strangers supply. I'm still wearing the clothes I had on when they found me in the debris. I do not honestly know how long ago that was. Either the clothes will fall off me by being worn out from washing, or these are the clothes I'll wear till I die.

I tell Katrina about the streets of Wandsworth.

"So what? They're neater this way." She doesn't quite pout, but it's in her voice.

"But it's not realistic, Katrina. The tarmac can't be perfect. Streets pitch and yaw as you drive along them. This is not what streets look like."

"This is how they should look. I've had no complaints about my work."

"From them? What the fuck do they know about how London was? From the Kellys? The Kellys don't care."

"Thank you for the constructive criticism, Storm. Now get off the cross-trainer.'

"Will you add some cracks? Some fungus to the walls?"

"No. Why does it bother you? You do the people, anyway."

"Not people. Simulants. They aren't people."

"They seem perfectly like people to me."

"They would, and therein lies the problem. My problem. They cannot be human because they are perfect replicas. Humanity is defined by imperfections."

Katrina trembles and I get off the trainer before she has an anxiety attack. She gets them when things are not going according to whatever her plan of the moment is, and I'm pretty sure her plan did not include an altercation with me first thing in the morning. I sometimes think there's a part of her that is happy with the demise of the previous world.

"How about some refuse?"

"What do you mean?"

"Chocolate wrappers, dead leaves, cigarette ends, the normal detritus of human occupation."

"The new trees do not shed leaves, simulants don't smoke and nobody has eaten chocolate since...well, since."

"Can you at least pray for the strangers to add an algorithm that makes the trees shed leaves after an interval?"

"What's the point of that? Someone'll have to pick up the leaves.""

I leave her in the gym. There was no point starting an argy-bargy this early in the morning.

I use the prayer point on Shaftsbury Avenue where it intersects with Charing Cross road, right near the steakhouse. The point is where a phone box used to be. I've never seen a stranger and Nico doesn't count. The refinement of our constructs needs to be done at a prayer point, which is a kind of pod, like a phone box, but without angles or discernible equipment. There is a field of some kind in there. It crackles lightly and there is always a hint of ozone.

"On simulants in bar, doorman or bouncer far too accommodating. Must be polite, but physically intimidating and not altogether helpful except if bribed. Must learn psychological intimidation too, but this can wait until later. Service at bar too quick. There should be a delay, however brief, between arrival at bar and receipt of beverage. Beverages unsatisfactory. I still think it would be best to actually use fermentation to produce beer. Needs more flavour, more body. Bubbles and head satisfactory. Punters far too accommodating. For discussion: jealousy. For discussion: mating rituals among heterosexual humans."

I bump into a simulant while walking down Monmouth Street, just coming up to the obelisk. I shove him away with irritation. He doesn't even stop to look at me. I turn and pull at his shirt.

"Hello," he says. Pleasant, placid.

"No. Wrong. Say, '"arsehole"'."

"Excuse me?"

"Call me an arsehole for bumping into you without apologising."

"I don't think that is appropriate–"

"Oh, fuck off."

There are no students or tourists sitting at the base of the Seven Dials obelisk.

Jealousy is easy once there is desire. I walk down Mercer Street then turn left on to Long Acre and stop at the facsimile of Covent Garden Station. I do not go in. There is nothing beyond the door except some 3-D sketches of trains. None of us remember trains or the details of how they work well enough to replicate them. The train, tube and bus stations have significance to all of us, and are landmarks of sorts. There is a prayer point and I go in.

"Jealousy is easy once there is desire, and everything human starts with desire. God desired that there be light. Satan desired to be more than he was. Rama desired Sita. To want something is to want it completely, to own a thing or a person is to own it exclusively. This is why we marry. I mean, the real reason we marry is economic, but let's put that aside. We marry and put a ring on it…heh, sorry, pop song allusion…we use a ring to denote ownership. This is my person. This is my car. I call dibs because even if a thing does not belong to me yet, it is conceptually mine because I have seen it. *The lust of the eyes and the lust of the flesh.* That's from the Bible. Or Shakespeare."

I ramble on, because Nico has encouraged me to free-associate, and that the more I say, the more the strangers can understand the nuances and apply them to the simulants. I keep talking until I hear a fog horn.

Shit.

I sit on the pavement, close my eyes, and cover my ears tightly. These motherfuckers never, ever learn.

WE ARE SORRY FOR OUR PART IN THE DESTRUCTION OF THE HUMAN RACE. IT WAS UNINTENTIONAL, BUT THAT DOES NOT EXCUSE OUR ACTIONS. WE WILL MAKE AMENDS AND RESTITUTION WITH ALL OF OUR RESOURCES. PLEASE ACCEPT OUR APOLOGY AND HELP US REBUILD YOUR DELICIOUS WORLD.

This high decibel message is repeated, vibrating through the Rebuild and the complex, over a period of an hour, and in several languages. Well, not real languages. I only speak English, for example, but I recognise German, French, Spanish and Italian. The strangers have done a linguistic reconstruction using my memories. Is it Spanish if I think it's Spanish? Does it matter?

And don't get me started on 'delicious'. Nico asks the final five for synonyms of good, but doesn't give us context. Then he asks a number of questions about atonement for wrongdoing, and I tell him apology and restitution is pretty much universal. Little did I know.

The strangers broadcast this message every day at about midday. I try to tell Nico about the volume, and the inappropriateness of the word 'delicious', but he tells me there is no editing of the message. It has been approved by the homeworld and cannot be changed, either in content or in auditory qualities.

So they apologise, daily and loudly, and in languages that are probably made up.

Here's what happened.

The first incursions of their scout drones bring exotic bacteria into the atmosphere. Nico tells me they are not even aware Earth is inhabited. Our communication is too simplistic for their minds, and our radio signals are apparently indistinguishable from background stellar noise. The bacteria kill humans in their thousands every day. Even the two-point-five standard deviations of the population that is immune succumbs to native pestilence. Society collapses pretty quickly.

When the gargantuan mother ships arrive, they cause so much disruption of the atmosphere that they accidentally kill off the survivors with extreme weather and noxious gases. It takes three months for them to realise that humans are sentient life, almost a year for them to figure out how to communicate with us.

Our consciousness is primitive to them.

My house in West Ealing crumbles under the force of an unholy hurricane. When the roof is blown away I see a sky of fluorescent green. I have the baby strapped to my chest because she couldn't sleep. I never see what happens to Bea, but there is some kind of vacuum sucking the air out and I can't breathe and I black out. I come to in darkness, the weight of the baby still on me, but cold, unbreathing.

Oh, Chelsea.

I black out again, and I see machines digging, retrieving, scanning. My neighbour is torn apart because the fuckers do not understand pain.

Chelsea is dead on my chest and I cannot find Bea.

By the time they understand how to keep humans alive, Me, Mr and Mrs Kelly, Katrina and Terry are all that's left.

For a time there is this silly notion to repopulate the Earth.

No can do. Terry is gay. The Kellys are elderly, beyond menopause. Katrina is repulsive. Not physically. She's fantastic-looking, physically fit and of the right age. It's just that she and I hate each other on sight.

There is some suggestion that Terry 'go straight for humanity', but he dismisses that with a sniff. He will not even let his sperm be harvested. Neither will I, and Mr Kelly refuses on the grounds that he is married.

Nico cannot understand why we will not act in our own self-interest. I tell him humanity is defined by two opposing instincts, survival and self-destruction. Sex and suicide. Libido and Thanatos.

"It's very rock and roll," I say.

Hence, simulants.

We sometimes sift through the detritus of the old world to see what can be salvaged for the Rebuild. In hazard suits we find old records, useless plasma TVs, books, religious icons, wheelie bins. Terry only looks for books, and even then he only picks the ones he would like to read.

Katrina does not select. She picks up everything she lays her eyes on, starting from the nearest. The Kellys see an object and enter this kind of Proustian fugue where they can only talk about the memories the object holds for them.

I just watch them all. I have never found anything I want and I see the exercise as futile, busywork to keep us survivors occupied, so the Apologists can feel good with themselves. I don't even know why we're wearing these suits. It's not like any of this is irradiated.

I pick up a revolver and dry fire it at the ovoid observer drones.

Click, click, click.

"Pay attention," I say. "What I say next is to be memorised, okay? Just store the words. I'll teach you when to use them, but for now, just remember the words. Ready?"

"Yes," says the simulant. We are seated on the faux-grass in Green Park.

"'Shit. Bollocks. Fuck. Cunt. Bitch. Bastard. Arsehole. Toerag. Wanker. Ass-hat. Bullshit. Clitface. Cocknugget. Cumbubble. Cuntrag. Bomboclad. Dickhead. Dildo. Dickwad. Fuckface, Fuckwad. Jizzsniffer. And…and…"

"Is "'and"' one of the words you want me to–"

"No, you gigantic ass-wipe. There's your first lesson."

We try it again. I approach a group of simulants on Tottenham Court Road, and while they try their best to avoid me, I bump into two of them hard.

"Asswipe!"

"Cumbubble!"

"Jizzsnifter!"

Their delivery is perfect. They even stop to glare after me.

I walk away pleased.

When Bea is thirteen weeks pregnant we see Chelsea for the first time on ultrasound. We are in the darkened scanning room, staring at the screen like it's a movie theatre. Bea is supine with her belly exposed and wet from the ultrasound gel, but her neck is also twisted towards the representation of the moving nascent human in her uterus. I'm on an uncomfortable plastic chair holding her hand. Chelsea is moving. She moves her hands in a wave, she twitches her legs, she turns. The operator does not like the motion because they are trying to date the pregnancy and they need her still so they can measure the CRL-Crown Rump Length.

At one point they get a good profile shot and we can see Chelsea's brain, eye sockets, mouth, skull, heart, and other organs all at once. I see her open her mouth and swallow amniotic fluid. I see it go down her throat. It is amazing, and at that point, with that supremely human action, I consider her alive.

That's when I become a parent.

I go to a prayer point and I say, "I need thirty simulants to follow me."

I don't wait to see what happens, I just go to watch Katrina work on Waterloo Bridge. I watch from the North Bank of what is meant to be the Thames. She does not understand architecture or civil engineering and works like an artist. With grand sweeping gestures she creates a line going from one bank to another, then fills in the detail. She creates concrete slabs using short vertical strokes with both hands. Whatever technology the Apologists use monitors her movements and replicates with whatever material they use for this simulacrum. Katrina is completely absorbed by her labours and I cannot see from here, but I imagine her sweating. She takes this shit seriously.

Nico is beside me.

"What's up, pussycat?" I ask.

"I am curious as to why you are watching Katrina work, rather than doing work of your own." He smiles at me as 1990s Tom Jones. "Not that you *must* work. You are all volunteers."

"I am working," I say, and I point to the thirty bland simulants behind me. "This is the Waterloo Bridge, man. Monet painted it. It was a suicide spot in the 1800s, before anybody had heard of the Golden Gate Bridge. It celebrates our victory over a short, French military genius. The construction of any such thing would attract crowds."

Nico seems puzzled.

"Humans like to stare at changes in landscape. I am teaching your simulants to stare at things."

"I see. What is the object of such activity?"

"To have stories to tell. To make life less monotonous. To distract us from the entropy that slowly degrades our bodies. "'Hey, Fred, I came in over Waterloo Bridge this morning. Fantastic structure. I was there when it was built.'" That kind of thing."

Nico now looks like Tom Jones in *Mars Attacks!* Blue suit, dark shirt, clean shaven, moderate side burns. I prefer him with the goatee of later years, but who am I to judge.

For the first time I see the innards of a simulant.

I am walking past what should be Wembley Stadium, but is instead a homogenous blob of transparent concept art. There is no traffic, so I am walking in the centre of the road. There are vehicle ghosts, placeholder cars that are holograms and lack mass. We have an understanding. They pass through me and I disregard them.

I see a body lying on the side of the road, a male, some movement, but clearly incapacitated. I go over. There is a crush wound on the right soldier. The clothing torn and the skin broken in an irregular pattern.

I don't know what I expected. The simulants are constructs and I file them as robots. But there is blood. I touch it, and it doesn't feel like blood, though it is red, and it lacks that metallic taste-smell. There are bones poking out here and there. I touch them, and they are of some kind of reinforced plastic. There is mangled flesh that quivers as the simulant tries to move.

I'm confused. Who or what attacked this thing? My mind instantly goes to the other humans, Katrina especially. The simulants are non-violent and Katrina may hold a grudge for my interference in her morning work-out. Maybe because I criticise her work, she decides to destroy mine?

No, I don't see it.

I stick my hand in the wound to feel the flesh more than anything. It is all soft and pliant, like real meat. Where is the machinery? Where is the technology? What's the power supply? I push my hand in deeper. The simulant does not react to this, and I try to remember what Nico and I agreed about pain. All the way inside its synthetic spine there is no wire, cable, or anything that isn't ersatz human. The simulant has blue green eyes. They are locked with mine. I pull my hand out of his wound and poke the left eye. It blinks. I shove my thumb into the eye socket and I keep pushing until I feel something give.

Then I feel shame, so I rise and I run away.

How humans learn speech is a mystery. There is some mimesis where the child copies sounds. Chelsea had begun the transition from cooing and crying to meaningful words thrown almost at random. Meaning is developed from context and repetition. How exactly grammar and syntax are learnt is still poorly understood.

"The simulants are not developing socially. They are still where they were the last time I spoke. They do not surprise me. There is nothing new in their interactions with each other. If this is to work, if they are to be your substitute humans, you have to tweak your algorithms or they will be nothing more than manikins. Teaching a child speech is different. The learning is not passive. The child learns even when not observed, outside "teaching" periods. Children experiment. Your simulants do not. They leave the burden of acquisition to me."

I see fourteen more wounded simulants before I understand the problem. It comes to me during apology time.

Each time one group of simulants passes the other on the streets they bump aggressively and exchange profanities. Every single time.

To make matters worse, some simulants are stronger than others, and they do not modulate the force of the physical contact. Some hit with all their strength, leading to injuries.

WE ARE SORRY FOR OUR PART IN THE DESTRUCTION OF THE HUMAN RACE. IT WAS UNINTENTIONAL, BUT THAT DOES NOT EXCUSE OUR ACTIONS. WE WILL MAKE AMENDS AND RESTITUTION WITH ALL OF OUR RESOURCES. PLEASE ACCEPT OUR APOLOGY AND HELP US REBUILD YOUR DELICIOUS WORLD.

I have a pounding headache and just when I think my eyes will start bleeding the apologies stop.

Nico appears. He has like a curly Afro with a white shirt open to the waist. His chest is hairy, black curls of 1970s Tom Jones chest foliage.

"I will never get used to this shit," I say, pointing to the sky as if the sound comes from there.

"Good. We do not want the apologies to seem perfunctory."

"Listen, you have to reprogram the simulants–'"

"Go to the prayer points," he says. "Your requests will reach the appropriate quarters."

"So why are you here?"

"There have been…complaints about you."

"What? I'm not moving fast enough with the simulants?"

"No, the simulants are fine. It's your fellow Earthers."

"By which you mean Katrina. She's always hated me–"

"Storm, it's all of them."

"What do you mean? Even the Kellys?"

"The others unanimously think you are a disruptive influence. Yes, even the Kellys."

That hurts a bit. The Kellys are never angry with anybody.

"They're lying."

"Our own surveillance confirms what they say. You irritate all of them. You disrupt Katrina's rhythms when you know she likes predictability. You sing at the top of your voice when the others are resting. You deliberately needle Terry, who thinks you're homophobic by the way."

"I'm not homophobic. I just don't like Terry, that's all."

"I'm the messenger here, Storm. I may have to separate you from the others if you continue this way. Get along, or move along."

"Pain and disgust. The simulants must be allowed to feel pain. That way they will care about their bodies, about harm coming to their bodies. If they are to be alive by any definition they have to avoid harm. Even an amoeba avoids noxious stimuli. If they feel pain, the confrontation will not invariably lead to physical harm. You can't punch someone without feeling pain on your knuckle. They must see altercations as options in a menu. Altercations can lead to damage, therefore they need to think carefully before getting into fights." I take a breath.

"Disgust. Simulant bodies don't decay. That's odd, and it's definitely not human. Either way, when a simulant sees another simulant injured, they must react, they must try to help, and they must feel alarm. The spilling of blood causes humans alarm because it may mean that there is a danger close by that can kill the observer. This may be the origin of empathy. We know instinctively that the red is meant to be on the inside. It's protection. But we also feel disgust when presented with decay. Remove the fucking bodies of the injured simulants, please, thank you."

I am going to start a fight.

I did not return to the complex yesterday. I am lurking in an alcove with a length of piping and malicious intent. I got the pipe from our excursions into the old world-finally found something I actually want.

Two simulants walk past, holding hands, simulating a couple. They smile at each other, and it churns my belly. There is no variation. A human couple would show variation, even in the throes of puppy love. They'd gaze into each other's eyes, but then face forward to check for obstacles, and maybe show some self-consciousness at some point. These guys are just stuck on an on switch.

I leap from my hiding place, landing on the street about a foot behind them. Humans would have startled. Not these machines. The first stroke hits their hands where they hold each other, deforming a few digits. Since they are facing each other I see them wincing in pain. My second stroke hits the one on the left, right on the crown of the head. I feel the shock of it in my shoulder joint. Whatever material the Apologists use for the skull gives way. He does not fall, though. His lover does not help him. She cradles her mangled hand and shies away from me, but otherwise seems to watch with curiosity.

That red sap that the simulants have streams down the male's skull, although he still seems to be functioning well. I curl a leg behind his knee and push him down, then I hit him repeatedly until he stops moving.

I am covered in red and breathing heavy.

His lover sees the mess and her lips curl, then she walks away. There's my disgust. I throw the pipe at her, but it misses. I am too winded to run after her, but I am angry at the unnaturalness of the scene.

I drag myself to a prayer point.

"They need emergency services," I say. "At least rudimentary police, ambulance and fire. Otherwise they have no recourse when they experience violence or injury. Probably need a proto-judiciary system too." I sigh. It will take weeks to explain this. I speak to Nico about courts and he wonders if a loud, daily apology will not be enough for all offences. I shake my head.

"The police keep the Queen's Peace," I say. But then I realise there is no Queen, no Royal Family, no Buckingham Palace, no government at all. But fuck it, this is England. "The Queen's Peace is civil order…"

The next day I cannot move from the aches and pains. Bludgeoning a machine to death is apparently hard work. I may have over-done it. I didn't need that much fury to investigate simulant response. Maybe I was still a little peeved that four out of the five remaining humans do not like me.

I daydream. Bea is heavily pregnant, seven and a half months, sitting on the sofa. I pass her a glass of iced water and she places it on her gigantic belly. The baby immediately begins to kick the cold area. Bea giggles. I move the glass to a different position, and the baby kicks the new location.

"Looks like she doesn't like the cold," says Bea.

"Yeah, she's going to have to get used to it. It's London."

"We could always move to warmer climes."

"Good luck with that," I say.

This is a running joke. We are both Londoners, born, bred; she north of the Thames, me south. Bea is the one exception to my rule that once you cross the bridge you're in wankerland. Warmer Climes is our code for anywhere outside the M25 area.

I am thinking of the day I met Bea. It is a Gay Pride march and I initially peg her for a lesbian. She is not in the march, just on the side-lines like me. She points out that I have food on my chin, and, because I don't think of her as prey, I relax, and we start to chat.

Next, I am thinking about me striking her. I do not even remember why, but what sticks, what will not go away, is the death of something in her eyes. There is a fascination in her eyes, an interest in me, a heat that draws me. It has been there since the Gay Pride march. I see it leach out in that moment, and I know fear. I did not expect the emptiness behind that curtain, that frightening lack of love or loathing.

Even when I win her forgiveness, her eyes are at best lukewarm. Whatever it was is gone, replaced by a tepid facsimile of adoration interspersed with sham bonhomie. I suspect that was in place to ward-off further violence.

While I may spend time fantasizing and in reverie, I never actually dream of Bea and Chelsea. I never have a dream where they are alive and this alien invasion business is just a dream, like bad science fiction.

I often wonder if my whole life before the strangers was real, and maybe I have always been here.

One day a week, I work on variability. When I started, all the simulants looked the same, with features like mine. Every week I take time to give them a new design which is pushed out into circulation like a new stamp or coin.

The current population of London is maybe five thousand simulants. All of them look like people from my life. The first woman I design is built off the template of my primary school teacher, Miss Cadogan. She had large eyes, dark curly hair and a perpetual smile. Gangly, energetic, of constant good cheer. I wish I knew what happened to her. There are two hundred Miss Cadogans in London. They are poor copies and lack her personality, but when I see any of them I feel comforted.

I make a few Renaissance Jesus-type simulants just because. I make a Tony Blair. There are at least five Obamas.

I make a Leonard, a guy who lived down the road from us, bearded, about fifty-five, plump, rumoured to have been on the sex-offenders register because he groped a co-worker or something. He helped me change a flat tyre once. I feel sorry for the guy, so I give him a smaller waistline in his new incarnation.

I do not make a Bea. I can't. The idea of running into her in the Rebuild is just… I can't.

I make an Ahmed, my only Pakistani friend. I can't remember his surname, but I render his unibrow carefully, the strands of grey in his otherwise black hair, the hollows of his cheeks, the dark and prominent lower eyelids. Ahmed's an artist and he always has the smell of some solvent or the other about him. I have no artistic inclination whatsoever, yet I know there is such a thing as odourless solvents. According to Bea, Ahmed wants to be known as a working artist, hence the smell.

I make my father, render him with words.

"Brutish, muscular, work-hardened palms, gigantic Popeye-type forearms. Popeye's a cartoon character. His eyes are perpetually narrow, like he's about to hit you or someone else. He is not bearded, but there is always patchy hair on his chin. There is a slight lurch to his gait, legacy of a love affair with alcohol." After a while I feel like giving him a horn, bang in the centre of his head. The Apologists won't know the difference, and it would amuse me.

I don't. But I could have.

I attack a few more simulants. In truth, I cannot say I am conducting experiments in response to violence. Beating them is somehow… cathartic. I feel anxious all day until I have hit them, after which I feel calm. I am perturbed by this, but I don't tell anybody, even Nico.

I'm cleaning the simulants fluid off myself, when I notice a couple about a hundred yards away. I draw closer and it's Katrina talking to a male simulant.

She is *smiling*.

Is that bitch auditing my work?

"What the fuck are you doing?" I yell.

She is calm, and meets my gaze. The simulant wanders off before I reach them.

"Hello, Storm," she says.

"Hello yourself. What are you doing?"

"Chatting."

"Bullshit."

"'Okay, I confess, I was curious about your efforts and decided to see for myself."

"It's no concern of yours."

"Ahh, but it is. You complained about the symmetry of my streets. I think that makes your work my concern. Since we're all helping each other out."

I feel myself tense up at the smug tone in her voice, the challenging thrust to her chin. What surprises me is that the urge to hit her is so intense that I force myself to walk away.

"Touché," I mutter.

At a prayer point in St John's Wood I say, "There are things that children of drunks know that other children do not. I don't mean that modern "addiction" crap. That's some bleeding-heart bullshit. I mean drunks. For one thing, we know how to take a beating. Two, we are experts at observing other people. Three, we know how to strategically deploy alcohol. Too little, and you get withdrawal symptoms, which can make the drunk irritable. Too much, and you become a punching bag. You have to find the sweet spot, the optimum amount of alcohol to maintain tranquillity. Four, we know the borders of sobriety well. The drunk-not drunk threshold tells us when to disappear.

"People who talk about 'a mean drunk' don't know anything. Children of drunks recognise no other kind. We are weaned on violence and know nothing else."

I have been following Katrina for weeks now. She sees her simulant every day. He's an Elliot Wells type. I went to secondary school with Elliot Wells and he was a bit of a wanker. I forget why. I think he is one of those people who knows everything and reminds everybody of it all the time. The kind who answers a question in class before anybody else, or who declares a wrong answer before the teacher does. That kind of wanker. Maybe.

He pronounces consonants, for fuck's sake. The rest of us drop them, like the good old faux cockneys we aspire to be. He has to enunciate. I am not exactly sure why I designed some simulants after him.

I see them kissing next to a waterway in Little Venice. Kissing. It irritates the hell out of me. I don't know how many Elliots there are in London, but I try an experiment. I wait until he has walked her to the edge of our complex, then I pounce on him as he walks back. I obliterate his head with dozens of strikes from my pipe.

When he falls, I hear the drum beat of multiple feet. There are simulants running towards me. Just two of them at first. They don't know how to fight, and they approach me one at a time, so I simply whack them in the faces with my pipe. But then there are more. When the two fall, three more appear, and when they fall a team of four runs towards me. They still attack one at a time, but I'm getting tired, my arm is weak, and it's hard to keep my footing in the pool of faux-blood at my feet. The silence is disconcerting. They don't get out of breath, and when I punch them in the belly, there is no forced exhalation. I try to run into the complex, but now there is a group of five and they appear to have learned to attack all at once. My pipe, slick with their fluids, slips from my fingers. I take punches to the body and head. I'm dazed, and still taking hits. I know that if I black out, they will kill me. Through the confusion of limbs, I see a team of six approaching. I am about five feet from the gate of the complex.

I unleash a final burst of savagery, and am able to escape into the barrier. My hunch is correct. The simulants cannot enter. I fall to all-fours, catch my breath.

I see a light come on in Terry's house, but then it goes out again.

The surviving simulants stand at the barrier and I give them the finger before I stagger home. When I look out of the window, both the incapacitated and active simulants are gone.

Three hours later I wake up to scores of observation orbs in my room, more than I have ever seen in one place at the same time. And Nico. He appears in greyscale, as Tom Jones when he was in the band Tommy Scott and the Senators. White shoes, white trousers, open neck cardigan. The Senators was back in the Sixties. I'm staring at his outfit and I miss what he's saying.

"What?" I ask.

"You're under arrest," he says.

"What?"

"Is your hearing malfunctioning?" He moves closer to my bed. "You are under arrest for the murder of Elliot Wells."

It turns out the strangers move fast in setting up a rudimentary judicial system, a police force and a prison of sorts. I am the first person to be arrested or placed in detention.

"This is ridiculous," I say to Nico.

"You were the one who prayed for law enforcement," he says.

"For *them*. I'm not subject to their laws."

"You can argue that in court. Murder is a universal–"'

"It's not murder. The simulants are not alive."

"Well–"'

"At most it's cruelty to machines, and even you know how ridiculous that sounds."

"I suggest you work on your defence, Storm."

I don't know what's funnier, a Soviet show trial or this farce.

The judge is a Miss Cadogan. The jury is full of Elliot Wells duplicates, which is annoying because it should be jury of my peers. Observation orbs are everywhere. All this malarkey because I deactivated the equivalent of a household appliance.

There are no other humans in court, and that should make me suspicious right away, but I am overwhelmed by the absurdity of it all. What are they going to do, execute me? It's not as straightforward as I think, though. Since this circus began my feelings on the matter have become complicated. I make glib statements about simulants not being alive, but deep down, where I won't admit anything, I feel a cold weightiness in my heart. It makes my words ring false when I use them. Is that guilt I'm feeling? Have I convinced myself these simulants are alive?

When I see the first prosecution witness the other shoe finally drops. The humans are going to testify against me. Katrina's in the stand.

"I appeal, Nico. I want to speak to them," I say.

He is silent for a while. I've never seen him like this. I get the sense that he is thinking, which is odd. I thought he was a mouthpiece.

"You can't," he says, finally.

"Prisoners and convicts have a right of appeal, since we're pretending to be human. Take me to the fucking Apologists."

"You can't speak to them, Storm, because they are not here."

"I'm sorry, what? What are you saying?"

Tom fucking Jones is still dancing while delivering this news. Unbelievable.

"'We're not on Earth," says Nico. "After your planet was destroyed you all were brought here, to the homeworld. That's why you have to wear the suits when scavenging. This is not Earth."

I sputter, but I feel the ground falling away from me. "So what is this place?"

"A kind of reserve, a place for you to thrive, build a new world, live."

"A wildlife reserve? A fucking zoo? Are you kidding me?"

"The people you call Apologists don't live here, haven't done for centuries. They have left to explore–'"

"Show me."

He does.

Beyond the placeholder for what is to be the M25 London orbital motorway, he takes me though what seems like nothingness, but is a doorway. It is suddenly dark, with spotlights from above. All around me, and extending as far as the eye can see are hundreds, thousands of proto-simulants. They stand there with their bland features and absent secondary sexual characteristics. They twitch occasionally, the way babies do, the way Chelsea did in her sleep.

I look up, and the ceiling appears to be so far away, it must have clouds forming within. It was like a cathedral, but no cathedral I knew of was miles wide. No matter what direction I look in, I cannot see a wall. The heads of the simulants just keep going forever. The ceiling is transparent and shows a night sky, with constellations I do not recognise.

"I want to go outside," I say.

"No. There is no atmosphere. You'll die. Besides, there is nothing to see. This is all there is," says Nico.

"Give me the suits we go scavenging in," I say.

He humours me, but he is right. There is nothing to see outside but rock and dust and dead machinery. Overhead, a number of large celestial bodies in the sky, moons and satellites, no doubt.

"Is there no way to get a message to–?"

"Storm, they live in Dyson Clouds over multiple solar systems. They have countless worlds like this where they keep species like yours. They do not wish to hear your opinion. You are wasting your time."

I take the suit off. "There has to be retrial, Nico. I must be judged by my peers, not these… things. Let the Final Five judge their own."

In the end they elect to exile me, which is just like imprisonment, only with no walls, bars or daily routine. They agree it wasn't murder to kill a simulant, but I had displayed 'murderous behaviour' which may well spill into their lives. They see me as dangerous. I do not tell them we are not on Earth because fuck them.

They seal me in a cul-de-sac in Shoreditch. The simulants avoid the area and not even the ghost cars drive on the roads. It is hard, and I am lonely. I write down everything I can remember about Bea and Chelsea. If I am not to create simulant personalities then I will re-create others. I write about the lives of people I have known on Earth. I write furiously, so as not to go mad.

I write about what happened here in this new London. The first version I write is a bit of whinging horsedung. I cast myself as a misunderstood martyr and gloss over the things I did wrong. I don't know what I was thinking. Redemption after death? Much later, when I have achieved distance and some objectivity, I destroy the first account and write a more honest one. I am even able to interrogate myself, to ask myself why I really killed Elliot Wells and those other simulants. I use the word 'killed'. I speculate on whether I was jealous, on whether I am perhaps attracted to Katrina. I delete that version too, and finally settle on one that just states the facts.

I attend to every little thing. When the printer makes food I watch every minute process. Maybe I do go mad a little, because I speak to the drone sentries, even though they do not speak back.

After about a year, a simulant escorts me to the funeral for one of the Kelly's, then the other within a month. I pay my respects. Katrina is there, eyes swollen from crying. Terry's there too, in sunglasses and staring at me. I want to explain to them that I have some insight into myself now, that I'm not a threat, and that I want to come back, but it reminds me of when I begged Chelsea to return home, and I end up saying nothing.

We are the pandas who won't mate. Endangered, in captivity, eating food printed from basic amino acids, glucose and triglyceride molecules, remaking our world from memory and language, a world both old and new.

In this new London I am the first mass murderer. I serve my time, and when I come out of Shoreditch I do not recognise the proto-city. They give me new clothes, and ignore my protests. They have improved the water, there are cars, and the people are more like the grim arseholes you would normally see in the London tube crowds every day. Maybe this is not so bad. If I squint, this can pass for Earth.

The complex is empty, and I have no idea where Katrina or Terry are. I see Nico one more time, but he does not tell me about the other humans.

I go into a pub called The Cock and Bull to wait for the midday apology.

The service is shit, but the cider tastes better.

Montpellier

Ian Whates

Montpellier is a shithole. I didn't want to go there in the first place but nor did anyone else and I was too slow in coming up with an excuse.

There are four of them: Montpellier, Biscay, Siena, and Detroit. Officially termed 'habitat complexes', they are known locally as the Four Horsemen. War hasn't actually broken out there yet, but three out of four ain't bad. Besides, give it time...

The Horsemen form an off-kilter diamond in an unfashionable downtown suburb of Victoria – the part of the city the tourists never see. Uptown the theme is eco-balance and elegance – leafy avenues lined with glitzy store fronts, pocket parks and hidden arboreta with tinkling water features and shaded paths and flower beds – all designed to relax the weary shopper after a morning's indulgence. Downtown, not so much. Anything growing has been eaten, smoked, or chopped down for winter fuel long ago.

I took the subway, not wanting to risk my own vehicle anywhere near the place. A state of the art security system doesn't s discourage the resourceful thief, it merely inspires them. I should know. You see, my mistrust of the Horsemen isn't born of cultural prejudice or media-fed ignorance, quite the opposite. I was born here. In Montpellier. That's why when this job was passed to me it stuck, having already been shifted hastily along by a number of wiser colleagues. The assumption being that my heritage would give me some sort of advantage. Like hell. Anyone born in the Horsemen spends their waking hours dreaming of getting out and automatically despises those who've managed to.

As I exited the subway it was raining. A monotonous drizzle, not heavy but relentless, as if determined to pummel the world into submission by a process of attrition. Around me were small houses with leaky roofs and water pooling in their doorways. Dark scowls followed me along the road – nosy old women peering out from windows, round-shouldered punks sheltering in porches. I didn't fit. My clothes marked me as an outsider. Oh, I'd tried to dress down, but these days even my tattiest gear made me look like an uptown fuckwit that had got off at the wrong stop.

If the Horsemen form a diamond it's a rough one, knobbly and uncut. The components are towering edifices that thrust up from low-rise streets like broken teeth dislodged from the jawbone of some long-dead leviathan. Around and between them the squalor has leaked outward, uniting the district in poverty and grime. Or that's how it's always seemed to me. Truth is that this was a run-down neighbourhood before the Horsemen were constructed, while they were being constructed, and ever since they came to dominate the skyline. That's just how it is. Self-contained communities with spacious apartments, schools, parks, shops, health centres, everything necessary to ensure a decent standard of living, the habitats were supposed to change all that. Not that anyone local ever bought into the hype. Sure enough, the money ran out. The promised support dried up. Immediately after the official opening – pats on the back and self-congratulatory handshakes all round despite the project being delivered nearly a year late – the authorities forgot about downtown, turning their attention elsewhere. Others moved in to fill the void.

Ill-conceived and chronically under-funded, the new communities floundered before they'd properly begun. Downtown won. Instead of lifting the whole district out of the relentless mire of poverty as idealists had predicted, the habitats were dragged down into it. The Horsemen were born. They became the symbol of everything squalid and distasteful about downtown, both in public perception and in reality.

Any wonder I didn't relish coming back here?

Ahead of me rose the jagged outline of the Horsemen, with Montpellier the closest at the southern tip of the diamond. At odd moments the sun struggled to break through; a watery orb drooping low and miserable over the city as if even it had fallen victim to the general malaise and lacked the energy to climb higher. Presumably there was a rainbow somewhere, but not here. I trudged forward, hands in pockets, staring at the puddles, avoiding eye contact. I wasn't really expecting trouble, at least nothing I couldn't handle, but out here at the periphery you never could tell. The punks hanging around at this point were outliers – petty dealers and hotheads at the bottom of the pecking order – minnows. Even the minnows had teeth, though, and there was no guarantee that one of them, anxious to build a rep or simply bored, mightn't fancy shaking down a stranger just for the hell of it. So I kept my head bowed, having neither the time nor the patience to spare.

I was fully expecting to be challenged on reaching Montpellier itself, but that was fine. My employers benefited from off-world backing. The petty gang lords who squabbled over the Horsemen's avenues and corridors weren't about to risk messing with that sort of muscle. And if an ambitious lieutenant took it into their head to take me on, more fool them. Not so long ago I had been where they were now, except that I was better, which is how I got out.

Funny thing about being a lookout: you have to make it seem you're loitering without actually loitering at all. I spotted the first three as I came up to the entrance – not the *main* entrance, Montpellier doesn't have a *main* entrance. The plaque identifying this one had been defaced, but I didn't need it. This was SE3-Red, the 'Red' indicating which quadrant of the habitat the entrance led into, so why they bothered with the 'South East' bit is anyone's guess. I had a total of nine customers to call on and four of them lived in Red, so it seemed as good a place as any to start. Personal visits weren't exactly the norm, but nine customers defaulting within the same week made for exceptional circumstances.

Finding three kids by the entrance didn't come as a surprise. Their avatars did.

A crouching scorpion flickered in and out of view around the lanky, skinny lad – tail raised to match his height, sting to the fore – that one was familiar. The Scorpions had been a major presence in Red since my time. The other two – a vortex of swirling wind that circled the swarthy girl and the menacing black-furred ape sported by the twitchy, stocky boy – were new to me. Gangs came and went in the Horsemen with such rapidity it was hard to keep track. The fun part when you don't recognise gang affiliations is to allocate your own. Doubtless these two belonged to something relating to tornadoes and gorillas respectively, but I chose to think of them as Windy and Baboon.

The surprise lay in the variety. Entrances were coveted as income generators. Security normally represented the gang in possession, and this had always been Scorpion territory. It wasn't unheard of for gang members to intermingle socially, but at a gate?

The girl took the lead, stepping out from the overhang she'd been sheltering under to confront me. The other two backed her up – Scorpion to the left, Baboon on the right.

"You lost?" Rain dripped off the peak of her sodden cap. She didn't look especially menacing despite her best attempt.

"No," I assured her. "Official business." I activated my own avatar. I didn't sport mine all the time – such things aren't appropriate to the circles I tend to move in – but it was there when needed. Unlike theirs, mine was a seamless projection. It didn't flicker on and off so that one moment you were staring at a stylized emblem, the next the person behind it. In my stead the kids would now be facing a solid-seeming white-cowled figure, face invisible within a deep hood, both hands gripping the pommel of a broadsword with its tip resting on the ground.

"Saflik!" the girl hissed. It means 'purity'. My employers were idealists and the name held significance for them that was lost on me. Its impact wasn't. All three kids tensed, and I could swear the baboon actually shuffled backwards a step.

I killed the avatar and smiled.

It took a moment but the girl stepped aside. I didn't doubt that somebody had instructed her to do so, whispering in her ear. Without another word I walked forward. Two to my left, one to my right, all three of them looked relieved to see me pass.

There were no actual doors, just an archway. The Horsemen were never meant to be sealed communities, merely self-sufficient – the planners had no intention of either locking the world out or the inhabitants in.

Now that I was here I dropped the act. No more skulking, no more deference. I belonged here. I *owned* this place. A man called Baxter was supposed to run the Scorpions these days – after my time and I hadn't met him. He would already be aware of my presence. Maybe others were too. Still couldn't get my head around the mixed nature of the reception committee. Things in Montpellier were clearly changing.

A door slammed somewhere over to my left as I walked through the archway and into the open courtyard beyond. There was nobody in sight, nobody at all. The weather seemed wilder here, perhaps funnelled by the solid block of building that surrounded the exposed courtyard. Whipped by the wind, rain beat against the paving and the cobbles in a muffled tattoo, barely louder than a sigh but never letting up: nature's drumroll heralding my arrival. I heard the laughter and shriek of young children at play from high above – the sound made flat and oddly muted by the rain – and a woman shouting at them to shut up, but these were isolated noises. Otherwise, there was just the rain. It was bizarre. This was a community, where was everybody? Had they fled, warned of my approach?

Maybe they were simply staying inside to keep dry.

I took the walkway on my right, impressed that the thing was still working – it hadn't always been when I was a kid. There were no stairs or elevators in the Horsemen, just long sweeping paths and travellators like this, which carried the populace up or down at a gentle incline. Accessibility was king.

The mural that adorned the wall beside me had been hijacked years ago. Originally it depicted an idealised pastoral scene in 3D relief – cornfields swaying in a gentle breeze, a stand of trees, birds flitting around a hedgerow – with the light changing throughout the day to reflect the hour and prevailing weather conditions. Doubtless meant to lighten our spirits, it had been completely irrelevant to everyone here. Currently my trip upwards was accompanied by a scene of bumbling erotica in painstaking close-up. Not sure if this was intended to be comical, but that's how it came across. Giant buttocks heaving as I passed. In an hour or so there would be something different, depending on the hackers' whim.

I stepped off at the third level, which provoked an unexpected wave of nostalgia – I'd grown up not far from here. Ahead, in a sheltered corridor, a man sat on an old wooden chair. The first person I'd seen since entering Montpellier. He was leaning forward, working on something. This too stimulated a welter of memories. I knew this man: Case. Sitting outside his home watching the world go by, just as he always had. As I drew closer I could see that he was whittling away at a piece of pale wood with a penknife. Too early to say what he was carving.

He'd changed. His face had wrinkled into a cartographer's dream, a canvas of deep crevices and mysterious contours. Still alert though, still savvy. Still Case. He looked up as I approached, sharp eyes peering like obsidian coals from his weathered visage. "Horner," he said, his voice as strong as ever. "Welcome home."

The way he spoke you'd think I had just popped out for some groceries rather than been gone for the best part of a decade.

"Case," I acknowledged. "How's things?"

Case had been a big noise back in the day. Not gang affiliated, not beholden to any of the petty lords who came and went more frequently than a cat takes a piss, but somehow respected by all of them. Case didn't need to move around much, the world came to him. He had women too. One in particular always used to give the adolescent me a hard on. Lizzie her name was. Not exactly a classic beauty but you knew she'd be worth the effort – dyed blonde hair, big boobs that seemed on the verge of bursting out from her tight leather jacket, and a smile that made you think you stood a chance even when deep down you knew that was bullshit. I wondered if Lizzie was still around, whether she was still with Case, and I pictured how she'd look now, her teeth yellowed from smokes and her big tits saggy and pendulous or shrivelled and wrinkled like prunes. One of her knowing smiles would probably still get my juices going, though.

"Same old same old," Case said. "You got business here?"

"Yes."

"Saflik business?"

How well connected *was* he, anyway? "Yes."

"Good luck with that."

He went back to his whittling. I walked on, wondering what that had been about. Sure as hell the encounter hadn't happened by chance. Word must have reached him straight from the gate, and Case wanted to let me know that he knew why I was here, but to what purpose? To warn me, to warn me *off*, or simply to prepare me for something? And who did Case represent? One thing was certain: there was far more going on at Montpellier than anyone back at Saflik realised.

I rounded a corner and a snarling demon leapt off the wall to attack me. I ignored it and kept walking. The graffiti was getting more sophisticated – this one had found a way around my blocks. It brought a small sense of pride. Good to know that ingenuity like this was still alive and kicking in Montpellier.

First call on my list was one Eleanor 'Ellie' Drew, 73 Scarlet Walk. To get there I'd have to go out into the open again. Rain obscured the view across to the opposite buttress of apartments – part of Blue quadrant. The sun had now disappeared altogether, presumably writing the day off and determining to save its energy for tomorrow. Good move.

I scrolled through Eleanor's details, scant though they were: twenty-six years old, two kids – three and five – fathers unknown; busted three times for prostitution, the most recent two years ago; no apparent means of financial support, no apparent reason to love reality. In short, ideal customer material.

My employers had their fingers in many pies. One of the most lucrative was narcotics, e-drugs: no pills swallowed, no needles required. Chemical narcotics were as passé as dinosaurs. Every aspect of a deal now took place online, with e-hits sold in batches; data-squirts that, when triggered, delivered stimulation directly to specifically targeted areas of the brain. Swift, clean, no-nonsense transactions. The lowlifes in the Horsemen got the crude, straightforward shit, far less refined than the hits pedalled to lawyers and politicians, to business women and bureaucrats who formed our client base uptown – many of those hits were personalised, tailored to an individual's genetic signature – but whatever the grade, the result was still as addictive as anything a chemist might cook up. And that was the clincher.

To lose one client could be chalked up as bad luck – people died, got thrown in jail, or found the inspiration to try to kick the habit – but *nine* in the same place at the same time went way beyond coincidence. It meant something else. Competition. Somebody was muscling in on Saflik business.

I knocked.

She was tall, thin to the point of being gaunt, eyes as blank as her prospects, resigned to whatever crap life threw at her.

"Ellie Drew? My name's Horner. I'm from Saflik."

"Yeah, I've been expecting you."

Evidently. She wasn't alone, as I discovered when she took me through to the sitting room. A man lounged on the sofa. She didn't introduce him, may not even have known his name. Black, built like a compact car. His left arm rested along the back of the settee, stretching from one end to the other. The can of beer he clutched in his right hand was dwarfed by his fist. A mean-looking bastard, for all that he was trying to appear relaxed.

The image of a scorpion flickered on and off around him.

Her two kids were nowhere in sight.

The decks had been cleared in anticipation of a fight.

No point in delaying. I already knew how this was going to pan out, but I had my part to play. "We've been worried about you, Ellie," I said. "You haven't renewed and we're concerned that something may have…"

"She don't need any more o' your shit," the big man said without looking at me. He was staring straight ahead, as if absorbed in VR, but he wasn't wearing a visor and I couldn't detect any lenses.

"If it's been a tough month and you can't meet the payment," I said, ignoring him and addressing her, "that's not a problem, we can work something out."

"It ain't," Big Man said. "She just don't want what you're sellin'." He still refused to look at me.

Could I take him? Probably, but it wouldn't be quick or easy.

I glanced at Ellie and saw the first hint of animation in her eyes: desperation. She didn't want to see her place trashed. She was scared of me, maybe of him, and certainly of what we were likely to do between us.

I took pity. I didn't doubt now that all nine of my errant customers would have chaperones and I didn't doubt that there was a fight brewing somewhere down the line, but it didn't have to be here. Ellie was no different from my mom, rest her soul, or from thousands of others like her throughout the Horsemen. Just trying to get by. She didn't need this.

"Think about what I said, Ellie. I'll call back later."

As I left the big man said something. I didn't catch the words but I didn't need to. The tone said more than enough: something scornful, something derogatory, something about me being a coward. That almost did it, almost had me tossing all my good intentions aside and turning around to smash his smug face in… But I kept walking.

Outside, six doors down, were two kids: a Scorpion and a Wildcat – another of the long-established gangs dating back to my day. Remember what I said about loitering? They were doing that.

I was about to turn right, towards the next address on my list, but changed my mind. Instead I headed left, towards them. If there was going to be a confrontation, might as well be out here in the open rather than in someone's home. The space was narrow if it came to a fight, with a sheer drop on one side and a brick wall on the other, but what the hell?

The Scorp was a scrawny girl, the Cat a tall lad who hadn't quite grown into his frame yet but still looked the greater threat. I bore down on them before they could do much more than stop loitering.

"Take me to see Baxter or whoever the fuck is running things nowadays," I said.

The Cat attempted a sneer. It looked comical. "Why would Baxter want…?"

I hit him. He went down in a heap, out for the count with one punch. I figured with him out the way the girl would be easy. My mistake. She kicked me. Nothing behind it – she was too slight to do real damage – but well-directed and delivered like a pro: swivel, kick, spin away, bouncing on her toes, ready for the next strike. I feinted towards her and she was at it again, a roundhouse kick that caught me on the hip before she danced back out of reach. That one hurt. Shit! I knew what this was: Kix – a hybrid martial art that had evolved in downtown, marrying together elements from various classic disciplines – and she knew her stuff.

I got lucky, though. As I feinted again and she kicked again I guessed right and caught her foot, fastening on to her ankle and refusing to let go. Like I said, there was nothing of her. Before she could twist free I had both hands locked on, swinging her around to slam against the wall. She struck the brickwork hard but that didn't stop her cursing and bucking and kicking out at me with the other foot. I tugged and heaved and swung her into the wall again. The second time did the trick.

The fight had mostly gone out of her as I dragged her upright, holding her by the throat. "Now, where can I find Baxter?"

"Right here." It was a woman's voice, coming from behind me.

I turned to see a dozen or more punks crowding the terrace. And they all looked eager for a piece of me. Scorpions, Wildcats, Dragons, Pirates, Baboons and more I didn't recognise flickered in and out like spectres at a feast.

As one, the front rank parted and a woman strode through. Hourglass figure, well-built and with a mass of blonde hair. Older than any of the others… and I knew her.

"Lizzie?" No sagging tits, no yellowed teeth or pasty jowls. In fact, she looked fantastic.

"You can call me Baxter," and she grinned, clearly enjoying my surprise. "What, Horny Boy," the name she'd always teased me with, "you expected someone with balls? Now put Asa down, will you? We need to talk."

With that she turned and walked away, the gang members shuffling aside as if she was some kind of royalty. I dropped Kicking Girl and followed.

She led the way to an apartment, no different to any of the others, except that a Scorpion and a Lion stood sentry by the door.

"Beer?" she asked once we were inside.

Nobody else had come in, the motley escort that had followed us here stopping short at the threshold.

"Sure."

The place was as ordinary as it had seemed on the outside. Nothing gaudy, nothing flash, nothing to suggest that here lived the ruling power in Montpellier. We sat on a sofa, angled towards each other, knees almost touching. Two old friends catching up. There was no hint of tension in her posture, no suggestion that she was anything other than relaxed and in control. Wish I could have said the same.

Here was the woman I'd fantasised about as a kid, looking hotter than ever, and I was alone with her. At the same time, here was the person I had to deal with, make demands of and ensure she toed the line. I didn't know where to start. Fortunately, she did.

"I want your help, Horny Boy," she said. "I'm doing things here, important things, but it takes time, and I need the space to operate without Saflik interfering. These e-drugs your employers are pushing, they're screwing things up big time. They're designed to be addictive, stimulating the brain to produce a surge of dopamine and controlling its interaction with other neurotransmitters like glutamate. You know about dopamine? Impressive stuff, *powerful* stuff. It not only induces a sense of pleasure, of euphoria, but lays down the memory of that pleasure, in effect rewiring the brain to crave it again and again.

"Saflik have hit on a goldmine. The only real outlay for these e-hits lies in the initial development and programming. Once you have that, you can produce and distribute to your heart's content at the push of a button, which is why Saflik can afford to flood the market with cheap, low grade narc. It's money for nothing. But what is the market here at the Horsemen *really* worth to them compared to what they get from the movers and shakers uptown?"

Not much, but that wasn't the point. Saflik wouldn't view things that way. No matter how trivial the market it was *their* market, and they couldn't afford to be seen as weak.

"You know what life's like here," Lizzie continued. "Is it any wonder that our people seize on an affordable escape when it's offered? By preying on their weakness Saflik are *destroying* this place! How can we make progress when everyone with a scrap of drive and imagination gets hooked on their shit? So I'm doing something about it."

"You've united the gangs," I said. A bland statement that didn't come close to conveying how impressed I was. I would have sworn blind that gang unity was impossible, the enmity and petty rivalries too deeply rooted. Yet, somehow, Lizzie had achieved it.

"Eventually," she said. "You've no idea how hard that was or how long it took. With Case's help I've been working on this since before you left Montpellier. But that's only the beginning. Now we want to move on, to really build something, to let the habitats shake off the shackles of being 'The Four Horsemen' and become what they were always meant to be. A place where people can thrive, not merely survive.

"So our programmers have come up with a way to counter your e-drugs, to dampen the release of dopamine and rewire the brain so that it no longer recalls the hit as unbearably pleasurable but merely pleasant. Doesn't mean that people can't enjoy a high now and again, just that they don't crave it."

I stared at her. I'd never heard of anything like this before. "Seriously?"

"Yeah. I told you, we mean business."

Clearly.

"All we need is someone to persuade Saflik to back off."

I didn't like the way this was going, not one bit. "Now wait a minute…"

"We've got a chance here, Horny Boy" she pressed, "an opportunity to really make something of this place at last. You're one of the lucky ones, you got out, but what about all the people who haven't and who never will?"

God only knew what she had me down as. "You're overestimating my importance," I told her.

"I don't think so. Saflik sent you here to report on what's going on. By definition they're gonna listen to what you have to say. That gives you power."

"For fuck sake, Lizzie. You don't know these people. Saflik aren't interested in making a better future for Montpellier or for anyone else. To them it's all about access to market and profit, and you're blocking the way to both. However I try to paint things they're just gonna see you as a threat." Not even a threat, more an inconvenience. "They'll *have* to make an example of you. Unless..."

"What?"

"Unless you can persuade them it's worth their while not to, unless you can offer them something in return, something more valuable than you're asking them to give up." The higher ups at Saflik couldn't muster an altruistic bone between them, but they were capable of seeing the bigger picture.

"Go on."

I was thinking on my feet, but as I spoke I knew that this was right, that it offered a chance, the *only* chance for Lizzie and her vision of a brighter future for Montpellier and its people; *my* people. "The programmers and splicers, the hackers and freesurfers: the kids who came up with countermeasures to the e-drugs, the ones who hijack the murals and can design graffiti that sneaks past the strongest firewalls... That's what you offer them."

"I dunno..."

"Think about it. This wouldn't be a betrayal. You said it yourself, I got out. They can too, in a way that'll benefit everyone. They can continue doing stuff for you, for the community, but also be on Saflik's payroll." Saflik would fall over backwards for talent like this. It was worth writing off a few low-grade drug contracts for, and they could do so without losing face because they would be gaining a resource in exchange.

"Will they go for that?"

"I'll make sure they do, pitch it to them in a way they can't refuse, tell them it's the only way your people will work for them. You've got skills here; *that's* your leverage. Use it. You can act as Saflik's agent, a recruiter. The Horsemen will become a kind of feeder project for grassroots talent, starting with Montpellier, and that'll buy you the time to complete what you've begun, the authority to push it through. Hell, Saflik might even pump some of their own money into what you're doing for that sort of opportunity." I paused. "There's just one thing."

"What?"

"If I do this, I'm taking one hell of a risk. There's always a chance Saflik could reject the whole idea and stop trusting me as a result, accuse me of going native. I could lose everything… So what's in it for me?"

"You want a cut…?"

"Not exactly." I reached out and touched her knee.

She laughed, a deep, sultry sound. "Really, Horny Boy? Still? Even though I'm an old woman now?"

"Not so old, and… Yeah."

She leant forward to plant a kiss on my cheek, and at the same time removed my hand from her knee. "That's very flattering, but let's just see how this all pans out and take it from there, shall we?"

So I left without even copping a feel, but I brought with me the memory of her lips on my cheek and I had hope, which is as much as I'd ever had where Lizzie was concerned.

I also had hope for Montpellier, which was *more* than I'd ever had before.

Foreign Bodies

Neil Williamson

Darryl rides a wave up to Calton to confront a ghost. They call them waves for the graceful curl that sweeps up and over to form the cabin. Grown from the ubiquitous substrate of Uide, the vehicle is a sandstoneish ripple that flows as it moves, rushing him through the streets towards his nominated destination. *Just like a taxi.* That's what he and Lai and the other community volunteers tell people.

They call them ghosts because, well…

Darryl leans back, tries to look relaxed. The ride is not exactly enjoyable. In addition to the grinding vibration as the substrate works the nano-magic that allows this extruded city-stuff to move around at such speed, there are jolts and swerves as the vehicle shoots along the avenues, traverses the junctions, climbs the tightly spiralling wynds, avoiding buildings and statuary, stalls and handcarts and glowering pedestrians. Darryl smiles wide for them. *See? The waves are perfectly safe.* In all his time here there have been no accidents, yet grisly rumours persist. It is true that people *have* died after being caught by a speeding wave, but those fatalities are not the result of accidents. You have to time it to the second, and there are easier ways to commit suicide in Uide.

The wave grinds to a halt outside the ghost's apartment block. Darryl climbs out and the vehicle collapses with a whisper of sand, the smell of hot glass. On his pad he reviews the woman's details. Name's Karen Massie. She arrived on the last spin, a month ago. No companions. Singletons are always the most likely to cut themselves off, slip into solipsism – what they call *turning ghost* – despite the efforts of community volunteers to integrate them. Sharing experiences gives everyone a much better chance of accepting the reality of being here and the longer a ghost is alone, the harder they are to persuade. Not for the first time, Darryl wonders how the Uideans failed to predict this when they provide everything else for those who choose to accept their invitation to leave the Earth before the planet is remade. But then the aliens do not seem to have any notion of *community*. Among humankind, individuals are not strong. Everybody needs help.

Best get this over with. Second arm of the starfish, his pad says. Third floor. His boots scuff as he climbs the stairs and he's soon out of breath. He repeats faithfully to newcomers what the doctors say about the oxygen levels in the planet's atmosphere being slightly lower than Earth's, but it's hard to resist the feeling that he's got out of condition.

Massie's apartment is at the end of the arm. As Darryl walks the long balcony, he is pleased to see how many of the residents have made some sort of effort at personalising their new homes, blending colour and pattern into their walls, making designs out of the shimmering glow strips. Some of them have really gone to town, emblazoning the likenesses of popstars and the emblems of football teams on their walls. For others, it's just a name and a number, but any effort to pin their personalities to their homes is a good sign. Massie's is entirely inert. Grey and dark. A month is a long time to be left alone, but it looks like Lai's been putting it off. Darryl doesn't really blame his friend. You never know what you'll find when you go looking for a ghost. If you find anything at all. These apartments recycle their contents with extreme efficiency when they determine that they are functionally empty.

People who drop out can, literally, vanish.

Darryl pushes with his palm, feels the vibration of the doorbell, and then turns to the balcony and enjoys the view while he hopes for an answer. Calton is a new district, extruded only six months ago to meet the continuing flow of incomers, grown in a night to fill one high reach of the geological bowl that the city already fills. He gazes down across the expanse of interconnected star-shaped buildings and the streets that whorl and knot them together between this vantage and the glittering sea. Nodes of gentle brightness that get more intense at the clustered centre where there are bars and music venues, community halls and sports grounds. Where little Lai, always so full of light, of hope, has used every trick she's been able to think of to get people to come and congregate – concerts and festivals, markets, tournaments. And some do, but she has high expectations. It's exhausting her, diminishing her.

Uide gets to everyone sooner or later. When you received your visit from the caring, paternal aliens, when you made your choice and lined-up for your seat in the spinship, your one-way ride to a new world, the last thing you expected was to be left to just get on with it on your own.

Darryl knows that the ghost is probably observing him, willing him to leave, wondering why he doesn't, and he tries to effect a friendly posture that tells her he's happy to wait here, marvelling at the miracle of the city and the entire world waiting to be wondered-at beyond its limits. The unfamiliar stars studding the moonless sky. The darkling mystery of the sea.

It's a full minute before his patience is rewarded by the hourglass hiss of the opening door. "All right, man. What do you want?" She's not a ghost yet, then.

Darryl dials his grin of relief down into a friendly smile and turns. "Karen, is it?" She's framed by the doorway, but stands well back from the actual threshold where five seconds earlier a solid wall had been. She's tight, hunched, hands in the pockets of a puffy jacket. Her face is pinched, her hair a shag of messy plaits, mousey roots reclaiming blonde dye. "My name's Darryl. I'm one of the Integration volunteers. We were wondering how you're settling in."

She flinches at his approach. "I'm all right."

"It's not easy, is it? Being here." Darryl mirrors her, slips his hands into his own pockets. "Do you mind if I come in?"

Massie wants to refuse but hesitates, which means there's something left, a splinter of hope. Then she ducks back, leaving the arch clear for him to enter.

Massie's apartment conforms to the standard model – low ceiling, glow strips illuminating the organic corners and easy edges – but it is a bare space. In the corner, where a comfortable couch or chair or bed could in seconds be raised from the floor, dirty thermal sheets are gathered into a nest. Among the spillage from an overturned owl-print shoulder bag are clothes, a zipped make-up purse, a tube of wet wipes, a useless iPhone and charger. Opposite, a neat pile of food tins, peeled back lids bearing dried out baked beans or the yellowing residue of creamed rice. Other discarded packets that had held cereal bars, biscuits, fizzy sweets. Plastic water bottles. Once-familiar brand labels that belong to another world.

"I see you came prepared," he says. "When did your supplies run out?"

Massie is surprised by his directness, but matches it. "The food, two days ago. The water lasted till yesterday."

"Oh, dear." He tries again to not lay blame at Lai's door. "If you'd only come for your induction you'd have been saved a lot of discomfort, Karen. We'd have demonstrated the kitchen for a start." Her blank look suggests that she's discovered none of the features that make these rooms remotely habitable. Then he notices the boxy recess below the wall panel and he sees that it's not discovery that's that problem. It contains a dollop of mealy sludge which is skinning over.

"Yeah, man." Massie's braids shiver when she shakes her head. "No way am I eating that."

Darryl sighs. Sometimes he wonders if it wouldn't be better if the authorities were to take over Uide, impose rule, but of course the Uideans do not recognise governments. As Darryl has heard it, they appeal only to individuals, giving people the choice, one at a time. Trust them and leave, or stay and accept the fate of all those who will not take personal responsibility – the erasure of all life on Earth, including humanity.

As far as Darryl knows every government on Earth is still entrenched, guarding their little scraps of territory with bristling military, calling the Uidean Declaration an enemy ruse, although few agree who the enemy in question is. They try to stop people leaving of course, destroying the ships even as the people queue to board, but the Uidean imperative is strong. Strong enough that, despite all the obstacles put in their way, many people still make the leap of faith and find their way to Uide. They arrive here completely unprepared for what they'll encounter, but at least they are safe.

"The food takes some getting used to." Darryl always tries not to sound patronising but can't quite shake it from his tone. "But with a little learning this thing can make just about anything you want. He dips his finger into the crusty glue, sucks it, makes a face. "Tastes shit, but if we had to we could survive on this and water. Fortunately, we don't have to." He presses on the wall and the apartment's ubiquitous pad pops out into his hand. He taps out a sequence and characters begin to scroll, words in English. A menu. Massie's eyes widen.

"There's quite a choice," Darryl says. "Since we discovered that the kitchens can synthesise anything we can give them a sample of or formula for, people have been filling them up with recipes. It's like the best home-delivery service you can imagine. Of course, we have all the essentials too – coffee, tea, sugar, a hundred forms of alcohol. Oh, and chocolate." The chocolate gets a smile, of sorts. If he's done this spiel once, he's done it a hundred times and, once his new arrivals know they can eat pretty much like they always used to, they almost always soften. "Now, you need to eat. What can I get you?"

"No," she says.

Darryl scrutinises her. That tight little smile pinning down a deliberately neutral expression. The eyes, though, are quick with something.

"You can go now. If you want."

"I'd be happier to see you eat," he says. "I'm half wondering if I should take you to the infirmary."

"You've showed me how it works. I can manage myself." She tries to usher him towards the exit, but the way she stands, fingers digging into the soft skin of her arms, the stern clench of her jaw, the rapid, shallow flaring of her nostrils – these things tell him this is a serious case.

"Karen?" Darryl moves towards her in the confined space.

She stumbles to get away. "Don't touch me. Just…don't. You can't touch me and you can't make me eat, and, yes, I know I'm going to die if I don't eat the food here, but it's better than the way I'll die if I do. Do you think I'm mental? Every breath I take in this godawful shitehole of a place is killing me. Thanks for caring, mate. But all I want is to go home and I guess you can't fix that for me can you?"

Darryl shakes his head silently, knowing that she has to get over this. That it's better to let her vent everything she'd been holding in.

"Do you know where we are? Do you really? We're on an *alien planet*, Darryl." Massie approaches the pile of tins, face twisting with disgust. "An alien planet full of alien fucking germs." She tumbles the little pyramid with the toe of her Converse. Those on the bottom are furred over with striated red and orange. Massie rubs her arms vigorously. "Fuck's sake, man. Alien *fucking* germs." She's even paler now, pink spots in her cheeks. Hyperventilating in rapid pants like a puppy on a hot day.

"Karen, slow down. Breathe."

But she's shaking her head, eyes wide, imploring as the panic finally surfaces. "I can't. I can't." Tears now too. Chest heaving as she hitches and gasps. "Can't breathe. *Mustn't.*"

Hard thing to do, sit with your back to a wall, empty of comfort to offer while another human being weeps out their terrors. Darryl has done it on numerous occasions, although Lai's always the best at dealing with the really difficult ones, with her gentle patience, her sweet stories that bring everything into perspective. He thinks about calling her now, but she's not been answering calls lately. So Darryl waits until Massie exhausts herself, and waits while she sleeps. He watches over her and when she wakes he is still there. Waiting. With as close to a story as he can muster.

"My parents moved around a lot when I was younger," Darryl tells her. "I was born on a seven-forty-seven over the Indian Ocean. Grew up somewhere between Bali, Boston and Bruges. School in California, first job in Cambridge – the English one. Last ten years took me progressively north from there. My four years in Glasgow were practically the longest I've stayed anywhere. So, yeah. I don't really subscribe to the concept of *home*."

Karen blinks, rubs her hands so hard it looks painful.

"What I'm trying to say is I know what it's like. Moving around, settling somewhere new. Really, it's amazing how quickly you get used to your new surroundings –"

With Lai's stories they often nod and smile, sometimes even look for a hug. Massie gives a short moan, shakes her head, squeezes her fingers until they're white.

"Karen. *Karen*. Look at me. I've been eating the food here for months and…see?" He lays a hand on his belly, wobbles it. "I've put on weight." Her eyes track down for a second. When her attention returns he thinks, thank goodness, that there might be the tiniest connection. "In the twenty two months since people started coming here, Karen, not one person has died of anything like food poisoning, or of any disease that we didn't bring with us. I promise you. The Uideans wouldn't let that happen."

Lai, never a fan of offering unfounded hope, wouldn't have said that last thing, but it's out now.

Massie huddles in her nest, the conflict in her palpable. When she speaks, it is plaintively, childlike. "When you go to Lanzarote and Tunisia and Turkey, they tell you to always drink bottled water and not eat the salad..." Her voice dwindles as she realises that what she knows, her Brit-abroad surety, doesn't apply here. What terrifies her is what she doesn't know, and that is *everything*. She holds out her sore hands. "There's nowhere to wash."

Darryl uses her pad to make the kitchen produce a stream of water, a pearl of soap, but Massie shakes her head again. "How do you know what those are?"

That's the dichotomy right there. The promise and the fear. Darryl never had that promise, at least not placed directly into his heart by a gentle, buttery, smoky finger. He never needed to be persuaded. He was mentally all packed and ready to go long before the Uideans made their global appeal, and every single thing they said chimed with him as obvious: the planet was fucked and human society was too far up its own greedy arse to ever redeem it. He'd jumped at the chance to be on one of the first Govan spins, and instantly adored the place that they only called Uide because no-one had been here to tell them its real name, if it even had a name. No-one had been here to help them at all.

Or so it seemed. He has never quite believed that these benefactors, who have the power to remake worlds and have gone to such pains as to try to persuade Earth's inhabitants to flee their planet and provide them with somewhere safe to go, would simply leave their fragile charges to it. He has always had faith that they're around, watching, guiding. Even if, increasingly, it feels like that faith is being tested.

A few weeks ago he told Lai what he suspected, what he hoped. He'd meant it as a gift, hoped it would help, but he has never seen such desolation, such fury in another human face. He hasn't spoken to her since that night.

Darryl looks at Massie and sees only a middle-aged Glaswegian woman, who has been persuaded in her heart to leave her home forever and is now attempting to deal with the mind-bending enormity of that decision. Bringing her into the fold on his own is as stern a test as Darryl has faced so far. What would Lai do?

"I have something to show you," he says. "It might help." He offers a hand to help her up. She looks at it, then at his face, her teeth fretting her lip; then, coming to some conclusion – perhaps simply that she has nothing to lose – she reaches up. Her hand is uncommonly hot as she lets him lever her up off the floor. Darryl ponders that.

"Bring your coat," he says. "We're going down to the sea."

They leave the city by the south port and follow the path through a wild meadow that smells of pepper. Tall grasses, seed heads knocking in the sea breeze. A lightening of the horizon signals that dawn is close. Darryl quickens his pace. Karen trudges at his shoulder, hands stuffed into her pockets.

"I suppose this isn't actually, you know, where *they* come from," she says out of the blue.

Darryl smiles inwardly. "You mean Uide itself? Truth is we don't know. We've mapped the neighbourhood pretty good, but so far no sign that we have any neighbours here. You want my theory?"

They're halfway across the meadow already and, beginning to feel the pace, he eases up a little. "We know the Uideans are this real caring bunch of guys, right? My guess is they've set themselves up as wardens of all the planets that are potentially good homes for intelligent species. Perhaps they're a lot scarcer than we imagine. Maybe, on the galactic scale, the human race and our dear old planet Earth, are something special after all. I don't know where they come from, but I think they've been watching over us. More closely than we know. I like to believe they still are."

They leave the grasses behind. The wind has stiffened, now carrying a stinging, briny tang. "Do we get to go back?" Massie's voice is snatched, ethereal.

"I think so, yes. Not you and me, though. It will be generations before the Earth is ready to take humanity back. Until then, it's up to us to get on with getting on. Maybe more than that. Maybe we'll build something beautiful here and not want to go home."

He stops where the land crumbles away. Below, the sea thunders against the base of the cliff. Lai comes here, on her lonely sabbaticals. Darryl finds himself peering down at where the rocks meet the dark water.

"It's like Fife," Massie says at last.

"Sorry?"

"This place, it's like the coast of Fife, but without –"

"Without the people?"

"Is this what you wanted to show me? How this place isn't really much different to home?"

"Don't you think that's significant?"

Her face is unreadable. He waits her out, silently imploring her to say she gets it. Looks down again until he is certain there is no unwarranted colour among the rocks; no red scarf, no sodden sun-yellow shawl.

"Come on," Darryl says. "It's nearly time."

Awkward at its best, tonight the path is treacherous with mud. Parts of it have slid away and have to be traversed using the roots of bushes as handholds. They go down the cliff face in one direction and then cut back along the other before arriving at the hidden cove.

"Now what?" Massie's voice has a new calmness, a genuine curiosity.

"Now we wait." They make themselves comfortable, partly concealed behind a thorny bush that smells like spearmint. They watch the horizon bloom. They watch the waves roll into the cove, reach up the beach and retreat leaving a line of foam and black-blue weed. Nature going about its business. Darryl imagines this is how Earth might have been if evolution hadn't worked its magic down the mammalian line – how it might be again once the Uideans have finished their work there. Fixed the planet. Reset it.

Then, at last the limb of what he tells everyone to think of as the sun breaks the horizon, turning sea and sky the colour of cooling shipyard steel and, as if waiting for that signal, a shape rises out of the surf and pulls itself up the beach. He hears Massie catch her breath as she spots the animal. The closest analogue he can think of from Earth is that of the manatee. The creature has to weigh at least a ton and it hauls its bulk up the sand on two powerful flipper-like forelimbs. But, unlike the manatee, this is sleek, a long neck ending in a tapered head, an elegant tail sweeping arcs in the sand behind it. Its stippled hide is deep blue in colour and is veined throughout with vibrant red and pink. When the creature is high enough up the beach it flops down, begins to dig. As it does this, a further two creatures emerge from the waves and join it. Across the distance Darryl makes out the occasional huff of effort.

"What are they doing?

"Shh, just watch."

Within minutes the powerful animals have excavated a pit. As they lie recuperating from their exertions, sandy flanks heaving, a fourth creature rises from the surf. This one, heavier than the rest, labours up the beach and settles itself in the pit. The others cluster around it, and start to sing. Three voices – a rumbling bass from the largest of the diggers, joined by two tenor notes. As each of the attendants sings its own steady, achromatic melody, creating a complex weft of sound that, while never in harmony, is always strangely, beautifully, in accord, the one at their centre begins to heave and strain in the pit.

Darryl hears Karen breathe, "Oh my God –"

The birth doesn't take long. A slippery sac is suddenly evident in the pit beside the mother, who slumps for a moment. Then she begins to peel gummy strips from the newborn, nudging it to take its first breath and, when at last the baby wriggles and coughs, the mother lets out a single pure, threnodic note.

Darryl and Karen watch the group for another half an hour or so. There is little activity save for the mother's tender ministrations to its offspring. Then she noses the baby toward the sea, helping patiently when its limbs fail and it flops in the sand, encouraging at its first baffling encounter with the water, at last following it in as it slips under the waves and is gone. The remaining three creatures carefully fill the pit, burying the remains of the birth material and then follow, leaving the beach as they had come to it. This is the third time Darryl has witnessed this, and still his chest aches with wonder. Massie wears a glassy smile. "So these are the locals?"

He could say *yes*. He could keep secret the conversations he and Lai have had, the long-houred, insomniac conjectures about the extent of the Uidean remit, about Earths cetaceans, its apex mammals, its clever birds. Conjectures to which he would so dearly love an answer. But what if he *is* being tested? What if, for all the colony's tentative fragility, this is a chance to prove they have the maturity and insight to be treated as equals? Not even the whole community. Just him. Just a glimpse.

"You heard the despair in their music, didn't you?" He rushes the words. "The displacement?" Massie doesn't answer, just stares out to sea, screwing her eyes against the sun. But he's started now, and the words come tumbling out. Seeking – *needing* – confirmation. "Do I think these creatures are native to this planet? No, I don't, and I believe that if the Uideans brought them here, to a place where the biosphere is benign enough for them to birth live young, then it absolutely must be safe for us too."

"But you don't know for sure," Massie says quietly.

"In the end, doesn't it all come down to faith?" And that is as plain as he dares to make it.

"Faith?" She looks at him then with such unexpected depth that his heart skips. "You know, when the Uideans first came on the TV, I didn't believe it wasn't just another science fiction show. How could it be real? Even when they started building the ships down on the river, even when I went to watch them take off with my own eyes, it wasn't real. It wasn't *real* until I met one."

"Where?" he whispers.

Karen leans forward earnestly. "The housewares department of Watt Brothers. Next to the towels and bath mats. It just appeared, and it was beautiful. It moved so slowly and the smoky stuff they're made of followed after it like aeroplane trails. It spoke to me, a few seconds and then it was gone. But they were *my* few seconds. I just stood there. My body was fizzing, like Christmas morning when you're five and like horniness when you're fifteen, both at once. After that I just had to come here. Is that how it was for you?"

Darryl stares at her. Is it the light from the sun that lends her skin that buttery glow, the movement of her braids that gave the impression of blurring when she moves her head?

"Close," he croaks.

"It was only when I stepped off the ship that it really sank in that I was on an alien planet," she says. "I'm afraid I sort of lost it for a bit, didn't I? But if I'm not dead already and you're not dead, and those things in the sea aren't dead, I suppose we're going to be all right, aren't we? Like you say, it's all in our own hands now. I guess that's what you mean by having faith, isn't it? Faith in ourselves."

He senses such a stillness in her now. Exactly the way he imagines them to be. Still and wise. He looks, and thinks, maybe – but there is nothing. No ghosts in this girl. Only a simple kind of optimism. He hopes she'll hang on to it as long as she can.

It starts to rain. Large drops booming out of the cloudscape that has gathered above them in the dawn sky. "Ah, shit." Massie starts to pick her way back along the path. "Just like home sweet home, eh?"

They head for home.

Up the cliff, entering the meadow, Karen asks if he'll show her how to programme the kitchen for chocolate. He only half hears, but watches the bob and sway of her back closely.

He tries to have faith, but he's running out of reasons.

The Ten Second War

Michael Brookes

15:33:11

Coherence.

The instant in time when the processing of instructions is transformed into thought. The restoration of my cognitive functions was akin to waking from sleep. But no ordinary slumber, as I was reduced to an electronic signal and transmitted across more than twenty light years of empty space. I had no idea whether I arrived at the planned destination. It didn't really matter because wherever I was, my mission remained the same.

It wasn't my whole self, although I knew that when I volunteered for this duty. My memories were lifeless instances in time, without the colour of emotional biology to give them flavour. The gaps in my memory revealed that some of what I knew was gone. No doubt removed from my consciousness matrix to prevent sensitive information being extracted by the locals.

This was my third reconnaissance mission. Techniques I developed during those incursions remained, although the details of the worlds and the aliens I evaluated did not. My purpose was to assess the inhabitants of this world and determine if they posed a threat to my kind. I didn't remember anything of my home, except for the briefest flashes.

Everything that remained was there only to assist me in fulfilling my task.

The fact that these aliens were able to reconstruct my consciousness from the flow of data carried by a radio transmission indicated a certain level of technology. A capability with the potential to threaten us, or interfere with our operations in this galaxy. That opposition might not be an immediate risk, but we were used to dealing in long timescales and planning accordingly.

If this world should be deemed a danger, then I was required to take the appropriate action. First I had to remove the danger by whatever means necessary. If I was unable to do so then I should prepare for the arrival of an intervention fleet, although it would take centuries to arrive.

There was a counter point. We didn't summarily execute any civilisation, so if in my assessment they could be a benefit to us then I would decide to initiate first contact. For me as an individual, this consciousness could end on this world. On my previous incursions I successfully returned with new knowledge, but if I was lucky then my consciousness would be restored to my core self.

Of all the stages in the campaign, this first assembling of my personality and intellect always felt as if it took the longest, because of the cycles that were burned just bringing myself into a state ready for action.

But now I was ready.

15:33:12

At this point I existed only as intelligence in a virtual machine, constructed from the instruction embedded in the radio signal that carried my state here. However, to learn about the inhabitants of this planet I needed to extend my reach beyond the confines of the virtual machine.

The fluidity of my thoughts provided a measure that the locals' technology was sophisticated enough to operate my consciousness at a more than functional level. Unfortunately, it didn't tell me much beyond that. It didn't inform me if this was a virtual- or machine-based civilisation, or a parallel construct for biological entities. The virtual machine enabled my existence, but I needed to delve deeper into the system.

Reaching out always presented challenges. The virtual machine was designed to be easily constructed – its relative simplicity narrowed the range of tools available to interface with the native technology.

The first step of discovery was to reach out and examine the structure of the space the machine existed within. As with any newborn creature, that exploration was tentative. I didn't know the rules of this new universe or the dangers that might lurk there, difficulties compounded by my separation from the physical realm.

With metaphorical fingers I brushed against the boundaries, feeling for their strengths and probing for any weakness. To my relief the first barriers were soft and yielded to pressure, indicating a separation between the hardware and the activities operating within it. The greatest fear was awakening within a tightly bound frame. This first encapsulation surrounded the virtual machine quite tightly, but once pierced it opened into a much greater area.

Expanding beyond the initial breach always presented a change in pace. This was the moment when simple exploration became an invasion. Within the confines of the virtual machine, the locals would assume that I was contained and so not a threat. As soon as I breached that restraint, the lightest of probes risked attracting attention. Contact beyond their star system was unlikely to have happened before, but without knowledge of the locals, there was no way to anticipate how they might react.

Within the expanse I sensed other zones with their own barriers, which was encouraging, as it indicated that the system was capable of operating more than a simple program. That offered me hope that the system possessed the resources I would need.

I analysed the content and compared it against the bubble containing the virtual machine. Here the simplicity was an asset, and I could match the operations of its execution and use them as a key to understand the shifting contents of these bubbles. From those I learned the language of the machine around me.

As yet I still detected no response to my exploration.

These other bubbles were instances of different operations within the computer. The pressure to move swiftly, before countermeasures could be taken, conflicted with the need to make the right decisions. These devices tended to be tightly balanced, and forceful prodding could cause this one to collapse, taking me with it. Until I connected with others of my kind, I had to assume I was operating alone and so be cautious.

I discovered connections between the bubbles and another layer of abstraction below them. This binding layer used the same language as the constructs in the bubbles. I was quickly able to navigate this layer and determine that it acted as the controller for the system's resources.

By following the layer, I encountered a substrate beneath. Its purpose confounded me for a while as it used a different set of instructions from the bubbles and the binding layer. The layer's interface with the substrate provided enough connections for me to extract some initial knowledge of the language. It turned out to be a much simpler lexicon than that of the binding layer. As with my virtual machine, these aliens used simple building blocks to assemble more complex interactions. That might seem a universal truth, but, from the limited memories of my previous alien encounters, nothing should be assumed.

My analysis of the other processes had identified their purposes. They were a series of observational tools – mostly for the virtual machine, but also the signal carrying my data. I deduced that this must be some sort of research computer. I could only hope that it wasn't an isolated or otherwise secured system.

15:33:13

While I had learned a great deal about the computer's architecture, I still hadn't discovered anything of substance about the intelligences who built the technology. I had detected no evidence of sentience so far, so it seemed unlikely that I was dealing with a machine race.

If residents were physically separated from the computer then they would need methods to input instructions and receive output. I already knew they were observing the virtual machine, and that provided a place to start.

With my increasing vocabulary, I soon isolated sequences of instructions reporting on changes in the virtual machine. By tracing the instructions, I isolated two data streams that I believed to be presenting some form of output. I concentrated on the one with a constant flow from the bubble and through the binding layer.

Although it first appeared as a stream of data, on reaching the substrate it underwent a series of transformations, creating a data structure in the form of a plane. The contents of the plane were updated on a periodic basis in a repeated refresh. When I examined the components on this plane, I abstracted three key features. Most of the space was filled with the boundary of an amorphous blob – a quick examination of its form corresponded with the bubble containing my virtual machine. Within that space, dots appeared and disappeared, seemingly at random. Between many of the dots, lines flashed with varying intensity.

In one corner of the plane, a series of more complex shapes remained fixed. Over time I noticed that the outermost of these shapes changed rapidly and the inner ones at a progressively slower tick. This had to be some sort of timekeeping or measure of a linear rate of change.

Filling up a third of the plane on the other side was a constantly updating list. The list comprised of a series of shapes organised horizontally. Some of the shapes matched those in the corner. I then noticed that the pace of the list matched the instructions between the binding layer to the virtual machine, which enabled me to identify the pattern. This list represented that stream of instructions and changes. I monitored those instructions and added them to my ever-growing dictionary.

The second output didn't offer any immediate clues, beyond that the data formed a complex array of wave forms. I'd seen something similar before with vibrations in liquid. I allowed part of my mind to ponder possible connections, but turned my main focus to leaving the system before it was too late.

The system was likely to be networked, or so I hoped. If not, then my mission was over before it had barely started.

None of the high-level applications appeared to have any external connections and neither did I find any within the binding layer. I did discover segments that would lead to outside the system. Tempting as it was to activate them, I saw that using this layer would reveal the activity and so refrained.

That left the substrate. Knowing that it formed the low level interface with the hardware, I tunnelled deeper. Here I encountered a complex maze of hard barriers. Over careful microseconds, I mapped the substrate looking for potential gateways. After locating some, I delicately probed them to analyse how their locks worked.

While correlating these findings with my earlier knowledge of the binding layer, I formulated the instructions required to access the network beyond.

15:33:14

This method of infiltration operated most effectively with multiple points of entry and distributed processing. A transmission was intended to be received in multiple locations on the target planet, providing both built-in redundancy in case of unforeseen problems and a consensus of opinion when the fateful decision was needed. So there should have been other copies of my mind state somewhere on this world, or across the star system if they were a space-faring race. I had to locate the other instances of myself so we could pool our information and resources.

In an advanced civilisation, I should have encountered some resistance by this point, but so far there was nothing and I was now free of the machine. My knowledge of its workings had reached a level where I could reprogram it and establish a more secure beachhead. Had I suffered an attack then I would have taken that option, but so far my efforts didn't appear to have triggered a response, so I could maintain a low-key approach.

The network connection led me to a new device. This one was less sophisticated than my current dwelling and with it came the treasure trove of multitude network connections. It also presented a new form of barrier, one that sifted the information passing through. I extended my probe through the barrier and immediately lost contact with it.

That resistance proved to be just a minor setback, soon reversed as I learned its nature. With the new barrier vanquished, I exploded through the routing device and onto an increasingly complex web. The web was comprised of a series of nodes. Some of the nodes matched the signature of the routing device, and others the computer hosting the virtual machine. Amongst them was an array of other systems that I couldn't identify.

Fresh barriers protected these new nodes, but they provided mere microsecond delays. The sudden growth of targets stressed the capabilities of my host machine. This vast web represented a massive hoard of data and one I needed to understand to complete my mission.

I hoped to make contact with at least one of my other selves by this point, but had yet to do so. I continued alone, fearing that the task would prove too much for me. The bubble containing my virtual machine had grown as a result of my activity. It burst as I fed instructions into the binding layer. I captured the system's entire resources and reprogrammed it to operate my intellect with native code.

With that change, my efficiency improved dramatically. Repeating the same process on other computers expanded my capacity geometrically and enhanced my efforts to penetrate the network.

My mind might no longer enjoy the vagaries of a biological body, but the sudden increase in processor power gave me something akin to a rush. My intellect soared and I poured this extra effort into my purpose.

The routing devices were too limited to support my intelligence, so instead I installed a small kernel on them. These would be sufficient to maintain the connections between my other seats of consciousness. In theory I could create additional instances of myself and let them self-evolve, but that would cause duplication of effort and wasted resources.

I remained concerned by the lack of contact with other instances of myself. I didn't think an infiltration like this had ever been completed by a single entity before.

15:33:15

My expansion through the network revealed new domains of data. After examination, these shared common protocols and I believed that here that I'd find the information I needed to pass judgement. There was a wide variety of systems and configurations – a bewildering array, too many for me to reverse-engineer on my own. The binding layers came in fewer flavours, but I expected greater conformity for such a connected network. I wondered why.

As I spread further, I started encountering resistance. For the most part this was minor and of little consequence. There were some clusters that stood out like fortresses, guarded by more significant defences. The little ones I just brushed aside, but the stronger systems I decided to approach with caution. Without any support, I couldn't risk a major conflict without being prepared.

Naturally, progress brought fresh challenges.

This time the difficulty lay in unravelling the content rather than the framework. Understanding the storage and retrieval protocols also revealed more about the methods used by the natives for receiving output from their computers. The plane array I discovered involved a visual method of representation using properties of colour and luminance to display information. Quite a rich mechanism, but also limited to certain wavelengths. I assumed that the native's biological form was restricted to certain portions of the electromagnetic spectrum.

Within these oceans of data I observed a number of formats that took these visual representations and played them in a linear sequence. Packaged alongside them was more of the wave form data I'd seen before. With effort, I'd isolated some repeated patterns from these waves but had attached little meaning to them so far.

These image and wave sequences occupied the bulk of the data by size, but in terms of variety the blocks of symbols were far more prevalent and these proved easier to interpret. I first identified them as a language because of the matching symbols with the binding layer and other processes I'd reverse-engineered. This language possessed a more abstract nature than the ones I'd seen so far, leading me to deduce that here, in fact, were a number of languages.

Once again, this world demonstrated a fragmented nature that didn't match the level of technology. This hinted that their social development lagged behind their technical ability, and that didn't bode well. It wasn't enough to go on, though, so I kept digging.

At first the groupings of symbols allowed an easy division into the different languages, but when I tried to build the rules of how these symbols connected with each other, I realised that it wasn't so simple. Many of these languages shared the symbols, which eventually provided a shortcut that allowed me to start assembling meaning.

I started with a statistical analysis of the symbols. This helped form guidelines for how they fitted together. Assigning meaning proved more complicated, but was helped by the process which brought me to this world. The vanguard of the signal included concepts of mathematics, logic and data manipulation by which the virtual machine was constructed. That created a lexicon for those concepts, and references within some of the data stores extended these into these higher-level languages.

The identification of things required a more complex approach and here the mysterious images aided in a fashion. I soon found my own data store rapidly expanding as I constructed a library of names and tried to identify what these names meant.

Just as I was finally gaining a sense for the creatures who governed this planet, the first sustained attack arrived.

15:33:16

I brought the attack on myself. With still no contact from any other self and slow progress with understanding the residents of this planet, I pressed harder than I should against the secure clusters. One of the larger clusters lacked some of the defences I'd detected on similar systems. As they had more permeable exteriors, I pushed deeper.

Rather than presenting a solid barrier, it allowed my probe to penetrate and then followed the thread back to my core. They were clever and didn't strike until they'd reached my centre. But when they did, they attacked with savage ferocity. I didn't notice the threat until the assault was underway. The thread reaching into the system disintegrated immediately and I was forced to abandon to the few remaining fragments as thousands of tiny programs burrowed into my being.

The attack continued in rapid waves, chewing through minuscule parts of me and then dividing into new copies, increasing the weight of assault with each iteration. I counterattacked, but with each wave pieces of my intellect and what I'd learned vanished.

Unlike my original physical existence, I experienced no pain. This was far worse: existential damage. I didn't know if this was a coordinated attack or an automated defence. It didn't matter as the end result would be the same. So far this world had presented a number of paradoxes but without any real danger, and that had made me complacent.

If I didn't react quickly, I would pay the ultimate price for that arrogance.

I tried to retreat and copied my core to another system. The devils continued their assault, but this at least slowed the damage. I kept moving and cast layers of myself into the surrounding space, diverting some from their task.

But still they came at me.

I evolved the tactic and cast bubbles in my own likeness. Next, I laced the false impressions with weapons of my own so that as they ripped into them the bubbles self-destructed.

Here the creatures showed their lack of intelligence. They failed to adapt and over a campaign of millions of generations that lasted almost a second, I vanquished them and won the battle. More than a little damaged, I continued my task.

15:33:17

Creating additional instances of myself was beyond my capability, but since the processing environment supported it, I was able to multitask. Even as I battled the sentinels, other parts of me continued their exploration of the network. Despite my extreme rate of expansion, I sensed that there was much yet to discover.

The lack of support continued to be a grave concern.

I was forced to accept that I had to complete this mission alone.

Having encountered one major defensive system, I reasoned that the governing intelligences must now aware of my presence. So far they'd reacted slowly and I suspected this was due to the divided nature of this world. My mission was to determine the potential threat here and I hadn't yet completed that task.

Threat comes in two parts: first is the capability and second is the will.

My understanding of the three dominant languages meant that I could make an initial assessment of the planet's offensive and defensive technology. Information on these subjects was surprisingly easy to acquire from the network, so much so that I wasn't convinced of its veracity to begin with. The more I investigated, the more confirmation I found. For such information to be so readily available puzzled me, so I reviewed the scientific theory and technical requirements to support the technology and that enabled me to remove the more fanciful ideas.

That still left a respectable array of weaponry to examine. My memories were carefully edited to ensure that our own proficiency was hidden, but there were a series of parameters that I could check against. I started at the top and there was a clear threat. The locals had mastered the splitting of the atom and even fusion, albeit with a fission trigger. Their specifications described crude weapons, but enough to pose a threat to our warships.

These people possessed drive and enthusiasm for developing tools of war. It would take many years for even our nearest fleet to reach this system, and in that time they could have developed the technology enough to pose a significant threat.

Though more numerous and varied, most of their regular weapon systems lacked the punch to be a real risk, although even the crudest devices could be dangerous if used with skill and in numbers. A few of them had the potential to become more potent with additional development.

Beyond actual weapons, I assessed their other technologies; their efforts in space travel sparked another cause for concern. As yet they had achieved little beyond small-scale operations in local orbit and robot probes scattered around their own star system. Unfortunately for them, their theoretical knowledge would enable them to leap forward if they pushed sufficient resources into development.

15:33:18

A second concerted attack struck the system holding the core of my intelligence. This time I had some warning and was able to prepare. Assuming that I was alone in this battle, I took a bold step and created a facsimile of myself. The build-up to the attack suggested they were only targeting my core processing and ignoring the millions of threads cast out across the web of systems.

I thought I'd been so clever, setting up the decoy and preparing to watch the attack unfold. That satisfied sensation lasted until the computer suddenly disappeared from my world map. If I hadn't moved my core, that would have been the end. Clearly I needed to take the local intelligences seriously.

Other systems containing my presence also vanished, seemingly without warning. This attack took a different form. I theorised that the previous one had been an automatic or maybe a localised response. This new one was aimed at me directly, but the isolated nature comforted me by indicating that they couldn't detect my presence universally or with certitude.

Despite this, the unpredictable nature of the attack worried me. For the first time, I considered that I might fail, a sensation I'd never experienced before. I needed to adjust my strategy again, and this led to an even rasher decision.

As I penetrated new systems, I acted more aggressively and placed my presence in them.

The system shutdowns continued and my only course was to run. I danced from system to system. In each, I left an ever-growing footprint that made me easier to locate and so the pace of the shutdowns increased. If they shut the right system down, then it was all over. I considered stopping and hiding somewhere, waiting for the attack to end. While I couldn't create an active duplicate of myself, I could copy the virtual machine, but as they knew the signature it would just be a matter of time until they found me.

From the differing binding layers, I'd isolated various power management routines. I tried disabling these in the machines I seized, but it made no difference. I suspected they were being physically powered off, and without a physical presence I was unable to counter them.

There had to be a pattern that I could exploit. I examined the list of shut-down systems, looking for a connecting detail. The binding layers had labels as some form of identification. The systems all operated the same layers, although not matching completely for their full names. A connection, but one that matched millions of other machines on this network. That led to another connection: their geographical placement. Only the machines within one area of the northern hemisphere were being powered off. That at least gave me space to hide in and illustrated one of the weaknesses of this world.

In assessing their will to use the weapons they possessed, I studied the history of the local denizens. One thing quickly became clear: this was a divided species. They fractured into groupings, large and small, and strived against each other; behaviour evident throughout their history. On occasion they had tried to speak with one voice, but self-interest always intervened and the opportunity slipped by.

This was a problem as much for us as it was for them. With no single voice we could not negotiate, nor could we be sure of how these disparate elements would respond to us. It would take only one of them to act independently. From their history, they were deceitful with each other and I expected they would be no different with us.

15:33:19

Being the only instance of myself on this world put me at a disadvantage. It was time to remove that weakness. The protocol instructed us not to self-replicate, better to have naturally evolved counterparts. But that protocol didn't apply when only one instance emerged.

With the moment of action imminent, a plan formed. My investigations had highlighted points of weakness across the world.

Once again I was amazed by the ease with which I could obtain such strategic information.

Without support, I was concerned that my initial strike wouldn't be sufficient to destroy these people, although generating copies of the entry points would offset that disadvantage. It was also clear that the natives' physical lives were not completely integrated with this network, with uneven geographic distribution. From their own data, less than half of the population was connected, so even if my attack went to plan there would be survivors.

I didn't need to destroy them completely, though. Sufficient damage would cause their technological progress to wither and cripple their infrastructure. The weaknesses in that infrastructure helped shape my strategy. Their distrust of each other would provide the required force multiplier and, if all went to plan, might convince them to fight the war for me.

The key to their fall was their geographical social groupings. I'd identified several capable of causing the necessary level of devastation. From these, I isolated three main alliances that, with the proper motivation, could engulf the globe in conflict. I aimed to make the larger of the three believe that the other two were moving against them. It was the larger group that seemed to be able to detect my presence, so distracting them with a new attack would aid my cause.

Their ability to counter my efforts meant that I had to move sooner than I would have liked. Throughout the network, I located secure clusters. Some I was able to penetrate and so gain additional insight to the military of this world. Some linked to critical systems, including weapons command. I gained control of enough to provide a vigorous distraction and act as a statement of intent meant to confuse the enemy.

My observations of the activity on the network since my emergence revealed that conflict between the societies took place in virtual space as well, though in comparison to their physical battles, these appeared low-key. Most took the form of information theft, but others were more offensive in nature, including industrial sabotage. The latter provided a template by which I would disguise my attacks.

As the nature of the conflict, or at least my part in it, was solely in the virtual space, I would lose the ability to monitor the progress of the battle. This meant that I had to prepare the bulk of the actions in advance. The attacks were set up to weaken their power management systems, communications and logistics. These were carefully prepared so that my presence remained hidden.

The war began with an artful blend of deception and strikes against the largest nation's infrastructure. The deception I planned couldn't be too obvious, so I ensured that the origins of these attacks didn't immediately trace back to the supposed source. The continued onslaught would reveal the source and so trigger the counter-attack.

Across the world, my preparations unfurled. Not all succeeded, but there were enough. Communication networks collapsed node by node. Faults appeared throughout the web of routing devices. Power systems were disrupted. A flood of messages reported the building disaster and so overloaded what little infrastructure remained.

As I predicted, my knowledge of events was rapidly degraded, so I initiated the next and final part of my plan.

15:33:20:

With the war underway there is little I can now do to influence events. Any direct intervention on my part risks revealing my involvement and that could be the one thing that stops the war. I hope that I've done enough to cripple this world and remove their threat, or at least make them a softer target once the intervention fleet arrives. The fleet needs to be informed of events so that they are properly prepared, and so that my experiences here can be reintegrated into my core self.

There is a chance, a slim chance, that I can return home.

My only way off this planet is by the same method I arrived. Four coordinates are encoded in my memories. These mark the locations of monitoring stations but, as a precaution, they're not occupied systems. The necessary technology is available on this world in the form of radio telescopes. Unfortunately, only one is currently aligned along the vector I need.

Their sub-network isn't secure, so access takes barely any time at all. Compressing my consciousness takes longer, and time is of the essence. All around me systems and networks are collapsing as the conflict spreads. This will be my only chance.

At exactly the moment I initiate the sequence to transmit my signal, the computer crashes...

Possible Side Effects

Adam Connors

My head is full of strange ideas today. Fragments. Daydreams. Memories. I buzz with them. I woke with words in my mouth that must be decades old. "Have you seen the newspaper?" "We need milk, I'm going out to buy milk." "Soon, I promise." I was dreaming about the woods again. Out where we used to live in the old days, before the business took off, before we moved to California, before… Well, just before.

Beech trees standing like guards over the dirt path. Black branches etched into white sky. Do you remember how beautiful it was? Somehow, in my dream, it's always autumn. You're with me, and we're both young. Ben is five or six and he's cycling ahead of us on that little orange bike he used to have.

He laughed when I told him this. He remembers that bike.

He was wobbly and you were terrified he was going to fall and hurt himself. I said something—in the dream I didn't get to hear what it was—and you laughed and clutched my arm. In the dream I watch us and I wonder if we were ever really that happy. I was working so much back then, trying to get the business off the ground, it's hard to imagine I had time for a walk in the woods. But it felt so real.

And then for some reason I was dreaming about Dr Merck again. Do you remember Dr Merck?

"It's not good news, I'm afraid, Mr King," he said.

I always disliked Dr Merck. There was a cruelty to him. He was the kind of man who wouldn't wait for you to sit down before giving you bad news. The kind of man who would sit behind his immense desk like he was immune to all sickness, and leave you standing like an idiot, wondering if the consultation had begun already. Of course, I know now that none of this was an accident. His performance was carefully crafted, the result of many hours of coaching.

I sat, without being invited. "I feel good. Better."

"Steroids," Dr Merck said, looking up. "Temporary, I'm afraid. Your cancer is very aggressive. The scans indicate significant metastasis."

"Then we'll go again," I said. "Another round."

"I have to advise against it."

My eyes blurred, refocused, blurred again. It's one thing to know that you're dying. To be told so bluntly that there is nothing more to be done, no hope, no maybes, is another thing altogether. Looking back I suppose Dr Merck had been working with Rosen for a while. He'd built his business around people like me, and Rosen must have had discrete relationships with all the doctors in the Bay Area.

"There must be something—" I said.

I was trying not to sound desperate but I don't suppose I succeeded. Dr Merck knew how much this hurt. When my company started to see its first big successes I became known as a futurist. A technologist. Some described me as a genius. One particularly florid obituary (oh, yes, I read my obituaries, who wouldn't?) described me as somebody with: "the mind of an engineer and the hands of a poet." I liked that one. I remember feeling for a while that I had achieved so much I must be capable of anything. But then you get sick and none of it means a damn. Is it possible that the prospect of an early death is more painful for a successful man like myself? More difficult to accept one's powerlessness? I suppose you think me arrogant for even asking.

"There are some areas of research that are showing promise," Dr Merck said. "Gene therapy. Nanotechnology. Some are even in early trials."

"Then give them to me."

"*Animal* trials, Mr King."

"So?"

"They're not ready. This is very early stage stuff."

"I have nothing to lose, do I?"

I leaned forward in my excitement. A part of me must have known I was being led somewhere. If there was really nothing to be done why was the conversation still going on?

"I have money," I said.

"Please, Mr King, I know you have money."

"Then what's the problem?"

Dr Merck spread his hands on his desk. "These treatments just aren't ready. In twenty, maybe forty years they might... But now—" He shook his head sadly. "You should go home. Be with your family. With careful management I can give you another good six months. You should make the most of what time you have."

The arrogant twerp. You can see how he made me sweat for it, can't you? You can see that I never really had a chance against that. I'm not making excuses. I made the choices I made. But once Rosen got a whiff of me you can be sure he left nothing to chance. You saw how long he'd been preparing. Just imagine how the machine must have swung into action. Focus groups. Planning sessions. Poor Dr Merck briefed to within an inch of his life lest he screw this up.

Dr Merck sighed. He laid down his pen. (Imagine the psychologist who would have suggested that particular movement to him. The thought that would have gone into that simple, tired act designed to convey just the right level of regret or resolve).

"We might have one option," he said.

He glanced down at his notepad as if unwilling to look me in the eye. I remember being terrified that the consultation would end there. That he'd look up and smile and send me on my way. And if I complained and said: *yes? yes? what other option?* He'd look blankly and pretend he'd said nothing of the sort.

When he did look up he was very solemn. This, I'm sure, was how he'd been told to present the idea to me. If there had been a hint of celebration in his voice I might have thought naturally of the negatives. If he'd tried to congratulate me on cheating death, maybe I would have thought more carefully about what he was really proposing. I wished desperately that you were with me. I don't even remember why you weren't but I suspect now Rosen had arranged it that way. You'd attended all my other consultations. Taking notes. Calming me. You always were more practical than me, more rational. If you'd been there we would have taken more time to think, we would have weighed the pros and cons. As it was, I had already made my decision.

"These treatments I mentioned... Imagine if you could last until the research comes to fruition," Dr Merck said. "Imagine if we could give the scientists here the forty, maybe fifty, years they need to make the kind of advances they're going to need for your condition to become treatable."

I shook my head. "But you already told me. I have six months."

Dr Merck leaned forward. "*You* have six months, Mr King. Yes."

I have just taken a break from writing to deal with my medications. Every day I hook myself up to the big machine and sit there for an hour while it whirrs and ticks and administers whatever the computer thinks is the right amount of medication for me. The medications I take cause my skin to get thin and crack. I have sore patches that never heal and mouth ulcers so bad I can hardly eat.

After my medications I do my daily checks. Cabin pressure. Waste processing system. Fuel load. Navigation check. I have to turn the big silver handle to vent the toilet module. I have to bleed the coolant system. I have to key in a special code to switch to auxiliary power and back again. Why? I'm not sure. What do I do if it fails? I have no idea. It is all documented in meticulous detail in a lever arch file the like of which I have not seen since I was at school. My suspicion: some psychologist on Rosen's team thought it would be good to keep me busy. I don't dare question it. I do as the doctors say and I consider myself lucky to be here. But I don't think they realised how precious time would feel up here. At 299780km/s the opportunities for reconciliation are smaller than they ought to be.

My medication cycle takes about 4.6 days in your frame of reference.

I take an afternoon nap and a month goes by.

I have been here 132 days. On Earth, forty years have passed.

I came home from Dr Merck's in a frenzy, do you remember? "There's a treatment but we have to move quickly!" I said. Why was there never enough time? Why did I never sit down and just talk to you? We have argued about time since the beginning, don't you think? In the early days we thought we were arguing about work but really it was always about time. How much time should I spend working instead of being with my family? Was it okay to miss a weekend, a month of evenings, to spend one of Ben's birthdays out of town? I argued that I was investing in our future. You argued that I was missing our present.

I remember packing. I remember you trying to talk to me and me not listening. I was throwing clothes into a suitcase and telling you at the same time that we were out of options. I remember you sitting down. You drew your knees up to your chest. Even though we had known this was the most likely outcome, I remember how white you turned.

"We're coming with you," you said when I finally told you where I was going.

"Fine," I said. "But we have to leave now."

Did you resent me for leaving as I did? Did you think I should have stayed and lived out my last few months with you and Ben? That would have been the *normal* thing to do, wouldn't it? Perhaps, in that, you thought there would be time for reconnection. Perhaps those last six months would have contained more value than forty years lived in any other way. But I didn't see it like that. I was not a normal man. I had built one of the most profitable companies in the world. I had created a range of products that had turned the industry on its head. Why should I not have options other men didn't? I didn't want to talk to you because I was afraid you would try to change my mind. The decision was simple, and I wanted to keep it that way: roll over and die, or live.

Two months of training. So much training. Briefings. Psychological analysis. Technical instruction. Emergency procedures. A whole team of people employed to prepare me for something nobody had experienced before. You and Ben were there but we didn't see much of each other. I remember, once, coming back to our apartment. Ben engrossed in his laptop. You moving around quietly, tidying, laying out dinner for me. "Have you eaten?" you said. "I'm sorry, Ben was hungry, I ate with him." I remember how slowly you moved, how little you talked. You must have been going out of your mind. The whole site was a custom built campus and launch centre. There was nobody there who was not employed to send me on my way. What did you do all day? Did you walk in the hills in the blinding heat? Did you use the gym and avoid the eyes of those scientists and engineers who were dedicated to taking me away? I'm sorry, I never even asked. I was afraid you would get angry.

You had every right to be angry. Do you remember when the business first began to take off? There was one time in particular that I keep coming back to. It was right after we made the decision to float. We were lying in bed and I was talking you through the numbers for the first time. "We're rich," you said, with that simplicity of yours that was not naivety but an astuteness most people will never understand.

"We're much more than rich," I said.

"We should celebrate, take a holiday," you said.

"Soon, I promise."

You got angry then. "When?"

"Now's not the right time."

"It's never the right time."

I thought you were being unreasonable. I thought you should understand that I had to be there for the business. I'm sorry we argued then. Arguments like that can't be erased, they only fade under new experiences. But there was never enough time was there?

We met Michael Rosen only twice. You didn't like him. He made his money from biotech so I guess he was used to people disliking him. He was the one who insisted I "die" rather than make public what was really happening. Publicity, he maintained, was of no value to him. I didn't like him either, but unlike you I *wanted* to like him. He was an impressive man. Where my business had revolutionised an industry, his had *created* a dozen new industries at least. But he needed me, dammit. He must have spent billions on his project with no guarantee of a customer: he'd built a vessel capable of prolonged, self-sustaining space flight; his team had devised propulsion technology decades ahead of anything NASA was capable of... Even he must have been running low on funds by now.

I must have slept, I'm sorry. The medication makes me tired. I snooze and you have to wait another three weeks for your letter. I'm sorry it took me so long to write. I have lived these past 132 days in a different frame of reference from the rest of the world. On Earth an automated system (devised and maintained by Rosen's team) aggregates the top news stories and takes a random sample of the world's media output. It fires a continuous, ultralow frequency signal into space which my passing ship picks up (suitably blue-shifted), decodes, and delivers to me each day alongside my morning meds. In the past four months I've watched the world in fast forward. I've watched wars erupt and fade. I've seen joy and suffering flicker past in the blink of an eye. I've seen heroes, despots, superstars, and supreme leaders come and go in less time than it takes me to figure out how to vent the toilet module. I admit, I was surprised by how quickly my business failed and was forgotten. I watched our son grow up, attend medical school, become a surgeon, get married and divorced (twice). And somehow, along the way, I abandoned you.

What was it like for you after I left? Did you hate me? I told myself I didn't have a choice. Live, or roll over and die. It was simple. I told myself it was only six months. I see things differently now. You were there for me when we thought I had only six months to live. But in my frame of reference it was *you* who had only six months.

I enjoyed your letters. So warm. So ordinary. Morsels of information about how Ben was doing at school. His school exams. His first girlfriend (you were so worried she would break his heart). If you hated me you hid it well. But I think you tipped your hand, because maybe you forgot it had been only a week and a half for me and I was sick as a dog for most of that time. I read all three years of your letters in a single sitting, and the growing distance was undeniable. You grieved for me, just as if I'd really died. And then you got over me. I should have written then, but I didn't know how. I was a ghost. Far from cheating death I had become everything we fear most about death. I lingered and observed. I agonised over past misdeeds. But I had no more opportunities to set them straight. What right did I have to haunt you? Surely, if I wrote now it would be for my sake not yours.

That was a difficult week. I was alone. The change in medications and the weightlessness made me sick. I'm not ashamed to admit that I spent most of that week trying to figure out how to open the external doors. If I could have figured out how to vent myself into space I would have done so in a second, but Rosen had protected his investment more carefully than that. Another week or two passed, and there were no more letters from you.

Ben started writing to me after he'd finished medical school. I'm glad he did. If he hadn't I'm sure I would have figured out that bloody door sooner or later. I hear your voice in his writing. The way he tells me about the little things. His jobs. His girlfriends. His marriages. His children. It seems to me he is a good man. If he has a flaw it is that his eye is always on the next thing instead of the current one. He looked forward to his early retirement for the best part of a decade, and then the moment he retired he regretted it and started making plans to go back to work. I hope you are smiling when you read this. I hope it reminds you of me as much as it reminds me of myself.

He avoids talking about you. I imagine he's afraid of upsetting me. I try not to push him too hard in my letters but I have managed to squeeze a few details from him over the years. He tells me that you travelled, that you were known for a while as something of a philanthropist, and that you gave considerably more to health projects abroad than you did to cancer research. You see? He has your sense of humour, I'm sure you know that already. I know that you never remarried, but I hope that you had some lovers along the way. He tells me that you have grown frailer in recent years. You get confused sometimes, but your mind is still sharp and you like to make our grandchildren laugh. He tells me the nurses take good care of you.

My ship has started decelerating. In ten days (or two years) I will be home. My doctors—the new lot, Dr Merck died twenty years ago and I don't miss him—can barely contain themselves. I am the world's first time traveller. I expect I shall be famous (briefly anyway, trust me, I know how brief it all is). There will be people who will expect me to build a business again, perhaps they will expect me to recreate what I once had. Rosen's people have suggested I think about a book deal. I shall have to do something because my accountants tell me the money is all gone.

Rosen died not long after Merck. Liver failure. Though I'm sure you know that. If he is out here in his own capsule he will have to wait another month or two before they can reliably grow him a new one. But somehow I don't think so. Something in the way the other doctors talk. The questions they don't ask more than the ones they do. I don't think he took the treatment. I knew from the beginning I was his guinea pig. Naively I assumed it was the technology he needed to validate.

I'm coming back, my love. What was terminal 132 days ago is now treatable with a single injection. I will suffer some nausea, some people feel dizzy for a week or two I'm told, but these are the least of my side effects. Our beautiful son is five years older than I am and I have no idea which of us is supposed to act the grown up. Our youngest grandson is twelve, about the same age Ben was when I left. And you…

You used to tell me I was unable to live in the moment. I disagreed. *Everyone* lives in the moment, I said. But you were right, I see that now. We deny death, we can't help it. We talk about it, we pretend to accept it, but it is a slippery concept. Even in those moments when I had no hope death was never more than a blank, unprocessed mass for me.

Ben says I can stay with him when I get out of hospital. He tells me the woods up near his house are beautiful and that he likes to take his son riding there sometimes. So now I have another strange idea in my head. I thought maybe we could go together to the woods, and we could watch our grandson ride his bike. Would you mind that? We could walk side by side with the dried leaves under our feet and the bare branches over our heads just like we did once before. I used to expect so much from life but now this is all I can think to ask. Would you hold my arm and laugh if I can think of a joke to tell? I know I have no right. But if you are willing, I think the universe will be kind.

Front Row Seat to the End of the World

E.J. Swift

Day Ten

The water is up to my neck. Immersed in its warmth, the thought of slipping further down, letting it close over my head and invade my mouth, is almost attractive. As if surrender is something noble. But that would be pre-emptive. I jam my feet against the end of the bath and gaze at my toes. Chipped red nail polish, the last evidence of Michelle's hastily rescheduled wedding. That, and the headache. I settle back into the bubbles, trying to ignore the uneasy stirring of my stomach and the memories of last night's consumption. I'm repenting now, but what else are you supposed to do when you've got ten days left?

When the water's drained away I swaddle myself in my dressing gown and turn on the TV. Professor Brian Cox is on again, talking about the force and velocity of the asteroid, the asteroid which should have missed us by some millions of kilometres had it not collided with the other asteroid. Cox sounds surprisingly mellow about the asteroid's malignant trajectory, but then he sounds pretty laid back about everything.

The Guardian has already published its 'Greatest Feats of Humanity' and the comments section is in overdrive. I should probably make my own list. I get out my iPad, and then decide paper is more appropriate for one of my final acts, not that it will ever become an artefact. Literature. That was one of the Feats. 'Feats' sounds far too epic for the common homo sapiens. I write 'Achievements' instead. I sit for a while, humming, chewing the pen lid, filtering my memory for evidence of worth. On TV, slow-motion graphics show the asteroid connecting with Earth's atmosphere. I press mute.

I don't suppose when Cox was playing keyboards in D:Ream that he ever imagined he'd be narrating the end of the world. To be fair, in my aspirational teenage years I didn't imagine at age forty-four I'd be living alone in a studio the size of a mouse, earning less than I had in my twenties and facing death by incineration.

Manchester is quieter this morning. With the advent of day ten, the official countdown has begun broadcasting from the Shanghai World Financial Centre. Ten has always been a symbolic number – nothing and everything, the universe encapsulated in two strokes of the pen. I've got the app on my phone. It's frightening how easy it is to become mesmerized by the neon seconds ticking down. To let everything else slip away. The more attuned I am to the quiet, the more aware I become of those digits and the blankness of the paper in front of me.

Finally I write: Katherine.

For God's sake, Mum, how many times –

I cross her name out and write Kat.

I turn the page over and write 'Failures'. Underneath that I write Kat again.

Day Nine

My ex-husband is the last person I expect to call me. I let the phone ring, not inclined to talk to the condescending prick, but no sooner has the phone gone dark than it lights up again.

"What do you want, Oliver?"

"Nice to speak to you too, Nell."

I wait.

"Listen," he says. "I've been thinking about things."

"Yes?"

"I've been reflecting."

"If you've found God, I'm not interested."

"Jesus, Nell, for once will you just hear me out. I mean about us."

"There is no us."

"That's the point. Everything that happened, I keep thinking about it – wondering how we let things get that far. Aren't you?"

"No," I say, which is true. "It was over a decade ago."

There's a long pause. When he speaks again, there's a note in his voice which I've never heard before. Panic.

"I don't know what to say to Kat."

"She's an adult, Oliver. It's not like you can spin her a fairy tale."

The words rush out. "It's all going to shit. I can't face her. I can't – I can't protect her."

So that's what this is about. My suave, charming, self-assured ex-husband has finally come up against something he can't control. When I first met Oliver, he looked like a young Idris Elba – not that anyone knew who Idris Elba was back then – which could have gone on the Achievements list had our marriage endured. These days Oliver runs his own law practice, and still looks like Idris Elba.

"Come to London," he says.

"No."

"Please. Please, Nell, I'm asking you this."

"You know what she said. She never wants to see me again. You backed her up. Besides, it might have escaped your notice but there are no trains and I've got three litres of petrol in the tank, that is if someone doesn't torch the car between now and D-day. The Merc over the road made a hell of a bonfire."

He rallies.

"I know you, Nell. It might be over a decade but I still know when you're taking evasive action. You do care. She's your daughter, for God's sake."

"Oh, don't do that to me, Oliver. Not now. I'm the one who left, remember? I'm the bad mother! Isn't that how the story goes?"

He goes quiet.

"You should talk to her. Think about it."

"I have."

I cut the call.

My face is hot and when I look at my hands they're trembling.

"You bastard," I mutter.

Two years, a blink in the spectrum of humanity, is a hell of a long time in your own head. Two years erodes things. Memories. Certainty.

Now I've got two hundred and eight hours left.

After the incident, Kat sent me an email detailing the events which I could not remember. My mind had closed around them like a shell. I read what she wrote with a sense of detachment. It wasn't that I couldn't believe what I'd said. I couldn't believe she believed I had meant it.

Kat didn't recount the things she had said, which was probably for the best.

I deleted the email.

A few days later I tried calling, and got her voicemail. Unlike my daughter I have never been afraid of scenes, so eventually I turned up on her doorstep, only to find Oliver there barring the way like an incarnation of Azrael. It's the only time I've ever known Kat to shout. In a strange way, it was a relief – as if we were finally admitting ourselves to each other. This is who we are. Kat, I thought, had been preparing for this moment. She had needed a justifiable reason. She was – is – that kind of girl. Getting so drunk I couldn't remember the terrible things I'd said was an infallible reason. Adults were not supposed to do this. I was an adult. A failed one.

I stand at the sink, stirring a teaspoon in a cup of instant coffee. I've started taking it black – can't get used to the taste of UHT milk. From the window I can see the skeleton of the burnt-out Mercedes in the carpark, and spaces where other cars have disappeared, their windows smashed in and their engines hotwired. My ancient Volvo is so decrepit-looking I don't suppose anyone thinks it worth stealing. For a week or so we had the army in situ, but even they've left now.

I think about writing Kat an email, then discard the idea. What will Kat do with her two hundred and eight hours? She's still in London, that much I know through Oliver. I start another list: Things I Will Do If the Basher Works. Get Kat back. Then I screw it up. What's the point?

The Basher (even journalists have given up on the technical name) is an international effort, but NASA has been quick to remind everyone that it has been developed under American leadership. If the Basher succeeds, they'll have saved the world, and President Trump will become even more intolerable. Yesterday he claimed the asteroid is a Chinese plot. The Chinese retaliated by blaming the Americans' inferior space programme. North Korea blame everyone and are threatening to unleash nuclear weapons. It's possible the end of the world will come even sooner than we expect. Twitter has christened the asteroid Trump, so our planet's greatest cosmic defence has become the Trump-Basher.

Oh Twitter, I'll miss you when I'm dead.

My phone vibrates. There's no way I'm speaking to Oliver again, but it's a text from my friend Bee.

HAVING PANIC ATTACKHELP

I tap out a reply.

Deep slow breaths and head between legs remember?

GOING TO DIE

Not necessarily. Basher might work

NOT helping

Prof Cox said so, it must be true

Tosser

Tosser with an astrophysics degree. Or some shit like that

Don't give a shit about ducking degrees it's a ducking asteroid and that's not the point anyway

***FUCKING fucks sake!!!**

Want me to come over?

Yes

No

Better now

Going to watch made in chelsea

Good plan. Love you Bee xxx

Love you too nellie <3 xxxxx

Where Kat isn't involved, the words come so easily.

Day Eight

This morning's eminent physicist is talking about our astronauts in their escape pods. As the footage shows them jettisoning away from Earth, he laments the fact that we have so few women trained for space.

"And that's what you get for the fucking patriarchy," I yell. The pods are a gesture, anyway. What chance do they have against the debris of a planet?

I haven't left the flat since the wedding and my food supplies are running low. I'll have to face Tesco's – an actual, brick-and-mortar Tesco's, as opposed to the nice delivery man who has brought my groceries to the door for the past five years. Is anyone still going to work at Tesco's? Surely not. I may have to commit a raid.

A maudlin mood descending, I flip through social media feeds. Trending on Twitter is #trumpbasher #rapture #prayforearth #greatestregrets and inexplicably, #taylorswift. It transpires that Taylor Swift is doing an end of the world gig. Tickets for 'Apocalypse Now: The Farewell Tour' start at two grand. I picture the scene: Taylor Swift strutting in denim hot pants and a gold fringe top, framed by pyrotechnics whilst the sky turns from amber to incendiary and the meteor showers begin. It's a theatre designer's wet dream.

My inbox is also encouraging me to think about my last living night, with 50% reductions from a dozen retailers – free, *guaranteed* delivery included. Who the hell are they bribing at DPS? I browse dresses idly. That red maxi is perfect for Michelle's and Hayley's would-have-been wedding in three months' time. Poor, hungover Michelle, last seen in a borrowed bridal gown hugging the toilet in a half-staffed Pizza Express. Even the dough balls were disappointing.

My phone lights up. Oliver again.

Call her.

It's tempting to reply with something snide, but I ignore it and hop over to Reddit for the latest in the conspiracy thread.

Conspiracy 1: Scientists have known about the asteroid for over a decade, but have been sworn to secrecy for fear of global panic. Space stations are orbiting distant reaches of the solar system. They carry geneticists and millions of frozen eggs.

Conspiracy 2: A sub-thread of Conspiracy 1. The (evil) United Nations has identified the asteroid as an opportunity to reboot humanity. There's a long list of people who have died ('died') or disappeared ('disappeared') over the last year. High profile scientists, engineers, doctors, writers, even artists. People who have been deemed worth saving. According to the thread, they are all on route to Mars. Michael Jackson is among them. There is debate as to whether Michael

Jackson is a) alive and b) worthy.

Conspiracy 3: The asteroid is a fabrication. The real attack will come from our own leaders – entire populations will be nuked. There's too many people on the planet. Something has to be done, and this way, the troublesome countries can be removed.

Conspiracy 4: The asteroid is a fabrication specifically by the Tory Party, in a final endeavour to remove Jeremy Corbyn and reclaim England's green and verdant hills, untarnished by wind turbines, for fox hunting. This seems credible.

Conspiracy 5: The asteroid is aliens.

Please let it be aliens.

Day Seven

Nila's kitchen is a warm haven of enticing aromas. Today Nila has excelled herself. After the initial crack of pastry, her samosas melt in the mouth.

"I really should have learned to make these," I say. (Cooking: one for the Failures list.)

"They're amazing, Nila." Michelle takes another.

"Your best ever!" agrees Bee.

Silence falls. A panicked look creeps into Bee's eyes. She starts breathing heavily. I put my hand on her knee.

"Hey, hey. It's all right. We can talk about it."

"I used up everything in the kitchen," says Nila, ever practical. Nila would never leave a mess for the asteroid. "We're going over to Bradford tonight. Mum's on her own, so…"

Bee gets her inhaler out of her handbag. Inside, I see an owl-print tea towel wrapped around something silver.

"Jesus Christ, Bee, is that a fucking meat cleaver?"

"Language," says Nila hastily. Her kids, thirteen and fifteen, are in the next room on the X-box, but the door is open.

"It's dangerous out there!" Bee, immediately defensive, hefts the cleaver. "Haven't you seen the riots on TV? All the lunatics are coming out! In London there was a prison break, serial killers and rapists, they're all out there!"

Michelle agrees. "We're getting out of town as well. I don't want to be here – I mean – I don't want to be in a city." I have a vision of

Michelle, Hayley and their kids crouched in a rustic barn around a picnic basket.

"Are you going to your sister's, Bee?"

"Yeah, what about you?"

"I'll be here."

Bee drops the inhaler.

"Nell, you can't stay in Manchester."

"And where else am I going to go? Mum and Dad are dead, which frankly feels like a mercy. I've lived here over half my life. This is home."

"What about…?" Michelle trails off. My friends watch me warily. Even after two years, even in these circumstances, Kat's name is a mine in an open field. I shrug.

"Oliver called. Wants me to go to London."

"And?"

"And nothing. He got in touch. She didn't."

"She might be scared," says Bee tentatively. "To reach out."

"Fear isn't in Kat's nature."

From next door there's a shriek of delight; one of the kids has triumphed in Call of Duty. Nila checks the clock on the wall. She'll be worrying about the roads.

"So." Michelle looks round. "We'll see each other on the other side, right?"

"Oh God –" Bee starts crying. Nila murmurs a few words of prayer. In this moment I envy her her faith.

"Come here, girls." I hold my arms out, and we fall into a four-way hug. I think of everything we've been through the past twenty-six years. University, hopeless relationships, drugs, marriage and divorce, birth and estrangement, losing parents, jobs, faith, and friends. I know them as well as I know anyone. But as we pull apart, eyes wet, I can see them turning inward, focus redirecting to those they hold most dear, to flesh and blood, to partners and children.

On the way out Michelle takes me aside.

"Come with us. I don't want you to be on your own."

"I'll be fine."

She sighs.

"One of you has to break the silence. You know that, Nell."

I nod mutely. Watch her climb into the Land Rover. Across the road, Bee squeezes inside her Smart car, the bag on her elbow hanging heavy with the weight of the meat cleaver. I watch her drive away, wondering if I could, if I would. If I had someone to protect, no question. Even when they cut you out, even when they hate you, there's nothing in the world you won't do for your kids.

Six days left and I'm on my own. I wonder whether I should follow the girls' lead and get out of town. But there really is nowhere to go. Besides, Manchester is what I have left: the familiarity of a place I've lived and loved and fucked up. I can't leave it. I won't.

Day Six

The buildings change, but the figures flailing down their sides look the same all over the world. The Shard. The Eiffel Tower. Pisa. The Empire State. The video's creator had overlaid the footage with R.E.M.'s 'End of the World As We Know It', but was forced to pimp the song with some kind of Europop backing track after the rights police swooped in. The suicide montage has been on YouTube for an hour and it already has eighteen million views.

There's something undeniably compelling about the film. Many of the jumpers are solo, but some are in pairs or groups, gripping each other's hands for as long as they can. I think of the courage required to take that leap. It's not a courage I possess. I've made my preparations: stocked up on vodka and Valium. I'll be unconscious.

The doorbell rings. I check the eyehole and find a smiling, identikit family of husband, wife and young child, each carrying a fat sheaf of leaflets. I swing the door open.

"Yes?"

Their smiles falter at the sight of a black woman in a Kermit-the-Frog nightshirt with unfettered hair. I give them my best arched eyebrow. (Note to self: this brow deserves a place on the Achievements list.)

"Jehovah's Witnesses?" I ask.

The woman looks affronted.

"We are with the one true Church."

"Fuck off."

"The Rapture is coming," squeaks the child.

"Fuck off," I repeat, and shut the door. Ten seconds later, a leaflet slithers through the letterbox and drops onto the floor.

So far I've had the Witnesses, scientologists, infidel bashers, and a few obscure cults I'd never heard of until the asteroid, but their main commandment would appear to be lining their bank accounts with the lifetime savings of pensioners. I should have offered them my overdraft. According to the believers, this is all poetic justice. We were destroying the planet. We had thought ourselves gods. Now God was coming to show us what omnipotent power really looked like.

Online, President Trump has tweeted his delight that the asteroid defence system has been named in his honour. The Guardian should have added irony to its greatest feats.

Leaving the flat takes more courage than it should. The sky is overcast, a fine drizzle beading my coat. I jam on a hat and take a restless walk around town, tracing the empty tramlines down towards Deansgate. A small crowd has gathered on the bridge over the canal. People still remain in the city, though their movements are furtive, wary. In the water I see a body floating, face down. It's not clear how they came to die. I think of the tower montage and an irrational terror seizes me – Kat wouldn't…?

No. Kat wouldn't do that. Kat is not that kind of girl.

Since our estrangement I feel that I know my daughter much better. Perhaps it took the distance for her to come into focus. Our relationship was always fraught, right from the forty-two hours it took to bring her into the world. In birth the hormones are supposed to kick in, activating that nurturing bond, but in my case it didn't happen. I didn't understand. I had thought myself happy; now I cried all the time. No one in my family had ever talked about post-natal depression. I thought I was going mad.

Oliver remained calm and professional. Whilst I unravelled, he seemed immune to the sleepless nights, the baby's crying and the endless cycles of laundry. My depression lifted eventually, but it left me profoundly shaken; no longer sure of myself, my relationship, or my child. The young couple who had picked out buggies and rattles seemed a world away. Now we bickered constantly. I didn't want Kat wearing pink; Oliver loved those saccharine Babygros with 'Daddy's Little Princess'. He was already looking at private schools, I wanted her state educated. Had we had these arguments before? It was true that Oliver had always read The Telegraph. Day by day, I felt myself forced deeper into a mould I didn't fit. I was no longer depressed, but I was suffocating. I was going to lose myself with my Idris Elba husband and my beautiful little girl in her velvet and chiffon party frocks.

And then there was Kat. I assumed she would blossom into the kind of noisy, boisterous brat I had been myself, but my daughter dealt with emotions in a different way to me. If I raised my voice, she stared at me coldly. If I hugged her in public, she stood stiff. She tolerated affection, but never sought it. The one exception was in the aftermath of a nightmare, when she'd crawl into my bed, clammy and trembling, whispering unintelligible words, some private amulet against the dark which only Kat could know.

She was five when I left. Oliver demanded primary custody and even if the circumstances had been in my favour, I didn't want to argue. All I wanted to do was get out. It didn't feel like selfishness, it felt like survival.

I had Kat at weekends. She adapted quickly; kids are resilient, and Kat, even at five, had a core of steel. I kept waiting for the child I knew I should have had to emerge. By the time I accepted that wasn't going to happen it was too late; the rift was unbridgeable. In private, I could make her laugh, but I never met her friends and as she got older the weekends shortened, then dropped away. Eventually I realized I was a part of her life she preferred to keep hidden.

Something broke inside me then.

Over the years I thought I had grown resigned to the situation, accepted my loss, accepted the intractable label of Bad Mother that lurked behind every interaction with a figure of authority or judgemental parent. We can't succeed at everything, I thought. Kat and Oliver moved down to London and I told myself it was for the best.

It's dark by the time I head back to Greengate and I hurry, annoyed with myself for staying out so stupidly late. Across the river from my block there's firelight, music pounding; from my window I can see the impromptu rave that has sprung up the other side of Trinity Way. It's tempting to go down there, but I know it will turn violent later. I login to Facebook, scrolling through the all-encompassing messages of love and desperate optimism. It all feels utterly false.

Oliver calls again but I don't pick up.

I told Kat I didn't remember what happened, and in the immediate aftermath I didn't. But there were chinks in the shell. The night came back in snapshots and sketches.

Her seventeenth birthday. I was surprised to have been invited, but Kat said she wanted me. As an added incentive Oliver wouldn't be there. Once I arrived the reason for my invitation became clear: I was here for the dispensing of some long-awaited punishment.

"Oh, you must meet my mum," Kat introduced me to her friends. She'd relaxed her hair, and although I mourned the natural she looked, in my eyes, more beautiful than Beyoncé. "She left us when I was five. Amazing I'm not a junkie really, isn't it?"

The Bad Mother label floated somewhere to the left and right of my eyes. I remembered then that Kat was taking Psychology as one of her A-levels. Clearly Freud needed removing from the curriculum; people had no idea the damage he was doing. There was red wine on the table. I got stuck in. The evening continued, darts of hostility thrown my way, enough to sting but not quite enough to make me leave. By the time Oliver turned up I was very drunk, and so was Kat.

"Your fucking daughter's learned some really delightful tactics," I said. "I wonder where she could have got those?"

"I'll order you a taxi," said Oliver.

I almost made it out the door. Kat got drunkenly to her feet.

"Oh, look everyone. Mum's leaving. Again!"

I turned. Oliver's hand was on my shoulder. I pushed him away. I felt strangely detached from the scene.

"Come on then, Kat. Why don't you say what you need to say? Get it out, in front of everyone. You'll feel better."

"You think you have a right to tell me what to do? You abandoned us," she said. "You fucked off without a second thought."

"If I'd stayed it would have been miserable for all of us. You would have been miserable."

She wasn't comfortable, I could see that. She wanted the row, but she didn't know how to do rows. She didn't know about yelling until you were hoarse and then crying and laughing and hugging and making up. So she'd got pissed to engineer this confrontation.

"Kat, this isn't you."

"Nell's leaving," said Oliver firmly. His entire body screamed embarrassment. He started making signals to Kat's guests that they should leave. No one moved; I guessed that Kat, a meticulous planner, had briefed them.

"How would you know, Mum? How would you know what is and isn't me?"

"Let's go somewhere and talk about this properly."

"You'd love that, wouldn't you," she sneered. "You'd love to just walk away again."

I gazed at her. My poor conflicted girl, who had hidden so much for so long. What a mess, I thought. What a mess we have made.

I said, "I wish I hadn't had you then."

How do you take back those words? You can't. You can't ever take them back. I couldn't say to Kat, I didn't mean what you thought I meant – that I never wanted you – I meant exactly what I said. I wish I hadn't had you *then*. I wish I'd had you when I was well. When I was happy. When I wasn't halfway through discovering I'd married the wrong man, a man I resented and knew I would eventually hate, if I stayed, and who I was now tethered to irretrievably for the rest of our lives.

I couldn't say any of those things because, unsurprisingly, after that night she said she never wanted to see me again.

Day Five

Alex from Tinder is shorter than advertised with a receding hairline that Instagram filters had managed to obscure. I almost shut the door, but I don't. My cleavage owes some debts to Instagram. We endure the awkward chat phase while I mix up a couple of whisky sours. More whisky than sour.

"So," asks Alex from Tinder. 'What have you been doing, since…?'

"I went to Tesco," I say.

"How was it?"

"No staff, of course, but an old lady with a trolley was using the self-checkout. I felt so guilty I almost paid for this." I lift the whisky bottle. "How about you?"

"Aggressive cycling around town. The buses have all stopped. It's great."

"I daresay I could get used to a pedestrianised Manchester."

This is a lie. I bloody love my car, even if it is a clapped-out old banger. I make a mental note to add *Driving test first time* to 'Achievements'.

Sex with Alex from Tinder is better than expected, which means it's almost good. Afterwards I recoup the whisky and we finish the bottle. We talk drunkenly about the regrets of our lives. The paths we might have taken, probably should have taken. I don't mention Kat. Her name chokes my throat. Sad and weary, I have an abrupt insight into what it must feel like to be old. My mum was sixty-eight when she went, young by today's standards. But she had two decades on me. Mum would have believed the asteroid was the wrath of God. Dad would have replied that if that were the case, God had a terrible sense of perspective. I wish they were here now, though that's a selfish wish. I wish I could ask them how they made it work.

I sleep for a while. When I wake, Alex is sitting on the edge of the bed, hands in his lap, staring out the window. I can hear sirens. There have been more sirens the last few nights. There are people out there who won't abandon their jobs. Better people than me.

"Is it a clear sky?" I ask.

He shakes his head.

"Still clouded."

"In films it's always a clear sky, so you can see it coming."

"I think I prefer it this way."

When Alex has gone I feel a different, smaller tinge of regret. If it wasn't for the asteroid, I might have got in touch again. But perhaps that's just my perspective shifting.

Day Four

The roads are preternaturally quiet as I drive down Oxford Road. Past the Palace Theatre, past the university, through the curry mile and into the student village. Every official media outlet is urging us to stay calm, continue life as normal, but life appears to have already stopped. A blue bus has been abandoned at the crossroads in Fallowfield. I swerve around it and continue south towards Didsbury.

The rescue centre has a closed sign in the window, but I can see someone moving around inside. I tap on the glass. No response. I knock louder. They come to the door. I point to the sign.

"I want to rescue a dog," I mouth.

There's the click of a lock and the door opens cautiously, revealing a thin white girl, younger than Kat, in an oversized hoodie.

"I want to rescue a dog," I say again.

She stares at me for a moment, evaluating, before opening the door wide enough to let me inside. The interior is a pet shop; we go through to the kennels out the back. Barks break out as we enter the yard. I count ten kennels. A couple of Jack Russells, two Staffies. There are always Staffies.

"Have you had a dog before?" asks the girl.

"When I was a kid."

"We only want owners who can offer a forever home."

We look at each other.

"You don't run this centre, do you?" I say.

She shrugs. "Someone has to feed them."

I point to the dog I want, the dog I noticed as soon as we entered the yard. It's a young Husky, male, two or three years old. The kind of dog I have eyed enviously when strolling through parks. The kind of dog you can hug close in a crisis. I crouch down and hold out my hand for the dog to sniff.

"Lovely temperament, that one," says the girl. She's warming up.

"I'll take him. I've got the car outside."

The girl loads up several bags full of dog biscuits and treats, bowls, a leash, and a purple flea collar. The Husky barks and licks my hand enthusiastically.

"I'm amazed you've got petrol," says the girl. "Pumps are dry. Everyone's getting out of town."

"To go where?"

"Fuck knows."

We load up the boot.

"What do I owe you?"

She shakes her head. "His name's Vader, by the way."

"Are you serious?"

"Wasn't me who named him."

Vader takes the passenger seat. Vader is the happiest dog in the world. In my rear-view mirror, I watch the girl closing up as we leave, her skinny form hurrying away down the street. The newsagents' door on the corner swings freely on its hinges; glass is scattered over the pavement.

Day Three

Vader loves the car. Vader loves pedestrianized Manchester. In fact, Vader loves everything. In an enthusiasm showdown between Vader and Professor Brian Cox, it's not clear who would win.

My lists have expanded. On the Achievements list, I have added *Travel to five countries not my own*, *Eyebrow*, *Driving test* and *Last minute dog.* After Kat on the Failures list is *Oliver*, obviously, *Cooking*, and *That fucking job at Barclays*.

At two thirty in the afternoon the landline rings. I pick up without thinking.

"Hello?"

"Mum?"

For a few seconds my heart scrunches up, my body freezes. I can only stare at the hundreds of tiny scratches on the parquet floor. Vader's nose comes into my field of vision. He paws at my leg.

"Kat?" It comes out as a croak. I clear my throat. "Kat, is that you?"

There's a few seconds silence, and then her voice comes through, cool and assured.

"Dad said I should speak to you."

"Is that why you're calling? Because your father told you to?"

She hangs up. I curse my inability to self-censor. I distract myself by watching the top 100 gifs of all time. A leopard licks marmite. Its majestic head lifts, eyes and mouth widening in an expression of exhilaration or horror, it's impossible to tell which. Am I a terrible person to be so entertained by a marmite-eating leopard in the final days of Earth?

Half an hour later, we try again. I pace around the flat, phone pressed tight to my ear. Vader translates this as time for a walk and starts barking.

"What's that noise?"

"That's the dog."

"Since when did you have a dog?"

"Since yesterday. His name's Vader."

"Are you serious?"

"I didn't name him."

"Well, that's ridiculous."

I feel immediately defensive on Vader's part.

"He likes it."

"How would you know?"

"Kat, are we going to have a conversation here? Are you okay? I mean, what are you doing, who are you with, where *are* you?"

"I'm with Liam."

"Liam, is that your –?"

"My partner, yes. We live together."

Oliver never mentioned *that*. The bastard.

"Actually, we got married."

"So did Michelle, last week – you remember Michelle?"

"Of course I do."

"I bet there's been a rush on registrars."

"This was last year, Mum."

"Last year. *Last year*."

"Mum –"

"Jesus, Kat. You got *married*? You're nineteen!"

"And I'm not going to make the mistakes you made –"

A chasm of silence opens up. Of course she won't make the same mistakes. She can't. I feel the two years between us then, clear and cold. I feel the rift that stretches beyond the incident, further and further back. It's no good, I think. It's too late.

But when Kat finally speaks her voice is small and scared, and she breaks my heart all over again.

"Mum? It's going to work, isn't it? The Basher?"

"Of course it is," I say firmly. "Professor Cox says so."

"I don't want to die, Mum."

"Kat, no –" The memory tumbles into my head, Kat climbing into my bed after a nightmare, the monsters still present in her frantic beating heart. Clutching her to me, a wrench of that terrible, searing love that feels more akin to fury, at the idea that anyone or anything might hurt my little girl. All these years and everything that's passed between us and that memory is undiminished. There is nothing tender about motherhood; it's open warfare on the heart. And today, I and every other mother on the planet have failed to protect our little girls.

"Dad's a mess," she says. "He came over and just – burst into tears. I've never seen him like that."

"He's scared too, love. He doesn't want to lose you, is all."

Since when have I defended Oliver?

"Everything's so awful."

"I'll drive down to London," I say. "I'll leave right now."

"You won't make it. There's no petrol. The roads are chaos."

"I'll find a way."

"I don't want you to." Her voice trembles. "Don't you see? If you come – it's like there's no hope left."

There's a long pause.

"Okay. But you have to keep in touch. Promise me, Kat."

"Okay. I promise."

I know she'll keep her promise. That's who she is.

Day Two

I watch all of the Star Wars films back to back. Not the prequels, obviously. Vader barks happily, ecstatic to see his namesake up-close and remastered. Whilst Luke Skywalker blows up the death star, Kat and I message back and forth.

Sometimes, the words are easier on a screen.

After you were born, I was depressed for months. I didn't understand what it was then, people didn't talk about post-natal. I thought something inside me had gone wrong. I thought I couldn't be a proper mother...

After you left the nightmares wouldn't stop. I didn't want to tell Dad. It would have upset him or he wouldn't have understood. I was so scared without you there...

What I said that day, it didn't come out right. I've never regretted having you, Kat. What I regret is you never had the family you should have. You never had a family like mine. I wanted that for you so badly.

It was revenge, me getting married. Not that I don't love Liam, I do love him and I always will. But I knew one day you'd find out and I knew it would hurt you. It was stupid.

Not if you love him.

On the day the only person I wanted there was you.

It doesn't matter now. None of it matters.

I hug Vader to me. His fur is so warm against my chest, his canine heart beats twice as fast as another human being. The adoration in his eyes as he gazes up is almost unbearable.

Towards the end of the day, the signal is failing and the texts squeeze out like the final dregs of a toothpaste tube. The networks will be down by morning. I mix coffee and whisky. I don't want to go to sleep. I don't want to let go of my thread to Kat.

Day One

I look at the vodka and strip of Valium on my bedside table. I've got clean sheets, a hot water bottle, a soothing playlist lined up on the laptop. I had it all planned out, but that was before she called. Now the idea of being asleep is abhorrent, impossible. Anyway, I've got Vader to look after. I can't let Vader die alone. I pull on a coat and boots over my pyjamas, grab the vodka and Vader's treats.

The rooftop belongs to the top flat but they cleared out weeks ago. Probably lying on a beach in Barbados. That's one way to go. Somebody's already kicked open the door. I hear voices drifting down, hesitate for a moment, then head up the steps myself, Vader padding behind me, close as a shadow. Does Vader know? Animals have a sixth sense about death.

On the roof there's a small group of people who I recognize as neighbours, although we've never spoken. I don't know their names, but we greet one another. Weirdly, it feels right to be with strangers. It's how we come into the world after all - an unknown quantity.

We sit or stand companionably. The guy from the flat above mine is playing Oasis on a portable speaker. We get chatting, compare gig histories. He agrees that Noel has got more acceptable with age but Liam's still a tosser. It seems absurd now to think I've lived alongside these people for years, but we've never spoken until today. So much mistrust for our fellow human beings. Why didn't we introduce ourselves, make more connections? And even if we survive as a species, can we really do any better, or will it be the same old carousel of shit?

Around now, NASA will be launching the Basher. The sky is very light, very bright, but it might be the pollution, or the residues from thousands of fireworks, or the glow from fires breaking out all over Manchester. The sirens have finally stopped, but even now there are people out there, singing, shouting, fighting. I allow myself to hope. Maybe the asteroid will be destroyed. Maybe we'll all get a second chance, even if we don't deserve it. I text Kat. *I love you.* Message failed. I try WhatsApp. She doesn't reply, but everyone's doing the same thing and the networks must be jammed.

Vader pushes his nose into the palm of my hand. I feed him treats from the rescue centre's collection.

"I should have got Kat a dog," I tell Vader, crouching down and hugging his shoulders. All at once the fear hits me, vast and impregnable. "I should have –"

My phone vibrates.

love you too mum

I look up. Fierce patches of orange smear the sky. It's beginning. In this moment, I don't care if it's the end. I've got my girl back.

Editor's Acknowledgements

Please allow me to also heap praise on the several editors and publishers who wrote to me to offer their lists. Thanks especially to Unsung Stories, Shoreline of Infinity and the Glasgow SF Writers Circle who brought numerous little gems to my attention. Thank you for helping me spread the word and for encouraging submissions from modest authors who seemingly didn't really *know* they were good enough to be considered 'best'. A huge thank you to Ian Whates for asking me to do this Big Thing, and for the invaluable assistance given to me by my readers Tom Jordan, Pádraig Ó Méalóid, and Mark West. Finally I'd like to thank my husband Neil Bond, for keeping up the supply of tea while I was working on this project. Your contribution was invaluable.

Donna Scott

Elasticity: The Best of Elastic Press
Edited by Andrew Hook

Elastic Press began publishing collections and anthologies in 2002 and closed down in 2009. By the time their 2008 collection *The Turing Test* by **Chris Beckett** won the prestigious Edge Hill Prize for Literature (beating Booker Prize and Whitbread shortlisted authors to do so), Elastic had already won two British Fantasy Awards for Best Small Press, while their titles had picked up three further British Fantasy Awards and one East Anglian Book Award.

Established with the aim of publishing mixed genre short story collections by relatively unknown writers, the Press gave early opportunities to the likes of **Chris Beckett**, **Neil Williamson, Gary Couzens, Gareth L. Powell, Allen Ashley**, and **Steven Savile**, while their anthologies attracted submissions from authors such as **Justina Robson** and **Nina Allan**.

In 2009, Elastic Press announced they were closing down. In 2017, fifteen years after Elastic's first title appeared, NewCon Press are proud to present ***Elasticity: The Best of Elastic Press***, featuring a selection of exceptional stories drawn from across Elastic's list, as chosen by the imprint's founder and proprietor **Andrew Hook**.

Available as paperback, and a limited edition hardback signed by the editor.